## GREEN GRASS OF WYOMING

This is the climactic novel about Ken McLaughlin, the horses which play so large a part in his life, and—this time—a girl. Ken, the dreamy boy who wanted his very own colt in MY FRIEND FLICKA, has grown into a sturdy, self-reliant young man eagerly facing a future full of promise.

## MARY O'HARA's

sensitive three-part study of the heart of an adolescent boy has already become a classic among the best-loved books in the English language. Her unusual knowledge of horses and her love for the Wyoming greengrass country enable her to write about them unforgettably on an age-old theme, that of the friendship between a boy and his horse.

The LAUREL-LEAF LIBRARY brings together under a single imprint outstanding works of fiction and nonfiction particularly suitable for young adult readers, both in and out of the classroom. This series is under the editorship of Charles F. Reasoner, Professor of Elementary Education, New York University; and Carolyn W. Carmichael, Associate Professor, Department of Communication Sciences, Kean College of New Jersey.

# MARY O'HARA

# *Green Grass of Wyoming*

Published by DELL PUBLISHING CO., INC.
1 Dag Hammarskjold Plaza, New York, N.Y. 10017
Copyright © 1946 by Mary O'Hara
Laurel-Leaf Library ® TM 766734, Dell Publishing Co., Inc.

Reprinted by arrangement with J. B. Lippincott Company
First Dell printing—April, 1967
Second Dell printing—December, 1968
Third Dell printing—July, 1970
Fourth Dell printing—December, 1971
Fifth Dell printing—October, 1972
Sixth Dell printing—January, 1974
Seventh Dell printing—November, 1974
Eighth Dell printing—February, 1976
Printed in U.S.A.

# 1

Contour maps of our country show a great hump somewhere west of the middle running irregularly north and south, and the trains of the transcontinental railway lines going through Wyoming slow up as they approach it, stop and take on an extra engine.

For scores of miles, as they crawl over this hump and down, the trains chug through an empty wilderness of low hills, dunes, plains; green in spring and early summer, fading to taupe and fawn as the season wears on. The ground is broken here and there by black bearded ridges and cones, or sharp profiled mesas of red granite, or huge pines standing solitary and twisted by the winds, like sardonic old men who know a thing or two.

This is the Continental Divide, and the trainmen call it The Top of The Big Hill.

Not far from the railroad tracks one September, in the hour of intense darkness just before the dawn, a horse had gone for water to a slight depression in the ground. To one side of it, a cluster of rocks hinted to the knowing that a spring might be there.

Old Pete quenched his thirst, raised his dripping muzzle and stood mouthing the water, turning his head this way and that, moving his ears, attending to a horse's business, which is to keep himself aware every minute of all that goes on near or far.

Pete was a heavy draft horse, seventeen hands high. His coat was light bay and dappled. His hair—tail, mane, forelock, even the little skirts over his hoofs—was thick and black. His calm, friendly, brown eyes looked out with a gentle scrutiny from hedges of dark lashes. He was not young and his movements were slow and deliberate.

There came the sound of a freight approaching from the east.

At the point where old Pete stood the ground sloped sharply up to the tracks a hundred feet away. The railroad made a quarter-turn here as it took its direction toward Red Buttes, the next station west.

The labored chugging of the freight grew louder, and Pete's head turned, his ears drew forward, waiting for the two great engines, spitting fire and smoke, which would appear in a moment. Trains had no terror for him. He had known them from birth, as he had known wind or hail or snow.

The train came nearer. With a roar it crashed into the curve and Pete was engulfed in the pounding of the engines, the squealing of the wheels on the tracks, the rattling of the cars. He stood quietly, watching with curiosity and enjoyment.

Suddenly he gave a convulsive start. Something was happening which was out of the ordinary. An enormous object had leaped off a flatcar and was sliding and bounding down the slope toward him.

At this strange attack, he crouched, every leg braced, his chin drawn in and ears cocked. Then he went up on hind legs, wheeled and thundered away across the plains.

At a safe distance he jammed to a stop, still snorting and trembling. The thing was not pursuing him. It had come to rest at the foot of the slope. The freight was behaving normally. The caboose had just appeared.

Pete waited until the tracks were empty and the chugging of the freight was muffled by distance, then he went back, stopping once to point his ears and snort again. It was an enormous box. He circled it—not too closely—lifting and placing his great feet carefully. Curiosity finally overcame caution and he went up to smell it. He was still gathered, ready to run.

What was this?—a deep whinny burst from him. Instantly it was answered from inside the box. The voice was high, eager, nervous, young and very feminine. A filly.

Now came a great scrambling and banging as if the filly were struggling to get to her feet and could not. She whinnied again and again, and whatever can be told in horse language, she made known to Pete in the next few minutes.

The crate was badly damaged by the fall. One corner was sprung and from this a hoof and leg and part of the filly's haunch protruded.

There was nothing Pete could do, but he rumbled his encouragement, and if a friend standing by is any help, he gave that help. And though, a little later, he moved off to graze, to stand broadside to the rising sun, to return to the water hole and finish his drink, yet he always came back to rumble his comfort and sympathy, to wish that he could share the grass, the water, the sun with her. Perhaps he knew that if help did not come soon, the filly would die.

When help did at last come, it announced itself by a loud, brassy neigh which rang down from the hills, causing the filly to whinny frantically in answer, to struggle until she was exhausted.

Pete knew a stallion's neigh when he heard it. And now he saw him coming, almost as large as himself, and pure white. The old horse withdrew a little and stood watching.

The stallion trotted swiftly with head up and stretched nose holding the scent. He threw his feet high, his tail plumed over his haunches.

Then there was bedlam around the crate. The filly struggled and thrashed and whinnied her distress. The stallion neighed and grunted, smelling at her haunch, at the whole box, plunging around it. He reared up and pawed it with great cleaver-like strokes, but still it held together. Furious, he wheeled away to charge at Pete.

Pete lumbered off. The stallion did not pursue him. At a safer distance the big gelding resumed his watching.

Now the stallion thundered upon the crate with his heels. It rocked and splintered. The great hoofs crashed again and again. Suddenly the side gave way, parting from the floor, and the filly rolled out. A flash of four black legs in the air, a frantic scramble, and she was on her feet—a sight which must have surprised the two horses for she was attired in a blanket coat and a hood with rimmed goggles.

She shook herself violently.

And now they made acquaintance, the stallion and the filly. They walked around each other, squealed, touched soft nostrils, nipped and nuzzled, reared and wheeled way, then, in intense excitement, did it all over again.

Suddenly the dalliance ended. The stallion seized the top of her neck in his teeth, folding his forelegs against her. Running on his hind legs he forced her to get going. She sidled away from him. Then he began his regular round-up routine, snaking around her, his nose close to the ground and his long neck undulating.

He plunged on this side, then that, nipping at her heels, giving her an occasional bite in the haunches.

She fled before him. Together they swept away from the tracks, southward. Pete stood there like a great monument, wistfully looking after them.

This part of the country, with its red clay soil, its ditches and water cuts, escarpments, long ridges or sudden jutting hills, was well named Red Buttes. It was dangerous ground. The stallion and filly raced over it as if the gulches and walls were obstacles in an easy steeplechase. At last they disappeared behind the shoulder of a hill.

Pete was alone again. He stood, occasionally looking south, occasionally at the railroad. He stamped a hoof and switched his tail. He wandered to the empty crate and sniffed it, but without interest now. He looked southward again and at last began to walk slowly in that direction. His big head plugged up and down. His pace increased. He broke into a pounding trot and the little hair skirts over his hoofs shook and swung.

He was no steeplechaser but he was a good pathfinder. He went down the gulches and up the other sides, he went around the ends of the escarpments. Finally, he too disappeared behind the shoulder.

And when, fifteen minutes later, another freight chugged up The Big Hill, the engineer leaning out of the locomotive window, idly wondered if anything ever happened on this empty and lifeless summit.

# 2

It was about five hours later that Ken McLaughlin was riding slowly along the ridge of Section Twenty-four which runs parallel to the railroad and about a quarter-mile south of it. He was a tall, thin boy of sixteen with a sensitive face and dark blue eyes that moved ceaselessly, sweeping the land—the characteristic far-reaching look of one who has been brought up on the plains.

He rode very much at ease, now and then addressing a word to the sorrel mare, Flicka, who carried him. She responded by turning an ear backward, or altering her pace at his command.

Ken was the son of Captain McLaughlin who raised sheep and polo ponies on the Goose Bar Ranch a few miles to the east. The boy had been sent by his father to the ranch of Joe Daly on an errand concerning the fifty registered Corriedale rams who served the ewes of the Goose Bar flocks. To keep the rams separate from the ewes until breeding time in October, Rob McLaughlin had boarded them with Joe Daly.

Although it was early in September, Flicka had already grown a respectable coat of fur. Saddling her that morning, Ken had noticed it and, roughing his hand along the side of her neck, had said, "Getting ready for winter already, Flicka? Isn't it a bit early for fur?"

But, judging by the cold west wind against which Flicka plodded, she was just showing good sense. Ken himself wore a tight-fitting canvas jacket and it was lined with sheepskin.

The wind veered suddenly and the icy tang of it, as well as the unmistakable smell of snow, made Ken turn his eyes to the threatening, timbered mountain range twenty miles to the north. "Sure cooking up something," he muttered, drawing the knitted wool collar of his coat up to his ears, and Flicka put one ear back as if she agreed.

The wind swung west again. Ken wondered why it was that when summer departed all color departed with it. The prairies were grey brown; the yellow and red of the quaking-asp in the little draws were hardly noticeable; here and there where a growth of pine stood, it showed up more black than green. It was the sky, he thought; if the deep glorious blue sky of Wyoming had arched over all this, then the colors would have sprung forth. But the sky was cold and withdrawn, a pale grey.

He hated the thought that summer was over and within a fortnight he and his brother, Howard, must leave for school in the East. He gave a sharp sigh— then pulled Flicka to an abrupt halt.

After a moment of silence in which, like a puppy, he put his head first on one side and then on the other, he addressed Flicka. "What in heck do you think that is?"

Flicka's attention also had been caught by the strange-looking object on the plains not far from the railroad tracks.

"Looks like a busted freight box of some kind," Ken told her, as he touched her side. "Let's take a look."

Flicka pricked her ears as she trotted to the crate. Ken dismounted and examined it.

It told its own story. It was a horse crate which,

somehow, had got slung off a freight car. He could see where it had slid and bounced down the slope.

Never had the boy seen such a de luxe affair. He crawled into it and saw that it was thickly padded, and that, sewn into the padding near the front was a card with the name and the picture of a filly.

"Crown Jewel." Ken read the name thoughtfully aloud.

Flicka, who was putting in the time snatching a few mouthfuls of grass, lifted her head and looked at him. "Hear that, Flicka? It's the name of the filly that was shipped in this fancy box—Crown Jewel—a three-year-old, it says."

The picture showed the filly's face and head, her expression of almost comical interest, the alert, forward-tilted ears, the narrow, curved lines of her face, the large white diamond between her eyes with a pear-shaped pendant hanging from the lowest point.

Ken placed his finger on this mark. "That's where she got her name." He was about to tear the card loose and appropriate it. But why not take the whole crate? —he could drag it home and fix it up. "How'd you like to have a ride in this someday, Flicka?"

He stood thinking. Could the shattered crate or any of its appointments be considered as belonging to anybody else? Certainly it had been discarded—no, it might have fallen off a freight accidentally; in which case, people sooner or later would come looking for it. Better leave it alone—at least for the present. Next week, if it was still here, he could take possession of it.

He got out of it and continued his examination. All around were the hoofprints of horses. What had horses been doing there? Just curious perhaps . . . the most curious animal in the world, his father always said . . . might have been here in the night looking

at the crate and smelling it over . . . yes, that was it
. . . there was dung in it and not so very old
either . . .

Studying the tracks, he saw that there had been
three horses there. A small, dainty, rounded hoof, a
larger one, and a third, still larger. Ken poked at it
with his foot. "Big as a bucket," he muttered. "Could
be Pete's. He's got the biggest hoof I ever saw."

Pete was a range bum. No one knew where he had
come from. He would work willingly for anyone who
roped him in, but few had harness big enough to fit
him. He wandered the plains, attaching himself to this
or that band of horses for a while, and sometimes
hanging around corrals and ranch houses, but for the
most part he went his way alone.

Just like him to have been smelling around this box,
thought Ken. He tracked the big hoofprints. They
went to the water hole and back several times. They
wandered a good deal. Finally they went away south
into the Buttes. But who were the other horses? The
tracks told him nothing. They also went south into the
Buttes.

Then Ken noticed the white lettering on the outside
of the crate:

TO: *Mr. Beaver Greenway, Blue Moon Ranch,
Idaho, U.S.A.*
FROM: *Lawrence Beckwith, Oak Farms, Nr.
Stroud, Glos. England.*

"Gosh! Beaver Greenway!"

It was a magic name! It brought back to Ken recollections of the most exciting experience of his whole
life, the race meet at Saginaw Falls just a year ago.
His father had allowed him to enter his white stallion,

Thunderhead, in Beaver Greenway's stake, the famous
Free-For-All. Thunderhead had lost, just because he
had preferred to act like a bronc, and buck and throw
his jockey and do some fancy fence-jumping. All the
same he had shown extraordinary speed. Everybody
had said he had it in him to be a steeplechaser. Once
again Ken felt the keen regret that had eaten at him
all the past year—if only he had ridden Thunderhead
himself! "Bet I'd have won . . . *I* could always manage him. . . ."

*Beaver Greenway . . . Blue Moon Ranch:* Ken
read the words slowly again. Blue Moon—he had
heard that that was the name of the great ranch in
Idaho where Greenway's racing stables were. *Beckwith . . . Oak Farms . . . England:* this busted crate
had once held a filly from England, consigned to
Beaver Greenway at the Blue Moon Ranch in Idaho.
Ken heaved a deep sigh. He could deduce no more,
but it was enough to make him feel that, by chance,
he had come in contact with important events and
important people.

He had a sudden sense of time passing. He was expected home for lunch and he had not yet done his errand at Joe Daly's.

He hurriedly mounted Flicka.

# 3

When Ken reached the Daly ranch house—a one-story
building of rough logs with a rickety porch—and put
Flicka's nose to the stack of hay in the yard, he heard

voices. Buck was home, then. He felt a little glow of pleasure. Buck Daly, Joe's son, was a friend. He looked like an Indian, small and swarthy and expressionless, and he had an Indian's skills. He had taught Ken and Howard McLaughlin how to trail animals on the prairies, how to trap beaver and mink, how to poison coyotes.

Ken's loud thump on the door was answered by Joe. "Come in! Come in! We're jess settin' down to dinner. Hev a bite to eat with us."

Ken greeted Joe and Buck and cast a glance at the repast spread on the kitchen table—beans, white bread and jam. He answered, "No thanks—I've got to get home for dinner. But I'll sit down a minute."

A big pot of coffee had been dragged forward on the stove. It sat, usually, on the back, half-filled with old grounds that were boiled up again whenever a fresh cup was wanted.

Buck set a cracked cup and saucer before Ken and filled it.

Joe Daly, who had a long quivering face with lips turned in, and colorless red-rimmed eyes, was bubbling with news. "Say! What d'ye think Buck seen this morning!"

Ken had been about to spring his own bit of gossip about the crate, but he stopped and looked at Buck's oily dark face inquiringly. Buck was shoveling beans into his mouth with his knife.

"Tell him, Buck," prodded his father.

Buck wiped his mouth with his hand and leaned back in his chair. "This mornin' early, I wuz up on the hill there," he made a wide gesture with one arm, "where I got my coyote bait put out. I wuz standin' fixin' the bait—rollin' the pizen into the balls of lard, w'en I heerd a stallion scream."

"A stallion!" Ken was interested. Except for Banner, his father's purebred stud, there were no stallions that he knew of in the neighborhood.

"An' I tuk a look aroun'," continued Buck, "an' way down by the railroad tracks I seen a queer-lookin' box—"

Ken interrupted excitedly, "I saw it too! On the way over—I was going to tell you about it! A bashed-up horse crate!"

"It waan't bashed up w'en I fust seen it. The stallion did the bashing. He wuz goin' round and round it and they wuz another hoss watchin' him—a big feller—looked like Pete. All of a sudden the stud turns hisself aroun' and kicks hell outer the crate. It opens up and out jumps another hoss, all dressed up in a blanket and they runs away together, and after a while, Pete follows 'em slow like."

Buck tilted his chair back, reached to the stove for the coffeepot and refilled his cup.

"Holy Cats! Then the filly was actually in the crate while it was rolling down the hill!"

"Sure wuz," said Buck, going at the beans again. "But wait—I ain't told ye the best part of it yet."

"Tell him, Buck, tell him!" chortled Joe.

Buck finished the pile of beans on his plate, then glanced up, his small black eyes expressionless. "Waal —here's the joker. Who d'ye think the stallion wuz?"

"Who?"

"Your stallion. Thunderhead."

It was a shock to Ken, for Buck said it with certainty. A second later, Ken shook his head. "No it wasn't, Buck—it couldn't have been."

Buck took a piece of bread, made a mop of it and swabbed his plate. "Why not?"

"Because Thunderhead isn't anywhere near here."

"That's wot I tole Buck," put in Joe. "He's up in that there valley in the Buckhorn Mountains, ain't he? What d'ye call it?"

"The Valley of the Eagles," said Ken and he said it with pride, for it was he who had first discovered the valley and given it its name. "Yep, he's up there and he can't get out and I saw him there not so very long ago."

"W'en?" asked Buck.

"I went up there when I got home from school in June—the last week it was, I guess."

Joe looked anxiously at Buck to see what he made of it. Buck shook his head. "That's quite a spell back, Ken. Thunderhead might have got out since then."

"He wouldn't leave his mares, Buck—you know that."

"That's right." Buck puzzled over this. "How many mares did he have?"

"About twenty," said Ken.

"Mebbe he come out to git some more. He wuz stealin' a mare w'en I seen him this mornin'. Mebbe he's ben out all summer, rampagin' around, stealin' mares like that old-timer, the Albino, uster—the mustang he's a throwback to."

Ken shook his head. "Nothing would make him leave that valley."

"*Couldn't* he leave it ef he tuk a notion to?"

"Not at the near end of it where I dynamited the only passage that leads into it."

"Ken," said Joe, "I never could figger why in tarnation ye done a thing like that."

Ken, always ready to talk about the exploits of his wonder horse, explained. "You see, he'd had that fight with the Albino up in that valley, and he'd killed him. And then he'd taken his mares and lived with them like a range stallion for a while. He wasn't just a baby colt any more. If we'd brought him home, and put him out at pasture with our other horses, what would he have done to Banner?"

There was silence in the dark little kitchen for a while. Every man there knew what would have happened to Banner; and it wasn't good to think of.

"I reckon ef Thunderhead did anything to Banner yer Dad would jess take his big Express rifle an' put a bullet through his head," said Joe.

"He sure would."

"I niver seen a man love a hoss the way yer father loves that red stallion of his'n."

"You c'd have gelded Thunderhead, Ken," said Buck. "Then he'd be safe."

Ken's mouth tightened. "I don't want him gelded— ever. It might kill him—it often does."

"Aw, Kennie—on'y now an' then," said Joe.

Ken's voice rose. This issue of whether or not Thunderhead should be gelded was one which had come up between him and his father over and over again. So far, luck had been with him. "Look here!" he shouted. "I saw that fight between Thunderhead and the Albino! Those two horses stood up on their hind legs and screamed at each other like prehistoric monsters! And then Thunderhead killed the Albino! Could he have done that if he had been gelded?"

Considerably overawed by Ken's large words and flashing eyes as well as by the picture he evoked, his listeners made no answer. Then Buck returned to his point. "Couldn't Thunderhead have left the valley at the other end, even ef he couldn't git out where you blasted the path shut?"

Ken calmed down. "Oh, sure! Down at the far end there are a lot of gorges and ravines he could get out of, if he wanted to, but why would he? He had everything he needed there—food, water, shelter. And what would he do with all the mares and colts?"

Buck thought this over, drawing the jam pot to him and taking several big spoonfuls.

"Must have been some other horse you saw," said Ken.

Buck said, "Ain't no white stallion round yer 'cept yore Thunderhead."

"How far away were you?"

"About two mile."

"You couldn't tell at that distance."

"Could tell it was a white hoss."

"Say," said Joe, "how about them two white work hosses of Bill Olcott's? They're often out on the range."

"I tole ye I heerd him neigh—an' not like no work hoss neither," said Buck.

"Did you go down to the crate?"

"Sure. Comin' home. I seen the cushions inside an' the photygraph an' all the fancy fixin's. Some class!"

"Son," said Joe, "pears to me like ye ought to git word to the station agent wot happened. They've likely missed that hoss awready."

"That's right. I could ride to Red Buttes!" suggested Buck.

"Fifteen mile there an' fifteen back!" said his father. "An' noon now, an' a day's work waitin' fer ye on the fences—no siree!"

Buck looked crestfallen and Ken grinned sympathy.

"But, " said Joe, "ye better take yer pony an' ride over to Satterlys'—that's on'y a mile—they'll let ye use their telyphone—and git word to the stationmaster at Red Buttes. This is gonna make some stink an' yo're an important witness. That crew in the caboose is gonna git hell, believe me!"

"Okay." Buck began to carry the dishes to the sink.

Ken got up and took a few steps toward the door. "Guess I'll be going, Joe."

"Ain't you goin' to take a look at yer rams?" asked Joe.

"Oh, gosh! Sure! That's what I came over to see you about! I almost forgot!"

While Buck made the few swift gestures which passed for dishwashing in the Daly household, Ken and Joe walked out around the house, past the barn and pigsties and corrals to the quarter-mile of good pasture land which Joe had fenced in with three-foot hog wire. They leaned against the gate.

The handsome Corriedales were grazing quietly, scattered over the pasture. Ken's eyes dwelt on the symmetrical, curving horns, rising from the thick curly wool. They reminded him of something he had seen once in the Valley of the Eagles when he had gone there to look for Thunderhead—a fight between two Rocky Mountain horned sheep up on a ledge on the mountainside. One had killed the other and shoved it off the ledge. Eagles had plummeted down into the forest, had torn the dead ram to pieces and carried huge chunks of it to their greedy eaglets in the eyrie.

"I bet they get into some big fights," he said.

"Sure. Ever' week, about, I hears them big booms! An' I have to go out with a club an' break it up."

"What I came over for," said Ken, "was to tell you, Dad wants them to have increased feedings from now until breeding time."

"Cotton cake?"

"Yes. He's ordered five tons. When it comes, Gus'll bring it over in the truck. He wants you to give them a sack a day."

"That'll put the juice into 'em."

They walked back to the house. Buck was just mounting his pony. Ken said goodby to Daly and the two boys rode together until their ways parted.

As Buck left him, Ken turned in his saddle and called, "Say! Buck!"

Buck halted.

"You don't really think that was Thunderhead, do you?"

Buck ruminated for quite a while before he answered. "Mebbe not, Ken." He started off again. A little farther on he checked his horse and called back, "But he wuz white. An' he wuz a white stallion."

Ken cantered homeward in so great a state of confusion that he forgot all about his dinner in spite of the pangs that were gnawing his stomach.

One moment he utterly disbelieved Buck's surmise; the next he was in agony for fear it was true.

On the subject of what should be done with Thunderhead, there had been a long running fight between himself and his father ever since the horse had been born, four years ago. Rob McLaughlin insisted that, the colt being a throwback, he would always be uncontrollable, and, unless gelded, a menace to Banner and no use as a saddle horse.

Ken's action in putting Thunderhead into the valley to take the place of the stallion, the Albino, whom Thunderhead had killed, and then shutting him in there with the mares, had seemed to solve the problem. Thunderhead was happy, all was quiet on the Goose Bar, and Ken, although he no longer had the daily use of him, yet knew that the colt was living the life of a natural, unaltered animal; and this satisfied the boy in a very deep way. He had been profoundly affected by the beauty of the valley and the way the

Albino lived there, like a king. If he could give such a life as that to the horse he loved so well, he would have given him the best there was.

But if Thunderhead had left the valley! If he were out!

Each time this thought came, there came with it an anguishing physical pang. He began to look desperately around for food. Tie Siding was not far away. He had meant, in any case, to pick up the mail before he went home.

He searched in his pockets for money. A dime in one—three pennies and a two-bit piece in another. Slightly cheered by this wealth, he altered his direction and soon was seated at the counter of the little short-order house in Tie Siding, wolfing sandwiches.

He looked out of the window. It was a dreary enough spot on the sunniest day, just the square box of a Post Office, the little store beside it and across the tracks, the station. Today, with the wind blowing dust and trash along the ground and no color in the sky or earth it was depressing and gave him a foreboding.

Suddenly Ken slid down from his high stool and ran to open the door. "Howard!" he yelled.

The tall fellow who was just getting out of the Goose Bar station wagon turned. "Hi, Ken! Why didn't you come home for lunch?"

"Didn't get through at Daly's," said Ken. "I'm having a sandwich here, now. Come on in. Got something to tell you."

"I'll get the mail first," said Howard, going toward the Post Office.

A few moments later, Howard, who had just finished a hearty meal at home, was ordering coffee and doughnuts.

Howard McLaughlin, at eighteen, was two inches

taller than his father. He had a merry, gibing face and
was considered handsome. His black hair was parted
in the exact center, his clear, light blue eyes had an in-
scrutable expression, his thin red mouth went down at
one corner.

"Hurry up," said Ken nervously. But his brother was
looking through the mail. There was a letter for him,
addressed in large feminine handwriting. He shoved
the rest of the mail into his pockets and opened and
began to read his own as he sipped his coffee.

Ken paid his check, went out and stood waiting by
the station wagon. This behavior brought Howard out
in a hurry—Ken was certainly being mysterious about
something.

The boys got into the front seat and Ken poured out
all he had seen and heard that morning.

Howard's eyes lighted with interest. "Gosh!" he exclaimed. "A filly of Beaver Greenway's! It sure looks
like your colt has got out of that valley and you're in
for it, Ken."

"Got any money?" asked Ken.

"What you want it for?"

"Want to buy some more sandwiches. I'm going up
to the valley to see if he's there or not."

"Without going home and telling Dad? You'll get
hell."

"I'm going to get hell anyway—and plenty of it.
Look, Howard, I've *got* to go. But don't tell Dad anything about it—about what Buck saw—about the
crate or anything."

"Why not? He's going to know, isn't he?"

"But Howard, he'll get all stirred up about Thunderhead. And maybe it wasn't Thunderhead after all. I
don't see how it could have been. I bet when I get to
the valley I'll find him there. But even so, Dad'll still

be stirred up and mad at me because he *got* stirred up."

"What'll I tell him?"

"Oh, tell him something—you know—figure something out."

For some time the boys argued about just what could be told their father with honesty and yet the proper amount of concealment. At last Howard promised, Ken stuffed his pockets with sandwiches, mounted Flicka and turned her head south toward the Buckhorn Hills.

# 4

The corral of the Goose Bar stables was full of men and horses.

Rob McLaughlin, called Captain because he was a West Point graduate and, if he weren't a captain, at least looked the part, had done his haying late this year. The hay crew had just been dismissed. Today, Tim and Wink, the two young hired men, had been working on the stacks, shaping them, binding them down with long wires upon the ends of which were fastened railroad ties as weights. They were now unharnessing Big Joe and Tommy from the light wagon which had carried their tools.

Ross Buckley, a broncobuster and wrangler, a bow-legged wisp of a man in faded, skin-tight bluejeans, was leaning against the fence, rolling himself a cigarette before he rubbed down Senator. Senator was one of six horses who were being prepared for sale to the Army, and Ross Buckley had been hired by Rob to do the job. Senator was weary after the going-over he had received, and stood near Ross with his head hanging. Knowing that Ross's arm was looped through the rein, he made no effort to move.

Rob McLaughlin was talking with Gus, the Swede, who was his foreman. Rob had just returned from a long ride and stood in worn and wrinkled leather boots that were mellowed to a rich old oak shade. Dust was thick in the creases. Heavy spur chains went under the insteps. The whipcord breeches were tight around his slightly bowed knees; a chamois-skin lumberjacket was snug around his powerful body. He was burned to a rich bronze up to the line where his wide felt hat gripped his brow. Deep under his black eyebrows were points of blue, keen and challenging. Howard and Ken often found it difficult to meet their father's eyes.

Two summers before, Rob had shipped East for sale every horse on the place except the spring colts, the yearlings, the two-year-olds, and four horses for the use of the family: Flicka, her son Thunderhead, her daughter Touch and Go, and Gypsy, Rob's own aged saddle mare, a relic of his youth. Of these four, there was now only one left, Flicka. Gypsy was dead, Touch and Go sold, and Thunderhead in the Buckhorn Mountains. But the young stuff growing up had provided them with new mounts. Rob had Mohawk, a big blood-bay gelding who was now standing at his shoulder. Howard had Sun Dog, and Nell McLaughlin, mother of the two boys, had a rangy sorrel who was named Redwing after one of the best horses ever raised on the Goose Bar Ranch.

Rob and Gus were examining the weather, planning the next day's work. "We'll bring Banner in to the corral in the morning," said Rob, "and get those two mares bred."

"Yah." Gus nodded slowly.

"Then in the afternoon we'll brand the colts."

"Gude weather fur branding," said Gus.

"Some time this week," said Rob, "Colonel Dickenson, the Army Remount Officer, is coming out to look over the geldings. Keep them all pretty close to the corral."

Gus nodded, his eyes roving observantly over the men and horses while he listened to his boss.

Kim, the yellow collie, lay on the grass outside the fence, panting violently, his long red tongue hanging out of the side of his mouth. He had been out with Rob and had gone off on some wild coyote hunts that had taken him far afield and worn him out. At intervals he heaved himself up, went to the horse trough which brimmed with cool spring water spilling a musical trickle out at the lower end, and noisily lapped, then returned and flopped on the ground again.

Pauly, a little brown tortoise-shell cat with long topaz eyes, appeared in the stable door, and stood there with dignity, looking out into the corral. In her mouth she held a large rat, still alive, and her head was high to carry the weight. She stepped daintily across the threshold, past the manure pile, and threaded her way between the horses' feet to the fence, jumped the lowest rail, and passed Kim, who turned his head to watch her and the rat but did not close his mouth nor cease his panting. Pauly plunged into the deep grass and disappeared from view. All eyes had followed her.

"See that big rat!" exclaimed Wink.

"She get one yoost about every day," said Gus.

"She's got kittens," said Tim, "and she hunts rats and bunnies and gophers all day for them."

A loud, indignant *moo-oo-oo* came from the east corral behind the barn.

Rob looked at Gus in surprise. "What in hell are the cows doing up here?"

"It ain't our cows, Boss. Some of Johnson's cows broke tru de fence in de corner of Section Eighteen. Nine white faces and some calves. Wink and Tim found 'em and corralled 'em. Want I should tell Wink to drive 'em back?"

"No. Wink's got to milk. I'll send Ken."

"Ken ain't home yet, Boss—leastways, Flicka's not here."

"Howard, then."

"Howard—" Gus looked searchingly around. "I ain't seen him neither."

"There's his horse." Rob pointed to a tall black, grazing in the pasture outside the corral.

"He tuk de station wagon."

"To get the mail?"

"Yah."

Rob gave an impatient exclamation. "And now it's milking time. When those kids get off the ranch they don't ever get home!"

"Dot's kids for you," said Gus, a slow warm smile crinkling his pink face.

Rob put the reins of Mohawk into Gus's hand. "Give him a good rubdown and be sure none of the horses can get out into the home pasture where they would get mixed up with Banner. Don't want any trouble."

"Yah, Boss." Gus took Mohawk's rein and led him into the stable.

Rob stood a moment, thinking, aware of the two blue jays squawking angrily at each other in the big pine south of the stables, of a flock of little birds splashing in the trickle of water that spilled from the trough, of the familiar smell of manure, of steaming horsehides, of corral dust—he was annoyed at the failure of the boys to show up.

He strode suddenly forward and Kim arose and ran around the corral to follow.

As they went down through the Gorge toward the house they were joined by Chaps, the black cocker spaniel, so named because of the long black curls on his legs. He was a tardy homecomer from the run with Rob and Mohawk. Chaps, in spite of his short legs, must be on every ride, every hunt, usually getting home long after the collie or the horses.

As a matter of habit, Rob lifted his eyes to the sky and examined the weather with thought of tomorrow's work.

The cows were waiting at the gate of the pasture to be milked. Formerly, Nell had taken complete charge of the dairy. But now there was the baby, Penelope Margaret, named after Nell's mother and his own, and her care took most of Nell's time. Rob had taken over the cows and the dairy himself. He thought with satisfaction of the fine crop of calves. The bull, a handsome Guernsey named Cricket, whom he had bought as a calf from a famous Star Valley, Wyoming, herd, was giving results. He was a four-year-old and already his first calves were milking and the butterfat was high. But the bull was getting bad tempered— better put a ring in his nose. He'd neglected that.

He reached the paved yard behind the kitchen door of the house. Nell would be upstairs with Penny. Soon now, she would give Penny her bath and her supper.

At the thought of Nell, he became motionless. There was a look of puzzlement on his face. . . . Nell! How quiet she was these days. She didn't look well.

She'd always had a tendency to have circles under her eyes but since Penny was born, they had been blue and transparent. Or was she worried? Dissatisfied? Had he fallen down on anything he should have done? She *couldn't* be unhappy now—not *now*—why, he had given her the piano! She had a cook! And two new bathrooms and a furnace had been installed since the new band of sheep had brought prosperity to the Goose Bar Ranch!

The look of anxiety was wiped off his face as his mind ran over the score. He beamed with satisfaction, took a rag from a hook inside the laundry door and wiped the dust off his boots. Leaning over the outside faucet, he let the cold water run and sloshed it over his face and arms. Then he scrubbed his hands and dried them on the towel which hung inside the door.

The Goose Bar ranch house was as pretty, these days of prosperity, and as cared for, as a lovely woman. It was a long house, for the most part not more than one room deep, and it went down in steps following the contour of the ground, one step down from kitchen to dining-room, another step down to living-room and Rob's study, another to the far wing which consisted of a couple of bedrooms and a bath. A twelve-foot terrace ran the full length of the house in front, the far end was shaded by a pergola. The terrace was supported by a low wall of beautifully laid stone and tucked under and against this was a wide flower border, a riot of color for all of the short summer, unless frost or hail cut it down.

The door of the house opened directly into the living-room from the terrace and was a heavy-paneled Dutch door, cut in half horizontally. The bottom-half was usually closed, the upper-half standing open. Window boxes holding masses of dark salmon geraniums were underneath the long casement windows which opened onto the terrace, and these boxes and the doors were the color of the sky, or of the bluebirds that came in whole migrations to swing over the Green or shelter themselves against the cold in the big barn. The roofs of the house were of the soft shade of red which is the standard color for American barns. The house itself was made of granite, a soft, dusty shade of pink. And the terrace steps, hewn of rough stone and flanked with lilac bushes, led down to the lawn, two acres of it, which Nell called the Green, after the little village greens in her native state of Massachusetts.

Beyond the Green was the hill rising abuptly, terminating in a sheer cliff, all of it clothed in pine. The tall points of the pines made a jagged outline against the sky. When there was a high wind, the pines roared like surf. At night, when the moon rose, it could be seen from the house or the terrace through the trunks and branches of the pines like a theatrical backdrop. Above, on the top of the cliff, there was a rocky, pine-studded terrain where the boys loved to climb and explore. The animals, too. Even the horses, put to graze on the Green, would attempt to climb the cliff. From the windows of the ranch house they could be seen, their large bodies pressed sideways against the cliff clinging to some invisible irregularities of rock, or defiling slowly through the pines, their golden hides glinting in the sun. It was up this steep hill that the cats vanished. From the top of it, on several occasions, had come the ear-splitting scream of a panther.

Rob went around to the front. Down the length of the terrace, he walked in fragrance and color between the geraniums of the window boxes and the massed flowers of the border beneath the stone wall. Still in bloom! This cold hadn't nipped them—not yet! But if snow came, goodby to the geraniums and all the rest. He remembered the autumn when Nell had laid blankets over the window boxes, hoping to tide the flowers through an early snow and have them for weeks more of Indian summer. The sweetness of the petunias filled his nostrils. He thought that the smell had the quality of innocence and that it drew one back to childhood. It went with his thoughts of Nell and little Penny. As always, when anything reminded him of Nell or he saw her unexpectedly, he felt happiness so intense it was like pain.

On the pergola which shaded the far end of the terrace a bluebird hopped nervously from pole to pole, but did not fly away as Rob came nearer. Behind the bluebird, half-hidden among the big leaves of the grapevine which straggled over the pergola, was his mate whom he brought to the ranch regularly every spring and with whom he reared a family and then left, around the time of the first snow.

Rob went into the house and stood at the foot of the stairs, listening, wondering if Nell were taking a nap, but no sound reached him. He returned to the living-room and paused beside the piano, his hand caressing the polished surface. His pride in this gift to his wife was accompanied by chagrin that for so many years of her life with him she should have been without one.

When he had taken her from her comfortable home in Boston twenty years before, and brought her to this ranch, he had never intended that she should be deprived of her music as well as all the other inevitable deprivations. He had intended buying her one that first year; then, the next year. Then came a baby; a year later additional investments in brood mares. Then another baby; then a year of losses and debts, and so it had gone. And for the last eight or ten years, things had been so bad that such an expensive and extravagant purchase as a grand piano was not even to be thought of. It was never mentioned. He had wondered if she had missed it dreadfully. You couldn't tell. She never spoke of it. He had believed, when he thought about it, that she was so perfectly resigned to the alteration of her life and circumstances, so absorbed in her daily work, so entranced with the wildness and beauty and epic grandeur of the country in which her lot was cast, and above all, so passionately loving of her two boys and himself, that not even within herself was there any lamenting.

All the greater, then, had been his happiness when he counted up the first crop of lambs from his new flocks, and realized that the time had come when he could give Nell a piano.

He had told her only that he had to go to Denver to arrange with a commission house for the sale of the lambs and that he might be gone for several days.

He had spent the time with the leading musician of Denver, a celebrated pianist, who went with him from one store to another. They sampled every second-hand grand piano of good make which was advertised for sale. The one they had picked, at last, was a reconstructed Steinway, twenty-five years old, embodying a number of advantageous features which newer makes did not have. The last owner had been a music teacher. Before that it had been owned by a virtuoso who had returned to Europe. It was he who had discovered the piano and had it completely reconstructed. Now it was standing in a storage house, waiting for a new owner—a long, shining, concert grand.

Rob maneuvered to have Nell away on the afternoon that the big truck rolled up to the front of the house and disgorged the piano. When Nell returned it was standing in place, the lid open. Rob himself sat near by in his pet armchair, in a carefully casual position, a pipe in his mouth, newspaper in his hands, his leg slung over the arm of the chair.

But he couldn't keep up the appearance of casualness when he saw Nell's amazement. He jumped up and kissed her hard. "Go try it!" he ordered.

She had gone slowly, almost fearfully, to the piano bench, pulling off her gloves. Then, a hand at each side of her gripping the bench, she had just stared down at the keys.

He had stood beside her, bursting with happiness. "Try it! Try it!" he had urged her.

She put her right hand on the keys, then dropped it in her lap. "I can't," she said.

He stood silent, aware of her emotion.

"If you would go out—" she said hesitantly, and he had gone out and stood on the terrace, looking around, drawing deep breaths of pride and triumph. But all his attention turned backward, listening for the first note of music.

It seemed a long time coming. A few notes, as if she were feeling for the tone. There it was! Rob's skin tingled! The glorious depth of it! The long sounding of the string! Then in a rush she played a few chords, a scale. Her fingers stumbled a little. Now she was playing just two notes, a fifth in a low register. She played it supplicatingly, over and over again, as if she were begging the piano to give her its real voice, not just to suffer her attack upon it. And at last through those two notes, Rob heard the true voice of the piano. He went slowly back into the room. She did not know he was there. Her face was rapt. She sat with one elbow propped on the rack, her head leaning on her hand, the other hand playing that low fifth with a deep, gentle touch, over and over.

At last he couldn't help asking her why she kept playing just those two notes, and why there were tears in her eyes. She tried to explain and every word made him happier because he saw how much it meant to her and how great a gift, therefore, he had been able to make her.

She explained hesitatingly, as if she were feeling her way through the thoughts. "I learned to do this when I was a child. By the hour. It is as if we know so small a part of life and of the universe and all that is. This world, all worlds, heaven, hell—whatever there is in the way of worlds and universes and life! How little we knew! We *cannot* know more. We're not constituted to know more, and yet we can't help wishing we could. Well, music hints at all that we cannot know but just dream of. If I sit playing one chord over and over, listening with an absolutely blank mind, it does something to me. Deep down. I don't know what, but it is a marvelous emotion. Everything falls away. And I begin to be aware of the depths of things—I don't know what to call them. Perhaps beauty. Perhaps love. Perhaps an immeasurable longing. Of the final deep and dreadful and marvelous things that would be too much for human beings to bear if they did know of them. Yes—that's it, through these two notes, I get a message, a promise, a terrible entice-ment."

As she talked, she kept playing the notes, and her voice died away and he saw that she had forgotten him again, sitting there absorbed, listening. . . .

A moment or two later she began to laugh and said, "I wonder how I can train Redwing to love my music?

I might tie him to the pergola out there so that he could put his head in the door and see me playing and hear it!"

And Rob had answered, "No, you'd have to be with him, close beside him, both of you hearing music together. Then he'd associate you with it."

"I'd have to be twins," laughed Nell. "Oh, Rob! I'm so happy about this I could die!" And she had jumped up and hugged him like a kid.

The animals had come to love the music. Even the cats. One day Nell had been playing the piano and Pauly had come through the dining-room, walking sedately with her five kittens obediently following in single file, and had laid herself down on her side under the piano bench. Her head was raised, bent over, listening, her dreaming topaz eyes half closed. The kittens nursed, their paws and claws going in and out against Pauly's soft belly, taking in the music with their mother's milk. Pauly, obviously, had considered this an important part of their training.

All this drifted through Rob's mind as he stood stroking the piano. He reached a finger down and pressed one of the notes, trying to hear in it the things his wife heard. At that moment there was the sound of the station wagon coming up the hill behind the house.

Rob went to the back door and threw it open.

"Howard!"

"Yes, sir—here's the mail."

"Mail! You left here at one to get the mail and now it's milking time! Where's Ken?"

"Well, Dad, he's gone up to the valley to see Thunderhead."

Rob's eyes narrowed. He kept looking at Howard without speaking. Howard continued. "You see the

haying's over and soon we'll be going back to school,"
Howard paused checking the truth of everything he
was saying, "and he was awfully keen on seeing Thunderhead again."

Rob continued to eye him as if waiting, but Howard
looked down and said nothing.

"Did he see Daly?"

"Oh, sure! Yeah—he saw Daly and told him about
feeding the rams up."

"Where did he eat?"

"At Tie Siding. I ran into him there when I went for
the mail."

"Well then, he won't get back tonight—" It was
more statement than question. Rob waited a moment.

When Howard merely shook his head, Rob's tone
changed.

"Howard there's something I want you to do. You'll
have to take your horse. A lot of Johnson's cattle broke
through the fence up on the corner of Section Eighteen. They're up in the east corral, nine white-face
cows and some calves. You drive them off our land,
put them back where they belong and mend the fence
before you come back."

"Yes, sir," said Howard with alacrity, jumping out of
the car.

Rob closed the door and walked toward his desk,
his lips tightening in an expression that was half grim,
half amused. He had some work to do on his accounts,
but before he began, he gave a few moments of
thought to Ken's behavior. Whenever Thunderhead
was concerned, or that valley up in the Buckhorns,
Ken was loco. If he had gone up there now, something
was wrong. Howard! Rob broke into a chuckle. Either
Howard was circumbobulating and didn't care who
knew it or he was making a bad job of it. It reminded

Rob of a time when Ken, a little fellow of five, had told him a lengthy, amazing, involved, impossible lie —going on and on—taking the greatest pains about it. And Rob had suddenly cut it short with a roar. "That's a lie, isn't it?" "Yes!" Ken had howled, sobbing. "What's the use of lying to me?" "No use!"

Well, anyway, Howard was shielding Ken. Wait until the kid came back—

He pulled his papers toward him.

Figures were reassuring these days. When he had put the sheep on the ranch, a couple of years ago, the worst of his troubles had ended. Now when he sat at his desk in the evenings, going over his accounts and making forecasts for the future, he could smoke his pipe in comfort, knowing that at last he was on the way to clearing off his debts. After sixteen years of losing money on horses he was now making money on sheep. This meant being able to educate his children properly, employ sufficient help to train and school those horses which he intended to keep, and give Nell the comforts and luxuries he so passionately wanted her to have.

Rob leaned back and took out his pipe. It was a wonder Nell still looked as she did, young, alert, slim and strong. And the way she walked! Light, really gay and young. The hard life at the ranch hadn't taken anything away from her. Thank God for that! But it was time things let up for her. Up to forty a woman can hold her own, but after that—well, things *had* let up for Nell.

## 5

Nell's life was quiet now, not so much riding, not so much to do with her sons and husband, nor with the ranch activities. And not so much activity in the house, either, for there was Pearl to do the housework and cooking, leaving Nell time to take care of Penny and to read and practice and to rest.

It was a great change for her, after having lived like a big sister with her growing boys for so long. Often she was surprised to find herself lonely. Penny was like a darling rose in her bosom, or like a thread of melody in her ear, but not yet a companion.

Nell suspected that part of her loneliness came from having a secret from Rob. It was something she was ashamed to tell. It was, merely, a premonition. When all was going so well with the family, with the ranch, the sheep, the baby girl they had wanted so passionately, could she be the one to cry, "It is all false! Trouble is coming!" No—of course not. Anyway, it was probably nonsense. She would get over it. But those dreams—always of disaster—

A slight shiver shook her. She was sitting in the deep chintz-covered armchair by the front window in her bedroom, one elbow on her knee, her chin in her hand, her eyes on the baby who sat on the floor playing with a red rubber ball.

The dream this morning, just at dawn, had been the worst of all—a nightmare. How real! Being strangled and unable to move, or to struggle, or do the least thing to help herself! And suddenly being awake enough to know that she was lying there in the bed, with Rob beside her, and yet the strangling and the terror and the awful presence that was beating down upon her continuing.

It had faded and she had come fully awake, panting, perspiration on her forehead, and, still the constriction in her throat and anxious not to wake Rob, but forced by her terror to do something to break the spell, she had slipped out of bed and gone through the open door into Penny's nursery.

Nell and Rob shared the large square room over the kitchen, warm in winter, facing the Green and the morning sun. The small room adjoining, Rob's dressing-room, had now been turned over to Penny and held her white-painted furniture ornamented with little clusters of forget-me-nots and pink roses and bowknots of ribbon. There was the chiffonier in which her clothes were kept, the large table holding scales, toilet articles and bath, there were her little table and tiny chairs.

Nell had gone first to the crib. In the faint light of dawn she could see the baby, lying flat on her back, head turned sideways so that her face was in profile, both arms out on the pillow, crooked at the elbow, the closed pink hands making tiny fists.

Nell felt them. Warm and relaxed. How exquisite she was with the high color on her peachy brown cheeks, the long silken lashes, the soft dark hair. Her physical loveliness seemed a marvel to Nell, a marvel that the world was full of infants and small children as beautiful as flowers, tinted like cream and roses, with eyes the color of the blue lilies that bloomed in the meadows early in the summer.

She longed to take the baby up and hold her in her arms and so assuage the fear within herself, but at this hour of the morning, if Penny woke she was likely to stay awake.

Nell had walked restlessly around the room, fussing a little with the baby's clothes which hung on the back of a chair, with the articles on the table.

Then she had gone to the window to look out and see how near it was to sunrise and there, down on the Green, were a man and woman dancing together. It was Pearl, of course, cutting up with a most decrepit object, shirttail flapping outside his baggy dark trousers, rolled-up sleeves showing thin, hairy arms, a battered black felt on his head. The clothes looked empty but they capered ecstatically, keeping pace with Pearl and the brisk wind which whipped her full cotton skirts about her aged legs.

Nell watched them a long time. . . . How happy they were . . . how carefree . . . drunk? Probably. . . .

Nell sighed. For how many years had she held out against employing anyone on the ranch who was not sober—and then at last given in. There were just not enough sober ones. . . . Was it because this was, really, a frontier? With frontier towns? Frontier waifs and strays? At any rate, if it had to be, let it be open. It was part of the agreement with Pearl that she would not drink while on the ranch, provided she was given a jigger of whiskey when she absolutely had to have one. The demands came at any moment, whether guests were present or not. "Captain McLaughlin—"; "Oh—you—want—"; "Yes, please—" Pearl would accompany him to the liquor cabinet, receive the glass of whiskey, drink it down and glide away with a soft "Thank you."

But this caracole of marionettes in the sunrise! It looked like an infringement of the agreement. . . . Where had the man come from? Where would he go when the dance was over? Was it he who had brought the bottle? Had they been out all night?

Of course something ought to be done about it. *Heavens no!* Suppose she should leave! She was priceless—she could cook anything. No matter how many guests, the meals went quietly. Pearl never seemed to think there was much to do. The kitchen was never in wild disorder. Pearl's speech was quiet and she agreed to all that was asked of her. True—she did have a good many husbands—always talking of Bill, or Jack, or Tom.

This fatal charm—in what did it lie? She was a woman of middle age, middle height. She had a voluptuous figure. Her greenish brown hair was cut all over her head and she arranged it in a halo of loose curls. There was always a cigarette hanging from the corner of her mouth, twisting her face and causing her hazel eyes to squint. Her skirts were short and her legs bare, and she moved with a smooth, gliding gait, her feet in a pair of felt slippers.

Nell wondered if the man dancing on the lawn was Tom. Pearl had spoken that name with romantic tenderness. Romance? Ah . . . Romance between the capering scarecrow and maudlin Pearl . . . dancing on the Green in the windy dawn . . . .

Nell had returned to the other room and slipped into bed again, moving closer to Rob's stalwart back, laying her cheek and hand against it to draw strength and courage from him.

All day, the shadow of that morning nightmare had been upon her. After lunch she had rested while Penny slept, and after that had not even troubled to dress and take the baby outdoors, making the excuse to herself that it was windy and cold.

But the room was warm. Thank God for the furnace. Heat in the house, at last, day and night. It stood down there in the deep earthen cellar, black and squat, feeding steam into the radiators, carrying warmth and comfort to every room. After a score of years spent in a Wyoming country house heated only by stoves and open fires, this furnace had made so great a change in the wintertime lives of the Mc-Laughlins that existence seemed a different thing, easier on a dozen counts. The time it had taken just to keep warm during the winters! The hours of work, replenishing woodpiles, hauling coal and stoking fires and stoves! Often on a very cold night Nell had picked up a pillow and put it on top of her head, leaving just a crack for breathing. All different now. She could sleep without being smothered by bedclothes. She could lie back on the pillow with one arm over her head, only a pajama jacket covering it. She could get out of bed on the coldest winter night, put on a robe and slippers and attend to Penny without fear that either of them would be chilled through. She could sit at the window, as she was doing now, with just a thin silk wrapper over her slip.

Penny, without being bundled up in woolens, was playing on the floor with her ball, rolling it, crawling after it, capturing it, hugging it, murmuring all the time in her strange language of sounds that were like bird notes. Nell wondered if Howard and Ken had made the same sounds. If they had, no one had noticed it. They were like the liquid notes of a hermit thrush. It seemed to her that most babies came when their parents were too young and perhaps too preoccupied with other things to enjoy them.

The wind was still blowing. Nell leaned her head to the window and looked out and her face went blank and detached. Meaningless, endless, pageant of wind and birds . . . wind and thrashing trees . . . wind and clouds . . . wind and little cones of dust and leaves that reeled across the ground. . . .

Way down the pasture a string of cows came slowly toward the barn. Nell's eyes came to life as she watched them. The bull was following Pansy. Nell began to count the months. How long since her calf was born—and how many months from now to June?—it would be nice to have Pansy come fresh in June—just about right—She thought about the bull, Cricket, with some anxiety. Was he getting bad tempered? He roared so whenever the men went near him, when he was brought in with the herd, when he stood in the corral waiting for his feed. They were all getting used, by now, to the morning and evening concert of deep bellowing roars. She had read in the newspapers not long ago that the most dangerous wild animal in America, with more killings to his credit than mountain lion or grizzly bear put together, was the purebred dairy bull. She had told Rob about it, but he had pooh-poohed it.

Across the Green, over in the long grass behind the corner of the spring house, a dark shape was lying— the black shepherd dog, the stray, who had appeared at the ranch some months before and had been there ever since. His head was lifted, pointed at Nell's window. Several times she had called to him and waved to him from that window. Now he lay there in the deep grass all day watching it, when he wasn't watching the front door for her to come out.

When the boys had first found him he was cowering under one of the hay wagons and no amount of coaxing or bribing had moved him to come out.

They had decided that there was something the matter with the dog, he was a psychopathic case. What had made him so? Some cruel mistreatment? Was he a sheep dog who had failed in his duty and been punished so that he would never forget it? Whatever it was, he had lost courage and faith. "He's cut his ties with man," said Rob, "he'll be a wanderer all his life." Nell had thought of the old hymn, remembering the deep, sad voice of her grandmother singing it. "I'm a Pilgrim, and I'm a stranger, I can tarry, I can tarry but a night."

Nell had put a platter of food as far under the hay wagon as she could push it, and had called to him. "Here, Pilgrim! Here, Pilgrim! Here's some dinner for you!" But the dog had not moved, and she had gone away and forgotten him. Later that night, before she went to bed, she had remembered him again, and had gone and sat down on the grass beside the wagon and called to him to come out. He did not move. Sitting there, she had half forgotten him and had fallen into a reverie, her face raised to the stars, her hands resting on the grass beside her. "I'm a Pilgrim, and I'm a stranger! I can tarry, I can tarry but a night!" she sang softly. Suddenly she felt a warm tongue licking the back of her hand. She did not move. The dog licked and licked, becoming more courageous and more impassioned as his terror diminished. Nell slowly lifted the other hand, and laid it on his head. He crawled into her arms, she held him tight, he laid his head upon her bosom and, trembling all over, poured out his terrible story in quivering, nearly inaudible cries.

She held him a long time. When she left him, he crawled back under the hay wagon. In the morning the plate of food was empty.

Once again he had a lifework. It was very important. It was to watch over his mistress whenever she took one step, or a thousand steps. To accomplish this filled all his time. For he must lie somewhere, hidden from everyone else, yet close enough to hear all that she did in the house. Of course the sounds she made were quite different from the sounds anyone else made—the way she opened the screen with a little push and let it fall shut with a bang, not a loud bang —not heavy striding steps, but all light and quick and easy.

It was necessary for him to have an understanding with Kim and Chaps. This was accomplished, no one knew how. The dogs knew where he was, perhaps they knew his story; they did not molest him nor expect him to play with them. They understood his duties toward Nell.

Pilgrim had several hideaways in which he concealed himself, all of them enabling him to keep his eyes and ears on the house. If Nell went out, then with half a dozen great leaps he would reach her, all bows and smiles and flourishes, every tooth showing. Now and then she had to say to him, looking at him with regret but still briskly and in a matter of fact manner, "No, I'm sorry, you can't come because I'm going in the car." At that point his tail would stop wagging and his smile would fade.

"But I'll come back," she would add. "And I'm not going to be long. You can just wait."

Even waiting can fill a life.

Penny's ball had disappeared under the dresser. She crawled to her mother and pulled herself up against her knee.

"Baw—Baw—" she trilled questioningly.

Nell caught her up into her arms with passion, crying, "Oh, darling! What if you are to be a baby growing up without a mother!"

Penny struggled. Nell put her down and leaned back in her chair sighing deeply. Penny gurgled a whole exciting story to the effect that she had known where the ball was all the time, as she crawled to retrieve it.

I shouldn't have said that, thought Nell. Her thick, fawn-colored hair was loose on the shoulders of her blue silk wrapper. She pushed her hands through it nervously, lifting the heavy bang from her forehead.

She scolded herself. What's the matter with me? *Something is.* Perhaps its physical. Perhaps it's just this fool premonition. An idea can get into you, and whether it's false or true, can make you awfully miserable. Lots of people before me have had the idea they were going to die. Nothing to moon about—*but those dreams.* It seemed to her that if only she didn't have the nightmares and the feeling of choking she could get hold of herself and be all right again.

She took from her table one of the books of mysticism and poetry which always kept her company. Just the feeling of it strengthened her. These books opened doors in the mind through which one could escape; they gave her courage.

Holding it closed upon her knee, she felt better.

Presently she heard Howard's voice outside. That was Rob talking to him. She put down the book, sprang up and began to dress.

# 6

Soon after breakfast next morning Rob, mounted on Reveillé, and Howard on Jester, and Ross Buckley on Senator, were schooling their horses in the practice field below the cowbarns. These were three fine geldings, conforming to Army specifications, four years old, fifteen and a half hands high, unblemished by barbed wire or any other scars.

A large black car appeared on the road and stopped, drawing up along the rail fence of the practice field.

Rob immediately swung his horse around. Howard followed him.

Descending from the car was a tall thin man, with a genial ruddy face under a thatch of grey hair, dressed in the Westerner's compromise between town and country, the tight-fitting whipcord trousers called "Cheyenne pants," a waist-length jacket, and wide-brimmed felt hat. He limped a little, there was an acousticon in his ear and a small microphone on the breast pocket of his jacket.

"Beaver Greenway!" yelled Rob, dismounting and going to the fence. "What brought you to this part of the world?" The two men shook hands and Rob's eyes took in the car, the English-looking fellow at the wheel with the checked cap and the look of a man who lives around horses—red face, receding chin, pop-eyes. Another man was getting out of the tonneau whom Rob recognized as the Cheyenne freight agent.

"Hackett!" exclaimed Rob. "Glad to see you!" Hackett advanced and shook hands.

"This is my son, Greenway, my older son—you met Ken a year ago—"

Rob motioned to Howard, who dismounted in one swift smooth step, looping the reins over his arm.

"Well," said Greenway, "I've got a tale of woe to tell, and Hackett here suggested you might be the man to help me out."

Howard looked interested and moved a step closer. But Rob said, "Well, Howard, you've got a morning's work on that plug—here, tie Reveillé to the fence for me, will you?"

Howard, obviously disappointed, did as he was told. Rob vaulted the fence and said to his visitors, "We can drive up to the house and be comfortable."

But Greenway had already seated himself on a

boulder by the roadside. "This is all right, McLaughlin. What I've come for—well, there's been sort of an accident."

The man at the wheel opened the door and emerged from the car. Dejectedly, he seated himself on the running board.

At the word "accident" Rob's eyes turned to the freight agent. "Not on the railroad, I hope? Anyone hurt?"

"Nothing as bad as that," said Greenway, "But I've lost a piece of freight."

"Oh." Rob was filling his pipe, carefully tamping the tobacco into the bowl.

Hackett braced one foot on a rock and leaned his arms on his thigh. His comfortable paunch, his cherub face, did not today convey their usual impression of affability. "I'm a worried man," he said. "McLaughlin, that piece of freight was valued at ten thousand dollars."

"Should think you *would* be worried!" Rob gibed at him. "Can't you fire someone?"

Hackett tried to grin back.

"Briefly," said Greenway, "this is what happened. A filly I had bought from the Beckwith breeding stables in England was lost off the railroad in transit. The crate in which she was traveling left the flatcar on the sharp curve this side of Red Buttes and rolled down the incline. I got to Red Buttes to meet her—no filly! No crate!"

"*Flatcar!*" Rob's amazed eyes turned to Hackett. "They wouldn't ship her on a flatcar—and with her crate so loosely lashed that it could swing off on a curve! The railroads don't do things like that—"

Hackett groaned, "Don't rub it in!"

Greenway made a disgusted gesture. "It was all my

fault. I was in too much of a damned hurry to see the filly. See here, this is the way it was. She was shipped from England in charge of Collins here—" his head tilted toward the car and as Rob looked at him, the groom touched his cap. "I can vouch for him. He has been in my employ for years. I sent him to England to bring back the filly. She was coming on a through train to Foxville, Idaho, which is the nearest station on the main line to my ranch. We followed her travels, of course. I say *we* because she's a present for my little grandneice, Carey." He paused a moment. "Carey is a grand little girl, McLaughlin. She and I are great pals. She's a chip off the old block, loves anything on four legs and has ridden since she could walk."

Rob nodded but said nothing.

"I've promised her the finest filly I could find, intending to breed from her later on. I've been interested in a line of horses that are bred at the Beckwith farms in Gloucestershire. Together, we picked this filly, Crown Jewel, from her pedigree and her record. So you can imagine that when she was actually en route, nothing else was talked of in our house. And I had the bright idea of coming down here to Red Buttes, which by road is only a few hundred miles from my place in Idaho, picking the filly up in a trailer and taking her home with me, so cutting off about two days' travel for her. The railroad makes a detour, you know, in going west from Cheyenne to Idaho. Carey was simply wild to do it. I wired them at Cheyenne to put her on the Red Buttes local—it's only a short run. They put her crate on a flatcar—"

Rob glanced at Hackett who protested, "It was the only thing we had in the yards—"

Greenway continued. "I met the train yesterday

morning at Red Buttes and she was gone! Crate and all!"

"Where was her groom?"

Collins shifted uneasily.

Greenway answered with a slight grin in his direction. "Just where you would suppose. In the caboose! Reciting her pedigree to the train crew!"

Collins looked at the ground—a man in misery.

Rob asked, "Wasn't the crate lashed to the flatcar?"

"It was," answered Hackett. "By a dozen boards. But the floor of the car was rotten old wood. The crate must have worked loose gradually—then the strain of that sharp swing around the curb—" he gave a sigh, removed his hat and passed his hand over his bald head.

Rob was stupefied. "I suppose you've found the body? Was she completely crushed? God!" he interrupted himslf, "I hate to think of it!"

Greenway's face brightened. "Wait a minute! From here on the story gets more cheerful! She wasn't killed. She wasn't even hurt!"

"What!"

Greenway continued. "You'll think it's a piece of fiction but here's what happened. A stallion comes along, kicks the crate to pieces, runs away with the filly."

"That doesn't seem like fiction to me," said Rob. "Hey! I've got a notion who the stallion is! I've got a big red fellow up on the Saddle Back there," he pointed with the stem of his pipe to the long indented hill above the ranch. "And he wouldn't pass up a ten-thousand-dollar filly! If he did, I'd fire him!" He laughed at his own joke. "And a crate wouldn't stop him—why he'd kick a *house* to pieces if there was a tidbit like that inside it—" He broke off suddenly, and then said, "Greenway, do you ride?"

Indignantly Greenway answered, "I ride better than I walk or hear! I broke my ankle playing polo and lost my hearing when the Turk kicked me in the head!"

"Fine!" exclaimed Rob.

Greenway put his hand ruefully on the side of his head. "Not so fine—I wouldn't say—"

"I mean—fine that you ride. You and I are going to have a ride, and I'll show you your filly! But wait a minute. How do you know this? Are you sure?"

"A young fellow told it to the station agent at Red Buttes. He saw it himself."

"Who was he?"

"His name is Buck Daly."

"I know him. He's the son of the man who keeps my rams for me. He's a good kid and he knows horses. If he says he saw that happen, it happened. But God, man!" he stepped forward to give Greenway a slap on the back. "What luck! The damndest luck I ever heard of!" Greenway slowly stood up.

Rob continued, "The filly's not hurt! Banner kicks her free before she dies of lying on her back, and brings her here where she is safe." He pointed again to the Saddle Back. "Up there, Greenway!" His grin widened. "Though I won't promise you won't have a colt from her a year from now that you weren't looking for! Come on, let's go—"

"Wait a minute," said Greenway. "What color did you say your stallion is?"

"Red," answered Rob promptly. "He was a chestnut when he was born, very dark with a tail and mane the color of cream. You never saw such coloring. But when he matured his body got lighter and redder and his hair darker. It's a perfect match now—red gold—wonderful!"

"But Buck Daly said the stallion he saw was white."

Rob put his pipe back in his mouth and leaned against the fence. His brows came down over his eyes.

Hackett said, "Now, of course, that's the strange thing about it—we all thought—" he hesitated.

Rob said slowly, "It's *very* strange. I've only known two white stallions in my life. One was called the Albino, a wild horse that used to roam these mountain states and steal mares wherever he could find them— he crossed some of my mares. If he was alive, he'd be the one that did this. But he isn't. He died a violent death a little over a year ago, killed by his own great-grandson—a throwback to him, a colt who was born right on this ranch out of Ken's mare, Flicka. We named him Thunderhead and he's the other white stallion I have known."

"Why couldn't it have been him, McLaughlin?" said Hackett eagerly. "He's the one we thought of right away."

"Because he isn't here any more. He's twenty miles away from here shut into a valley in the Buckhorn Mountains with all of the mares and colts that used to belong to the Albino."

"How do you mean—shut in?" asked Greenway.

"Well the valley is in the crater of an old volcano. It is surrounded by a rampart of volcanic stone. A fissure in this was the entrance to the valley. Ken simply blew up that pathway with dynamite and completely closed it so that Thunderhead could live in there as the Albino had—a sort of king. The natural, wild life."

"With his great-grandsire's harem," grinned Greenway. "To the winner belongs the spoils! Is that it?"

"Exactly!"

Greenway thought a moment. "Is there no other way out?"

Rob did not answer immediately, then he said, "The valley is ∪-shaped. Down at the other end where the ∪ is open, the wall is gone and there is an eruption of the ground in every direction covering a hundred miles or so. Ravines, mountains, gorges—he could get out of there if he wanted, a long, hard way. And of course, if he left the valley, he would have taken his brood along. A stallion never leaves his mares."

Hackett cleared his throat. "I think it was Thunderhead, McLaughlin. I think he left the valley."

"Hah! Sounds as if you know something! Let's have it!"

"My wife was down in Colorado visiting about a month ago. She heard a lot of talk about a stallion that had been raiding the ranches around there, and stealing mares. Folks thought the Albino had come to life again, because it was a white stallion."

There was a moment's silence.

"When was this?" Rob snapped.

"July—August. A dry farmer down at Glendevy, Jeff Stevens, had his two work mares stolen from him—the only work team he had. It pretty near broke him up. Two fine Morgan mares. And over at Steamboat Springs, the man that owns the daily paper, name of Ashley Gildersleeve, he lost a fine saddle mare he had put out at pasture. And he wrote a piece in the paper and called him the 'White Raider' or something like that."

"I'll be damned," exclaimed Rob. "Thunderhead! Out of the valley! All the way through that mountain country!" He leaned forward, picked up a stick, went to the middle of the road, and in the dust began to draw a map. "Look here!" The men drew near.

"See? Here's the valley—here's all that mountainous country south of it, then here are the grazing lands that fan out from it to the south—that's way down in Colorado—then over here to Steamboat Springs, and back through Rabbit Ear Pass, up through the Red Feather country to Fox Park, and then Sherman Hill and the Buttes! A great big curve!"

Greenway straightened up. "And home again. That's natural."

Rob rubbed his chin thoughtfully. "But why would he leave that valley? And all his mares and colts?"

The men stood around in silence for a few moments. Then Greenway asked, "Where is your boy now, McLaughlin? The one who owns the white stallion?"

As Rob turned to answer him an odd expression of surprise dawned on his face. "Strange coincidence! He's up in that valley!" His eyes turned to Howard who was painstakingly putting Jester through a series of figure eights in the middle of the field. "I'm beginning to think everyone knew about this before I did. Howard!"

Howard cantered over to the fence and dismounted.

In a few sentences Rob acquainted Howard with the situation, and asked if Ken had known about it.

"Yes, sir. Buck told him. Buck thought it was Thunderhead. Ken went up to the valley to find out if he was there or not."

Rob turned to the others with a little shrug of his shoulders. "So that's it! We'll know for certain when Ken gets back! That's all, Howard." Howard mounted and cantered away again.

"The thing is," said Greenway, "whoever the stallion is, I want the filly back, if it's possible to find her. There would be tracks to follow. And, by the way, this boy, Buck Daly, said there was another horse near the crate—a horse he called Pete."

Rob nodded. "An old farm horse. Big fellow."

"Buck said Pete was with the filly before the stallion got there." Greenway laughed. "They way he put it—he said he guessed they had talked all night and become friends!"

Rob did not laugh. He said gravely, "Quite possible. Horses form these attachments. Just like human beings. I've seen it happen over and over again. I had a cow once who lost her calf. A yearling heifer that belonged to a different cow got nursing on her. We couldn't break it up. Even when she got older and stopped nursing, or almost stopped, for that's a hard habit to break them of, those two animals were inseparable. I put them in different pastures, but there was only a fence between and they would stand close together, pressed against the fence, licking each other, or the heifer with its head through the wires, nursing. So at last I separated them still further, put another pasture and two fences between them. Damned if they didn't stand against those fences, looking across the pasture at each other, bellowing all day long, with real tears streaming down their faces. We called them Ruth and Naomi."

"It's so human it's gruesome," said Greenway. "Perhaps, then, the filly has two suitors with her. Buck Daly said Pete—if it was Pete—followed them."

Rob puffed at his pipe for a few moments. "It ought not to be too hard to follow that trail,'" he said.

"That's what I came to see you about."

"I couldn't go myself," said Rob. "I'm expecting the Remount Officer, Colonel Dickenson, out this week to inspect some horses I've got ready for the Army."

Greenway made a deprecating gesture. "And of course I couldn't go on such a ride, I'm too old. I can't stand the gaff. But a bunch of young ranchers or cowhands—I'll pay well."

Rob looked at the sky and the pace of the clouds. "Yes, I could get you some men," he said. "The weather's threatening, but if this wind holds I don't think it'll snow. This will have to be carefully planned. If they find them, then there's the job of catching them and that won't be easy. They would either have to build a corral or drive them toward someone's ranch and corral them there."

Hackett seemed more cheerful. He straightened up and blew his nose. "You just leave it all to the Captain, Mr. Greenway. I told you he was the man to come to."

"That's settled then?" asked Greenway. "How soon can you let me know about the men?"

"I'll get right at it," said Rob. "Why don't you stay here? I can put you up."

"As a matter of fact," said Greenway hesitantly, "I am not alone. My sister, Mrs. Palmer, and my grand-niece to whom the filly belongs are at Red Buttes, waiting for news. The child was almost out of her head when the filly turned up missing."

"Where on earth did you spend the night?"

"In a terrible little dump near the station."

"Well, you must come here and stay until this matter is settled. We can easily accomodate three guests."

Collins coughed conspicuously and Rob hastily added, "And there is always room in the bunkhouse for an extra man."

"I accept with pleasure," said Greenway promptly. "And I'm very much obliged."

"You'll be over then—at what time?"

"This afternoon, I think, if that's convenient?"

"Perfectly."

As they got into the car, Rob added, "And I think

it'd be a good idea to get on that trail without losing any time. I'm going to telephone the station and have them send someone over to tell young Buck to get on his pony and see if he can follow those tracks through the Buttes. Then, if we can get the men together by tomorrow morning, we'll have gained time." He grinned at the freight agent. "Don't let it get you down, Hackett! There's always the insurance!"

Hackett leaned out of the window and said, "Lucky for you the law don't hold a man responsible if his stallion rustles mares!"

Rob stood watching as the car, turning, demolished the map he had drawn in the dust and then sped away. His mind was racing. Thunderhead! Yes, probably this was his doing. He'd know soon, when Ken got back. And if it was—how about that old farmer down in Glendevy—Jeff Stevens—who had lost his two work mares?

He ground his heel into the road. Yes—he'd have to lend him a work team—truck them down there. . . .

He glared at the back of the vanishing car as if it had been the culprit.

Ken was standing on the rampart of the valley, looking over it to the mountains in the south that guarded it, range after range blanketed with a fresh fall of snow—Kyrie and the Thunderer and Epsilon and Lindbergh and Torry Peak.

He was glad that he was alone so that no one could see that he had been crying.

There was no longer that band of beautiful horses and handsome colts in the valley. There were, instead, carcasses and bleaching bones with vultures and coyotes still busy about them. The birds were heavy and slow as if they had fed to repletion.

How many had died? All? Ken had walked the floor of the valley for hours. It was impossible to tell how many, for the bones were scattered widely. But not Thunderhead. Not even coyotes eat tails—there would have been a white tail.

It was as if, from one of those high mountain peaks, a breath of poison gas had been released to creep down the gorges and cover the floor of this valley and bring death to every living thing in it. No, not every living thing, only those that ate grass. And not poison gas, but poison *grass*—it must have been that. Loco weed, larkspur, frozen alfalfa, some one of the murdering weeds. It wouldn't be the first time.

Ken looked at the valley with an almost bewildered expression. This had been part of his life—a kind of horse heaven. Just to think about it—and about Thunderhead reigning in it—had made him happy. He used to dream about it.

A cold wind hit him and made the tears on his face turn to ice. It filled him with such loneliness that it was like a sickness.

To look at the mountains made him more lonely, but he kept looking at them. Perhaps, if he looked long enough, they would give him the answer. . . . No. . . . They were indifferent. This meant nothing to them. At last he began to be comforted by their indifference. Time—what was it? How long had they been standing there like sentinels? Perhaps often before some pestilence had wiped life from the valley, and still the mountains stood in their places, and they didn't care, and the seasons and the years had come and gone and rains and storms and snows and sun and wind had taken away the horror and foulness and decay, and washed it clean. This could happen again. And again, into the valley could come a beautiful tribe of horses looking for some place where they could be safe and happy. And there could be a kingdom once more, as the Albino's had been, as Thunderhead's had been.

As he thought about this, it seemed to Ken that those great sweeps of time were rushing through him. It was as if he were struggling to reach across the death in the valley to the mountains. He wanted to stand there until he could feel strong again, as indifferent as they; and not as if he were going to burst out crying every time he thought of it. After all, Thunderhead was not there rotting in the grass, he was out! He was on the rampage! He was forming a new band! He was stealing mares!

And then it all seemed too much for Ken, and he put his hands over his face and sobbed. It was just for a second. And next he did a little clattering dance on the stone of the rampart. And then he looked up at that highest peak of all, the Thunderer, and yelled, "Hi, Thunderhead!" so loud it almost split his throat and the slow echoes wafted it back to him in the living voice of the mountain, "I Underhead!" Then he rushed back to Flicka, mounted her, and rode home as fast as he could.

Sweet, fresh-cut hay, still green from the meadows, and a boy worn out with excitement and sorrow and hope and hard riding—he dove into it head first. He rolled close under its protecting walls.

But sleep would not come immediately. The images still danced in his brain. The ride home, the pouring out of the whole story to his family, his mother's gentleness, his father's concern. And all that he had heard from them—Beaver Greenway—A ten-thousand-dollar race horse owned by a child—Guests coming to the ranch—"Go and get some sleep, Ken, you and Howard can go on the hunt for Thunderhead and the

English filly."

He burrowed further into the hay, then turned on his back.

Ah, the sweet smell of it! His eyes were full of the sky. There was one bird in it, not a vulture, just a little fellow crying "Killdeer! Killdeer!" swinging, playing with the wind, having a tood time. His eyes swung with the bird. He was lifted up, he went higher and higher. At last he was up there in the clean sky . . . free . . . untroubled . . . swinging in the wind, both wings spread . . . "Killdeer! . . . Killdeer!" . . .

# 7

When Ken awoke he did not know where he was. Piece by piece the memories came back to him, and at last he sat up wondering how long he had been there. He leaned against the hay waiting for the heavy load of sleep to lift.

It had been early in the afternoon when he had come to the haystack—now it had the feel of milking time, or even later.

He was hungry. He had eaten something as soon as he had arrived from the valley, but he hadn't wanted much. Now he felt as if he hadn't eaten for a week.

He stood up, stretched, brushed the hay off himself and looked around, coming back to the world from the far journey which he had made in spirit as well as body.

A glance around told him the time. The dogs were waiting outside the kitchen door to be fed. The cows had been milked and were standing by the corral gates placidly chewing their cuds. His eyes were arrested by the sight of a large black car drawn up behind the house—Ah! The guests had arrived! The child—Ken began to feel quite himself again, alert and eager. But first to get something to eat. There was still an hour or more before supper.

Buttermilk—there was likely to be a big can of it standing in the cold-water trough in the spring house.

At the door he almost collided with a girl who was coming out, very carefully carrying a tray on which there was a small pitcher. She was walking slowly, her eyes on the pitcher.

"Oh!" exclaimed Ken.

She looked up, showing no surprise. She had a quiet, child face, direct grey eyes under dark eyebrows that went up at the tips like swallows' wings, and straight brown hair in a smooth, shining fall to her shoulders. It was held out of her eyes by a blue velvet ribbon.

"Hello," she said gravely.

"Oh," Ken said again, embarassed, "who—well I guess—oh, you're the child."

"I am Carey," she said quietly.

"Oh." Ken stared at her, thinking he had never seen anyone like her before. What was she anyway? Child or young lady?

Seeing the question in his eyes she gave her full name sedately. "Carey Palmer Marsh."

"Oh. Well. I see. Well—is your mother here too?"

"My mother is dead."

This came in the same quiet way.

"I'm sorry." After that Ken could think of nothing to say. She stood now and then looking right at him, now and then down at the pitcher of buttermilk. Perhaps she was wondering why he did not step to one side and let her pass, but he simply could not move.

"Is your father here?"

"My father is dead too."

"Oh, excuse me! I'm terribly sorry."

"You don't have to be sorry. All that was long ago. I never knew them. I've always lived with my grandmother. That's Mrs. Palmer. And then when I was five, Grandma and I left Philadelphia and came to live with Uncle Beaver. You have met him."

"Oh, yes. I met him a year ago at the races. Oh, I'm terribly sorry about the filly and my stallion's stealing her. She's yours, isn't she?"

It seemed for a moment as if Carey would be unconcerned about this, too. She made no reply, keeping her head down. Then it turned sideways as if to hide from his eyes, and he saw big drops sliding down her cheeks. She strained still farther away from him, and then suddenly her face contorted, her mouth went square, showing most of her teeth, her eyes closed tight, and tears drenched her cheeks. Still she made no sound. Now Ken knew that she was just a child.

"Oh, I'm sorry! But don't cry! We'll get her back. Here—you'd better give me the tray—you'll spill it—" He seized the tray, but she recovered herself and clutched it tight.

"No, that's for my grandmother. She wanted some fresh buttermilk."

"I'll take it to her."

"No. She always wants me to wait on her."

"I'll carry it to the house for you then."

"You can hold it for a moment, please."

Ken took the tray and tactfully turned and surveyed the Green while she took a handkerchief from the pocket of her jacket and wiped her face.

When she had regained her composure but was still mopping she said, "What did he steal her for and how could he?"

"That's what stallions do. They get a band of mares and then they take care of them and of all the colts and take them where there's good food and shelter."

Carey showed signs of weeping again. "Maybe he'll kill her."

"Oh, no, it's not like that. He wanted her for his band of mares. Those are his wives. A stallion has a lot of them—about twenty. It's kind of like falling in love. He knew she was a winner and he just kicked the crate to pieces till she was free and ran away with her—kind of eloping."

"But what if she didn't want to go?"

Ken grinned. "Well, he'd make her. That's what a stallion does. But he'll take good care of her—Oh, the very best care! You don't need to worry about her coming to any harm!"

Carey's tears were drying and she looked at Ken, intrigued by this strange tale of wild-animal romance. "You really think he fell in love with her?"

"I'm sure he did."

"What's he like?"

"Well, he's just the most wonderful horse you ever saw! He stands sixteen hands high and he's so perfectly formed, like a carved statue! And he's pure white. And he's so strong, so full of power—you just can't understand what he's like until you see him."

"*Thunderhead*," she said softly, savoring the name, "*Thunderhead*. That's a good name for a horse like that."

"He's named after a cloud," said Ken eagerly. "From the day he was born I wanted him to be a racer and I asked Mother to give him a big important name, that would be right for a white horse, and she looked up into the sky, and there was a big white thunderhead creeping slowly up, so she named him that."

"It's beautiful," said Carey slowly. "I wish I could see him."

"Oh, you'll see him! We'll get them both!"

Carey looked at him, thinking of him, now, and not the horses. "You're Ken, aren't you?"

"Yes."

"You've just come back from that place in the mountains where you had them shut up and you found a lot of dead horses there, didn't you?"

"Yes." Ken looked down. He didn't want to talk about it.

There was a silence in which they seemed to be feeling each other out. Then Ken asked, "How old are you?"

"I'm fifteen."

"Oh, are you?" Nearly as old as he. Ken did not know whether he was surprised or not. She had cried like a child and yet there was a curious dignity and composure about her—almost an authority, as if you would have to do whatever she said, and who was it that she reminded him of? It came to him with a shock. Heavens! It was his mother! Carey had something of importance about her like his mother!

"Are you sure, Ken?" she asked.

"Sure of what?"

"What you said. That you would get Jewel back for me."

"Yes."

"How can you be? You're not much older than I am. *I* couldn't get her back."

"Well you see, she's with my stallion and we're

going to get him back. We have to. We couldn't leave him out loose on the range."

"Oh. Well then there's nothing for me to worry about, is there?"

"Not a thing."

She stood thinking this over and suddenly the most enchanting smile dawned on her face. Those shining white teeth gleamed again, not framed in a square mouth this time, but between two full lips that went up happily at each corner.

"Thank you," she said, taking the tray from him, and walked off toward the house.

Ken stood watching her, his mind in a whirling confusion, all thought of thirst or hunger or buttermilk gone. Her short tan kilted skirt swung against her bare knees, her legs were brown and slender, terminating in well-polished light moccasins, her tailored jacket matched the skirt, and the round white collar of her blouse framed her neck. She looked a very important, well-cared for little affair altogether. Watching her go, the only part he could see that was really herself were those smooth brown calves, so slim and childish, and that glossy fall of brown hair.

Suddenly she stopped and half turned, calling back to him, "I have met your father and mother and the baby and I just love them. Particularly the baby. Your mother said I could help give her her bath. That is what I am going to do as soon as I have carried this buttermilk to Grandma. I think your mother is beautiful. So I have to go now, Ken."

Turning again, she continued her way to the door, now and then taking a few running steps as she came out from the lee of the spring house and the wind hit her. She mounted the steps of the terrace, carefully held the tray with one hand while she opened the front door, and then vanished from Ken's view.

Ken did not know how deep a sigh he heaved, did not know that he sighed at all. Did not know how long he stood leaning there against the stone wall of the spring house. Fragmentary thoughts zigzagged through his mind. In the house . . . she was there . . . soon he would be going in . . . she would help his mother bathe Penny . . . upstairs near his own room . . . up there himself soon, taking a shower and dressing for supper . . . might actually run into her in the hall or on the stairs . . . Oh, Gosh, Oh, Gosh . . . was it real? . . . perhaps he had just imagined it all . . . no, no, the filly . . . Thunderhead. . . . It had all happened and everything was different . . .

# 8

Mrs. Palmer kept her eyes fastened on the door, looking out from beneath a cold compress which covered her forehead. She was resting on the wide double bed of the McLaughlin's downstairs guestroom, her head and shoulders supported by pillows. She had removed shoes and dress and put on high-heeled red velvet mules and a red silk wrapper.

She removed the wet handkerchief from her brow, dropped it into a bowl of ice water which stood on the night table and again directed her eyes to the closed door. She was still a handsome woman; the outstanding features of her face being a delicate, aquiline nose, and high arched eyebrows which were black and finely pencilled, over light, rather cold, grey eyes. Her expression was one of restrained fury.

At last Carey's footsteps were heard, the door opened and Carey stepped in, holding her tray carefully, her eyes going swiftly to her grandmother's face as if to gauge her humor.

"What do you mean by keeping me waiting so long? What have you been doing?"

Carey carefully closed the door behind her and went forward to her grandmother's bedside. She made room for the tray on the table, at the same time saying contritely, "Oh, Grandma! I'm sorry! Something delayed me—you've taken off your compress. Oh, I think you should have it on—your head is so bad." She squeezed the ice water out of the compress and was about to lay it on her grandmother's forehead again but the old lady's head was quickly turned aside.

"I'm sorry," murmured Carey, dropping the compress back into the bowl.

"You're sorry! That's what you say! But here I lie, ill and helpless on this bed in a strange house. And you cannot even do me the one small favor of bringing me a drink of buttermilk without getting sidetracked and 'delayed.' What have you been doing all this time?"

Carey hesitated a little. "I didn't get sidetracked or do anything else, Grandma. It was just one of the boys who was coming into the spring house when I was bringing your milk. One of the McLaughlin boys, and we stood there talking a moment. It wasn't really long. It's just that you're so tired and nervous and thirsty. I'm sorry." And she tenderly put her hand on her grandmother's forehead and smoothed it.

When Mrs. Palmer again turned her head away Carey went softly around the room, picking up garments, hanging them in the closets.

She saw that her grandmother had taken her fine embroidered handkerchief and was pressing it against her eyes. Carey hurried to her side and sat down on the edge of the bed. She put her hand over her grandmother's. "Oh, don't, Grandma! You'll make yourself ill!"

"And who cares if I am ill?" The anger had gone from her voice. It now quivered pathetically. "What difference did it make to anyone that I didn't want to come on this trip?"

"We wanted you to stay home, Grandma."

"Oh yes, I know I wasn't wanted— You don't love me, Carey, you say you do, but you don't act it."

"Oh, Grandma!" Carey slid down and laid her arms about the old woman.

"No, you don't! And you're all I've got in the world, Carey—" her chest heaved.

Carey comforted and protested, laid her soft young cheek against her grandmother's and her own eyes filled with tears.

"Oh, Grandma, don't feel like that, it isn't true. Why, we all love you, we couldn't get along without you."

Mrs. Palmer wiped her eyes and became quieter but when she removed the handkerchief from her face she looked dreadfully sad. "Do you, Carey, my darling? Do you really love your old grandmother?"

"Of course, of course!"

"Better than anyone else in the world?" And as she said this, there crept the hint of a teasing smile across her face.

Carey heaved a sigh of relief. "Oh, yes, Grandma!"

Mrs. Palmer put out a hand, a thin, white, aristocratic hand ornamented with several rings and smoothed the girl's hair. "Do you love me the very best? Better than you love your uncle?"

Carey's smile broadened. "Oh, I love Uncle Beaver, too. Lots. But—but you're not well, Grandma, and you need me, and I've got to take good care of you and I feel so badly when you are upset like this."

The old woman was calm again. She lay back on the pillow and looked at Carey.

"How about a little of the buttermilk now?" suggested Carey as if to a captious child. "It's so nice. I had a dipperful in the spring house before I filled your pitcher. And it's an hour yet before supper."

She poured a glassful and Mrs. Palmer began to sip it. "And what do you think," Carey said, "Mrs. McLaughlin said I could help give the baby her bath."

The glass of buttermilk stopped halfway to Mrs. Palmer's mouth. "When?"

"Soon, now."

Mrs. Palmer made no answer. The glass of buttermilk did not move. Even her expression did not change. Carey hastily added, "But I don't think I will. Not today, anyway. Perhaps tomorrow."

Mrs. Palmer finished the buttermilk and set down the glass. "How long do you imagine we are going to stay in this god-forsaken place, anyway?"

"Well, it might be for several days. They're going to try to find Jewel, you know."

"All this fuss about a horse! You have horses enough at home. It would be better if you studied more and practiced your music more and rode less."

"Oh, but Grandma! This one is special! And she's just for me and she's come all the way from England!"

Mrs. Palmer made no more protests. She held out her glass for some more buttermilk and drank it down. Then Carey asked her what she would like her to do until suppertime. Read to her? Or, if she wanted to be quiet, perhaps she could rest better if Carey left the room?

"No," said Mrs. Palmer, "you need a rest yourself. Take off your suit and lie down here on the bed beside me until it's time to dress for supper. Pull the window curtains."

Obediently Carey drew the chintz curtains then stood fingering them, fascinated by the pattern of miniature bucking broncos and stage coaches.

"Stop mooning," commanded her grandmother.

Carey left the window, removed her gabardine suit and her blouse and flung herself on the bed.

"Put your wrapper on."

"I'm not cold."

"Do as I tell you."

Sighing, Carey rose, found her pink wrapper and slipped it on. Then she lay down again, flat on her back. Her feet and legs were bare. She propped the heel of one slim, brown foot on the toes of the other, contemplated them a moment, then jacked up her knees and cupped them with her hands.

The only sounds in the room were the measured and rather heavy breathing of Mrs. Palmer, and the wind making strange noises, like a subdued chattering around the chimney.

Mrs. Palmer said drowsily, "What a terribly windy place! But Mrs. McLaughlin is a charming woman and a perfect lady."

"Uh-huh," said Carey, wondering how her grandmother could be sleepy when there was so much to think about.

Her thoughts slipped back to early yesterday morning when they had risen at five, expecting to find Jewel at the Red Buttes station and load her on the trailer. Her uncle's face, when he had heard what had hap-

pened, had told her instantly that he considered the
filly as good as dead, and she never would forget the
sick feeling that had gone through her.

But she wasn't dead! All sorts of strange things were
happening to her. It bewildered Carey. She understood race horses and horses that were brought up to
the door saddled and bridled. But horses that eloped,
that kicked each other out of crates, that lived exciting
lives, off in the wilds, independently of men—

"And *Mr.* McLaughlin," continued Mrs. Palmer in
her sleepy voice, "is one of the finest-looking men I
have ever seen."

Carey did not answer this. Her hands were playing
a happy but silent little tattoo on her bare, brown
knees. Ken was going to get her filly back for her! He
said he would.

Her hands came to rest on her knees. Her eyes
widened, seeing faraway scenes. She saw Jewel and
Thunderhead racing with incredible speed over the
prairie. She saw a band of mares with little colts. Saw a
crowd of men, Westerners like the posses in the
movies, galloping after them. Suddenly she saw just
Ken's face, close to hers, looking at her, and she knew
that she would never again feel just the way she had
felt before she came to the Goose Bar.

Looking backward through life, one can see the
points of change, like great locks through which one
glides on a flood wave, so smoothly, on such irresistible power that one is hardly aware of any movement.
But life is never the same again. One has gone
through the lock and lives on a new level.

# 9

Sunset filled the dining-room where the McLaughlins and their guests had gathered for the evening meal.

Nell stood behind her chair at the far end of the table and Beaver Greenway pulled it out for her and then seated himself at her right. He talked, thought Ken, in the silly way that old gentlemen talk to ladies, about the way her blue dress matched her blue eyes.

Ken himself was on the other side of Greenway. He placed his napkin across his knees, determining that he would never talk to ladies like that, but Nell seemed to like it. She smiled and chatted with Mr. Greenway so charmingly, and smoothed the blue silk dress over her bosom. Ken glanced quickly across the table at Carey and met her eyes. This embarrassed him so he looked at Mrs. Palmer who sat next to her, at his father's right hand.

Ken had noticed that wherever Mrs. Palmer went there was a sort of rustle and bustle about her. People paid attention to her. Her father had bowed as he pulled out her chair. His mother made gracious remarks to her. She was something like a queen with her head held so high and importantly, and her smiling, condescending way of talking that now and then changed suddenly to fierceness.

He had noticed, too, that Carey was very attentive to her. Carey sat at Nell's left with her grandmother on the other side of her, and Mrs. Palmer kept glancing down at her, her face changing from the gay way she looked when she talked to Rob, to the sharp way in which older people look at children when they want to find something to correct. Perhaps this was what made Carey seem so young.

Ken answered almost grudgingly when they asked him more questions about his trip to the valley. They knew it all anyway. There was nothing more to tell.

"What seems strange," said Greenway, "is how poison grass suddenly got into a secluded mountain valley when it had never been there before."

"I think," said Rob, "that the mares must have taken alfalfa seed in there from the outside range. They were out on the range near here a year ago—and it sprang up the following spring. Then there might have come a cold spell. We've had snow here on the Fourth of July. The alfafa got frozen, the horses ate it, and that was the end of them!"

"Oh!" exclaimed Mrs. Palmer, shuddering. "Dreadful!"

While the men discussed this possibility, Nell watched Ken, amused at the effect Carey had produced upon him.

Nell had wanted the boys to meet more young people of their own age during their vacations and she had said this summer she was going to have company at the ranch for them, and insist on their accepting invitations to visit elsewhere. But it had not worked out that way. As usual, there was endless work to be done. Rob believed in keeping them busy in some useful way. So this, now; the way he was looking at Carey, this was something new!

Pearl was serving the dinner in the most exemplary manner. Every time she came through the swinging door she cast a glance at Nell as if to say, "How'm I doing?" The slip-slap of her felt moccasins was almost inaudible as her voluptuous figure slid around the table passing platters of deliciously fried chicken, hot biscuits, crab-apple jelly. Nell missed the cigarette hanging from the corner of her mouth.

The telephone jangled noisily and Rob went to answer it.

This telephone was another of the conveniences the sheep had made possible. Rob had set posts all the way from the house to Tie Siding and strung them with wires. A telegram could be sent or received without driving five miles or so to the station. A luncheon date could be arranged for Nell in Cheyenne or Laramie in an hour. Rob could send a message asking for more men from the employment office or put in a hurry call for the veterinarian. The world was nearer and life was easier. And for local messages, it served as a kind of clearinghouse.

Rob returned and took his seat. "That was from Reuben Dale," said he with satisfaction. "He's got six sons, all fine horsemen and clever with ropes. He and two of his sons will go—they'll be over this evening to talk it over."

Gus had said he thought the wind would hold, and as long as it held the snow would not come. Perhaps not for several weeks yet. There was snow in the sky, plenty of it, but not immediately threatening, unless the wind dropped.

Now the wind had dropped. Rob and Greenway, too, kept turning to look out the window. The lowest layer of clouds which had been grey were now crimson and edged with gold, and behind them were swirling depths of fiery color, changing in hue every minute.

"But the wind always drops at sunset," said Nell, "and then it rises again in the evening or during the night."

"Well—everything depends on the weather," Rob kept saying.

"I can imagine you are a fine weather prophet, Mr. McLaughlin," said Mrs. Palmer archly.

Rob glanced at her, "After all these years, I ought to be!"

"Where do your worst storms come from, Mrs. McLaughlin?" asked Greenway, then, "Oh, my! Look at this dessert!" Pearl was passing a bowl of peach shortcake, piled high with cream. "Um—um—don't that look good!"

"By far the worst one is what is called hereabouts the easterner," answered Nell. "It lasts three days as a rule, and it's really dangerous. But we get bad storms from the north too. They come from that big ridge of mountains to the north of us."

The dessert reached Mrs. Palmer and she helped herself liberally. "Your winds must have given me a big appetite, Mr. McLaughlin!" She tossed her head, leaned back with both hands pressed against the table laughing heartily, displaying all her fine teeth. And Nell was amused to see Rob assume a gallant manner as he leaned toward the old lady.

"I wish I could go along on the search," said Carey wistfully.

Nell answered, "At any rate, Carey, you must have some riding while you are here."

Mrs. Palmer's face lost its expression of affability. "She has no riding clothes with her."

"Oh, but we have plenty," said Nell. "That closet under the stairs is just full of old boots of all sizes and blue jeans and riding pants. She'll easily find something that fits her."

"I think," began Mrs. Palmer, "that with strange horses—" but Mr. Greenway interrupted.

"A swell idea! We'll ride together, Carey, you and I, while the rest of them go off on the horse-hunt. It'll be like being at the Blue Moon together, won't it?" He turned to Nell. "Carey and I ride together often."

"Mr. Greenway," asked Howard, "why did you call your ranch the Blue Moon?"

"That's quite a long story, Howard," said Greenway, smiling.

"A story!" exclaimed Ken, his face lighting up.

"Let's hear it, Greenway," said Rob.

"Goes back a long way," protested Greenway, "all the time to when I was a young man, and that's many a year."

"All the better," said Nell.

Greenway glanced at his sister and she at him. Their memories stretched back together to that far-distant time, and their eyes sparkled in sympathy.

"All right, here goes. We were born and brought up in Philadelphia. Five of us. One girl—here she is," he ducked his head and Mrs. Palmer tittered self-consciously, "and four boys. All the older members of the family had died off and we were left an enormous fortune. We didn't know what to do with it, or with ourselves. We had always ridden a lot, loved horses, owned our own. As young people will, we thought it would be great if we made a business out of the thing we loved. We decided to get a ranch out West, stock it with horses, live there and breed race horses and race them. We spent many days discussing just the sort of place we wanted. It was hard to agree. Everyone had a different idea. At last I was sent out to scout around and find it. And I found it there in Idaho, such a place that, as I examined it from one boundary to another and remembered the expressed desires of every member of the family, I realized it was made to order. I went back and announced to them. "It's only once in a blue moon that you'd find a place made to order like this one. And it was Terry, the youngest, the one who was killed at St. Mihiel in the war, who said, 'All right, then! It's a go! The Blue Moon Ranch.'"

The boys stared at him, fascinated at being able to see into the storied past of a different family than their own.

"A fine name for a ranch," said Rob smiling. "Are your older brothers still there with you?"

"No. Mark was killed at Verdun. Harold got through the war all right, but he spent a lot of time in England, fell in love with and married an English girl and finally became a British subject."

Nell turned to Mrs. Palmer. "And how did you like the Blue Moon Ranch when you first went out there?" she asked in her gracious and interested manner.

"Very much," said Mrs. Palmer. "But I didn't stay there long. I was leaving all my friends behind in Philadelphia, you know."

"Yes, and soon she deserted us," put in Greenway, "and went back to Philly and married her best beau and lived there."

Mrs. Palmer pressed her napkin to her lips. "Yes, my dear husband died there. And my daughter, my only child, was born there."

"And grew up and married," said Greenway cheerfully. Mrs. Palmer withdrew her napkin from her lips.

"And had me," put in Carey.

Mrs. Palmer's expression became tragic again as Greenway said, "And when Carey was five, both her parents were killed in an automobile accident and I've had them ever since. And what a fine little horsewoman Carey turned out to be! It's in the blood, of course, and she has her share of it."

"Carey rides very well," conceded Mrs. Palmer, "but her greatest talent is her music. She practices two hours every day."

Everyone at the table looked at Carey with a new interest. This caused her no embarassment.

"I see that you have a fine piano here. After dinner," said Mrs. Palmer, "Carey will play to you."

"Do you groom your own horse?" asked Howard.

Carey shook her head. Her grandmother, with a flash of her dictatorial spirit, answered for her, "I do not like her to be in the stables."

"Wouldn't do her a bit of harm," grumbled Greenway, "no use in wrapping a child up in cotton wool."

"Carey is not strong," said Mrs. Palmer firmly.

"Oh, Grandma, I'm all right. I'm never sick."

As if amazed at this contradiction, Mrs. Palmer looked angrily at her granddaughter. Carey's cheeks were flushed, her eyes bright. She was looking, not at her grandmother but, eagerly, first at one of the boys, then at the other.

Mrs. Palmer began to cough violently. As the paroxysms continued, all conversation ceased and she became the center of attention. Rob offered her a glass of water. Carey half rose out of her chair and looked at her anxiously, "Is it your asthma, Grandma? Shall I get the medicine?"

Mrs. Palmer emerged from her napkin smiling, waving them back to their seats, apologizing. She made Ken feel uncomfortable. What was it that kept everybody fussing about her?

The entrance of Pearl with coffee brought things back to normal, but when Nell told Ken that after supper he ought to take Carey out for a walk and show her the ranch, again there came over Mrs. Palmer's face the shadow that appeared whenever Carey was tempted from her side.

For the moment she said nothing, but as Carey accompanied Ken to the door her grandmother said very pleasantly that she must not go out again—the day had been too long—it would be too much for her.

"Oh, I'm not a bit tired, Grandma," pleaded Carey.

Everyone was looking at Mrs. Palmer. She smiled unpleasantly.

Beaver Greenway waved his hand and said genially, "Go on with you! Trot around with these young fellows and see what's to be seen. Caroline," he turned to his sister, "let her have a little fun now and then!"

Mrs. Palmer cast one furious glance at her brother, then said, "Put your coat on, Carey," and Carey ran to obey.

Rob said to Howard, "Take the car, Howard, drive over to Crosby's—I haven't been able to get word to him. See if he will come over tonight."

Nell suggested that Carey and Ken ride out to the highway with Howard and then walk back.

They got into the new Studebaker which was standing on the hill behind the house. Howard took the wheel, Carey and Ken sat in the back. Howard watched Carey in the little mirror over the windshield. She looked at him, now and then smiling. Ken noticed this and fell silent, sitting morosely in the corner. At the highway they got out and walked slowly back together.

The sunset colors had died down, the wind was blowing hard again, and there was a feeling of wildness and desolation in the strange twilight that was shed from the cloud-covered heavens.

"Oh, I love the wind!" cried Carey, spreading her arms wide and running before it. Ken grasped one of her hands and they ran down the road together.

A big jackrabbit leaped out of the brush, sailing on the wind with long jumps, and Carey stopped short. "Oh, look! I thought it was a deer!"

"Look over there," said Ken.

She gave a scream of excitement. "What is it? Where? Is it Jewel?"

He shook his head and pointed. She saw the three deer then, feeding quietly by the stream and near them, a black colt grazing. Ken went to the barbed wire fence and whistled a soft, far-carrying trill. Deer and colt raised their heads, then the deer resumed feeding and, as Ken continued to whistle, the colt came to the fence.

"This is WhoDat," said Ken, stroking the colt's face.

Carey laughed at the name, and Ken told her how it had come to be given to the foal who, on the very day of his birth, had lost his mother in a blizzard.

"It's a wonder we raised him, but he's a beauty. He's going to be our stud when he's old enough. He gets special feeding and care."

"But what about Banner?" asked Carey, who, when she had first arrived at the ranch that afternoon, had been taken with her uncle by Rob to the pasture to see Banner and his mares and colts. Banner, Rob had explained, was usually out on the range, but yesterday morning had been found by Gus waiting at the pasture gate. Obviously the stud had come down from the range to pay a call on the family and of course would not think of moving without the entire brood. Carey had stood looking at the big stallion, who remained aloof, watching the strangers. His hide was red gold, the smooth elastic muscles rippled on haunch and neck, his bony, strongly modeled face was full of intelligence. Rob had explained that Banner had never been broken, he was a range stallion and nothing else, that the greatest concession he would make was to eat oats out of a bucket if Rob held it. "No one can even touch him, see?" Rob had said. He had approached the stallion with outstretched hand. Banner's body trembled, he drew his weight back without moving his feet, his ears strained forward, his chin drew down and back. The whites of his eyes widened. It had been, Carey thought, as if he had struggled to hold his ground and allow that well-loved person to caress him, but at the last moment could not, and retreated with dignity, slowly, step by step.

"Banner's getting old and tired," said Ken. "A range stallion has tremendous responsibilities, you know. He has to care for the mares on the range, keep the band together, keep any other stallion away even at the risk of his life. He's got to protect them from wild animals and guide them to good food and shelter and water. Dad says it would take two or three cowboys, working day and night, to give the mares and colts as fine care as one good range stallion."

"I never knew stallions could do all that."

"But you see it's awfully hard on them," continued Ken. "And when you think of the weather, too, the hard winters, the terrible storms and blizzards, it's no wonder they wear out sooner than stable-kept stallions. Banner has fewer and fewer colts every year. That's why we have to have a junior stud coming along."

They walked farther, turned a corner and here came a big piebald to meet them from another part of the pasture.

"He heard my whistle," said Ken, stroking him. "This is Calico, the nursemaid of the colts."

"The nursemaid!" exclaimed Carey.

"Yes. He takes them from their mothers when they are six months old and teaches them manners. He's just crazy about colts. Dad says it's because he's a risling. Hereabouts when there's an old animal that's crazy about babies he is called a 'Granny.'"

Carey clasped her hands in her ardent, childish gesture. "I have a Granny! Isn't it funny that colts have them too?"

"And lambs," said Ken. "A Granny is always appointed by the herd to take care of the young ones. In the spring soon after the lambs are born the grannies take them to places high up on the hillsides, like nurseries, whole flocks of them, while their mothers graze down in the valley. They curl up under rocks and snuggle against each other and sleep. Often they pile on top of the granny—several of them at once. She leads a hard life."

"How does Calico teach the colts manners?"

"He teaches them not to be afraid of their master, and to come when they are called, and to obey. They are put in the calf pasture with him. They see that he obeys the whistle, so they follow him. And that teaches them that the whistle means something good—oats and hay, or water and shelter, or just a little loving. It gets to be second nature for them."

They walked on down the road and presently Carey said, "Why don't you take Thunderhead for your range stallion now that Banner's getting worn out?"

Ken answered, his face clouding a little, "Dad doesn't like Thunderhead much. Doesn't like the Albino's blood line. He says it's a wild, bad strain."

"But Thunderhead's not wild and bad?" Carey looked up at him questioningly.

Ken glanced at her and then quickly away, shaking his head, as he remembered all the trouble he had had raising the colt, the constant running away, the fighting against control and training. "Pretty wild, pretty bad," he admitted, "and still—" he looked at Carey again, at the wide, questioning, grey eyes, so eager, so childlike.

"And still—" prompted Carey. They smiled at each other, as if, without words, they could understand how lovable a wild, bad horse could be.

"But I'm awfully sorry he stole your filly, Carey. I wish he hadn't."

"Well," said Carey, "it wasn't all his fault. Her crate fell off the car. He wasn't responsible for that. Anyway, we're going to get her back. You said so. Ken, tell me about Thunderhead."

She was climbing a great irregular rock that sloped up to the base of a hill. She turned and fitted herself into a cranny of it.

Ken stood before her, his foot propped up, his arm leaning on his thigh. "He's the most *wonderful* horse in the world," he said slowly.

"You don't know Jewel!" exclaimed Carey.

"Neither do you."

She laughed. "Well, I know *about* her. She won her maiden race as a two-year-old at the Craven Meeting. And she won the three-year-old hunter's class at the Dublin horseshow. And that's something, let me tell you! She has four blue ribbons. And in her ancestry there are some of the finest race horses that ever were. She goes back to Eclipse."

"Race horses," said Ken slowly, "are different. Thunderhead isn't a race horse even though he *could* win a race."

"What is he then?"

Ken was silent quite a while. "I don't know. We all wonder. He's just like a great person, different from anybody else. But oh, Carey, how I wish I could ride him in another race!"

"Do you, Ken?"

"More than anything else in the world."

"If you get Thunderhead and my filly back, we'll ride races on them, shall we? Just you and I?"

"Gosh! That would be swell!"

"I wonder which is the fastest?" she sat up excitedly. "I bet mine is!"

"I bet mine is!"

Carey burst out laughing, and Ken joined in. Then Carey said, "Tell me some more about him. What is the fastest he ever went when you were riding him?"

Ken thought back. "Oh, I don't know. The fastest we ever clocked him, he made a half-mile in forty-seven seconds. But I'm sure he's gone faster than that with me when we were just out riding for fun. Once— when he was rounding up his mares after he had killed the Albino—"

"Killed the Albino!" exclaimed Carey. "He *killed* a horse?"

"That was his own great-grandsire, a kind of outlaw horse, white like Thunderhead, and Thunderhead is a throwback to him."

"But why did he kill him?" She gave a shudder. "Ugh! That's awful."

"It *was* awful, and terrible, but still wonderful to see." Ken told her how he and Howard had gone to the Valley of the Eagles riding Thunderhead and Flicka. And how Thunderhead had got away from them and challenged the old stallion and killed him.

"And what then?" breathed Carey.

"Well then I got on him to try to get control of him again, and bring him home because we were going to enter him in your uncle's Free-For-All at Saginaw

Falls. But he wouldn't come with me."

"Why not?"

Ken looked at her with a deep strange look. It seemed to him that he knew so much more, had experienced so much more than she, that she could not possibly understand. The Valley of the Eagles had entered into him and nothing like that was in her life —just carrying trays to an old sick woman, and changing her clothes, and being obedient to the old harridan and riding a horse that was cleaned and saddled by a groom and brought up to the front door for her to mount.

But he tried to explain. "There were all the mares there. The mares and colts that had belonged to the Albino's band. Now they were Thunderhead's. That's what he had fought for and risked his life for. Now he was the victor and they belonged to him so he took them."

"How?"

"I jumped up on his back and tried to make him come with me. He had always obeyed my command before but now he wouldn't pay the slightest attention to me. He began to round up the mares. Did you ever see that, Carey?"

She shook her head. "No."

"Well, a range stallion, when he wants to get a band of mares running, rounds them up. He puts his head down low to the ground—it sort of snakes along in front of him. His ears are so flat back you can't see them at all and his eyes bulge out. He runs around and between them, whipping them, nipping them, gathering them together—in and out, like a whip lash. They try to get away from him, and he's only one, and there are a lot of them trying to go in all directions at once, but he's faster than all of them, and quicker to turn and twist, and so he gets them together."

"He did that with you on his back all the time?"

"Yes, I hung on. I had to. Then he got going, going like the wind straight down the valley, with all the mares pounding along with him. By that time I was all in. I just finally slid off."

Carey's eyes were wild with excitement. She was silent a long time, envisioning that ride. At last her face changed and she looked at Ken as she had not looked at him before. "I've never done anything like that, Ken."

Ken said nothing, taken out of himself, as he always was when he remembered that morning in the Valley of the Eagles.

After a long silence he added, "It tells about Thunderhead in the Bible."

Carey looked up to see if he were kidding her.

"Sure enough," insisted Ken. "Mother read it to me out of the Book of Job and I learned it." He struck an attitude and declaimed, *"Hast thou given the horse strength? has thou clothed his neck with thunder? . . . He paweth in the valley, and rejoiceth in his strength . . . He mocketh at fear. . . . He swalloweth the ground with fierceness and rage."*

Carey's mouth opened in amazement. "Why I never heard of such a thing!" She gave a burst of laughter. "Why, Ken!"

He nodded at her, they looked into each other's eyes and the effect of the words he had just spoken seemed to grow and spread within both of them. They felt a thrill, a prickling of the scalp.

"And that isn't all," said Ken, "there's another about the eagle." He told her of the eagles in the valley, of his own battle with the one-legged eagle, and how when the herd had been poisoned, the eagles had come down, with vultures and hawks, to feed upon the carcasses. *"Doth the eagle mount up at thy command, and make her nest on high? She dwelleth and abideth on the rock . . . and the strong place. From thence she seeketh the prey and her eyes behold afar off . . . and where the slain are, there is she.* Gosh!" exclaimed Ken as he finished the verse, "where the slain were, there were the eagles all right!"

Again Carey was astonished and thrilled. "By whose command?" she asked. "It says, 'at thy command.'"

"It means, God's command."

"Oh."

For a moment they were silent. Then Ken said abruptly, "I wish it was the beginning of the summer instead of the end."

"Why?"

When Ken stammered, "Well, d-d-don't you see, you're here now, and if it was the beginning of the summer you c-c-could stay and—" Carey caught embarrassment from him and ducked her head, her brown hair fell forward and Ken could see nothing of her eyes except the straight up-tilted brows and the full smooth lids and dark lashes.

There was silence for a long minute. Then she picked up a little stone and with it began pounding at the rock she was leaning against. Then she glanced at Ken and gave a little smile, her mouth going up at the corners and drawing together in the center. That was the way she had smiled at Howard.

Suddenly she tossed the stone carelessly. It bounced against a rock and a little brown cottontail shot out and streaked away. They both laughed.

A car whizzed past on the road. Ken looked after it. "That's Reuben Dale. I bet he's going up to talk to Dad about going after Jewel."

Carey jumped up. They did not want to miss any of the talk and planning. They hurried to the house.

# 10

Fourteen men were to go on the search. This included Ross Buckley. Gus and Wink and Tim could not be spared. Howard and Ken were to go but had to be back at the ranch by September eleventh whether or not the search was successful, for they were to leave on the twelfth for school.

All evening, cars drove up to the ranch house. The living-room gradually filled with tall weather-beaten men in boots and spurs. Outside there was the blustering wind and the clashing of trees, and strange noises, like voices, around the chimneys. Inside was the crackling of logs in the stone fireplace and Rob's deep, harsh voice explaining and planning and an occasional word or short question from one of the men. They seemed to communicate with each other by monosyllables and glances and silence.

Reuben Dale was there with two of his six strapping sons, all fine horsemen and clever with ropes.

Crosby had finished his haying and he and his two hired men would go. Others had been reached by relayed messages, the country grapevine, which, as effectually as the South African's mysterious method of disseminating news, had spread the knowledge of this interesting event over the countryside.

And the men were glad to go. Work or no work, they would snatch at any excuse to get away from the monotony of their daily routine. Besides, in this case, there was real excitement. They were thrilled at being actors in a drama that was, as you might say, of international importance. A ten thousand dollar filly! She must be made of gold.

But even, Nell explained to Mrs. Palmer, if it had been nothing exciting, if it had been a real chore, they would all have answered the call and put aside their own interests to help in an emergency. That was the way they were.

Collins was there, but very lugubrious. Sitting in the living-room with the McLaughlins and Mrs. Palmer and his master offended his English sense of propriety. Besides, he had played a somewhat ignominious part in the loss of the filly, though where he should have been riding except in the caboose was hard to say. Moreover, it was up to Collins to state whether he would go on the search or not. He well knew that he could not undertake such a ride, and yet it was not an easy admission to make. A man likes to boast a little, it is practically his duty to, but Collins could not —unless he boasted about the virtues and exploits of Crown Jewel. Yet this hardly seemed the time for that either. So he sat on the extreme edge of the piano bench, his head down, his arms supported on his thighs, his hands hanging between them twirling his plaid cap, a very hangdog object altogether.

The men preferred hard wood to soft cushions, sheering away from these almost in alarm, so when the supply of chairs gave out, they found seats on wood-box, piano bench, or tables, while the davenport was occupied by Mrs. Palmer and Nell with Carey between.

Mrs. Palmer was stimulated by the masculine voices and the many long legs, standing, stretched out, tucked back under chairs or crossed one over the other, all of them terminated by boots and spurs and encased in the faded and shrunken blue-jeans which somehow made the most of the muscular limbs underneath.

Rob was particularly pleased that he had got Milt Norcross to go on the search. Milt was an old man, but then, he always had been. He never shaved, and little of his face could be seen between the thatch above his eyes and the whiskers below. But no one could stay in the saddle for more hours at a stretch than he, no one knew the country better, nor the habits of horses, nor the likely places to pick up tracks. Milt held his clothes together by safety pins, and, if he had two old coats, never troubled to buy a new one but pinned the better half of the one to the better half of the other. And with, say, the front of an old sweater added to reinforce the back, he was quite satisfied. As the room grew warmer, Nell asked him if he would not take his coat off, and they all watched him unwind and shed the pieces, saw the different layers come off, the sleeves unpinned and taken off separately, and all the while Milt explaining the peculiarities of his methods of dressing, half-embarrassed, half-proud.

But it was Gus, Rob's foreman, the old Swede with his round pink face and his halo of grey curls and the childlike spiritual eyes whose opinions carried most weight.

A message came in over the telephone which created a stir. It was from Joe Daly. His boy, Buck, had been able to follow the trails of Thunderhead, Jewel, and Pete, through the Buttes. Then they had headed west, and only three miles away joined up with a band of eight other horses.

"Gosh!" exclaimed Ken, "he had his band of mares not three miles from where we were!"

Daly's boy said the band was moving west, straight toward the desert-like expanse of country south of Laramie. If they kept on, they would end up in the Snowy Range. They were moving slowly, grazing as they went. Also, near the Monument which commemorated the massacre of a troop of cavalry by the Shoshone Indians, he had found the filly's blanket coat, torn and filthy. Looked as if it had been ripped by the stallion's teeth.

Following this message, there was more talk. There seemed a good chance that the search party might come up with the horses quickly. Then what to do? What ranches were in the neighborhood? Which ones had the highest and staunchest corral into which the horses could be driven? And if this proved not to be feasible a new corral must be built. Where could they procure the wood? Tools must be taken along for such a contingency.

Gus said thoughtfully, "There's no water in that country. Not till they get near the mountains. They'll have to start moving fast—unless snow comes. We shouldn't lose no time."

But Carey was thinking of something different. She started to get up. Her grandmother's hand pressed her knee. "Sit still, dear."

"I just want to ask Collins something," said Carey urgently, and her grandmother let her rise.

Carey sat down on the piano bench on the other side of Collins—young Georgie Dale, blushing scarlet, rising to make room for her. "Collins, will she catch cold? Jewel, I mean, without her blanket?"

Collins made one of his weary and discouraged gestures. "Gawd knows, Miss. She's wore 'er blanket hall the trip hout, hin 'er crate, hin the hexpress car. Now she's aht hin the wilds with nuthin honl" He shook his head.

"Out in the wilds with nothing on," repeated Carey in a wondering murmur as this picture unfolded itself to her mental vision. And suddenly Jewel looked not like a filly but like a little naked, shivering girl.

Ken came over to them. "What's that you said, Collins? Do you think she'll catch cold?"

"She's never 'ad a cold hin 'er life, but wot's appenin' to her naow runnin' abaht with hall them wild beasts hin Greenland's hicy mountings, 'oo can sye?"

Several of the men went out on the terrace to inspect the weather. Collins joined them and Ken sat down on the piano bench beside Carey.

Sitting there he could think of nothing to say. Carey turned to him and he raised his eyes and met hers. That made his heart pound and he felt almost frightened, but Carey just looked at him searchingly and wonderingly for a moment, and then looked down. The dark lashes lay on her cheek and she smiled the way she had smiled at Howard, that bewitchingly sweet but mischievous smile when the centers of her lips seemed almost to draw together while the corners went up.

"I'd better take de horses in de truck," Gus was saying, standing in the middle of the room, talking to Mr. Greenway and Rob.

"Yes, that would save time," said Rob, and added with a grin, "motorized cavalry."

"Start early," said Gus, "pick up all de horses and get to de Monument about eight. Unload dere."

"It would save a whole day's riding," said Rob.

The men gathered around.

"Have to start by daylight," continued Rob.

"We'll be ready."

"I'll drive to all de ranches," said Gus, "and load on all de horses. De truck'll hold fifteen head."

"What about the men?" asked Reuben Dale. "If they all drive their own cars, likely some'll have engine trouble or tire trouble."

"Howard can take the men in the station wagon. He'll follow you, Gus. Hear that, Howard?"

"Yes, sir."

"And the saddles?" asked Reuben.

"Ken!" called Rob.

Ken woke out of a dream and leaped to his father. "Yes, sir!" Carey followed and stood behind him.

"Gus is going to pick up all these fellows' nags at daybreak tomorrow and load them into the truck and drive them to the Monument. Howard will take the men in the station wagon. You'll take the saddles and equipment in the pick-up. Set your alarm for three o'clock."

"Yes, sir."

"Oh, Ken!" Ken heard the soft whisper behind him and turned to look into Carey's face. "I wish girls could do things like that! I wish I could go along!"

Mr. Greenway heard the remark and turned to put his arm around Carey.

"You couldn't," said Ken, "not just one girl with a lot of men."

"But I could go in the pick-up with you, just as far as the Monument, and then come back with Gus."

Someone said, "How about the chuck?"

Provisions for the trip, however long it might last, would have to be carried in a chuckwagon. There was a big beef outfit in that part of the country, owned by Bill Beasley. He had a number of chuckwagons and teams, always stocked and ready to start out at a moment's notice.

Rob went to the telephone and fifteen minutes later came back with the word that Beasley would provide a well-stocked chuckwagon, a good team, a cook, and have it meet them at the Monument tomorrow morning at eight. In case a corral had to be built, tools could be carried in the chuckwagon.

"Beasley's got good horses," said Georgie Dale, "and they'd better be, for rough country like the Buttes and the badlands."

Greenway suddenly took Ken and Carey, one by each arm, and drew them away from the crowd. There was a larky conspiratorial expression on his face that intrigued both of the youngsters. "Carey, how would you like to drive out with Ken in the pick-up to the Monument—then come back with Gus in the truck?"

"But that's just what I said, Uncle Beaver! I'm just dying to!"

"Well, *would* you?"

She drew her breath in and squeezed her hands together. Her mouth opened and closed soundlessly, her whole face was ecstatic.

"Okay! Then we'll fix it."

Carey found words, almost horrified words, "But, Uncle Beaver! Grandma would never, never let me!"

Greenway's face took on its intimate winking expression and he held her elbow tight. "Carey, by the time you get to be ten or twenty years older, there will be a few larks you can look back upon—things you did you weren't supposed to do, nights or early mornings when you skinned out and went gallivanting somewhere without anyone's knowing—everyone's entitled to that. I can look back on quite a few escapades of that sort and—tell you a secret—" he put his mouth close to Carey's ear, "Your Granny can, too!"

Carey looked utterly shocked, "Oh, Uncle Beaver, I don't think so!"

"I'm tellin' you! And this will be one for you! A barrel of fun, and not a bit of harm."

Again Carey's breath lifted her breast in a great gasp. "But, Uncle! I sleep with her in the same bed!"

"Didn't I hear that you were to set your alarm at three o'clock, Ken?"

"Yes, sir."

"Well, your Grandma is a very heavy sleeper, Carey. Especially at three in the morning. You can slip out of bed, go to the bathroom, have your clothes there, dress there, and presto! What's to stop you?"

"Clothes!" gasped Carey, visualizing all this, "Oh, Uncle Beaver, may I really do it?"

"You not only may, but I insist upon it, and I'll have no disobedience."

"When we unload the horses," said Ken, "I'll give you a ride on Redwing."

Carey looked from one to the other completely carried away.

"Come on with me," said Ken, "and we'll pick out some riding clothes for you, boots and pants, then you can stow them away in the bathroom."

"Give her a lumberjacket, Ken," said her uncle, "it's going to be mighty cold at three o'clock tomorrow morning."

"There's a black leather jacket there," said Ken. "Mother used to wear it. Lined with plaid wool."

"No," said Carey suddenly with decision. "I can't do it." The expression of her whole face changed. "Uncle Beaver, it would make Grandma ill—I know it would. And I can't do that."

Greenway turned her around by the shoulders, gave

her a little spank and shove. "Get along with you! Your Grandma is my sister, remember that, and if she is ill, I'll take care of her. I did it before you were born. Go with Ken and get yourself fixed up. This is going to be fun for everybody. The best fun will be for me, tomorrow at breakfast. I'll have some tall talking to do!"

The men were preparing to go. Rob handed every man a glass, and the bottle went from one to the other —some of the tumblers were filled to the brim.

Ken and Carey sat on the floor in the big closet under the elbow of the stairs. Piled about them were jackets and jodhpurs, boots, sweaters, bluejeans. Carey stood up and held one pair after the other against herself until one of the right length was found. She sat down, took off her shoes, tried the boots on, and finally found a pair.

Ken dandled them in his hands. "I think I wore those when I was about six. Carey, how are *you* going to wake up? *You* can't have an alarm clock."

"Grandma has a nightclock with a luminous dial. If I happen to be awake I can see the time."

"But if you don't?"

Carey was sure she would. She was so excited she thought she would not go to sleep at all.

"What side of the bed do you sleep on?" asked Ken.

She looked up at him. In the dim light his face looked gentle and beautiful.

"The side nearest the window."

"Leave the screen up a little. I can put in my hand and reach your shoulder."

Her head sank. It was a gesture of assent, but that was not all. There was something tremulous that moved between them. For a few moments they sat so, in silence. Then they got to their feet and returned to

the living-room where the men now were pulling on
their coats and making ready to leave.

"By the way, boys," yelled Rob standing on the terrace, while the cars in front of the house were filling
up. "I take it for granted none of you is planning to
ride a *mare* on this trip?"

There was a moment's astonished silence, as if none
of the men had happened to think about this.

Crosby said, "Sure, I'm ridin' Becky. Bought her
from you. Best little hoss a man could have."

There were several guffaws from the other cars.

Rob grinned and said, "Well, you're after a stallion.
And one who doesn't care what the odds against him
are. If he wants a mare he takes her. Advise you to
leave the ladies at home."

The guffaws spread from one car to another as they
winked on their lights and moved out to the road.

# 11

The winds returned to their lairs. The brisk southwest
wind, which for weeks had been chasing clouds and
mists eastward, turned tail and fled home. The movement of the lowest layer of clouds ceased and all the
crosscurrents above them ceased, too, and the cloudy
sky became one solid heavy mass and sank lower and
not a living thing on the plains but knew that a threat
hung above.

What moving air was left came from the east as
there drifted softly back all the mists and moistures
that had been pushed eastward. There was not much

pressure behind this drift from the east. It was slightly stuffy. A harmless-seeming thing, but, even during the breakfast in the bunkhouse before dawn when everyone, including Rob McLaughlin and Beaver Greenway, was filling themselves up with coffee and hot cakes, oatmeal, sausages and fried eggs, Gus made several trips outside to stand in the darkness and feel the air, to sniff at the weather, to lift his head as if he could by some sixth sense examine the heavy sky of which not a glimpse could be seen. Low and full of snow. He could smell it and feel it. But how near? How soon? And the nearness of the snow was to be balanced against the nearness of the horses they were going in search of. They were near, too. But how near?

Carey's uncle said to her, as he put her into her seat in the pick-up, "You'll want to see all you can," and hung his binoculars on their leather strap over her shoulder. And as she was thanking him, he leaned closer and whispered that the only reason he wasn't going along himself as far as the Monument was to leave her free to have her little spree without supervision. Carey suspected that the stiffness which he was feeling as a result of his ride yesterday had something to do with it, too.

At the same moment Rob was telling Gus, "Watch out for the little girl, Gus." And Gus said, "Ya Boss," and their eyes met on the promise.

And then, just as Ken was letting in the clutch of the pick-up to follow the station wagon, Rob jumped on the running board and Ken pulled the car to a stop.

"Yes, sir?"

"Keep the same order you are in. Don't pass Howard."

"Yes, sir."

Rob dropped off the running board and Ken let in the clutch.

"Why did he say that?" asked Carey curiously. "Why couldn't you pass Howard? You don't have to stay behind him just because you are the youngest, do you?"

Ken gave a funny little embarrassed laugh, tucking his chin into his collar. "No. It's just that Dad didn't want—well, he didn't want us to be racing each other and trying to pass each other on the highway."

Carey thought this over. Then suddenly she began to understand. She had seen other boys do that. Weaving in and out at top speed, yelling at each other as they passed, taking the most horrible risks, frightening everyone who saw them. Howard and Ken McLaughlin, too, then—just like other boys! And suddenly she began to scream with laughter, flinging her head down into her lap, then back again.

"No!" she gasped. "I should think not!" In the half-light and half-shadow of the cab she looked at Ken and he at her, and they laughed together wildly.

Carey actually jounced a little on the seat. How exciting this was! Nothing had ever been like it before. It was dark. It seemed like the dead of night, and here she was, cooped up along with Ken, all sorts of adventures before her.

There was the wildest feeling of escape. It was escape, of course, from her grandmother. Mrs. Mc-Laughlin was sweet. Maybe that was the difference between mothers and grandmothers. If her own mother had lived . . . Anyway, soon she was going to help Mrs. McLaughlin give Penny a bath. Maybe not tomorrow, because her grandma would still be angry, but the day after.

The lights in front of them curved off. She felt the

rough-going of a country road; then other curves, awkward and tilted; then some terrible chuckholes through which Ken eased the truck expertly, then suddenly they were in a wide yard before the black shape of a house, parts of it picking up outline from the lights of the truck. A window sprang into light as a blind flew up, and there was the silhouette of a very fat woman clutching a gown around her. There were little sharp knobs all over her head.

There was a chorus of yapping dogs.

The air was torn by the sound of a horse neighing and several answering from a distance, the rough, harsh voices of men shouting, then came the clatter of the horse's hoofs as he pounded up the ramp into the truck. There were more shouts, and then the slamming of wood and iron as the back of the truck was closed. Howard's car was already moving, backing to get out of the way of the truck. A man appeared at the side of the pick-up. He was a grotesque shape, loaded with saddle and an armful of equipment.

"Hello, Ken."

"Hello, Hal."

The saddle and equipment were dumped into the pick-up and the man vanished.

There was too much for Carey to take in. Everything happened so quickly. They were on the move again and in a moment she felt the same chuckholes, the same uneven road, the same tilted curves before they resumed their order on the highway, Ken behind Howard's station wagon and the station wagon behind the truck.

This was repeated many times, with small variations of more or fewer chuckholes, barking dogs, neighing horses, women leaning out of windows, or standing outside shouting at the men and kidding them.

More and more the smell of leather and horses filled the pick-up and made Carey's nose tingle. She loved it.

Then Ken said, "That's all." And curving away from the last ranch house, Carey caught sight of the truck, crowded with horses packed in head to tail, the frightened, excited faces staring wildly over the high wooden side as the headlights from Howard's station wagon for a moment played over it.

And now they were on the highway. Smooth going. And Gus increased his pace.

Ken suddenly said, "We're not going to see each other hardly any more, are we, Carey? Maybe not at all."

Carey looked at him in astonishment. "Why not?"

"Well, I'm going after Jewel with the men, and you'll go back to the ranch with Gus. And the minute we find her we'll bring her back, and then you'll go away with her, won't you?"

After a little silence, Carey answered, "Yes, I guess we will. But—maybe you won't find her so soon."

"Anyway, I'll be out hunting, and you'll be at the ranch, and in eight days we've got to leave for school."

There was a silence for a few moments, then Ken added heavily, "Yes, I guess this is just about our last time together. Carey—will you write to me this winter? The address is Bostwick's School, Duncan, Mass. Or you can write to the ranch and it will be forwarded."

Carey slowly nodded her head.

"And I can write to you at the Blue Moon Ranch?"

She nodded again.

Ken said, "Of course, when I said that, that this is just about our last time together, I mean for *now*. Because I'll see you again. Sure. Probably next summer."

Ken had said all this without taking his eyes from

the road. Carey stole a look at his profile. How handsome these two McLaughlin boys were! Ken looked very manly and responsible. Carey sat in silence, her thoughts confused.

The darkness was fading and farms and sheds and mountains and the shapes of animals on the plains were coming into vision as if they were just being created and had not been there at all in the darkness. This she had never seen before, and it gave her a feeling of wonder. If you were always on the edge of light, moving out of the darkness, then you could see world after world being created.

"You didn't wait for me to wake you," said Ken, breaking the long silence. "How did you manage to wake up without an alarm clock?"

"But I have got an alarm clock!"

He glanced at her in surprise and saw a face of teasing mischief.

"I've got it inside of me," said Carey. "Uncle Beaver says it's my subconscious, because if I know I am to wake at a certain time, then I wake up of myself just about five minutes before. I did this morning. I woke at just five minutes to three."

Ken was silent a few minutes. His mother had said the child would probably not sleep at all, for excitement.

"Did you sleep?"

"Like a log," said Carey. "I didn't think I would, because there was so much to think about and to look forward to, but I guess I passed out the moment my head touched the pillow, for I don't remember a thing until I woke up suddenly, and it was pitch dark, and Grandma was snoring, and I got up on one elbow and looked over her to the night table where her little clock is, and I could see the luminous dial and it was just five minutes to three."

"Gee!" said Ken. "That's like me. I always can wake up when I want, but Howard can't, no matter how hard he tries."

"Does he try to?"

Ken laughed. "Sure. You miss out on things sometimes, if you can't wake up when you want."

Carey sat thinking that she wouldn't have missed out this morning, because Ken would have put his arm through the window and wakened her. She wondered if he had come to the window.

"Didn't your grandmother hear you when you got out of bed?" he asked.

"She didn't hear a sound. I didn't *make* a sound. I took a long time to open and shut the door. I was afraid it would squeak, but she was snoring so loud—" Carey stopped abruptly. Perhaps it wasn't really quite kind to speak of her grandmother's snoring.

"Of course, it's because of her asthma," she explained. "Those little pipes in her bronchial tubes are a little swollen up and don't give her room enough to breathe."

Ken did not seem interested in her grandmother's little pipes. "I went to wake you, you know."

"Did you?"

"Yes, the way I said I would. I got up at quarter to three. I went out around the house to your room, but when I passed the bathroom, I saw there was a light in the window and then I knew you were in there dressing."

"Yes."

"You've got my baby boots on. How do they feel?"

Carey crossed one foot over her knee and wiggled her foot. "A little stiff, but they're just the right size." She was wondering if Ken had gone around to her window after all, and suddenly she asked him.

"Did you go to my window, anyway?"

"Yes, I went around."

"Well, why? When you knew I was dressing in the bathroom."

She asks such a lot of questions, thought Ken; that's because she's a child. All children ask questions all the time.

"I dunno exactly why. Just wanted to see if you *had* left the screen up, so that I could wake you, like we said."

"Of course I did," said Carey, "because supposing my inside alarm clock hadn't gone off?"

"I heard your grandmother snoring. She sure tunes up. And I put my hand in through the window, too."

Carey made no answer to this. It seemed as if this action of Ken's lacked a reason, and he must have thought so too, for presently he said, "I just wanted to see if I really *could* have reached you to wake you up, *if* you hadn't waked up of yourself."

"Well, I guess you could, all right," said Carey, inspecting a piece of loose leather on the heel of one boot.

"Yes, I could have. I felt the pillow."

The car drove on through the thinning darkness. It seemed not a true dawn, but a sort of lowering greyness that was all the day would bring. And it was a long time before Ken finished his thought with a few simple words, "The pillow was warm," that made a strange, tingling embarrassment go through Carey. She replaced her foot on the floor, turned to look resolutely out the window and was silent. The words still played upon her nerves. She wondered if Ken were embarrassed too.

When he spoke again it was very impersonally.

"Looks more like late October than early September."

"What does?"

"The grass." He motioned toward the sere and yellow plains. There was not a particle of color in the landscape. "Winter's coming early this year and it's going to be a tough one."

"How do you know?" Carey never failed to come through with a question, but Ken was coming to feel that there was really something to be said for it, because it gave a fellow a chance.

His voice was deep and firm—quite like his father's —when he answered. "Haven't you noticed the animals? The cows and horses have got fur two inches long all over them! They've been getting ready for it. They know!"

"Two inches!" marveled Carey.

The cars ahead swung off the highway, crossed the railway tracks and took a dirt road that went southwest. It was not a very good road, and Gus slackened speed a little. Carey could see that the country was changing. They were getting near to the Buttes. Would there be ways to get through these badlands without bringing danger to the horses in the truck? Her thoughts flew to Jewel. All of this effort and work and risk was for her. Carey thought back— Was it only day before yesterday that Jewel had been lost? So much, so awfully much had happened it seemed as if she had lived a year since that moment when she had dressed herself in her tan kilted suit in the early morning, expecting to go out and see Jewel taken off the train and loaded onto the trailer.

Then she thought back further still, much further, to the day when she and her Uncle Beaver had had their heads together over the papers and letters and pictures from the Beckwith farms in England, and

Uncle Beaver had at last leaned back and said, "You want her, honey?" and she had nodded her head, and he had said, "She's yours, then."

From that moment, up until the moment when she arrived at the Goose Bar Ranch, there had been only one thing she had wanted: Jewel. Now her life had spread out like an open fan upon which were painted scenes of new and fascinating places and people. She no longer knew just what she wanted most of anything.

# 12

The chuckwagon, in charge of one of Bill Beasley's cooks, was at the rendezvous before them. Carey did not know exactly what she had expected the Monument to be, but certainly not just a great rock sticking up out of the plains, roughly shaped like a small pyramid, with one face smoothed off and inscribed with a brief tale of the massacre of a troop of American cavalry by Shoshone Indians in the year of 1873.

Cookie had already made a fire. Over it hung a big coffeepot on a tripod. The back of the chuckwagon had been let down, forming a table upon which were a can of sugar, a pile of tin cups and spoons, a few dozen doughnuts and some cans of evaporated milk. The team had been unharnessed and, together with a couple of other horses, was hobbled and grazing at a little distance.

When Ken and Carey got out, Howard was already studying the tracks on the ground and he called Ken to him. Ken, with a hasty word of excuse to Carey, went to his brother.

Gus, leaving the horses still in the truck, walked slowly to the chuckwagon for coffee. Some of the men did likewise, others were following the example of Ken and Howard, studying and discussing the hoofprints that were plainly to be seen pressed upon or cut into the ochre-colored, dried up grass. Here and there was a pile of dung.

Howard suddenly gave a yell that brought the men crowding around him. "See here? That's Pete's hoofprint! As big as a bucket! He's still with them!"

A horseman appeared galloping toward them from the southwest. It proved to be young Buck Daly who had arrived at the rendezvous some time ago and had followed the tracks southward a few miles.

He dismounted and told his news. Jenny, his father's mare, had disappeared. Thunderhead had come in the night and stolen her.

There was a roar of delighted laughter from the men at this. They began to banter each other as to what mares had been left behind on their ranches. They crowded around Buck and asked if he had seen the tracks? Sure, he had seen the tracks, coming and going, Jenny's going away with him. He had been out since daylight, following them. Hadn't seen the horses, but the tracks were plain. They were heading toward the Snowy Range and they were traveling faster than they had yesterday.

Carey noticed that the men were noisy and hilarious, as if they were out for a good time. It *was* a good time, of course, a picnic, horseback riding, a chase, how could there be any better fun for these men or for anybody? Suddenly there came to her a strong sense of closeness to earth and grass and the smell of the horses and men. Emotion made her tense. There was something else—it was freedom, wild and soft and sweet and exciting.

The men, stamping about, kicking at the tracks on the grass, talked and bantered as they had not done last night at the ranch house. They argued about the weather, stood looking at the sky, making empty bets as to how many hours it would be before the storm hit them and how much of a chance they had to catch up with the horses. They strained their eyes to the southwest. The low grey sky acted like a shade or hat brim and increased the visibility. Every object stood out as clearly as if magnified. They could see a herd of cattle grazing far away—it might be five miles. There were ridges, solitary trees, upstanding rocks and knolls, the endless plains, and in the far distance the gradual rise of ground toward the Snowy Range. That was at least fifty miles away. Its summit—a table top —was hidden in the clouds.

Buck thought hard riding might catch up with the horses before the day was over. No tellin'—they might be tucked away in some depression of the ground or some little draw within five or ten miles of the Monument. It was worth a try anyhow.

Thinking about this—that Jewel might be somewhere quite near, Carey squeezed her hands together in excitement.

Gus brought her a cup of coffee. "Awful black, but give you strent, Carey." Carey went to Cookie for sugar who, with a beaming smile which showed absolutely toothless gums under his drooping brown mustache, poured sugar into the thick black fluid.

She stirred it into her coffee and listened to Gus and Leonard Moody talking. In every such a group of men there is one who takes command naturally. This seemed to be Moody, a tall, lean, tow-headed man with an angry expression on his handsome face. He and Gus were deciding just what should be done.

Every man had a cup of coffee and a couple of doughnuts. They came and went, joshing with Cookie.

Gus and Moody were talking about the weather. A storm was sure coming. It was getting cold fast. But they might catch up with the horses before it broke. This sky—it was getting lower—looked like it was going to be fog pretty soon. If they didn't get the horses now, before this storm came, they wouldn't get them until spring. This wasn't just a storm coming. It was winter. Look at the thick fur on the horses. Been getting ready. A hard winter and an early winter. Thunderhead was taking his mares to the foothills of the Snowy Range, and when they once got there, goodby.

*Spring*, thought Carey, her heart sinking. Into her coffeecup fell a big feathery flake of snow. For a split second she saw the star shape of it, then it was gone. She raised her face and looked for more, and saw them here and there, drifting softly. And the wind was more than a drift now, and it was from the east.

"Here it comes, boys!" yelled Georgie Dale. "We better get moving!"

They bolted the last of their coffee and doughnuts, picked up their bridles and crowded around the truck. The back was lowered, the horses clattered down and each man took his own.

Carey wondered if Ken had forgotten that he had said he could let her have a ride before they got off. No, there he was coming toward her leading a big sorrel. "Here's Redwing, Carey. You're going to have a ride before we leave."

But Carey shook her head. "I don't believe there's

time, Ken," she said. "Look at them. They're all mounting."

Gus raised his voice. "Looks to me like you're licked. Dis is an easterner an' it's comin' fast. You can try, but you may be wantin' me before noon, so I won't go back to de ranch right away. If you don't stay away too long, I'll be here to take you home."

Leonard Moody swung into his saddle and turning his head said, "Come on, fellers."

"Go on, Ken," said Carey. "I'll be seein' you."

For a moment he hesitated, looking at her. This was the end of seeing Carey. The faded bluejeans fitted her neatly. Her hands were stuffed into the pockets of her black leather jacket, the collar was turned up around her glowing face and all covered with the fall of her glossy brown mane. Her eyes were starry with excitement, her cheeks red, and a snowflake fell and melted on the tip of her nose. An old blue linen hat was pulled down over her head. Ken could not look away from her. The big sorrel with his head high over Ken's shoulder pricked his ears and looked at Carey too, knowing that this was somebody new. It went through Ken's mind that yesterday morning he had not even known of Carey's existence, and now—at the thought of leaving her—

"Come on!" It was an impatient yell from Howard, who was already mounted.

"Goodby," said Ken. He put out a hand and they shook hands gravely. Their eyes met.

Then Ken mounted Redwing and joined the others.

The whole troop moved off. The boys waved to Carey. Ken kept turning in his saddle to look at her. Over and over again they put up a hand to each other, until suddenly the men and horses seemed to disappear into a hollow, then emerged on the other side, cantering on in an indistinguishable mass.

Gus had hardly watched them leave. He had the hood of the truck open and was inspecting the engine which had been missing. Wink and Tim, who had come along to drive the pick-up and station wagon back, were cleaning the manure out of the truck.

Carey felt very deserted and her face quivered. The wind was terribly cold and it cut through the cotton of her trousers to the skin.

"Don't the little gal have a horse to ride?" asked Cookie sympathetically. "See that roan pony over there a-grazin'? Ye can take a ride on her, as good a pony as there is in Wyoming. I've had her eight year."

"But," said Carey quaveringly, "she's yours, and you'll be taking her along with you. I've got to go back with Gus."

"Gus ain't goin' till noon or so. An' I'm not startin' after the boys just yet. Ain't had my breakfast."

"You mean your second breakfast!" yelled Tim.

"Or your third!" contributed Wink.

Cookie ignored them. "When everybody else is fed, then I get mine. I won't be leavin' for a while yet. I'll saddle the pony for ye and ye can get a look around anyways."

Carey pointed to a group of cone-shaped hills to the northwest, one quite high. "Think there's time for me to ride up to that hill? I could see from there, I could see the men riding." She lifted her binoculars. "With these," she added.

"Sure, sure, plenty of time," said Cookie amiably and went to saddle the roan for her.

Gus sang out, "What you saddling up for, Cookie?"

"The little gal wants to try my pony," shouted back Cookie. "She kin be ridin' around while I eats my breakfast."

The Swede nodded and put his head under the hood of the engine again.

Carey mounted the roan. It pranced a little, feeling the strange hands and the unaccustomed lightness of the rider. Carey slid around in the far too large saddle.

"The stirrups are too long," she said and held the mare while Cookie shortened the stirrup leathers. Then she took command of the pony, got a firm hold with her knees, touched her heels into its side and swung it in a small circle.

"Say! You're right handy with a horse!" exclaimed Cookie admiringly. He stood watching, his arms folded over his stomach underneath an unbelievably dirty white apron.

"What's her name?" asked Carey.

"Name's Mamie."

"Well, come on, Mamie. We're off." They cantered away.

Cookie watched them a moment, then turned to his wagon and busied himself at the table. He mixed a quantity of honey and butter together on a large tin plate, stirring it with the flat of his knife as a painter mixes paints on a palette, then cut himself a thick slice of the white bread which he made himself once a week, and placed this on top of the mixture, pressing it down, lifting it with a fork and soaking the other side.

Gus left the engine and walked over to him.

"Better keep away!" warned Cookie jovially. "When I get started everybody better have a bathin' suit on!"

But Gus had something else on his mind. "Dot pony she's ridin'—is it a mare or a geldin'?"

Cookie hastily swallowed his mouthful of bread and honey and wiped his mouth, looking at Gus.

"It's a mare, Gus. I never give it a thought."

"Well, that ain't so gude with this stud around." The two men turned and watched Carey cantering toward the group of hills. Gus spoke in a worried way, "Dot white stallion of Ken's is nuthin' to fool with."

"Sure, I know all about it," said Cookie, "but say, she ain't goin' in that direction." He pointed at the troop of men, riding southwest, still clearly to be seen.

Gus took off his hat and scratched his head. He looked first at the riders, then at Carey who, even as he watched, disappeared behind the nearest of the cone-shaped hills. He looked back at the riders and spoke his thought. "When horses is out free dey don't go in a straight line, unless dey be headin' fur some place. T'underhead an' dose mares cud have circled around and be watchin' us from behind our backs, right now."

"Say!" said Cookie. "I jes' remembered. The mare's with foal, anyway."

Gus stood so long thinking this over that Cookie turned to the dish of ambrosia for which his tongue and toothless gums were longing and began to lap it up by the technique called slurping.

On rare occasions Gus thought up a joke, or handed out a bit of the type of joshing which is current coin with American boys.

"Waal," he drawled, "T'underhead never pays no attention to any mares but de best ones anyways." He put his hat on again and walked back to the truck, leaving Cookie sputtering indignant words mixed with honey and butter.

# 13

The wind died down again and the snowflakes that had been drifting through the air seemed to have been sucked up from the earth. It became much colder, and once again the air was crystal clear under the lid of the sky, and far objects seemed near.

As Carey climbed the little peak she realized that no more feathery little stars or gauntlets were falling on her sleeves or face. She kept turning to watch the riders. They progressed in a close pack and a cloud of dust followed them.

When she reached the summit she halted her mare, put the binoculars to her eyes and tried to see if she could pick Ken and Howard out of the group. Then she swung her glasses to the right and left, studying every detail of the plains which, because seen through the round circle, took on a startling significance. They seemed not real at all, but something created and planned especially for her.

There slid into view a beautiful picture, framed in the narrow circle: the statue of a horse, pure white, standing on a sharp crest. He was motionless, slightly turned, his head twisted up, every muscle taut and ready.

Carey lowered the binoculars. Her heart was thumping. Was it Thunderhead? No—it wasn't real at all; it was just something in the binoculars—

She sat a moment trying to gather her wits. She looked, without the glasses, at the hill where she had seen the horse but could see nothing new except the barren-looking plains, the ridges and rocks, the Snowy Range far away. No, there it was! A speck of white on a hilltop!

She put the binoculars to her eyes again, seeking him, swinging the glasses in small circles until she captured him. She adjusted the focus with painstaking care until every detail of the stallion was revealed as if in an etching—the intent, white-ringed eyes, the sharply cocked ears, the widely flaring nostrils with a hint of scarlet inside. They palpitated. Was he actually smelling her? Certainly he was watching her—examining her and the mare inch by inch just as she was examining him.

It seemed to Carey that she had never seen anything so beautiful, so wild and so pure.

Then, as she watched, the low sky sank lower. A mist dimmed his shape—he was completely blotted out.

Astonished, she let the glasses fall on their strap and looked around her. Everywhere the sky was sinking. Mist, clouds, fog, snow enveloped her.

She heard a whining in the air. It was in the wind. The snowflakes were not big feathery stars now, but a cutting frozen mist, a horizontal sheet of powdered ice that bit and burned.

She whirled the little roan mare and put heels into her side. "Get back there to camp, and get there in a hurry!" Mamie plunged willingly down the slope.

At the bottom, Carey found she had forgotten just how she had reached that central, highest peak. On every side there were these steep cones going up. The snow was thicker. She could not hold her eyes open against it. Mamie plodded forward. She seemed to be going up another peak. Carey stopped her and tried to remember. Sitting still on her horse for that moment, she chilled through. Where the wind drove the snow against her leg it melted and instantly froze so that as she tried to brush it off, it was a thin sheet of ice that shattered beneath her hand. And immediately there was another sheet of ice forming on her thigh. Then on her cheek. She kept brushing the ice off. Mamie started forward of her own accord. Carey remembered now that she had gone up and down one small hill before she had reached the central peak. It was this small hill that lay between her and the camp. Mamie was right. They must go up this hill. She urged the little mare forward, bending low, shielding her face and eyes with one arm. She tried to see where she was going but there was only the thick white smother. She thought wonderingly. Why, it's like a sheet wound around me!

They went up the hill and down. Presently Mamie started up another hill. Carey halted her. That's wrong, she thought, there weren't two hills to go up and down. Mamie pulled restlessly at the bit. Carey thought of the wind. It was an easterner, she remembered. The wind was driving from the east. That should direct her to the camp. But here amongst the peaks, the wind was swirling from every direction. You couldn't tell a thing from the wind.

Her teeth were chattering and her body shaking violently. Automatically, she touched her heel to Mamie's side and loosened the reins. The mare plodded forward, up a hill, and Carey didn't know why she let her, for there had not been two hills. It was then she realized that she had no idea where the camp was, and no way of finding it. She was lost.

Mamie plodded part way up the hill, then began to circle it. Carey stopped her again, turned her and forced her to retrace her steps. She was more cold than frightened. She wondered if her face were really freezing as she kept shattering the ice on her cheek and ear. She was glad she had found warm felt gloves in the pocket of the jacket.

The cold drove at her on the whining wind as if it were determined to destroy her. Again, in complete uncertainty, she stopped the mare; Mamie was discouraged and stood with her head hanging. Carey leaned forward and patted her neck and spoke to her, glad to hear the sound of her own voice even though the wind whipped it from her lips. Mamie could hardly have heard it, but still she lifted and turned her head as if comforted.

Everyone knows that horses will find their way home if given their head, thought Carey. But I want to go to the camp. Will she feel that is home because the team and the chuckwagon and the other horse and her master are there? Or will she head for her real home, the Beasley ranch—and how far away is that? She did not remember, but thought it was seven or eight miles. If Mamie had real sense, real horse sense, she would go to the nearest place; she would go to the Monument. . . . She gave her her head again, and said, "It's up to you now, Mamie, you find the way."

Mamie went more briskly, in and out the little cones, winding around some, going over others. So chilled that her brain was getting numb, Carey wondered dully if this could really be the way to the camp. Of course, when one is cantering along on the way to a place it doesn't seem any time at all before you're there. Now, fighting back through the blizzard like this, it could seem far, far longer, and still be all right.

But maybe it was wrong. Maybe they were going farther from the camp. Why move at all? Wouldn't it be better just to stay in one spot and wait for Gus or Cookie to come looking for her? But you couldn't stay still. She wondered why no one ever stayed still when they were lost, but wandered on and on.

If she weren't so cold.

She had no idea how far they had gone or how much time had passed. There was nothing to measure by. No change of light. No landmarks to be seen. Just the utter sameness of white driving snow and wind, and the cold getting deeper into her.

Coming out from behind a hill, the wind was behind Mamie and she began a slow trot. She went down a little gulch abruptly, making Carey pitch forward. Up again on the other side. In unexpected places there were big drifts of snow already, then a space swept perfectly clean. Mamie ploughed through some of the drifts, skirted others. Carey knew now that beyond any doubt this was not the way to the camp. They had not crossed any gulches coming. This was more like the badlands. Mamie was going to the Beasley ranch, or she was lost and not going anywhere. Carey decided they must go back and tried to stop the mare. But Mamie fought for her head. When Carey pulled her more determinedly she reared, then plunged. Her foot slipped and she crashed to the earth. Carey rolled free, still holding the reins. But her fingers were stiff and when Mamie scrambled to her feet, one jerk of her head pulled the reins from Carey's hand. In a second, the mare had vanished, and there was no further sight nor sound of her.

Carey sat on the ground a moment, turning her back to the wind, shielding her face, then got to her feet and started forward. It was, she realized, just an aimless wandering. She had not the faintest idea where she was going. But you can't keep still in a

storm like that. You'd freeze. Really freeze to death.
People did. It was on the front pages of newspapers.
Farmers froze to death trying to get from their own
barns to their houses. Or people caught in automo-
biles on the highways. You've got to keep your blood
circulating. You've *got* to keep moving. . . .

She kept at it a long time, then, worn out, flopped in
the lee of a rock on a hillside and told herself she
would just rest a minute or two, get a little strength
back, and get going again. If only someone would find
her now, before she had to move.

It seemed impossible to get going. She tried once,
but decided to rest a little longer. Then she did get
up. She was shaking all over. She weaved as she
walked. She was stiff with the cold. She must sit down
again and rest a little longer. Sitting there, her
thoughts took a different turn. . . . Perhaps she was
not going to be found. Perhaps she was going to be
one of those headlines on the front page. "Grandniece
of Beaver Greenway lost in the Badlands during a
blizzard, frozen to death!" Then she thought of Ken,
and hot tears stung her eyes and she had to swallow a
lump of self-pity. For this to happen, just after she
had met the McLaughlins and all these exciting things
had come into her life!

She whipped herself back to reality. A fine thing to
do! Just to sit there with her head hanging on her
chest, letting herself be frozen to death!

But she could not take another step. Anyway, her
only hope was for them to find her. Shout, then! Help
them find her! So she opened her mouth to shout and
heard the words, "Oh, Ken!" come from her lips and
ride away on the wind.

Her head sank on her chest again. She would do it
regularly, at intervals, the way a foghorn blows. So,

every minute or so, she raised her head and sent the
cry of desperation out to the boy who had ridden
away to the southwest in search of her filly.

She made herself a little more comfortable where
she was crouching in the lee of a rock. There were
longer and longer intervals between the calls. She was
really getting rested. She didn't feel so cold. For long
minutes she slept profoundly. Then the command she
had given herself to call for help, and not to cease
calling, flogged her awake again, and she raised her
head and cried as loudly as she could, "Oh, Ken!"

Having performed this duty, she smiled happily as
her head sank to rest on the arm which was between
herself and the earth. She did not wake to cry again.

It was Gus who found her an hour later.

It was as if he had known exactly what to expect.
He jerked her to her feet, shook her as hard as he
could, shouted at her. Her legs collapsed. Her head
rolled on her shoulders. Dropping her to the earth, he
took a flask out of his pocket, leaned over her, forced
some whiskey into her mouth and massaged her
throat. She choked on the strong liquor. He pulled her
to her feet and shook her and jounced her up and
down.

No one could know more about the snow sleep than
Gus. In Sweden, in the dead of winter, not a month
passes but one hears of someone sleeping themselves
to death. Not from fatigue. Not from cold. But from a
mesmerism that comes from the ceaseless white passes
of the snow, binding the will, forbidding effort, bringing peace.

"Und now you git goin'!" thundered Gus, shoving
her ahead of him. When she fell, he lifted and shook
her and shoved her on again.

She did not whimper. Her eyes flashed open at him

now and then; and saw a strange, snow-encrusted being who was shouting at her, pushing her and forcing her to wake and walk.

Enough consciousness was roused in her to know what was happening. Agony crept into every limb as her blood began to move again. She must obey him; she must keep going, when she fell, she must get up.

It was a struggle that seemed endless to her, the more she woke and moved, the more pain flowed through all her veins.

Other men joined them before they reached the camp and she was aware of the riders coming galloping in, horses and men so coated in snow that they were unrecognizable. There was much shouting. Gus lifted her and put her into the cab of the truck which was warm because the engine was going and the heater was on. Gus left the door open and stood outside, talking to the men. Cookie had harnessed the chuckwagon.

She could hear what they were shouting—to make for Beasley's ranch. Cookie knew every turn of the country and could lead the way—a safe way for the truck to follow, and the station wagon and pick-up, and the men on their horses since it was impossible to load them into the truck. Some of the men shouted that they would make for home.

Suddenly Gus slammed the door shut and she was alone in the cab. The feeling of comfort and security was almost too much for her, and again her eyes were hot with tears. She stuck her fists into them. Her body still felt queer.

The door opened and Gus put Ken into the cab beside her. "Keep her movin' and talkin', Ken, shake her if you have to, I'll be back."

Ken's face was both awed and frightened. He took

her hands and rubbed them as if he feared they would break. She tried to smile at him.

The other door opened, Gus climbed in, speeded up the engine, opened the window to stick his head out and shout some last orders, then the truck was under way. Gus closed the window, without a word handed the flask to Ken and told him to make Carey get some more down her.

Carey obediently gulped the strong stuff, Gus looked down into her eyes searchingly and said, as the truck lurched on, "You be all right now, Carey."

Carey nodded at him but still did not speak until she turned to Ken and suddenly said, "Oh, Ken, I called you and called you and called you!"

"Gosh, Carey!" Ken mumbled helplessly as he fastened the top of the flask and handed it back to Gus.

"Ken! I saw Thunderhead!"

The boy stared at her, wondering if this was part of her snow-sleep dream.

"I really saw him, through the binoculars, standing way off there on a crest, like a white statue, just what you said."

For a long moment their eyes met, sharing all that had happened, for Carey's mind had gone all of the way toward death—the rest would have been easy—and her eyes clung to Ken's and she leaned toward him putting the burden of this on him too, to help her carry it, and suddenly the long-held tears and sobs burst through and she cried, "Oh, Ken!" and flung herself on his breast. He put his arms around her and held her tight.

The cars carried no lights. They followed one behind the other close after the chuckwagon. It was the team in the chuckwagon that led the way, knowing it well, going at a smart trot, their heads turned away from the storm, and their backs hunched slightly, heading for home.

Gus glanced sideways at Ken and Carey and said with a little grin, "Looks more like huggin' dan shakin' —vell—so long as she don' go to sleep again."

Fifteen minutes before the little cavalcade turned into the Beasley ranch, Mamie trotted up to the bunkhouse, her reins dragging. She stopped before the lighted windows and gave a beseeching whinny.

# 14

Thunderhead brought his band back across the plains, heading for shelter from the blizzard in the strange tortured hill formations of the Buttes.

Thunderhead's band now numbered fourteen. There were ten mares and three colts aged two or three months. The colts belonged to three of the mares he had brought from the valley with him, a bay and a sorrel and the large black mare Ken had named Hagar.

These mares had also had yearlings, but when the new foals came Thunderhead had driven the yearlings out of the band.

It is the common law of horsedom that when a mare drops a foal the yearling running at her side must be banished. One is enough for her to nurse and care for. The stallion sees to it and drives them away. At first they try desperately to get back and the struggle continues for days. They cannot conceive of life, separated from their dams. Eventually, bitten and bleeding and scarred, they accept their first serious defeat and stand at a distance in woebegone postures with heads hanging, eyes turned wistfully back toward the herd. But soon comes consolation, for they band together in their affliction. Often permanent attachments are formed. They learn a new and independent way of life, find their own food and shelter, and glorious fun begins.

But Hagar's yearling, who was the Albino's only white colt, could not adjust himself to this fate. There must have been in him, together with his white coat and his magnificent conformation, the same stubbornness and wilfulness that had characterized his sire. Thunderhead had driven him away with the other yearlings, but he returned and clung to the mares as close as he dared, half a mile or so away. So he truly deserved the name Ken had given him, Ishmael, driven out of his own band and yet without the companionship of any other. Now and then Thunderhead made a sortie to drive him farther off and, if he could catch up with him, punish him for his presumption. Then would Ishmael's long slim white legs—as strong as Thunderhead's own—take him floating off over the prairie to a safer distance, and Thunderhead would return to his duties.

Thunderhead's lead mare was a dry, rangy black named Lady Godiva who had once belonged to the owner of the Steamboat Springs daily paper.

There were the two handsome brown Morgan mares which Thunderhead had stolen from Jeff Stevens. These were also dry. There was a pair of beautiful two-year-olds, stolen from who knows where, not fully grown, one a pale honey color, one a warm russet, quite chunky. Evidently they had Palomino blood in them. These would have their first foals the following spring.

There was Jenny, Daly's mare.

And there was Jewel.

Jewel alone of all the band had no warm coat of fur. Her hair was short, close, glossy from much graining, and her hide was thin. She had never experienced snow, let alone a blizzard. All her winter nights had been spent in her comfortable box stall in the Beckwith stables. During the mild spring and summer and fall nights she had browsed and drowsed in one of the small fenced pastures. She had never had to fight against a stiff wind. Now she was beaten upon by a blinding white blizzard that bewildered her, burned her eyes, and struck its fingers of ice into the very marrow of her bones.

Already, within her, the supernaturally intelligent mechanism of her body was hastening to repair the deficiency. The signals had been given. But it took a little time. In a week the lengthening hair would be visible. Meanwhile, she was an object of half-frozen misery if she ceased moving even for a moment.

But Thunderhead kept them all moving. He was sometimes ahead, leading them, sometimes behind, driving them. To Jewel he was as much a part of the horror as the cold. She veered away from him when he was near her. She had several sore spots in her haunches that would be bleeding now were it not that they were frozen. Occasionally she felt that the stallion was the whole trouble. If she could only get away from him and these mares all the other troubles would vanish too and she might find herself in the padded crate warm and snug again with Collins' familiar voice coming to her, his firm, accustomed hands smoothing her neck, tying the bag of oats on her head, petting her while the stream of delicious heat and strength poured down her gullet and gradually filled her with new life. Yes—escape! That was what she wanted! More than once, with this idea, she broke away from the herd and dashed off at an angle. But fast as she was, Thunderhead was faster, and in a moment she would be screaming with terror of the white monster behind her who drove his cruel teeth into her rump. More sore places now. More even than his teeth she feared himself and would swing away from him and find then that he had calculated on that, and that she was once again in the band of mares, going along obediently with them. But there was no peace for her with the mares either. One and all of them bit at her, shouldered her, swung their haunches and kicked her.

So she ran out to one side of the band and galloped there alone.

Jenny was being hazed, too.

Newcomers in a band of horses are always persecuted exactly like the new children at school. The newcomer has to prove himself and win his way. At last he is accepted. Jewel and Jenny were "new girls."

The three foals ran close under the sides of their dams, as well able, in spite of the short time they had been on the earth, to bear up under the cold and wind as their dams; perhaps better, because the mares had to rustle for their feed. A colt need only to thrust its nose under its dam's belly if she should pause for so much as a half-minute. Moreover, food came warmed exactly to the colt's needs, whereas the mare had to paw up the snow and eat the dry cold grass beneath it.

Long icicles hung from their nostrils and lips, their bodies were encrusted with white, only the manes and tails were dark. These moving constantly in the wind, were kept free from snow.

Suddenly the wind seemed to drop. Thunderhead slackened speed, the band stopped running and stood grouped in the lee of a high ridge of ground, one of the Buttes. Here was shelter. This was what Thunderhead had been leading them to. The colts immediately began to nurse. The mares were thirsty and ate the snow. Thunderhead himself pawed the snow and disclosed, under the cliff, a good-sized patch of green buffalo grass, sub-irrigated. The mares crowded to it and ate ravenously. Jewel tried to do the same, but the mares kicked her out. Frightened and forlorn, she moved to a safer distance and stood there, taut and humped in the icy wind and snow that curled over the peak of the ridge and just caught her where she was. But she dared not return. To freeze was better than to be kicked and bitten.

The night wore on. Vitality died down in Jewel. Her legs did not hold her up very well but seemed to bend. Her head hung very low.

The scent came to her on one of the currents of wind that whirled around the ridge. It was a warm scent, a horse scent, and a friendly scent. Oh, better than that! It was the scent of a champion, a refuge, a god! It was the big Clyde, the gentle monster with the brown eyes and the heavy, black forelock. It was the scent of Pete!

Jewel raised her head as if she had received new life. A wild nicker of recognition burst from her. Every mare and the stallion, too, turned and looked.

Something off there in the whiteness! A huge, bulky shape standing, a little timid, a little humble in the presence of the stallion as every gelded creature must be timid and humble in the presence of the unaltered male. Jewel fled toward him and in spite of his knowledge of the danger an answering whinny rumbled up out of his deep throat.

Jewel reached him and flung herself against him. They pressed their faces together, their nostrils touched and clung. Pete's deep, tender rumblings continued.

At that moment the stallion fell upon him, reared and pawed him, bit him, and whirled to lash out with his murderous heels. But Pete was not there to receive the blow. He had faded off into the impenetrable whiteness. Not a sound—not a rumble more came from him. Jewel felt a vicious nip on her withers and fled back to the mares. They presented their haunches and kicked her out of the herd.

Again she found her cold and lonely place on the outside and took her stand there.

A half hour passed. Then again that warm friendly smell of Pete! Again the irrepressible nicker burst from her and she dashed off to meet him. Again the stallion pursued. But this time Pete waited only for one touch of his nostrils to hers, one deep whinny—a promise not to desert her—then whirled and pounded away, his great hoofs shaking the earth.

Jewel went meekly back to her place and Thunderhead returned to his frantic chopping of the buffalo grass with his thick, white teeth, feeding voraciously, needing the nourishment and heat that comes from it to maintain his strength and vigilance and the fire of his stallion-kingliness.

The next time Jewel smelled Pete she did not whinny nor run out to him. She raised her head and looked through the driving snow to that spot of looming darkness. He came nearer but not too near, and warily, casually, as it were, began to paw the grass and nose beneath it for food.

He did not fool Thunderhead. The stallion's ears were flattened even though his head still hung low over the grass and he continued to eat, but he was alert to every move Pete made. Then his ears relaxed. He gave over being concerned and concentrated on his feeding.

Jewel too began to paw the grass and nose underneath it for food. Her grazing brought her nearer to Pete. He stood in an unsheltered place taking the full force of the wind and snow. Step by step she approached him, at last ceased any pretense of grazing, moved close and placed herself against his towering bulk as a colt is close under its mother's side. She felt the heat of his great body and was comforted. He did not waver, but stood staunchly, the blizzard beating upon his windward side and coating it with ice.

The snow with which Jewel was encrusted gradually melted and dripped off. The heat from the gelding's body penetrated her own. It was delicious. She was safe. She began to drowse.

Hours passed.

The prairie wolves were out seeking for victims of the blizzard. Now and then their long-drawn, mournful howls were carried on the wind to the horses, but they were not near, the stallion did not even raise his head.

Not quite so brave were the little yearlings who were seeing their first blizzard out, alone, sheltered under the lee of an overhanging cliff four miles to the north. They swung their heads nervously as the howls drifted to them, joined in sinister dissonance to the whine of the wind. They strained their ears to hear, held themselves taut and trembling.

A half mile away a solitary horse shape, the young Ishmael, stood motionless by a sheltering hill. He was shrouded in ice and snow, as white as his own hair and hide. His head was turned toward the band of mares. His ears were pricked, listening for the sound of Hagar's voice. And so he stood while the night passed.

Jewel did not cease to cling to Pete. And he leaned his great head, his rough black mane streaming over her.

# 15

Crown Jewel might not have survived that first blizzard had it not been for Pete. In all the storms of the hard winter which she spent with Thunderhead's band on the plains between the Buttes and the Snowy Range, Pete was her protector.

As soon as the first blizzard had ended and also the terrible ground blizzard which followed it, Thunderhead led them south into the open. Here, ground would be bare of snow because of the wind which incessantly swept it. There would be grass, dry and brown but extremely nourishing. There would be shelter enough and water enough in the little draws and depressions of the plains.

Elk and antelope and deer were on these plains for the same reason. Jewel was a comical picture of surprise when she first lifted her head from her grazing and saw, not very far off, a group of these strangely shaped animals sharing her pasture. But it soon came to be a natural and a pleasant thing. Occasionally, moved by irrepressible curiosity, she approached them tentatively. Sometimes, equally curious, they would come hesitantly to meet her and stand at a little distance, staring, stamp a hoof nervously, whirl away, run for a few seconds, then calm down and begin grazing again.

Sometimes the deer and horses grazed together, paying no attention to each other.

On winter days the true Wyoming gloriousness, when the sun, in a cloudless sky of deepest blue, blazed down through crystal air and poured its heat and energy into the horses like charges of electricity, Jewel was almost bereft of her senses with excitement and happiness. Nothing like this had ever been known by her before. She frolicked like a yearling. She bucked and frisked and tossed her head, stood on her hind legs and pawed at nothing.

The little group of yearlings a few miles away could easily be seen through the clear air. Jewel went flying off to make friends with them. Thunderhead, without even lifting his head kept an eye on all they did. Jewel returned. She always returned now. She had learned her lessons and got no more bites in her haunches. She no longer feared Thunderhead except for a seemly attention to his wishes. Once she found herself grazing close beside him. They moved slowly, almost keeping step, their sharp teeth jerking left, then right, another step, and with a full mouth, the stallion raised his head high tossing his eyes in a wide circle, a glance which took in every moving thing within a radius of many miles. *All's well*—and he lowered his head and again went step by step along with Jewel, their muzzles almost touching. He was not greedy. He willingly left her the good tuft of grass they were approaching. She came to feel a confidence in him. She knew that when he watched and stood guard, he stood guard for the whole herd.

But Pete was her true friend. He never entered the herd but accompanied it wherever it went, remaining always at the respectful distance of a few hundred yards. Most of the time Jewel was with him. Thunderhead had now accepted this friendship. In wintertime, when the mares are with foal, there is not so much to fear from an intruder. Besides, Pete was a gelding and not young, either. It is the young stallions a herd leader fears.

So the formation of horses was like a constellation. Thunderhead the central sun with the mares his close satellites, Pete and Jewel moving on an outer circle, Ishmael all alone on another ring, the yearlings on the farthest ring of all.

Still farther, but out of sight of this band, were other groups of horses, many of them the inbred small "wild" horses which are to be found in all the mountain states. But the centripetal force emanating from Thunderhead and binding his constellation together did not reach to these others and they ranged free of his control.

Jewel was acquiring greater strength and health than she had ever had before. Her lungs deepened and gained in power. She grew taller, longer-legged. The luxuriant growth of her mane and tail and her thick fur made her look, at first glance, like a wild horse of the plains, but at second glance, there was that superb head of an English thoroughbred, the fine sensitive ears, and four most perfect black legs. The only white mark upon her was the diamond and pendant upon her forehead.

The winter was long. The mares grew thin, their bellies were low, there was a sag in their backbones.

The storms continued with lengthening periods of

good grazing weather between. Sometimes there was a day when the air was balmy.

As spring approached the snow melted quickly after storms.

Thunderhead changed his pasture constantly. He was approaching the foothills of the Snowy Range, country that was new to him. He investigated every rock, every hill, every little hollow, really surveying the land like an engineer, so that when he was leading his band, either for food or safety, he knew where to take them. If they had to be concealed, he knew draws in which they could be invisible to anything moving on the plains. He spotted each rise where he could stand and see the country for miles around. Wherever he went, his entire constellation went with him until one day when Jewel, looking for the yearlings, could not see them. They had drifted away to a farther range. The bond between them and the mother-herd was cut. But Ishmael, now a magnificent two-year-old, still clung to his orbit, still stood at night with his head turned and his ears pricked toward Thunderhead's band. Thunderhead eyed him with increasing disfavor. This could not be tolerated much longer. But Ishmael was fast on his feet, and Thunderhead knew it.

With the approach of spring, Thunderhead's temper became short. Stallions would soon be roaming. Spring would put wanderlust into their feet. They would be looking for mares.

Sex was awakening in him and brought its characteristic restlessness, pugnaciousness, suspiciousness, flaring temper. It was as if through the sexless wintertime, he had enjoyed a period of peace, his care of his herd having a quality of father-love and protection. Now he watched ceaselessly for rivals, for the scent of a mare to be found and bred and appropriated, for someone to pick a fight with.

He trotted around his mares, erect from his springy hoofs to his high, sharply pricked ears and uplifted tail. Savagely he drove the colts out of his herd. These were yearlings now. The forlorn youngsters went through the usual period of agony before they accepted defeat and formed their own little band a few miles from the mother-herd.

For hours at a time, Thunderhead stood on his high point of vantage, looking for trouble. No challenger came, but there was still Ishmael.

One day Thunderhead's anger crystallized. He shot out of the herd, a bolt of fury aimed at the white two-year-old. This time he would have his way and punish the youngster so he would never return. But Ishmael knew beforehand just what was coming and was off and a mile away before Thunderhead reached the spot where he had been.

From that day on Ishmael no longer clung close to the mother-herd but neither did he join the band of his fellows, nor any other band. He found a new range for himself, a range which had a high peak from which he could see Thunderhead's band of mares. If the wind were right, he could smell them; now and then, he could get a whiff, or at least the sense, of his dam. This was all of life for him. Here he was safe from Thunderhead, could watch, move as they moved, keep his distance, yet have them within sight.

There came a day when Thunderhead, incessantly on the lookout and sniffing the messages brought on the wind, got notice of some mares in the neighborhood, one newly foaled, open. He left his band and trotted away, his high-held muzzle undulating from side to side, playing with the scent, feeling it bathe his sensitive nostrils. His tail plumed, his feet stepped high.

When he returned with two mares, one with a foal at foot, Hagar had vanished. Well he knew what had happened. In his absence, Ishmael had swooped down on the herd and stolen his mother. Thunderhead's nose made a careful survey of Ishmael's hoof prints and of Hagar's. He pawed at these. Furious snorts rippled from his nostrils. He came upon a pile of dung. It still smoked. Thunderhead moved a step or two forward and covered it with his own. Then, following the scent with his nose, he went in pursuit.

When he came upon them he went first for the mare. A few vicious chops separated her from her son and turned her backward. Then Thunderhead snorted his challenge to Ishmael. Ishmael stood up to him and faced him bravely, twenty feet or so away. Thunderhead pawed the earth, raking up clouds of dust, Ishmael did the same. His proud young crest lifted, his chin was dragged back and in, he seemed to swell. He had never fought before. When Thunderhead lifted a foot and took a step forward, Ishmael did likewise. They neared each other slowly, deliberately, the breath coming loudly through the flaring nostrils of their drawn-in muzzles.

Just as they were about to touch heads, Ishmael swerved, reared, wheeled; and, as Thunderhead faced about and lashed with his heels, the young stallion fled away. Even as Thunderhead, when a yearling, had fled the Albino, now Ishmael fled from Thunderhead. Not yet could he engage such a warrior. Thunderhead pursued him. The two horses flew over the plains on wings. Was Ishmael the faster? Or was Thunderhead halfhearted in the pursuit? The distance between them grew wider, at last Thunderhead turned in a short circle, abandoned the pursuit, headed for Hagar who was nibbling at the grass as if she had never had such a thought as an elopement in her head. Reaching her, Thunderhead gave her a few mean chops which put her into a gallop, then he forgave her and raced by her side.

When they reached the band of mares, the two "new girls" were already being hazed by the other mares. Jenny and Jewel did their part.

# 16

At last the mares began to shed their winter coats and drop their foals.

To make sweet, nourishing milk, high in protein content, they needed grass—fresh, young grass, green and luscious and tender and new. They needed an abundance of it.

It showed first as a soft tint on the southern slopes, then deepened until it was like emerald velvet. It covered the world.

The history of the state of Wyoming is the history of its grass. First the buffaloes had it and the Indians and the wild mustangs.

Before Wyoming was a state there had come to it large numbers of English and Scottish younger sons to make their fortunes. And they made not only fortunes but a most picturesque period of history.

There were hunts, with the coyote and timber wolf taking the place of the red fox. There were gathering

places in Cheyenne, the famous Stockman's Club, the
Normandy and the Cosmopolitan, where fine old
British names were spoken across the bars. There
were handsome homes on the great ranches and much
visiting back and forth in huge coaches drawn by four
or six horses. There was afternoon tea drunk out of
beautiful old china, there were heavy English pud-
dings on the dinner tables. At Yuletide, clear, sweet
English tenors sang the Carols; sang, as often as not,
on horseback. And from that custom, to this day, the
cowboy Carol singers ride out on Christmas Eve,
breaking the silence of the frozen plains between
ranch and ranch with the joyful ringing of the hoofs of
their galloping horses; and, arriving at some sprawling
huddle of dark walls and snow-laden roofs, announce
in "close harmony" that, Hark! the herald angels are
singing, and that, Oh, little town of Bethlehem, the
hopes and fears of all the years are met in thee tonight.

There were no fences in those days, no national
parks. The range was for those who ran their thundering herds of beef upon it. Red Hereford cattle, with
their distinguishing mark of the white face, were im-
ported from England and became the standard beef
cattle of the United States.

When sheep were introduced, there was enmity
between those who ran beef and those who ran sheep.
The cattle were there first. The sheep nosed in. "Fire-
mouths," they were called, from the way they nibbled
the range close. In spite of many and bloody conflicts
between beef owners and sheep owners the sheep
were there to stay. It was finally understood that they
did not spoil the range for beef, they ate a different
grass. They liked sage and gamma grass, not the native
hay or buffalo grass which was the preferred feed for

beef cattle.

Eventually there came to Wyoming the dry farmer with ploughs and fences.

For a few years these dry farms existed as a camel lives off its hump, feeding on the accumulations of moisture that the green grass roots had preserved in the soil.

But the plough cut and divided the sod, turning the roots up to the sun. The usual periodical drouths were more severe. Dry winds swept the plateau country and there was nothing to resist them. Moisture went out of the soil, springs and streams vanished, rivers became trickles. The range dried up and blew away.

The dry farmers starved. They packed their families and beds and stoves and pots and pans and mattresses in and on the tops and sides of their rusty, ramshackle Fords, and fled from the murder they had committed, joining the processions of dustbowl refugees that rattled along the highways of the country.

The whole story was told by the gaping, windowless walls, the sagging roofs, the banging shutters of the abandoned farms. Weather beat them into insensibility. They yielded themselves to the tumbleweeds and the tin cans.

The general calamity threatened to engulf the stockman as well as the farmer. Hundreds of thousands of cattle were slaughtered to leave more of the dried grass for the few that could survive. But, thanks to the foresight of the federal and state governments and certain public-spirited citizens in reserving almost one-third of the state of Wyoming for national forests, the watersheds of the United States were protected from the ignorance and rapacity of man. There was still grass in the mountains. And the surviving herds were trailed higher and higher, following the receding snows.

The lakes, mountains, snow-covered peaks, dense forests of the national reserves saved the remnants of the herds. The eternal threat and seduction of the desert, which had almost had its way with the grasslands, could not creep beyond the foothills.

The lesson was learned. Grass! Oh, for grass again! A country halfway between tillable farm land and desert is cattle land. Heal the ugly scars by planting grass seed on the ploughed fields. Coax the prairie to put an end to the dust storms by creeping back over the gaping earth and laying over it a luscious cover of greensward. Give it to the cattle and sheep and horses who enrich it as they feed. Let it be grass again!

And now, when spring comes in Wyoming, the children in school ask each other, *"Have you got green grass yet? We have!"* And there are jubilant answers, *"We have! We have, too."*

It is an event. Newspapers publish it. The whole tempo of life and business throughout the state changes. Now the mortgage can be lifted or a new one procured. Grandmother gets out of bed. Children get well of their winter ailments. Old quarrels are forgotten and forgiven, new ones start.

On the range, every living thing, small and large, knows that the world is new again. Clouds of bluebirds swing over the land, migrating to their northern summer homes. Rabbits and ermine change their winter coats of white to fawn and amber. The little lambs frolic in clusters and make abrupt jackknife dives into the air. The fleet wild mares of the plains gallop with loose jointed, gangling foals beside them. The slow-moving Hereford cows drop their chunky white-faced calves on the spongy turf and lick them

dry. All the world is filled with faint innocent bleat-
ings and cries and moos and whinnys the like of which
has not been heard for a year on the plains or in the
mountains.

The grass thickens and lengthens until it is a lush
green lawn of unbelievably vivid color as far as the
eye can see. There are patches of pink and blue and
lavender made by the forget-me-nots, mariposa lilies,
bluebells, larkspur, delphinium. Over all, the heavens
deepen into cobalt and are cupped like a bowl. The
big, sculptured, white ships of the sky take shape far
off in unseen caves, come drifting up from the western
horizon, sail slowly across and slide down the eastern
slopes. The heavens are patterned with them from
north to south and east to west, and the soft wind
blowing steadily, but sweet-tempered now and
smiling, keeps them ever a-moving.

The clouds cast their shadows upon the prairies,
mysterious pools of amethyst color. They wander,
they drift slowly eastward, their shapes are distinct
and clean-cut upon the grass but constantly changing.
Two cows are grazing side by side, two red Hereford
cows, one inside the edge of the shadow, one outside.
The one within is dark and cool looking, the one
outside is brilliant and bright, its hide flashing with
glints of fiery color.

There is a windmill upon the horizon, squat brown
shape, with sturdy arms that wave and posture against
the sky.

There is nectar in the cool, steady wind—nectar of
sage from the hillsides, of wildflowers from the gulches, of snow from the mountains, and of miles upon
miles of young greengrass.

The great mountain ranges, the Neversummer
Range in the southwest, the Snowy Range in the west,

the Buckhorn Range in the south, are still snow covered; the peaks, rearing up, are still as dazzling white as the clouds they touch noses with, but the snow line is higher. Here and there a bare, brown ridge runs clear to the top. They are far away, ringing the world.

Thunderhead often stood with his nose up, his ears pricked, looking at those far mountain peaks, aware of all the life that moved, openly or hidden, between himself and them. He wanted more mares. For a young and kingly stallion his band was short. Occasionally he made a foray and captured another, and once again men began to talk of him and look for him and to pass the word if anyone caught a glimpse of him.

And so the news came to the Goose Bar that the stallion was somewhere near the border of Wyoming and Colorado. Rob McLaughlin sent Buck Daly out scouting, and a week later wrote Beaver Greenway that Buck had picked up the trail in Fox Park and was following it south.

# 17

It was Saturday, the twelfth of June.

Ken McLaughlin was out on the Saddle Back filling his eyes and his nostrils and his lungs and his heart with sky and plains and wind and grass.

On the peak of a ridge they stood in silent companionship, the tall, thin, seventeen-year-old boy and his mare, Flicka. He had dismounted and was leaning against her. So had they been standing for the last fifteen minutes.

They were just looking around.

The look reached to the rampart of snow-covered mountains across the state border fifty miles south; and to the gilded dome of the State Capitol building thirty miles east and two thousand feet down; and to the long, level, sun-blinded plains to the west, pathway of the prevailing winds.

All this he had seen since he had been born, every summer when he came home from school, and in the winter vacations. Never did he come back to the ranch after a long winter's schooling without going through a strange state of consciousness, blissful but dislocated, unable to find his place.

The young do not know that this sense of strangeness is a universal feeling. It wears off. They think, almost with despair, that they have come to the end and their misery will be forever.

Flicka turned her head and pricked her ears.

Ken heard the faraway thunder of hoofs and looked alertly in every direction, until Flicka's head, pointing at a bare ridge several miles south, gave him the cue. Concentrating on it, he saw the little specks, like ants, running along the crest. Just a bunch of wild broncs. He would not have seen them, but for Flicka. He realized, this morning, he had not really been looking.

As a small boy Ken had been an addict to daydreaming, one of those children who, when they are preoccupied with their thoughts, can walk through their days seeing nothing, knowing nothing of what is going on. In fact, the filly, Flicka, had been given to him in the hope that her reality would overcome his love of the unreal. And it had. Ken could be wide awake enough now when he wanted to, but he could still dream.

Today he had just been dreaming. There were two ways you could look at things. One way, you really saw nothing at all, because you looked at it as one whole thing and just drifted away into it and forgot everything. The other way you took it apart and looked at everything separately and then it came to life.

Now he looked around and took it apart. The stones turned into squat gray bunnies almost underfoot. Those nubbly points on top of rocks were whistling pigs standing on their hind legs and looking searchingly out of little, old men's faces. Those big tufts on the wild currant bush were two hawks watching for gopher. The twist on the top of the trunk of the big pine was an eagle. All this was familiar. All this was home.

In his looking and searching, there was also the wonder of what was not yet to be seen but might show up at any moment.

The sheep, for instance. There was not a sign of them. His father had given him a message to deliver to Jeremy, the sheepherder, camping near Section Twenty-seven water hole.

Ken searched the hill above the water hole some miles to the east, but it was bare of life. His eyes wandered away again, losing their focus, falling back into their dreamy contemplation.

A sound from overhead aroused him, the steady, distant drone of an airplane. He searched the deep skies. They were partly obscured by processions of clouds on their slow way across the zenith. He found no plane, only a hawk that wheeled with a harsh, sad cry, and the lovely iridescent broken-off piece of a rainbow, hanging inexplicably in clear blue. Left behind, he thought, from the last storm.

He counted the colors. Pink and mauve and gold and green.

Then an exciting smell made him turn. It was the metallic smell of rain and of dust on the wind. Down southeast a storm was boiling up. The tangle of blue-black thunderheads seemed on a level with him. Lightning split the blackness again and again, and he could see the clouds colliding and wrestling with each other, and curtains of rain falling.

It was not coming toward him. Up here in the sun, with the gentle breeze and the drifting clouds and the hanging ribbon of rainbow, it was a perfect summer afternoon.

He must not forget his errand. Again he turned his eyes to the barren hill above the water hole and in spite of its apparent emptiness he kept on looking. There were two small black bushes on the hillside near the top. Suddenly they moved. One made a dash. They were sheep dogs. Then it looked as if a wave of grey water washed over the hill and rippled down. The sheep. Three thousand of them. The whole band.

He mounted Flicka and rode slowly toward the water hole.

Jeremy, hungry, as all sheepherders are, for a breath of the outside world, was standing out in front of his wagon, eagerly awaiting his visitor.

Greetings were exchanged as Ken dismounted and threw the reins over Flicka's head. Jeremy's eyes went to the saddle upon which several packages were fastened.

"Did ye bring me any magazines, Ken?"

"Sure. And some candy and a couple of records." Ken took the bundle off Flicka's saddle and handed it to Jeremy. "This one's a Spanish rumba. Hot stuff. This one's a Western."

The herder took the two records in his hands and looked at the writing.

"The Western," said Ken, pointing, "it's about—all this." He swung his arm wide.

"All what?"

"The grass. The greengrass. See the title? *Green Grass of Wyoming.*"

Jeremy read the title slowly aloud and stood thoughtfully looking at it while Ken, stretching himself, gazed around with his far, dreaming gaze.

"Must have been a guy that saw all this—the greengrass, and so much of it—and wrote that song about it."

"Grass is awful plain stuff to write poetry and music about," said Jeremy thoughtfully. "Still and all, come to think about it, we live on it."

"Not us," corrected Ken. "The animals do."

"Well, the beef eats the grass and we eat the beef."

Ken laughed. "That's right." Presently he said, "I know why he wrote about the grass."

Jeremy looked up.

"It kind of—gets you," Ken explained. "I always feel that way when I've been off at school and then come back. It's so awfully big, so awfully different from anything else in the world—and yet, it's—*just grass.*"

"Wait while I play it," said Jeremy and went into the sheepwagon and put the western song on his little phonograph. Ken stood outside listening.

"Oh! It's the green grass!
On the hills, in the spring, that keeps me a-roaming,
Ridin' all day on the prairie,
On the green grass rolling range of Wyoming.
     Lonely plains,

Wide and still
On the skyline
An old windmill!
Oh! It's the galloping hoofs
On the green grass rolling range of Wyoming.

"Oh! It's the west wind!
It's the wind that sweeps the grass of Wyoming,
Scented with snow from the mountains
And the pine and silver sage of Wyoming.
Saddle up!
Winter's done!
And I'm trailin'
The settin' sun.
Oh! It's the galloping hoofs
On the green grass rolling range of Wyoming!" *

"You can keep it if you like," said Ken as Jeremy shut off the phonograph and came to stand beside him. "You can give it back to me when you come down for the shearing."

"There's gonna be a good clip," said Jeremy seating himself on one of the steps of his wagon and taking out his pipe. "Any news down at your place?"

Ken threw himself full length on the grass. "Well, I came up to tell you," said he, "that Dad's got Garcia and his men for the shearing. It'll be in about two weeks. He wants you to keep the sheep where they are until then if there's feed enough."

Jeremy took a deep pull at his pipe. "There's plenty grass here yet—the lambs are lookin' fine. Your brother home too?"

"Sure. Say—did you know Howard passed his exams and is ordered to report at West Point on the Fourth of July?"

"That ain't no news! He took them exams last January. He got the notice he had passed in April, the wire to your Dad came through the telegraph agent over to Tie Siding, an' he spread the news—I bet I had it afore your Dad did. And I kin tell you somepin' else too. Your Dad went into Cheyenne and painted the town red. Waal, he ended up at the Post, and the Army officers give him a dinner of congratulation, and they did say your Dad got tight as a tick. But, say! Who'd blame him? Sixteen thousand dollars! That ain't a minnow—that's a good big wad of dough."

"Sixteen thousand dollars?" said Ken. "What you givin' me?"

"Sure. That's what it takes to put a boy through West Point. When Howard passed them exams he put sixteen thousand dollars in your Dad's pocket, or words to that effect. Say, Ken, any other news down at your place?"

Ken thought hard, then shook his head.

"Your baby sister baptized yet?"

"Nope. That's comin' off soon, though. Howard and I are going to be godfathers."

"I heerd yore Maw was set to have it done last summer an' yore Paw didn't git around to feelin' ready for it and yore Maw was real mad. That so, Ken?"

Ken looked a little worried. "Something like that," he said.

"Any other news, Ken?"

Ken shook his head.

"What about that Pearl woman?"

There was always news about Pearl. Ken told how she had gone to town for her day off and had disappeared. His father had found her in jail as usual.

Told the Sheriff to leave her there for two days more, till she was good and sober, then he'd come for her.

"And I bet," chuckled Jeremy, "the Sheriff was glad to oblige. Ef yore Maw and Paw didn't keep her here on the ranch the state would have her board and keep to pay at the House of Correction."

"Sure," said Ken. "That's the luck of it for us. Zowie! the pies and cookies she makes!"

"Fond of cookies myself," said Jeremy, smacking his lips. "Did she sober up all right?"

"Sure. They took her out of jail and put her in Dad's car and he brought her right to the ranch."

Jeremy chuckled. "Didn't give her no chance to cut loose again. Say! I wonder how many times your Dad's done that!"

"Plenty," said Ken. "It's lucky she's home again now because we've got company coming."

"Company?" Jeremy pricked up his ears. Company at any ranch was a good news-item.

"Carey Marsh," said Ken importantly.

"Say! Ain't that the leetle gal was nearly lost in the blizzard last fall?"

"That's the one."

"Daughter of Beaver Greenway? The fellow owns the race track over to Saginaw Falls?"

"Not daughter, grandneice. Mother wrote and asked her to come down to visit us and she's coming tomorrow."

"And wot about that horse of hers got lost in the Badlands? The English race horse? Milt Norcross was over here yestiddy asking me was you going out again this summer to hunt her?"

"Sure we are. And this time we'll get her. And my stallion, too. Dad sent Buck Daly out two weeks ago to locate them."

"Locatin' a little band of horses somewhere in Wyoming, Montana, or Colorado is a big order, Kennie."

"But we know where they are. A lumber outfit over near Fox Park sent word to Dad they'd seen them over there near the North Platte. That's where Thunderhead wàs a year ago when Howard and I trailed him. It's one of his hangouts."

"If anyone can trail him, it's Buck Daly. As good as an Indian scout any day."

They continued to talk until the light changed. Most of the sheep were drawing nearer to the fold for their evening feed of cotton cake.

Ken slowly got to his feet and stretched again. Jeremy stood up and walked out from the wagon to look at his sheep. A mile away a group was lingering in the valley. Jeremy turned to his dogs. Ken saw how both the collies had their eyes on their master, waiting for orders. Jeremy pointed toward the sheep and made a gesture with his hand. The two dogs shot down the slope, ran across the fields and curved around the sheep. The sheep, startled, looked up, and with their smooth flowing motion, rippled across the floor of the valley. But there were still some which the dogs had not seen beyond the shoulder of the hill. The two collies, glancing at Jeremy for orders, received this information from a few free gestures of his hand. They investigated behind the hill, rounded up the sheep and brought them to the others. Jeremy waved his arms again, telling the dogs not to hurry the sheep, let them take their time coming in. The dogs lay down, panting, and turned their faces away, and the sheep quieted, grazing slowly as they approached the fold.

When Jeremy came back, Ken said, "I've got to go."

He put his hand in his pocket and took out a small paper. "Here's the receipt for the letter Dad took to town and had registered for you."

The herder took it and rummaged in his pocket. "I owe your Dad fifteen cents for the registration fee."

"Yes, he told me to bring it."

"Here's two nickels and three pennies and a two cent stamp. Sorry I haven't got it all in cash. Don't lose it."

Ken put the nickels and pennies and stamp very carefully in his watch pocket and mounted his horse.

"So long, Jeremy."

"So long, Ken." The old man stood watching the boy ride away, then went into his wagon and played the Western again.

Ken heard it as he rode slowly along the crest. The music had a poignant wistfulness, drifting to him across the space.

Before he turned Flicka down the slope he drew rein for a last look around up here on the Saddle Back. Quite close were two antelope, running along the antelope trail which led from the water hole. Seeing him they sheered off to the south. They so perfectly blended with the colors of the range that Ken would not have seen them but for the white, heart-shaped shields which were their rear elevations.

An ermine, in summer dress of rich brown fur with black-tipped tail, undulated over the grass and disappeared into a hole near a rock. This small aristocrat of the plains was a rare sight and Ken kept his eyes on the hole, hoping to catch another glimpse. Presently he saw the head and long neck come up, stare at him a moment, then pop back in again.

Ken looked for the storm, the rainbow, the ridge

runners, the airplane—all gone now. And the world
had changed because the light was changed. There
were long shadows. Every outline was soft and mysterious. The colors were richer. There was a new
exciting coolness in the wind.

Ken drew a deep sigh, but it was not of sadness, it
was of emotion. Because Carey was coming, because
his life trembled on the brink of this exciting event,
everything was significant, everything was important.

There drifted to him, from far away, the deep
belching roar of the bull. . . . Milking time, and
Cricket acting up, as usual. Didn't like to see the men
coming to drive the cows in. A good thing they'd put
the ring in old Cricket's nose; fastened him with
chains out on both sides of his head and down to a big
bolt in the floor of the barn. Couldn't move any way
but down. And then Gus had opened the big copper
ring on its hinge, and driven the two points through
the cartilege of the bull's nose. Cricket had squirmed
and roared, gone down on his knees and rubbed his
nose on the ground. But that hurt! He got up again
pretty quick, Gus greased the nose, kept turning the
ring in it, then undid the chains and led the bull away,
squealing, but as obedient as you please.

That roaring! Just a lot of bluff, now. . . . Ken
touched his heel to Flicka's side and turned her down
the slope.

# 18

Eastward bound Number Twenty-One roared into the
Cheyenne station at 6:45 P.M.

The McLaughlins, with the exception of Nell and Penny, were on the platform to meet it; Rob, very conservative-looking, in an English tweed suit, Howard in striped blue flannels and a sport coat, Ken in his best suit of grey French flannel. The two tall, sun-burned boys were bareheaded, their dark hair a little rough, their collars open, their blue eyes eager.

The train slowed down and the white-coated porter stepped off and swung the luggage down. Carey was the first passenger to be seen.

Ken hadn't dreamed that he was going to feel like this when he saw her. His heart hit him a thump under his throat. He felt that he would choke if he tried to say anything. With one look he took in every detail of her as she came down the steps. There was that grave smile, as of a child being very sure to be correct and remembered everything she had been told. It pulled her full lips together in the middle and drew them up at the corners. Her dark eyebrows tilting up over her temples made her grey eyes look questioning. A wide-brimmed Breton sailor hat curled back from her face and her heavy, glossy hair fell like a mane to the shoulders of her white linen suit. Yes—there was *the child*. Ken was glad she hadn't changed. Sometimes, from one year to the next, girls and boys changed so you could hardly know them. He realized vaguely that she was very smart. What was it about the suit? The jacket was short and the blouse, dark blue. There were the same lovely long legs, slim and brown and smooth.

"How's the girl?" cried Rob helping her down and giving her a kiss.

"Hello, Mr. McLaughlin."

"Hello, Carey."

"Hello, Ken; hello, Howard."

"Hello, Carey." They all shook hands. She gave the porter the tip she had ready, the boys grabbed her suitcases and there was the usual scramble of talk which said nothing and made Ken feel both uncomfortable and excited.

Rob McLaughlin took her by the arm and steered her across the platform. "We're going to have dinner at the Plains Hotel."

"Mother didn't come, because she didn't like to leave Penny," said Howard. "She sends her love."

"How is the baby?" Carey addressed this to Ken, looking over her shoulder at him.

"She's okay." He tried to think of something else to say. "Gee, Carey—" It seemed inadequate and ridiculous, but Carey gave him a glance, and it went through him and warmed him. Perhaps she knew all that "Gee, Carey" meant.

The hotel dining room was crowded. They had a round table in the middle of it. They asked the correct and formal questions of each other at first, little by little gathering up the threads of each other's lives and beginning to feel at ease again. Then Carey wanted to know if they had had any news of Buck Daly? Had he located Thunderhead and his band of mares? Had he seen Jewel?

Rob explained that he was in Fox Park trailing them, had not yet seen them, but might at any time, and asked, "What races are you going to put her in, Carey, when you get her back?"

"First, the American Grand National at Belmont Park, in November," said Carey calmly, and Ken gasped.

Rob laughed. "Two-and-a-half-mile steeplechase! That'll be some going for a youngster."

"That is," said Carey, "if she's in condition. We

don't know if she's been hurt. She mightn't be able to run."

"You don't need to worry about that," said Rob. "She's been in charge of a range stallion, remember, and she's on Wyoming greengrass."

"Wyoming greengrass," murmured Carey, feeling the lilt of the words. "It sounds like something magic."

"It is, believe me!" said Rob. "This country up here does something for horses that is out of this world. Gives them strong lungs, staying power, makes them hard. Jewel will be in better condition than she has ever been in before."

*"Oh, it's the green grass!"* sang Howard softly.

Ken opened his mouth to say that Jewel, in all likelihood, was about to become a mother. He glanced around, thought better of it and shut his mouth again. Carey was telling Rob of the other races her uncle was thinking of for Jewel. Jewel was to be entered in all the big stakes.

Some Army officers whom Rob knew came by and stopped to speak. The boys got up and stood. Again, the talk was of Jewel and the expedition which was to be sent out to get her and of the races she would run in. Her fame, and the interest of her story, had gone all over the state. The officers asked who was going to get her?

"We're all of us going," said Howard.

Colonel Harris looked at him. "This is the Cadet, isn't it?"

Howard grinned and nodded. "Yes, sir. My last vacation here for two years."

Colonel Harris shook him warmly by the hand. "Welcome to our midst, Howard. Rob, couldn't you find a better fate to wish on him?"

Rob went over to their table for a few minutes and

now the boys talked more freely. They wanted to know about last fall, after the blizzard, when Carey had left the ranch with her Grandma and uncle. Had she got an awful bawling out from her Grandma for having gone with Ken in the pick-up to the Monument?

Carey shook her head. Her face was contrite. "Oh, it wasn't like that, it was just that it made Grandma ill, she was so worried about me. I shouldn't have done it."

"Is she coming down here with your uncle when we go out after the horses?"

"Of course," said Carey, "your mother has asked her."

The boys looked at each other. Ken said, "But this summer, won't you go along with us?"

Carey looked doubtful. "I don't think Grandma would ever let me do that. There won't be any other woman along."

"But Dad is going this time! And your uncle!"

"Look what happened to me last fall. She'll never get over that."

"But that was because of bad weather. Now it's summertime. It'll just be like going off on a summer horseback trip with a lot of fun and excitement thrown in."

Carey heaved a deep sigh. "Oh, I wish I could! I'd give anything to!"

Howard said firmly, "There isn't a reason in the world why you should not go. Any other girl would— any other girl's mother would let her. You ought to show a little spunk. If your uncle says you can go, then just take a stand!"

"But it might make her ill!"

The two boys looked at each other. What would

you do if someone got sick every time you did anything that was fun?

"Cripes, Carey!" said Howard, "You've got a problem child on your hands. I don't see how you can take it!"

Carey's wide grey eyes took on a worried expression. "Well, but Howard," she said, "*you* obey your father—and your mother too!"

"But they're *reasonable!*" exclaimed Howard. "Your grandmother treats you as if you were a little girl."

Ken said persuasively, "Mother says that everyone in the world has a special problem to solve. I guess she's yours. I don't think you *ought* to knuckle under when there's no sense in the things she makes you do."

"But she's not well," Carey staunchly defended her.

"I think she just puts half of that on to make you do what she wants!"

Carey looked doubtful. "That's what Uncle Beaver thinks. At least, sometimes he does. He says I ought to assert myself. I *would* like to go to college."

"However did you get to come down and visit us?" asked Ken.

Carey laughed. "Well, it was just luck. You see, when your father wrote to Uncle Beaver to tell him he had sent Buck Daly out to locate the horses he said at the end of the letter that your mother was writing inviting me down right away for a visit. And that same day my Grandma received the letter from your mother, inviting me. Grandma was writing to say I couldn't go until they all went. But Uncle Beaver wired your mother and said I could come, and then told Grandma what he had done. So there wasn't any use in her finishing her letter."

The boys laughed loudly. Howard seemed to have a morbid interest in the strange psychology of Mrs.

Palmer. "Was she mad?" he asked hopefully.

But Carey would give him no satisfaction. "She didn't like it very well," she said in her reserved manner.

"Gee! I'm glad you came," said Ken.

"So'm I." Carey's eyes were on her plate.

"We'll have a lot of fun!" said Howard.

"I want to do everything different from what I do at home," said Carey. "I don't want to be wrapped up in cotton wool. I want to wear pants and groom my own horse. And bathe Penny. And cook and make dumplings and doughnuts and strudels, and have a pair of pliers in my pocket and everything."

"Howard and I are training four spring colts," said Ken. "You can help us do that."

The boys explained how this was done. Carey listened, her eyes shining, feeling as she had last year, that she was being taken into a new world.

Rob returned, they finished their dinner, and got into the Studebaker. Rob stopped at the Creamery for some ice cream to take home to Nell.

On the drive home, Carey sat behind, between the two boys and asked them why the officers had called Howard "the Cadet." They explained. Carey looked at Howard almost with reverence, then gravely shook his hand and said, "Congratulations, Cadet McLaughlin."

Ken writhed inwardly. Was it going to be like this? Would Howard be the one she looked at and admired? It was tough having your girl see you always with your elder brother who was handsome and full of teasing talk and funny ideas and would soon have a West Point uniform on.

"He's got a girl," Ken blurted out.

"Oh, has he?"

"Hey! What are you giving us!" exclaimed Howard.

"Yes he has, her name's Barbara Bingham and he's got her picture in a case in his pocket and a big one in his room and he gets two or three airmail letters from her every week."

Ken got all the evidence out before he could be interrupted. But Howard was nonchalant. He winked at Carey and said, "So what?"

Carey kept looking at him smilingly and wonderingly. Ken leaned back in his corner and sat silent and glum.

At the ranch, Nell took the girl into her arms and gave her a warm embrace. Carey had fallen in love with Nell the summer before. To be taken in her arms now and hugged and then kissed on both cheeks, with Nell's tender, dark blue eyes smiling a welcome, almost made a lump come into her throat. This was the way mothers were. She felt her own loss as if it had just happened. She could have put her head down on Nell's breast and cried because she had no mother and had never known one. Just think what these boys had!

"Come out to the terrace," called Nell, "when you have put your things away."

"And we'll have some ice cream," added Rob.

Nell sat there with Rob, while Howard and Ken carried the suitcases in for Carey, lit the light, opened the closet doors, and then left her.

It was the same bedroom in which Carey had slept with her grandmother the year before. Carey stood in the middle of the room sniffing. The room had a smell. Every room has its own smell. This seemed to be of wood and something spicy that hung around the big mahogany bureau, and a wonderful freshness and sweetness that came in the open windows. Associated with it were thrills, excitement, fun. It was definitely a smell of happiness.

Carey looked out. There was still a soft twilight. She could see the undulations of the plains, the point of a timbered hill running down to the road across the stream, the mountains so far away, the bluish misty color of the sky above the horizon, three faint new stars.

A soft wind blew in the window, billowing the curtains, the same chintz curtains with tiny bucking broncos printed on them that had been there last year.

That night, when Carey put her head on the pillow, she heard a hoot owl calling plaintively. The next moment, it seemed, she rolled over and stretched her arms, yawning, and the blue-and-white striped sleeves of her pajamas slid to her shoulder, and it was morning, and there was a different smell, smell of coffee and bacon, and the faraway sound of a bull roaring.

# 19

"He's simply nuts about her," said Howard at the end of the breakfast, as Carey and Ken left the room together on their way to the stables.

"Ken, you must remember, has a one-track mind," said Ken's father. "He's a lad of one idea. He takes hold and he can't let go." Rob pushed his plate away and gave his undivided attention to Penny who sat on the table just to the right of his water glass, her customary position at breakfast. He took hold of her tiny waist, his big hand almost ringing it, and squeezed a little. Penny chortled and grabbed his fingers.

"It's all right with me if he is," said Nell.

Rob said dryly, "Judging by the way he is crazy about horses, it would be quite something to see! Ken crazy about a girl!"

Nell said, "That's just it! It's time he knew there was something in life to fall in love with and dream about besides horses."

"Have a heart, Mum!" cried Howard. "You know Ken! If he really falls for a girl, he'll be all the way loco, not just halfway."

"Ken is possessive," said Rob, "far too possessive."

Nell glanced at him thoughtfully as she refilled her cup with coffee and placed one elbow on the table.

Howard looked from one of his parents to the other. "Possessive? How do you mean?"

"Whatever he loves or wants," explained Rob, "has to belong to him completely and exclusively."

"That's right!" exclaimed Howard. "Do you remember how he was about Flicka?"

Nell remembered. When she had asked Ken why, when he could ride any horse on the ranch, he was so set on his father's giving him a colt, he had answered, "Oh, Mother, it isn't just the riding. I want a colt to be mine—all my own."

She said aloud, "And do you remember how he was about the canaries?"

"The canaries?"

"Perhaps that's too long ago for you to remember, Howard."

But Rob began to laugh. "Ken and his 'freemale'!" he said.

Nell explained. "It was the canary year. At the little school you both went to, they were raising canaries, so then all the children wanted to raise canaries at home. You were seven and Ken was five. Ken heard all the talk about males and females and began to beg, 'But I want a little freemale—couldn't I have a little freemale all of my own?' "

They laughed. Howard said, "I bet he got his little freemale."

"He did," said Nell. "We raised canaries. *Did* we raise canaries! They were all over the house."

"And then he wanted another little freemale, Flicka."

Pearl came in and started to remove the dishes. Rob got to his feet, and lifted Penny in his arms. She seized his nose and squeezed it as hard as she could. "Ouch!" he said, ducking his head against her. She gurgled and grabbed a fistful of hair.

"Hey! Just a minute," yelled Rob, and the baby burst into one of her hearty laughs, so infectious everyone had to laugh with her. "You're going to wreck me!"

He carried her to Nell who took her on her lap.

As Rob and Howard left the room, Howard turned at the door to look back with a grin. "First the canary, then the filly, and now another little freemale!"

Nell laughed and when they had gone, sat stirring the sugar into her coffee, thinking. . . . For all that they say about possession and possessiveness, who is there that isn't? Who that loves, really loves, would be willing to share? If they were willing, it would mean that they were lukewarm and indifferent. The possessive ones are the ardent ones, the all-out ones; the ones who can give themselves wholly, utterly. Possessiveness is the sweetest part of love, and it's *all* of sex! All the same—her face became grave as she remembered how deeply Ken, the ardent, the possessive, had suffered, and would suffer again.

Her thoughts ran ahead to the future. She thought

of Carey as Ken's wife, as her own daughter. Of course it would be years yet, but so often the love of young people is intense, wholehearted, pure, deep and lasting. Many a man marries his first love.

Nell had turned over Redwing for Carey's use. This time Carey was equipped with her own riding clothes. They were all unpacked, and hung neatly with her other things in the pine-scented closets of her room, with her boots and shoes in a row underneath. In the mornings, with riding and stable work ahead of her, she wore bluejeans and a cotton shirt. In the evenings, she would put on one of her ruffled summer dresses and win an approving smile from Rob.

Carey was not only happier than she had ever been in her life, but she knew it. Every day was packed with interest and fun, the more precious because, when her grandmother arrived, the fun would be over —unless she screwed up her courage—as Howard was always urging her to do—and took a *stand!* and insisted on being allowed to go on the expedition with the others. If she didn't—her mind envisioned the departure of the expedition—on horseback or in cars; the boys riding away; herself left behind with her grandmother and Nell; and the baby—and Pearl —a lot of women.

So she made the most of this interlude of freedom and did the things she had always longed to do. She helped Nell give Penny her bath and dress her. She put on a big apron and, under Pearl's direction, made an excellent batch of doughnuts. She made acquaintance with all the animals and learned their histories.

A cocker bitch had been procured some time ago as a mate for Chaps, and now the pups were six weeks old, as beautiful a litter as could be desired, with soft, curly hair all over their bodies and sweet little domed heads from which depended long silky ears. Daisy, the bitch, was not in favor. Recently she had dug a hole under the fence of the chicken yard and devoured eighteen baby chicks. For a bird dog, there was no excuse. Stern frowning looks were Daisy's portion. No such thing had ever happened before on the Goose Bar Ranch and it was a disgrace. Daisy knew it. She had formed the habit of slinking, her belly low on the ground, casting hang-dog looks at her master. Rob didn't feel it was good for a dog. Nobody knew what to do with such a dog as Daisy.

There were stories for Carey to hear about the cats, too. Cats, it seemed, both wild and tame, inhabited the woods, and appeared without notice at the door of a ranch house when they wanted a little domesticity. A gentle, grey tabby cat, white-breasted, who looked like a stuffed cat to be set on the mantelpiece, had appeared from nowhere one day. They called her Susie. She got a litter of kittens about the same time Pauly got hers, but Susie's were born dead. Nell decided that Pauly could spare a couple of her five husky kits to assuage the pangs of disappointed motherhood in poor little Susie. So she fixed up a box for Susie and gave her two of Pauly's kittens. But that wasn't enough to suit Susie. one by one she stole every one of Pauly's kittens and carried them to her box. Then Pauly stole them back again. Then Susie stole them. It was all they did—carry those kits from box to box. At last, one morning, they had worked it out. Pearl had found the two mother cats and all five kittens in one box together. They brought them up in partnership, both nursed them, both licked and washed them, both hunted for them and fed them.

The boys were training four colts. Carey helped them. They spent the morning doing this, halter-breaking the foals, teaching them to lead, to obey orders, to eat oats out of the hand.

Then, at noon, they would go into the swimming pool which was really a reservoir for the irrigation ditches. Carey loved this. To float on her back staring up at the deep blue sky, watching the clouds moving so slowly across the heavens, the hills going up around her so that she seemed to be at the bottom of a cup; and she would muse about these new friends and all the things she was doing here. Nell—what was the matter with Nell? You never seemed quite to get at her, as if she was shut up in herself with some secret.

Carey's reverie was broken by a vigorous splashing as the boys tore past her—just showing off.

They rode their horses down to the pool, bareback, in their bathing suits and rode them back again, soaking wet. More than once they put the horses into the pool and made them swim, too. They took long rides over the plains, or to do errands for Rob, or to inspect the fences. They gossiped with the men and heard of all that was going on in the country.

The evenings were long and light. It seemed as if, in the gentle twilight hours, the fruit of the day was gathered up and eaten. Sometimes Nell and Carey played duets. Sometimes they all sat on the terrace and talked while the animals hung around, turning their curious and affectionate eyes upon the different members of the family.

On one such evening Ken suggested to Carey that they walk down the meadows to Castle Rock.

Carey glanced around. She was sitting on the steps of the terrace, watching the puppies playing.

Nell was indoors at the piano. Rob was near by, occupied with Penny, a highball on the table beside him. He had drawn the baby between his knees, her tiny hands were busy with the buckle of his belt and there came from her lips a stream of talk without intelligible words but of so pure and birdlike a tone, so innocent, so mindless, that Carey wondered at the sweetness of it.

"How about it, Carey?"

Carey had heard about Castle Rock. The boys had told her of the finding of the carcass of Rocket's foal there, half-devoured by the wildcat, and of all the other skeletons and grisly remains in the caves under the rock. She would like to see it. And an evening walk alone with Ken through the meadows—the thought slightly quickened her pulse. Still, there was a deliciousness about this family group on the terrace after supper and she was reluctant to leave it.

Howard, chinning himself on one of the poles of the pergola, said, "Why don't you take your gun? I'll come along and we'll get some cottontails."

Nell was coming out the door. "Don't shoot any cottontails today. We have more meat on hand than we need. I want to talk to you, Howard."

Nell sat down in the hammock and Ken and Carey started off.

Howard stood looking down at his mother questioningly. Her face was merry as she looked back at him. There was a little teasing grin. She patted the hammock beside her and he fitted himself in, flung his arm around her and pulled her against his shoulder. "Why," she said, taking hold of his hands which were clasped across her chest, "do you want to cut out Ken with Carey?"

"Wha—a-at?" exclaimed Howard. "Why, Mother!"

"Don't 'Why Mother' me," she said trying to pull out of his arms, but he held her tight. "I'm on to you. But what I really want to ask you about is Barbara

Bingham."

All her senses were alert, and clasped against his chest as she was, she could feel the slight reaction of his body to this name—a tension, a waiting.

"Howard, you are so secretive!" she cried. "Why do you make a mystery about this girl?"

"I don't make any mystery." He rubbed his chin on her hair tenderly.

"Yes, you do! All these important-looking letters coming! Air mails! Special deliveries! Although who could specially deliver a letter to us here on the ranch I cannot imagine, unless a coyote or an eagle."

Howard laughed, but even though Nell waited, he volunteered nothing.

"Is she *the* girl, Howard?"

"Well, I guess she is, Mother."

"More than Carey?"

"Carey's just a kid."

"I like Barbara's looks, judging from the pictures of her you have around, but if she is to be my daughter-in-law, I'd like to know it."

Howard made no answer to this, and Nell muttered impatiently, "Oh, you make me tired!" She struggled to free herself, Howard released her, stood up, then stooped, gave her a quick kiss and leaped off the terrace. He walked down to the cowbarn. Nell sat, touching her foot to the ground, so that the hammock swung a little.

Now and then, her eyes rested on Rob and the baby. She felt something moist and warm on her bare ankle. Looking down she saw one of the curly-haired cocker pups. The little red tongue was licking her ankle. She picked it up and held it close. The puppy thrust its nose inside the collar of her dress and heaved a deep sigh. They were very sweet, she thought, but there were too many of them. Every one of them had been spoken for, they were old enough to be given to their new owners. We will keep one, she thought, perhaps this one, little Willy.

There came a deep roar from the corral of the cowbarn. Usually, after evening milking and feeding were over, the bull was quiet. Sometimes he went out to pasture with the cows, sometimes, even when the cows had left him, he remained in the corral where he had received his feed, standing there motionless in one of his dark meditations upon the primal joys of blood and lust. He appeared to live in a chronic state of smoldering fury, viewing any person, any moving thing, any life outside himself, as something which it was his duty to put an end to. Even the calves were not safe with him. Only the cows.

"Rob," said Nell, "I wish you'd sell Cricket, or have him butchered."

Rob made no answer. He was absorbed in trying to discover what Penny had, shut up in one small fist. He tried to open the wee fingers. She resisted him and squirmed in his grasp.

"Rob!" said Nell.

"Oh, he's all right," said Rob, "now that I've put the ring in his nose. It's Howard he's yelling at." He raised his voice. "Howard!" he shouted. "Cut that out!"

"I'm not doing anything," Howard shouted back, then wandered up from the cowbarn to the bunkhouse. The men were sitting out-of-doors on the wooden benches which flanked the front door. Here they gossiped the long evenings away, falling into silence when music came from Nell's piano. Howard joined them. Cricket ceased his bellowings. And Nell's foot touched the ground, and gave her hammock a little push, and another, and another. . . . She wondered where Pilgrim was and her eyes wandered, searching. She knew he was looking at her from some hideout, from the grass behind the spring house, from the trees under the cliff, or the edge of the path leading up to the barn, but she could see no sign of him. She put Willy down. Willy picked up a leaf, lifted his head proudly and trotted down the terrace carrying it with an important air.

Beyond the flower border a strange performance was going on. Daisy, the mother cocker, had conceived a maternal passion for Pauly. She took the cat by the neck with her delicate spaniel hold. She dragged her and carried her as she had carried and dragged the puppies whom she no longer permitted to approach her. And Pauly furled all her talons and curled in her paws and went limp, her eyes half closed with the ecstasy of returning to the helplessness of her kittenhood.

There was a movement farther away on the Green. It was the black cat who, one day last summer, had suddenly emerged from the woods to pay court to Pauly. But Pauly already had a lover in the person of the large yellow cat who had been named Matilda before her sex had been known. When, after a night of terrible feline screams, there was silence, and thereafter Matilda came no more but the black cat came instead, the battle on the cliff opposite the house had been guessed. The boys named the newcomer Bagheera, after Kipling's black panther. They all wondered if Pauly had been watching while the two tomcats fought for her. She might, thought Nell, have been lying stretched out on a rock in the moonlight, relaxed and pleased, purring, casting only occasional glances at her suitors while they tore each other to pieces. After Matilda had been eliminated, Pauly and

Bagheera had fallen in love and would lie looking at each other for hours at a time, about ten feet apart, their paws tucked in, all the world forgotten.

Bagheera, now, was creeping with silent panther steps toward a little pile of fresh dirt on the lawn which marked a gopher hole.

Willy caught sight of him, dropped his leaf, burst into blithe yappings and frolicked forward to have a game. He flung himself on his back in front of Bagheera, batting his paws in the air.

With glaring eyes the black cat rose up, delivered a flurry of lightning swift slaps on the puppy, then turned his dignified back and slowly walked away. Willy rolled over, unhurt, but puzzled, twisting his head first to one side, then the other.

While Nell swung gently in the hammock and watched the intelligent play of the animals, her thoughts wandered. . . . Guests coming before long . . . rooms to get ready . . . long talks with Pearl . . . how was the old lady going to behave . . . Ken . . . Howard . . . Fourth of July. . . .

# 20

The long winding hay meadows of the ranch had their names, names which had never been given them, which had just come to be. The closest to the house was called the Home Meadow. The next was Crooked Meadow, because of the tortuous twists and turns of Lone Tree Creek winding through it. The farthest meadow was called Castle Rock because, overhang-

ing the aspen grove at the far end was the great rock,
jutting up seventy feet high, as big as a house, constructed in the strangest manner with parapets and
turrets and balconies and peaks and minarets and
domes, and underneath it the chambers of horrors
which the boys had described so vividly to Carey.

Now she stood in one of them, in pitch darkness.
Ken was there beside her but she could not see him
and he did not make a sound. It was frightening. She
made a little murmur of fear and felt Ken's hand
reaching out, asking for hers. She gave it to him and
he clasped it tight and then, standing so, the fear left
her. It became a thrilling experience, and it was hard
not to breathe in such a way that Ken would know
how she felt. Gradually her eyes became accustomed
to the dark and she was able to follow him about from
one cavern to the other, inspecting the bones and skeletons, listening to him tell her what each animal had
been. But though she looked at them she was really
thinking of Ken and wondering why she was always excited when she was alone with him, wondering why, mostly, she chose to go with Howard when
she really liked Ken best.

Then they climbed the great rock, Ken helping her
in the difficult places, and at last they were up on one
of the high platforms at the very top, lifted into the
freshness of the evening sky.

Carey skipped about. She put her head back and
lost herself in the soft, indigo depths of the heavens.
She scanned all the wideness of the plains and the
rolling hills. And she chattered to Ken.

They were never tired of discussing the events of
last fall. It was like having the adventures all over
again. Carey told Ken what she had done at the Monument after he had ridden away with the men. How

Cookie had saddled the roan for her and told her to go off and have a ride, and how she had gone, and climbed up the little cone-shaped hill, and then, at the very top, had taken out her binoculars and had seen Thunderhead ten miles away or so, standing up on the top of a peak like the statue of a horse, looking right back at her.

"You've seen him since I have," said Ken jealously.

"But you'll see him soon now, Ken. You're going to get him back."

"Maybe," said Ken, who was in a despondent mood.

"That's what you want more than anything else in the world, isn't it?"

"I don't know."

"You said last summer the thing you wanted more than anything in the world was to get him back and ride him in one more race."

"I know I did."

"Don't you still want to?"

"Yes, but," he turned his face to look at her with a glance half wary, half bold, "but now—what I want most has something to do with you, I think. I feel as if I would want most in the world to do something for you."

Their eyes met timidly, slid away again. It seemed a huge admission Ken had made and he hastened to cover it up.

"What do *you* want most? Oh, I know! You want to be a singer."

"No."

"Then a concert pianist."

"No."

"Well, what then? Or don't you know, either?"

"Yes, I know perfectly well. I want to be a mother and have about eight lovely children! Oh, I think that would be the most wonderful thing in the world!"

Ken frowned. "You're too young to be thinking of things like that, Carey. Why, you're only sixteen."

"But my mother married when she was seventeen, and she must have been thinking about it before then, so why can't I? Why, I'm a woman, Ken!"

"But Carey, I haven't even finished school yet. And then I have to go through college."

Carey looked at him in amazement. "But, Ken! What do *you* have to do with it?"

"Well, *somebody* has to be the father, hasn't he?"

Carey covered her embarrassment with a careless laugh. "Oh, you just don't understand girls, Ken."

Ken turned away. On the floor of this eyrie lay a branch of dead wood. He picked it up. "How the heck do you think this got here? The wind must have brought it, I guess." He took his knife out of his pocket and began to whittle it as his mind raced, trying to figure out what he could say next.

"I see what you mean. It's just a kind of make-believe." He glanced at her questioningly, and she became serious and then nodded doubtfully. "Well, let me be in it, too. Wouldn't I do?" He laughed gaily and presently Carey laughed too, hesitatingly at first, then more hilariously as their emotion found an outlet. They roared together.

Carey said, "Uncle Beaver told me that when I was picking out a husband I must be sure to see that he wasn't spavined and to look at his teeth."

This caused more uproarious laughter, then Ken said, "I pass on both counts. Anything else?"

Carey gaily counted the points on her fingers. "He'd have to be a good physical specimen—"

Ken flexed his arm and showed his muscle. "I'm the wiry kind. I had pneumonia when I was ten, but I'm all over it."

Carey was giggling. "He'd have to be religious, but I know you are."

Ken asked, "How do you know?"

They were beginning to forget that it was a game of pretend.

"Because your family is. Your father says grace and you all go to church. But," added Carey, "I don't know if you yourself are, are you?"

"I don't know."

"Why don't you know?"

"Well, how can you tell?"

"Do you say prayers?"

Ken gave a moment's thought to this. He and Howard had always knelt down to say their prayers, night and morning. He prayed at other times too, when he was in any sort of trouble. Just short prayers, like, "Oh, God! Please get me out of this!" or "Don't let it happen, God." or "Please fix it up, God." Not very dignified prayers. He'd always done it. Kind of a hangover from when he was a little boy. His mother said it was all right. The Bible said it was right to pray all the time. But was he really religious? As for thinking about God or reading and studying about Him the way his mother did, he never did that. When he did think about Him it was like Sunday School talk, nothing very close or real. All the same, now and then, he knew there was something beyond and above him, something mysterious. And some day he would have to meet it.

"Well, do you?" repeated Carey.

"Sure," said Ken.

"Then you're religious. Why did you say you didn't know?"

"Well, I thought you meant, sort of, if I was *good*."

"Oh, no! I don't think it's the same thing at all. Well —so you are religious. And healthy enough, I guess—"

"Do I pass?" demanded Ken.

Carey laughed, sighed, reverted to her first theme. "Just think of naming them all! And the color of their eyes and hair—all different!"

Ken felt shut out again. These children of hers!

She straightened up, the soft wind blew her hair back from her face. Clasping her hands she looked far off into the western horizon as if she could see several of the little ones sitting on the small clouds that were gathering around the sun. "I just hope one of them will look like Penny. I think she is the most beautiful baby I ever saw."

"Well, if I am the father, maybe one of them will. She's my sister, you know."

He said this so seriously that Carey was brought up short. She gave a little embarrassed laugh. "That was just pretending, you know."

"I know," said Ken.

"I know some other boys," she added.

"Do you? Who?"

"Well, not many, because Grandma won't let me go around the way other girls do. But I know two. I know Paul."

"Who's he?"

"An awfully nice boy I met in the observation car last time we went East. We sat on the back platform. I got to know him very well."

"Do you write to him?"

"Yes."

"Who's the other boy?"

"Howard."

"Howard who?"

"Why, Howard McLaughlin, your brother."

"Oh, Howard!" exclaimed Ken with the utmost contempt. "Well, you don't know *him* very well!"

"Well, he is a boy and I know him."

"As well as you know me?"

Carey looked away, holding the top of the parapet, swinging against it. Ken watched her intently and angrily. Suddenly Howard was an intruder in his life—a menace.

"Well, I've known him as long as I've known you, haven't I?" evaded Carey. "Longer. I met him about an hour before I met you."

"That doesn't mean anything," said Ken surlily.

"Oh, Ken! Just think of giving them all their baths and putting them to bed!"

Ken gave an exclamation of annoyance. "Those children of yours! You don't think of anything else! You're just a little girl playing with dolls! I really don't think it's exactly proper!"

"It certainly is," Carey defended herself. "It is a subject that is of the greatest importance to all young people, especially girls, and one has to study and think about the things that are important."

"Let's go back," said Ken abruptly. They went down the rock. Ken stumped home in bad-tempered silence.

It was still light. Cottontails and jackrabbits were out for their evening runs. One tiny pale star twinkled in the sky over the eastern horizon. As they got near to the house they heard hilarious laughter and men's voices shouting. It seemed to come from the corrals of the cowbarn.

"What the heck's up?" said Ken, pausing and listening.

"Let's hurry and see!"

They left the road and cut across to the cowbarn. As they came around its corner they saw Gus and Tim and Wink perched on the fence of the corral, watching Howard who was giving a performance designed to take the starch out of Cricket. Pearl leaned against the fence, adding her screams of mirth to the chorus.

Cricket was still in the corral and Howard had closed the gate to the pasture. In the adjoining corral, separated from Cricket's by a three rail fence, he was engaged in a bull fight with a young steer.

He was a rakish toreador. The long braid that flew from the back of his head had been made out of a horse's tail. A wide sombrero tilted over his eyes. Apparently he was in long black tights and it would have taken close examination to disclose the fact that they were made of a pair of stockings attached to his mother's black jersey silk bloomers. The cape also was Nell's, a full, red, peasant skirt. This he was flirting about on an outstretched umbrella.

The little steer charged. Howard flitted out of his way bending over, turning a mock-terrified face over his shoulder. The men roared. Pearl screamed with laughter. Howard then turned and charged the steer, opening and shutting the umbrella at him, and the steer fled to the corner of the corral but came out of it again the moment Howard turned his back. Howard whirled to face him, charging with the cape and umbrella but the rollicking steer came on, caught the cape on his little horns and galloped across the corral with it. Howard pursued him with long leaps.

"Oh, *look* at him!" screamed Carey as she, too, scrambled up on the fence. Ken climbed up beside her, feeling peculiar, not knowing whether he should be with Howard in the arena or watching with the spectators.

Cricket stood with lowered head, his eyes fastened on the red cape. Now and then Howard, as he rushed past the fence which separated the two corrals, waved the cape over it insultingly. Cricket never moved.

Rob came down from the house, wondering what all the laughter was about. He stood with a grin on his face, holding his pipe in his hand.

Nell joined him and watched, too, but she was anxious. "I don't think he ought to do it, Rob."

Rob made no answer. In a wild run away from the galloping steer, Howard leaped the fence into Cricket's corral, ran around Cricket at top speed, and leaped back into the steer's corral.

Cricket did nothing to punish this insult. He seemed puzzled.

Howard saw that his audience had increased in number. Carey was on the fence and was laughing excitedly, his mother was standing near, his father had a grin on his face. Delightful sensations went to Howard's head. He felt light as air. He leaped the fence into Cricket's corral again and stood directly in front of him at a distance of about fifteen feet. Erect and haughty as a dueler, he doffed his hat and bowed, replaced it, fussing a little to get exactly the right angle. Carey screamed with suspense, and Pearl, watching the bull closely, gave a loud yell of warning. Still Cricket did not move.

Howard squared his legs, took the dueler's position with left elbow bent, left hand gracefully elevated. He slowly extended the umbrella across which hung the red skirt until it pointed at Cricket's nose and gathered himself to charge.

"Oh, Rob! Stop him!" said Nell under her breath.

"Be quiet," said Rob. "Cricket'll teach him a lesson."

Nell's hands wrung together.

"If he gets roused," added Rob.

Howard charged. Cricket lowered his head. Howard leaped back. The bull came at him with a great bellow that blasted the dust of the corral. As nimble as a flea, Howard was back over the fence again. To Carey's amazement Cricket sailed over the dividing fence as easily as Howard had.

Rob chuckled. "I knew he'd do that," he said.

Howard had not figured on this but his reflexes were quick. He crossed the steer corral with long leaps that barely kept him in front of the charging bull's nose. Umbrella and cape went sailing. His hands seized the top rail of the high outer fence of the corral and he went up and over it like a pole vaulter.

While the onlookers yelled with laughter, Cricket nosed and tossed the red cape, gored it with his horns, dropped it, kneeled on it and ground it into the dirt.

Nell's hands were at her heart, trying to stop its terrified pounding. "There goes my skirt," she said.

Howard kept his toreador suit on for the rest of the evening. He was the center of attraction.

That night, lying in bed, Ken could have groaned out loud. He could not figure out what had happened to depress him so. It was partly the talk with Carey. She had talked to him as she would talk to another girl. Would she have said such things to Howard? No, with Howard she was shy and even a little flirtatious, the way girls are with boys they really like. And after Howard's stunt with the steer and the bull, Carey had hardly known anyone else was around. Kept asking Howard if he hadn't been scared to death, and what he felt like when he saw the bull coming over the fence after him. And everybody had examined Howard's costume and there was great hilarity. If only *he* could do something which would make him glorious in Carey's eyes. Not something which was just a silly, show-off stunt, but something really heroic. If he

could save her! If only it had been he who had saved
her in the blizzard, but it was Gus. Maybe he could
save her some other way. Maybe on the horse-hunting
expedition—if she went. Maybe on that trip, her horse
might run away with her and Ken overtake it and rescue her. Or one of the men might get fresh with her.
Georgie Dale, last summer had stared at her every
minute. And he, Ken, could dress him down. If need
be, knock him down.

Lying there in bed Ken gritted his teeth and looked
at his knotted fists—they weren't very big. Ken had
the long, slender hands of his mother. Well, anyway,
*something*—

Then he had a still more thrilling idea. Carey must
see him win a race on Thunderhead! That would be
heroic enough for anybody! This excited him so that he
sat up in bed. This was really possible. He lay down
again and went on with the dream . . . Himself in
jockey's silks mounted on the prancing white stallion
who was the object of universal admiration. . . .
Thunderhead's chin held in by his master's strong
hands on the reins . . . the whirlwind of power waiting to be unleashed . . . the exquisite young girl
standing by his side . . . "Good luck, Ken! Ride to victory for me!"

There came to him through the walls of the house
the sound of his father's laughing and it brought to
mind what he had said the other day when Ken had
hinted around at this idea of entering Thunderhead in
another race.

"Catch him first, Ken!"

# 21

Carey was in the delightful state of mind that any girl is in when two handsome and attractive boys vie for her favor and there is always someone, a male some-one, looking at her. She was as gay as a lark. She was always laughing, always singing, always running off with one or another or both of them. Rob and Nell tasted the joy of having a grown girl in the house.

In the evenings she sat at the piano, the boys leaned against it, and they all sang together or shouted or wailed modern blues songs. She knew both classical and light music. She could play an accompaniement by ear. They sang the Westerns, "Green Grass of Wyoming," or "The Last Roundup." Or they cleared the dining-room and danced there.

"I'd like to shake Howard," said Nell to Rob at that time when husbands and wives talk intimately to each other. She took the pins out of her hair and began to brush it.

"Now don't interfere," said Rob as he stuck his heels, one after the other, into the bootjack and removed his boots.

"But you can just see how Ken is feeling! He's at a disadvantage!"

"He has the same chance Howard has."

Nell turned around on the little dressing-table bench. She had on a thin pink negligee that fell in folds to the floor. Her cheeks had an unusual color, her dark blue eyes shone. "No, he hasn't the same chance."

"Why not?"

"Because he cares, and Howard's just having a good time."

"*Cares?*" exclaimed Rob. "Aren't you taking this too seriously?"

Nell smoothed the folds of her gown with the back of her silver brush, then resumed the brushing of her hair.

Rob watched this process, as he never tired of doing. The fine fleece of tawny hair followed the brush until it was in a shining halo around her head.

"I suppose I am," she admitted, "but you only have to see his face, watch the way he sighs, to know that it's serious with him—at least for the time being. And I think Howard's doing a lot of it on purpose."

"I don't," said Rob. "It can't last long anyway. Howard will be leaving for West Point soon."

"Yes, but that's no help," said Nell. "When Howard leaves, Ken may feel he's just a second best with Carey. It would be better if Howard stayed and they fought it out squarely."

Rob put his head back and roared. "I see," said he, "that we are entering a new phase. Mating season approaches. And our two young stallions are beginning to arch their necks and look over the fence."

Nell burst out laughing.

Actually Carey distributed her favors without partiality. But it seemed to Ken that Howard received them all.

One morning a message came from the Mexican shearers that they would arrive at the Goose Bar Ranch next day, and Rob went down to the corrals where the boys were working with their colts, and called out that one of them should ride up to Jeremy that afternoon and tell him that they would be moving him down to the ranch the next morning early for the shearing.

The two boys looked at each other, then at Carey.

"Which of us?" asked Howard.

"Ken can go." Rob walked back to the house.

Ken looked at Carey. "Will you ride up with me, Carey?"

Howard said quickly, "I'm going fishing. Carey, you said you wanted to do some fishing."

Carey decided that she would prefer the fishing to the ride, and soon after the noon meal she and Howard were out digging in the flower beds for worms, while Ken saddled up.

He was coming home late in the afternoon when, without intending to spy, he saw a strange scene on the big flat rock which overlooked one of the best pools on Deercreek.

From where he was riding highup along the Saddle Back he got almost a bird's-eye view of it. First there were two figures, then there was one figure, then there was some sort of a scuffle.

A flame of anger poured all through Ken. He didn't want to spy. He turned his face away, took another tack down the mountainside and rode slowly home, knowing what it was to hate his brother, to hate the hate, to feel an utter misery.

He unsaddled Flicka and walked down through the Gorge, going toward the back door. Then he heard them coming up from the stream. They were behind the house and Howard was laughing as if he would burst. Ken stopped walking and stood still. In a moment or two he would be face to face with them. He was trembling.

Howard said, "But, Carey, I didn't mean—"

Carey's voice interrupted him—it sounded as if she were half crying.

Then they turned the corner and came into Ken's view. Carey was soaking wet and covered with mud. She was in a sobbing fury. "Don't you ever speak to me again as long as you live, Howard McLaughlin!" And she rushed in the back door.

Howard turned. The two boys looked at each other. "What did you do?" demanded Ken. "You tried to kiss her!"

"I did not," denied Howard. Then, angry at himself, he gave Ken an ugly look. "What's it to you if I did? Whose business is it, I'd like to know?" And he threw up his hands into boxing position and shuffled his feet threateningly.

The gesture was half in earnest, half in pretense, but it startled Ken and made him jump. He threw himself into the position of defense. Howard shuffled his feet again and began warily to circle Ken. Ken lit out, Howard countered, they began to spar.

After a moment or two Pearl came to the back door to see what was doing.

"Why, you two boys!" she exclaimed. "You ought to be ashamed of yourselves!"

The make-believe fight was becoming a real fight. To Ken particularly it was an outlet for pent-up feelings. He landed a stiff arm jolt in Howard's midriff.

Pearl danced with excitement. "Good for you, Ken! Give it to him again! Oh, cripes! My spuds are burning!" She vanished into the kitchen, but a moment later was at the back door again. "Hi-Ya! Go it!"

They did not need to be spurred on. They were fighting as hard as they could now but in deadly silence, their ears on the alert for the sound of their father's step or voice. The hot blood poured up into their faces. Their eyes blazed.

"Where's Dad?" asked Howard as he landed one on Ken's eye.

"Around on the front terrace," said Pearl in a stage whisper.

"Watch him, will you?" grunted Ken, swinging as hard as he could.

The sound of their father's voice came to them.

Kim came around the corner of the house, stopped at sight of what was going on, and stood watching. At first he wore his big grin and his tail waved softly. Then he got the bitter taste of the conflict, his head and tail dropped, he turned and crawled unhappily away.

"Cheese it!" exclaimed Pearl. "Your father's coming!"

"What's the matter with supper, Pearl?" called Rob and his steps came loudly along the terrace toward the back of the house.

"Just goin' to ring the bell, Captain McLaughlin!" said Pearl.

The boys vanished behind the house, and a few moments later were at the supper table. So was Carey. All three had high color. The boys' hair was plastered down in the fashion which meant a lightning session with head and comb under the water faucet. Carey's hair, too, was wet, and she said little and kept her face turned to Nell.

One of Ken's eyes was slowly closing and a purplish hue surrounded it.

Howard had a place on his lip to which he kept touching his napkin.

Rob glanced from one boy to the other but no ques-

tions were asked and all the talk was of the shearing
which was to begin next day.

# 22

It was still night when Jeremy reached out an arm and
silenced the racket of his alarm clock.

In the grimy long underwear in which he slept, he
opened the door of his wagon and stepped out. He always did this—one deep breath of that fresh night air
which had swept over hundreds of miles of uninhabit-
ed land, one glance around—

The day would be clear, the stars were low and brilliant. Their light illumined the whole vast scene,
stretching through illimitable distances to low
horizons, the contours of the hills far away, the belts
of timber, the thick willows along the winding stream
way below in the meadows. Closer by was the grey
mass of the sheep, faint shadows picking out the
curved lines of their backs; here and there was a lifted
head of incomparably tender shape.

They were silent and motionless. Not even the bell-
wether tinkled.

Suddenly, close beside Jeremy, another face was
lifted from the ground. A grinning, toothy face, with
shaggy cocked ears and wild brown eyes, bright and
questioning. *Is there anything for me to do?*

"Go back to bed, Shep."

The dog returned to the warm spot under the
sheepwagon where he had been sleeping, but he kept
one eye open, one ear pricked and both nostrils on the

alert. There would be the smell of food soon.

Jeremy returned to his wagon and shaved and dressed carefully, for he was going into society today; he would be consorting with ladies—the highest in the land. He cooked his bacon and eggs, his coffee and oatmeal. He sliced and ate innumerable pieces of bread piled with strawberry jam which he dug out of a big can. He fed his dogs.

It was getting darker. The stars were paling. At last there was no more starlight, only a ghostly grey tinge that came from nowhere and changed and saddened and made mysterious the face of the world.

Jeremy stepped out of the wagon.

"Get 'em going, Shep."

Shep shot at top speed away from the wagon, roused the other dogs and gave them the message. They glanced at Jeremy, seeing even in the darkness that he waved his arm westward. They knew without being told that the sheep must always move with their backs to the sun, westward in the morning, eastward in the afternoon.

The lambs began to nurse and there was a great baaing and bleating. Gradually the band spread and scattered to graze.

In Jeremy's hand was a nursing-bottle with a large nipple. The bottle was full of condensed milk which he had warmed.

"Here, Pinky, Pinky!"

There ran out of the flock to him, bleating, a four-months-old lamb, husky, thick-wooled. It was one of the motherless little ones which are called *bummers* because they grow up on the flock, learning to dodge the indignant butts of the mother ewes who have no intention of nursing any except their own lambs. A suck here, a suck there, ducking and running from one to the other—so they manage to survive. Occasionally the sheepherder helps them along.

Jeremy seated himself on the step of his wagon and held out the bottle. Pinky eagerly hitched on. Presently Jeremy lifted the lamb up, sat him on his left knee with one arm around his middle. The lamb leaned back, resting his head against Jeremy's shoulder, his front legs dangling like arms over Jeremy's wrist. Jeremy's right hand, with the bottle, was held high, feeding him the milk. Pinky sucked the bottle dry. Jeremy set him down, and he ran away and disappeared in the flock.

All was ready: Jeremy closed the door of his wagon. He was dressed in his best and newest bluejeans, a plaid shirt with a vest buttoned over it and a ten gallon hat. A heavy gold watch was in his watch pocket and from it dangled a chain of gold nuggets. The watch was one which told time by chimes, very convenient for sheepherders whose eyes so constantly are watching the far places that they forget how to see at short distances. He carried over his left arm the slicker without which no sheepherder ever moves, and in his right hand a light cane which he had cut from one of the quaking-asps.

Gathering up his sheep, he emitted sharp cries, he yelled messages to his dogs, he waved his arms. The sheep increased their pace. They nibbled rapidly, ran a few steps, nibbled again.

At last they were moving along the mountainside at a fairly good pace.

The sheepwagon stood alone and deserted.

Down under the eastern horizon a sea of color was washing upward. Already forerunners of it, wide banners, raced toward the zenith. The last star melted away. One hilltop after the other sprang into light.

Every cloud flushed pink or red. A blazing sickle of gold edged up over the undulating line of hills in the east and from it shot a circle of dazzling rays.

The glorious June day came in like the roar of a symphony.

Big Joe and Tommy, Rob McLaughlin's heavy team, blinked their eyes as they jogged along the top of Saddle Back, going up to the sheep camp to get Jeremy's wagon and bring it back to the ranch for the shearing.

They trotted side by side, festooned with harness. The braces were looped up, the big collars were loose on their necks.

Astride of Tommy was Ken. Astride of Big Joe was Carey. Big Joe's trot was long and rough. Without a saddle, and unable to post or knee-grip, she bounced madly and often had to grab the hames.

The wind was cool, the sunrise filled their eyes, they were on the top of a wide and empty world and they should have been friends but Carey's face was turned away from Ken and his heart hurt him.

It was his own fault, he knew that. He had been mad at her ever since she had chosen to go fishing with Howard the day before. It had made him still angrier that something had happened between them that he was shut out of. This ought to be thrashed out and explained, she *had* to tell him all about it, and until she did, things could not be right between them. His manner toward her, hurting her and showing her plainly that he was affronted, was what would make her try to conciliate him; she would want to win him over, and then he would understand and forgive, and take her back into his friendship, and, oh—love her, love her—

But Carey had not played her part in this imagined scene at all. From the moment when they had kept their rendezvous, so early that it seemed practically in the night, she had been bright and sweet and oblivious to his mood and his attitude. This had made him scowl more fiercely, though, in the darkness, what use was it? She ought to be able to tell by his voice, by the short sharp sentences he spoke as he led her from the house up to the stable corral where Big Joe and Tommy were waiting.

He had put the harness on the two horses, carrying each piece of the equipment from the stable and slinging it over the wide backs while Carey stood talking to the big beasts. They ate their oats, she patted their thick necks.

"How'll I ever get up on him?" she had laughed, looking up at the towering shape.

"I'll lift you up." Ken longed to lift Carey. There was not a day that he did not try to think up some event which would necessitate his lifting her or carrying her—perhaps across the creek, but she always skipped ahead, as spry as a little frog; or getting over a fence, but of course she was up and over while he was gathering his nerve.

"Why, you couldn't!" she exclaimed, laughing. "He's way over your head too! I know what I'll do!" And she climbed up the corral fence to which Big Joe was tied, slipped her leg over his back and slid onto him.

They rode out of the corral.

He wondered if she had no notion that he was angry. She prattled along excited by being out so early and showed not the least consciousness of anything wrong.

So then he had begun to upbraid her. He had burst out, demanding to know what had happened between her and Howard yesterday. And why, before that, she had gone fishing with Howard, anyway. And why she showed such favor to Howard at all, and why, and why, and why—

Carey had made a few surprised, stumbling rejoinders at first, then had fallen silent, her face turned away from him. Finally she had given a little cold laugh. "Well, you don't own me, do you?"

Ken could not answer, and they had ridden up the Saddle Back and along its crest in silence.

He felt that he did own her—that he *must*—and finally, quite humbly, he tried to explain, "I guess it's because of last year I feel that way—don't you remember? The blizzard, and your being lost and seeing Thunderhead. Oh, Carey—I can't help it—"

It was no use. Riding with his head turned to look at her he saw an impassive profile. There was nothing to do but go along, trot—trot, jog—jog, now and then breaking into a lope—the trip seemed endless. The sun got higher and higher. Now that Ken had had his outburst everything within him was melted into tenderness. If she would only look at him, give him one smile, one soft glance.

But Carey was shut into herself and away from him.

They arrived at the wagon and before Ken had got to the side of her horse to help her she had slipped to the ground.

He hitched the team to the wagon, they got in, and Ken took the reins. Carey sat quietly beside him. They started off. Halfway along the mountainside they passed Jeremy with the sheep and left him behind. They arrived at the ranch in time for breakfast.

Already Garcia, the Mexican, and his men were there. Bunkhouse breakfast was over, the men were busy preparing the shearing pens.

# 23

Rob heaved a deep sigh, shoved his hat farther back and scratched his head. Then, squinting, knotting the impatient lines which crisscrossed his forehead, he looked slowly over the heavens, the horizon, the far mountains.

It was his habitual, almost automatic gesture.

There was nothing to demand his attention. It was a placid day in late June. The scene was peaceful, meadows and rolling hills covered with lush grass, the farther hills with pine, glimpses of mountains in the distance, and at his feet the little stream, its clear brown water rushing busily over the rocks and twisting under the banks.

The shearing was over.

The grinning, half-naked Mexicans had gone on to their next job. The mess they had left behind them had been cleaned up. The incessant baaing and bleating which had laid an unaccustomed blanket of sound over the ranch for five days had faded into silence as Jeremy and his dogs headed back to the range with the three thousand naked and ridiculous-looking ewes and their lambs.

Many of the ewes had long bloody scars on them where the shears had torn into the flesh. Several of them had died from their wounds. The skinned carcasses were hanging in the wind cage to dry and cure. There would be roast mutton, tasting almost like venison, and deliciously flavored with garlic, for some time to come.

It had been a good clip, as Jeremy had foretold. There were eighty of the long wool sacks. To fill these a platform had been built, supported on eight-foot stilts; it had a large hole in the center through which the sack was thrust hanging to the ground below, the edges of its gaping mouth fastened around a steel hoop which ringed the edge of the hole. About thirty-five of the fleeces went into each of the big sacks. The truck had made five trips to town with the wool. It was sold, and the check was in the bank. Everybody could relax.

Rob heaved another sigh, pulled his hat down over his eyes and concentrated on his fishing. He reeled the line in, frowning heavily, cast the bait to a likely spot downstream under the farther bank, watched a moment with intense determination, impatiently yanked it out, got to his feet, walked upstream, found himself another place, and sat down to fish again. His bait was gone. Cursing freely, he got the can out of his pocket, forced a worm on the hook and dropped it under the bank. His eyes wandered. Again he recalled his thoughts to his fishing, peered into the water for his hook, saw it, lifted it, dropped it in another place, and again forgot it while his eyes wandered and his lips pursed, whistling the air to, *"Oh, it's the galloping hoofs! It's the green grass rolling range of Wyoming."*

At some distance from him, Rodney Scott, his friend and doctor, leaned around a bush, wigwagging for silence. Rodney took his fishing with appropriate seriousness. No worms for him! Few were the Saturday afternoons that did not provide him with an outing and a creel full of trout.

But Rob's short patience was exhausted. He pulled in his line and walked up to Rodney.

"How the hell a grown man can waste his time in such foolishness!" exclaimed Rob.

"How do you expect me to catch anything if you come stamping and shouting around?" complained Rodney bitterly. At that moment he felt a strike, played his fish and drew out a shining ten-inch trout.

Rob watched him glumly as he took it off the hook and dropped it in his creel. "What do you think I got you out here for?"

Rodney looked at him suspiciously, "Well, you *said* to come out and fish but I had an idea you had something else in the back of your head. If you want to consult me professionally why don't you come to my office when you're in town?"

Rob shrugged. "Go on and get your fish. I'll put in the time doing something that'll be of some use to me. Call me when you're through." He walked a little way off, flung himself down on the grass, pulled his hat over his eyes and composed himself for slumber.

"Who is sick?" asked Rodney as he gathered up his things and moved upstream a little way.

There was no answer. A gentle snore came from under Rob's hat. Rodney smiled and carefully cast under the farther bank, then relaxed in the true fisherman's attitude, a blend of a constant alert and a dreaming peace.

Fishing, one can think of many things at once. Thoughts dart through the mind, different topics, as fish through the water. Who was sick here at the Goose Bar? The baby? Nell had had Penny in his office regularly. The baby was thriving. Howard? Ken? Nothing was ever wrong with Rob or Nell.

He moved silently up the bank. His creel filled. Six, seven trout, all good sized. What luck to have a trout stream like this right in your own backyard. But Rob didn't fish. When he wanted relaxation he went to town, went to luncheon in the hotel restaurants with a lot of men, sat at bars and drank, visited the Army Post, swapped yarns, talked of weather, crops, politics, local gossip. It was the town men who went to the country for their relaxation.

Who was sick here anyway? Nell. The conviction hit him hard. She had been sick a long time. Why hadn't he seen it? He had carried her through her pregnancy and confinement with standard care, standard remedies, standard advice. Nothing had gone wrong. They had been crazy for the baby, over-anxious. When she came she was tiny. All attention had been centered on her. But certainly, now, looking back, he could see that Nell was not herself—had not been herself since the baby came. Before that? His thoughts went probing back into the past. Certainly Nell had been terribly run down that year before her pregnancy began—white and thin and silent. Before that? He couldn't remember. Nell was a hard person to know about. So very controlled. Always the same in her gay manner, in the way she was adequate to every demand, and if anything was wrong, covered up.

Zing! Another strike. As Rodney played the fish a deep, bellowing roar reached him. Rodney looked about nervously. In these big pastures, a mile or more square, you never knew if there were cattle in it with you or not, but the bulls knew, instantly, if there was a stranger on the place. That bull was a terror.

Then Rodney saw Cricket, who had already seen him. The bull was a quarter-mile away and, fortunately, on the other side of a barbed-wire fence. Cricket was pacing the length of it, his head turned so that he could keep his eyes on this stranger. Now and then he paused to rake the dust and roar.

From the other direction came Rob's lusty snores. Rodney felt reassured and continued to fish until his creel was full. Then he reeled in his line, put away his folder of flies and went to Rob and sat down beside him. He shook him by the shoulder.

"Now tell me who is sick?" he asked.

Rob sat up, stretched, shook the sleep out of his eyes, addressed Rodney with jovial profanity, examined the heavens, took his pipe out and filled it, demanded to see Rodney's fish and finally settled down to talk about Nell.

Cricket paced the length of the wire fence and back again, his eyes on the two men. The sun was low, shadows lengthened. Sounds from far away drifted to them, the moo of a cow, the sound of a bus on the Lincoln Highway two miles away, the honk of a horn. And Rob talked and talked, pausing occasionally to answer questions, and the burden of it all was just that Nell was *not right*—hadn't been right for several years—was getting worse—others were beginning to notice it—the boys—something *wrong* with her—just the other night woke up screaming and wanted Rob to "Hold me! Hold me!" God! It gave him the shivers.

After he had stopped talking, Rodney was silent a long time. He had a stalk of timothy grass in his mouth. He pulled at it and chewed it, his eyes far away.

"And you say she's never been ill?"

"Never a sick day in her life," said Rob proudly.

Rodney shook his head. "That's hardly fair. Being sick is often a rest for a woman. These women that never give in—"

But Rob disagreed. "No, she was *really* well. It wasn't put on. Nell is strong as a horse. Things were hard for her, I know that, *awfully hard,* for many years."

"Were they?" Rodney turned to look at him.

"You bet they were."

"For how long?"

Rob grinned. "Ever since she married me. Before that she lived the kind of comfortable, luxurious, easy life that most girls live, city girls."

"And she came right from that to the life on the ranch here," said Rodney thoughtfully. "And you didn't have running water or electricity or a furnace, at first, did you?"

"We had nuthin'," said Rob grimly. "Nuthin' but babies, debts, bills, hard work and one disappointment after the other. But she wasn't sick *then,* Rodney, she was swell. She did the work of ten. She never gave up, never collapsed, never broke down."

"Never," said Rodney slowly, "until *now.*"

"Yes. *Now* when everything is going so well. Furnace in, a cook for her, plenty of help, no worries!" and Rob finished with a helpless, bewildered gesture.

"Perhaps that's just the trouble," suggested Rodney.

Rob turned to look at him questioningly. "How?"

"Perhaps she's one of those women who never gives up as long as the going is tough. When everything is easy for them, they go all to pieces."

Rob screwed up his face and shoved his hat back to scratch his head.

Rodney added, "That just means that they let go and give in at a time when they can afford to. They've been drawing on their reserves all the time. Sooner or later the bill has to be met."

"That seems pretty far fetched, Rodney."

"You'd be surprised," said Rodney, "it often happens. In fact, it's almost sure to happen. I had one patient, all through the depression her husband was out of work, they nearly starved, were evicted from one rented house after the other. She was a tower of strength. Never sick. Her husband got a good job, she had a nervous breakdown."

Rob rubbed his chin reflectively. "Nell hasn't had a breakdown—I wouldn't go so far as to say that."

"She might be better now if she had had one," said Rodney. "If she had let herself go to pieces—get a nurse—give up everything—be really sick, perhaps go to the hospital and then get over it."

Rob shook his head. "Nell just couldn't," he said simply.

"Then," said Rodney, "we know what's the matter with her. We've diagnosed the case."

Rob was silent a few moments digesting this. "That amounts to saying that it is mental," he said.

"The glands are all tied up in whatever is mental and emotional. And when they get out of balance, then there are physical results. I could kick myself," he added. "I should have studied her more closely and given her some tests. But I never noticed."

"That's just it," said Rob, "one doesn't notice anything wrong with her. That is, one *didn't*. But now I think even the boys notice it."

"How?" asked Rodney.

"Oh, it's not like Nell to go pewling and mewling around. About her food, for instance, she's so picky about it. She never used to complain if I happened to bring out something from Cheyenne that isn't just exactly what she put on the list for me to get."

Rodney chuckled. "Gives you back talk, does she? Good for Nell!"

"Back talk!" Rob was aggrieved. "She says that I ought just to stop using my own judgment and obey orders for a change."

Rodney laughed outright.

"You can laugh," said Rob doggedly, "but it isn't like Nell."

"No, I guess it isn't, at that," said Rodney.

They sat a moment in silence, then Rob added. "There's one thing—perhaps I should tell you—that a year before Penny was born Nell and I were at outs with each other. In fact we almost came to the point of separating. Did you know that?"

"Never dreamed of it," said Rodney, chewing his piece of grass. "How did that affect Nell?"

"Well, she really went down then. Anyone could see it. She didn't eat. Got thin as a rail. Didn't sleep either. It went on a long time."

"Of course a thing like that plays hob with the whole system," said Rodney. "Then you made it up?"

"Yes."

"And what happened to Nell? That's when she should have had her breakdown—leave you for a while—get a rest somewhere, hospital maybe."

"Well—" said Rob hesitantly, "we had been so keen to have a little girl—another baby—and that's when Penny started."

"She went right into a pregnancy," said Rodney thoughtfully, "and she didn't have an easy time either when Penny was born."

"I know."

"And now since the baby came she hasn't had her out of her sight—how old is Penny?"

"Twenty months."

"Nor been off this ranch."

"No."

Rodney acted as if the case were closed. He removed the grass from his mouth, took his hat off, passed his handkerchief over his thinning hair, then opened his creel and began to count his trout.

# 24

Nell had spent the afternoon at her piano.

She had a large repertoire as a girl. Her mother had believed that only a repertoire acquired in the teens is a permanent possession. If you hear an old woman playing the few remaining pieces she can remember, they are almost certain to be the first pieces that she liked and learned. And they must not be too difficult. Otherwise they will be lost as life goes on.

Chopin provided an inexhaustible supply of the kind of music one could play all one's life.

Nell had known by heart his "Etudes," "Preludes," "Nocturnes," the "Maiden's Wish," the "Berceuse," the "Funeral March." All of these and many others by different composers she was in process of "getting back."

This wonderful piano! At the thought of it she felt a warm rush of happiness and gratitude toward Rob. How good he was to her! How constantly he thought of her and did things for her! One of his great pleasures, since his finances had improved, was giving her presents. The beautiful new silver set on her dressing-table. The little bedroom clock with its soft chimes. The clothes he insisted on her having—why, he never even passed her, if he was eating something good, without offering her a bite!

Love itself is a virtue, she thought. If love is in the

heart of a man or a woman they are the better for it. And what love was in the heart of Rob! A great lover, ardent and tempestuous! There was a flame in him, greater than any flame in her, and it blew steadily upon her, warming her whole person and lifting her to an intensity of feeling and living which she could not have known without him.

She was practicing the "Berceuse." Strange that so free and rich a melody should have been set to an accompaniment which consisted of one bar played over and over throughout the entire piece. . . .

She wondered if Howard, if Ken, would ever know love as she knew it. How would it come to them? It comes, she thought, not as affection or admiration, or any sentiment, but as if one suffered a blow, an impact; as if two elements rushed together and became one. It is all one can do to hold up under it. One is changed, and struggles along as a blinded, bewildered, changed being.

Her thoughts clung to this theme. How little of such love there was in the world, how few husbands and wives, as the years went on, retained that deep power of emotion for each other. Why should this be? Life separated them—that was the reason. Their interests, so often different, drew them apart. And most married people, especially those living in cities, simply did not spend time enough with each other to nourish their love. Love cannot survive if you just give it scraps of yourself, scraps of your time, scraps of your thoughts. "No Time For Love." It could be a song! But if you *do* consider marriage important enough to be worked at, then you can build a happy marriage just as you build a house. You build it out of patience and forebearance, determination, understanding, self-sacrifice, and appreciation. You shine like the sun on anything you

can shine on or smile at or love. You forgive and forget and by-pass the things you cannot shine on or
smile at or even endure. It ought to be taught in the
schools, she thought suddenly, it's so important. It's an
art and it has a technique which should be learned.
And when you have made your successful marriage,
though you've paid a big price, yet the reward is out
of all proportion. A house of happiness. A safe refuge.
An enduring, living harmony that sounds in the ears
like a bell! She must tell the boys that. She must train
them so that if the true mating should come to them
they would know how to cherish it and keep it, sac-
rificing themselves and everything else, in order that
it might always be nourished and live. *Tell them these
things quickly so that, no matter what happened to
her . . .*

She pulled her mind back to the "Berceuse." This,
too, was love—the composer was expressing the love
of a mother for her child—yes, a mother's dream over
the cradle of her child.

. . . So many kinds of love in the world . . . it was
a force, like electricity, it was a creative power . . .
*any sort* of love, the love between men and women, or
children and parents, or friends, or love for music or
art or beauty or work or God. . . . Could there be happiness without it? And, provided it was there, could
there be any real unhappiness? Could life exist
without it? Would not all life wither away and die if
love were withdrawn?

Somewhere she had read an essay about those modern nations which proclaim that they can, and will,
live without God. The author finished his essay by
raising the question: How will they like it when they
try to live without love?

That was the interesting idea. Did all love proceed

from God? Without God, would love vanish from the earth and from the hearts of humanity?

While the liquid dreaming notes of the "Berceuse" rippled from under her fingers she tried to strip love out of the world. But it was impossible. As long as there was color in the sunset, as long as there was music, as long as human beings clung to each other—no.

Howard came in, pulled up a big chair to face his mother and sat down to listen.

She glanced at him, smiling, went on playing.

He laid his head back, slung one long thin leg over the arm of the chair. He had obviously been doing something violent, looked tired and hot, his neckerchief twisted under one ear, black hair plastered to his head.

Nell wondered what he would say, what was in his mind. Would it be about Carey? or Barbara? Perhaps he was about to tell her.

"Only eight days more," he finally said.

That was it. He was counting the days before he left home.

"Mother, isn't it the darndest thing the way I always have to leave just when something is happening? Two summers ago, remember? I missed out on seeing Thunderhead in the race at Saginaw Falls. And the year before that, right after I left, Ken went up to the Valley of the Eagles and got tangled up with the eagle and had all those adventures. And now this year I have to leave just before we go out to find Thunderhead and Jewel. Damn the luck!"

Nell's eyes were upon him, smiling, while her fingers continued to play.

"West Point is a pretty big adventure, it seems to me."

Looking directly into her eyes, taking her along with him, as it were, into his future, the trip on the train, up the Hudson to West Point, feeling her excitement, her sympathy, he was comforted.

He relaxed in his chair. "Play the 'Polonaise,' " he said. "It always makes me feel like doing things—big things."

Nell played it. When she had finished it, he said, "Mother, do you remember when I went away to school the first time, you gave me a talk? Kind of a lecture?"

"Did I, son?"

"Well—I did it."

"Did what?"

"Did the things you told me to. Two things."

"What were they?"

"You told me to pray. And to be honest."

Nell bent her head over the piano and began to play again to conceal the feeling that surged up in her. Mothers talk so much, advise so much, are all the time correcting and pointing out and lecturing, but if out of all that flood of talk a few things can be remembered and acted upon, a few such things as that—to be honest, to pray. . . .

"What I was thinking," began Howard hesitatingly, "will you tell me something this time, too? This is even more important, isn't it? Going to West Point? I won't be back for two years. Well, it's over, isn't it, Mum, being a boy at home here?"

Nell glanced at her son with a little rueful smile and nodded.

"Will you, Mum?"

"Why do you want it, Howard?"

"Well, when you're out in the world, it's kind of comforting, to have things like that to remember and to go by."

"Of course, darling, I'll talk to you—tell you anything I can."

"What'll it be about?"

She dropped her hands in her lap. "It'll have to be about whatever I am thinking most about—have been thinking about for a long time."

"What?"

There was a silence before she answered. "Love. I seem to have been thinking about that."

"What kind of love?"

"All kinds. But it all leads up to the final love—the love of God."

Howard was dumbfounded. He jumped to his feet. "Oh, mother!" he exclaimed. "Do you think that would be any help?"

Her expression was quizzical. "I think it would, dear. A lot of help. Maybe not right now. But some day."

He straightened himself up, stuffed into his belt the tail of his shirt which had come out, and said, "All right. Don't forget. I'm going for a swim before supper." He leaned over, kissed her, padded out of the room on his sneakered feet and vanished.

Nell sat in silent thought for a while, experiencing the deepest tenderness for her son, for both boys, feeling that there was so very little she could do for them, wonderful that she could do anything when within herself she was so confused, so full of fear, so inadequate. But she had noticed that when any demand was made upon her it strengthened her, as if that power of God or power of love rushed through her to them, leaving a deposit in her.

She began to play again. The "Etudes" now—the "Butterfly," then the "Black Finger"—strange! Actual-

ly her technique was better than before she had
talked to Howard, she was stronger.

# 25

Nell went out to the terrace. Penny was there in her
pen and she did not like her pen. But the pen was a
necessity for, though she was small for her age, she
was swift as quicksilver. She ran with little twinkling
feet that reminded Nell of the sandpipers on the Cape
Cod beaches. She was here, there, and everywhere, so
quickly it was impossible to keep track of her.

Now most of the baby's toys had been hurled away
and she was sitting in one corner, sucking her thumb.
Her blue eyes were angry, her vivid face was flushed,
her mouth was a scarlet ring around her tiny thumb,
her dark hair with its glints of gold was a mass of tou-
sled curls over her forehead.

When she saw Nell she plucked out the thumb and
held out her arms with a torrent of the soft and liquid
bird notes which were her special language. Nell
picked her up and took her in and sat her on top of
the grand piano and coaxed her to sing. Nell would
sing a note, Penny would open her mouth with an
excited, delighted expression on her face and emit an
"Oh!" an octave higher. Nell sang a song. Penny sang
along with her, not the right notes, but an ecstatic
warbling.

She suddenly stopped singing, turned her head and
listened. Nell did likewise. There came to them the
deep sounds of the bull roaring.

Penny looked questioningly at her mother. "No more?" she suggested. Nell did not know whether she wanted no more singing or no more bull roaring.

"Come, honeybunch, let's go for a walk," said Nell. She lifted the baby off the piano and set her on the floor. Penny trotted to the door and pushed at the screen. Nell took her by the hand and they went down to the Green.

They wandered around. Penny's miniature world was close to the earth. Every few steps she found something to interest her, a clump of dandelions, a beetle laboriously climbing a grass blade, a brightly shining piece of quartz. She would sit down in the easy manner of infants, without bending of the knees, just a little plump and there she was, her hand slipping out of Nell's.

Nell seated herself on the stone coping of the fountain.

Kim, the yellow collie, came slowly across the Green, his ears flat because of the love he was feeling at sight of Nell there and the baby sitting on the grass. He looked, smiling, from one to the other, and then went to Penny, standing with his pointed nose close to her face and his brush of a tail waving gently.

"Doggie! Doggie!" exclaimed Penny, and patted the top of his head with a little fist.

Kim lay down close beside her so that this delightful game might be continued. She picked the dandelions, one by one, and sprinkled them on him.

Cricket's roars were getting closer. He was being brought to the barn with the cows for evening milking and feeding.

A wave of fear went over Nell. It was not the bull. It was the meaningless fear she had had this last year, always accompanied by a feeling of helplessness to avert whatever fate was impending. It was as if suddenly she were going to be run over . . . a locomotive was bearing down upon her . . . or a crowd of men with uplifted axes were hurling themselves upon her . . . or she was drowning . . . or someone had her by the throat . . . or she was going over a cliff in an automobile.

She put her hand to her throat. There was that terrible feeling of constriction. Could there be the slightest reason for this or was it pure hysteria? Was it true, as she thought, that she really had not long to live? Howard—this little talk he asked for—was it farewell? Would she ever see him again? Two years—

The conviction came to her that she would not live that long. She was not getting better, she was getting worse.

She stood up and walked nervously down toward the cowbarn. She saw the cows coming around the shoulder of the hill in the calf pasture. Tim was driving them. She noticed the pitchfork in his hand.

Cricket maneuvered to get behind him.

Tim turned, held his pitchfork in charging position and yelled, "Come on, you!" making a gesture as if to go for him.

Grunting, Cricket ran nimbly forward into position with the cows, then paused to drop his head, paw up a cloud of dust and give a bellowing roar.

Tim yelled again and made pretense of going for him. Cricket subsided and walked through the corral gates.

Wink was in the barn, measuring out the feed for the cows. Now he threw open the doors into the corral and the cows filed in to take their places at the long manger.

Nell knew what was going on in there. Wink was

going down the line, closing the stanchions. The cows were perfectly quiet and at peace, munching their grain. Pansy; Peaches—whose name, inelegantly, had evolved from Peaches to Peach, Pitch, Bitch—; Moon, who was a big pale Jersey, the color of the moon; Demitasse, as dark and brown as coffee; Dolly; Sassafras; Willow; Kiki—well-named, standing always for milking with steel clamps and chain on her hocks.

There were three dry cows who did not come into the barn but had their feed in the corral with Cricket.

Tim filled the feed cans for these and then went into the barn to do his share of the milking.

Nell watched Cricket eating his ground oats.

The sturdy corral fence was between them. She went to it and leaned on the top pole. Cricket licked up the last of the grain and stood there in profile to her.

He was a large Guernsey, a dark reddish brown shading to white on the belly. If you parted the hairs and looked at the skin you saw it was the color of an orange peel. Hoofs, horns, ears all a rich orange.

They had bought him as a two weeks' old calf. Nell had raised him, feeding him with the bucket. He had learned to feel for her fingers in the pail of warm milk, and sucking on these, to draw the milk into his mouth. Soon he had learned to take milk alone. But if ever she wanted to call him to her and get him to follow her, all she had to do was hold out her hand, he would seize it in his mouth and then, sucking it vigorously, follow wherever she led.

And now he had turned into this, a monster who knew where everyone on the ranch was at any time. If they moved out of the house, he knew it. If anyone walked in the meadows, Cricket paced along the nearest fence, which might be a mile away, watching them, threatening them with his fearful roars, now and then pausing to examine the flimsy barbed wire as if, some day, he might take it into his head to ignore that ridiculous thing and charge through it. He hadn't —yet.

He stood now in profile to Nell, his head hanging over the empty feed can. To judge by his attitude and position he did not know she was there, but his eye was turned back, looking full at her, crafty and dangerous.

She was still standing there, watching the bull, when Rob and Rodney Scott returned from the meadow. Milking was over and the cows were in the corral. The gate stood open to the calf pasture. A few of them were moving out. Cricket was quiet.

"I want Rob to sell that bull or have him killed, Rodney," said Nell as they approached her. "Don't you think he should?"

"I should say not!" exclaimed Rob. "We raised him from a calf, and now he's proved. His first calves are milking and giving higher butterfat than any of our other cows. Sell him? Don't be silly."

"I really mean it," said Nell. "Rodney, you know the awful things that happen. You're always reading in the papers about thoroughbred dairy bulls goring their owners. You hear tales on every farm. If a bull turns bad-tempered, as Cricket has, sell him! And sell him the *day before* something happens—not the *day after!*" And suddenly her voice was shaking.

Rob was exasperated. "Nell! I can't make out what's got into you! You didn't used to be such a scare cat. This is a PROVED BULL! We're lucky to have him. A new young bull would not be proved and might never turn out to be any good. What if he is bad-tempered? The men can watch out for themselves!"

"Those flimsy barbed-wire fences," stammered Nell.

"Nell, if we started being afraid of all the dangerous things that happen or can happen on a ranch, where would we be?"

This silenced Nell. It was true. Every day was full of danger. Horses—weather—lightning—bulls—ropes —machines—they lived on sufferance. She drew a deep breath.

Rob changed his tactics. He put his hand on her arm and beamed at her.

"Listen, honey, Rodney and I've been talking about you. You're a nervous woman. That's why you worry about the bull and everything. We want you to go to the hospital and take a long rest."

Nell looked at him as if he were crazy. Then at Rodney.

Rodney seemed embarrassed, but presently he nodded and said, "How would you like that, Nell?"

"I wouldn't like it at all," said Nell with a short laugh. "I think it's the silliest thing I ever heard of. Go on up to the back door and get the fish smell off yourselves, then come to the terrace and I'll have something cool for you to drink."

In the back yard, the puppies swarmed over Rob. He gathered them up into his arms and held them against his chest. In a frenzy of love they strained upward to lick his face.

"Just old enough to be cute," said Rodney.

"Just old enough to begin to be loving," said Rob.

Rodney went to the trough up by the spring house to clean his fish.

Kim had followed Rob and now stood watching him playing with the pups. His tail waved gently, enjoying vicariously the tenderness, the petting. There was a quizzical, tolerant expression on his face. Rob put the pups down. They rollicked over to Kim, clambered at him, pawed and bit his legs. The collie moved quietly away and sat down.

As it was nearly suppertime all the small domestic animals were assembled, the cats and kittens in a frenzy over the entrails of the fish that Rodney threw them.

The cocker bitch, Daisy, poked her face around the corner of the building watching Rob as he opened the faucet and sloshed water over his hands and arms.

She looks guilty as hell, he thought, wonder what she's been murdering now. But he said, "Hello, Daisy," and Daisy crept fearfully forward to cringe beside him.

As he stood wiping his hands one small pup lay sprawled across his boot, relaxed and adoring. He gently disengaged his foot and walked away, stooping to give Daisy a careless pat which threw her into a squirming ecstasy.

The Green lay bathed in the vivid golden light which comes late in the afternoon, laced with long pointed shadows from the pines on the cliff. Two bay mares with their foals had come down from the pines and were grazing there.

Nell was reclining in a long canvas chair on the terrace. Before her was a low table with a pitcher of tea, a bottle of Scotch, a bowl of ice and some tall glasses.

Penny, talking to herself busily, went up and down the three stone steps which led from the terrace to the Green. She was dressed as Rob wanted her to be, in an embroidered white nainsook dress with lace on the edges of tiny petticoat and panties.

One of the mares moved slowly to the fountain in the center of the Green and began to drink. Her foal followed suit, tasting the cold water and then lifting its head and shaking it from its lips.

Penny reached out her hands toward the mare and called, "Doggie! Doggie!"

"Horse," corrected Nell. "That's not a doggie, darling, it's a horse."

"Doggie," insisted Penny. She got up, started rapidly down the steps, slipped off the side and plunged headlong into the lilac bush.

Rob, coming around from the back of the house heard the howls and reached her before Nell did. He fished her out of the lilac bush and carried her down onto the Green, high in his arms.

Penny sobbed pitifully, "Dad-dee's ba-ba—"

Howard came round the corner of the house. He had been swimming. His hair was wet, his towel was over his arm. At that moment the telephone rang. Howard said, "I'll answer it!" and ran indoors.

Presently he came out holding a sheet of paper upon which he had written down the message.

"It's from Buck, Dad! A telegram from Westgate, Colorado! They telephoned it from the station! He's found the horses!"

Rob set Penny on the terrace and held out his hand. "Let's see," and took the paper Howard held out. *Have located Thunderhead and seventeen head of horses west of here. Will wait here till you come.*

                              *Buck.*

After dinner they got the maps out and studied them. Westgate was on the North Platte near the headwaters.

Rob knew the terrain. It was treacherous country, winter country really, the snow lay deep in those valleys, the mountains ran every which way, there were all sorts of cover, canyons and ravines and thick forests.

"There are plenty of ranches in that country," said Rob. "That's a piece of luck. We might find a corral near the horses and not have to build one." His pencil pointed to two dots on the map, which was spread out on the dining-room table. Howard and Ken and Carey, at his back, followed the point of his pencil with their eyes. "These are towns, Walden and Cowdrey. They're not far from Westgate. I've heard of them. We can get men from there. I've never heard of Westgate. It must be a little dump. But this is government land and it's forest country. There's plenty of lumber if we have to build."

He pushed away the maps, turned his chair from the table and put his pipe in his mouth.

"Shouldn't we wire Uncle Beaver, Mr. McLaughlin?" asked Carey.

"I was just thinking," said Rob, "if he met us at Westgate it would save him many miles. Is your Grandmother coming with him, Carey?"

Carey nodded her head very slowly, trying to think what this change of plan would accomplish. It meant that she would go to Westgate with the McLaughlins! She would be there when Jewel and Thunderhead were caught. Her eyes brightened and she raised her face to Howard's. He smiled back at her.

Rob was thinking out loud. "But I don't know if there's a hotel or any sort of accommodations at Westgate. Probably a trailer camp! Your Grandma might find that rather rough. I think I'll drive over there—it's about a hundred and fifty miles. Look around. Talk to Buck. See what we have to do and what men we can get. See if there's a hotel in the town, and wire your uncle from there. I'll start early tomorrow morning."

"Not tomorrow, Rob. Tomorrow's Sunday, and it's

the day of Penny's baptism."

"Oh, that's right. Well, the next day. Howard, you want to come?"

"You bet."

"Carey, how about you?"

"Oh, I'd love to go along, Mr. McLaughlin!"

Rob glanced at Ken. "Want to come, Ken?"

Ken was silent. His face paled. During the five days of the shearing he and Carey had not really got together, whereas Carey and Howard had. If she had been angry at Howard for whatever it was he had done, in the intimacy of being amongst the sheep, watching the work of the shearers and helping Jeremy move the sheep from one pen into the other, she had forgiven him and forgotten it. They were thicker than ever. They seemed to have something new to laugh about. And Ken was completely in the dark. If he went along in the station wagon it was certain Howard would have the inside track with Carey and *he* would be the gooseberry. A whole long day of that!

He said he didn't want to go along.

"Suit yourself," said Rob, and gathered up the maps.

Nell carried Penny upstairs and undressed her. As she laid her in the crib she stood looking down at her a moment. "You're going to be baptized tomorrow, my small daughter," she said. "How will you like that? And how will you behave, I wonder?"

She put into the crib, beside Penny, the small white lamb which was the baby's favorite toy. But Penny pushed it away. She gave a deep sigh, turned her face sideways upon the pillow and said, "No more."

# 26

Nell had several favorite spots on the ranch where she would take a book or her sewing and spend quiet hours away from the hurly-burly of the house and the corrals.

One of them, not very far from the house, was just above the spot where the stream ran under the barbed-wire fence into the Long Pasture. Here a great cottonwood tree sent its roots down a bank toward the stream, making a tilted cradle in which one could sit, comfortably supported. On the opposite bank was the greensward, running up to the line where the pines of Number Sixteen clothed the hill. To the right, across the barbed-wire fence, was the pasture, spreading up from both sides of the willows and cottonwoods which bordered the creek. Everywhere were the great clumps of rocks, characteristic of this country, looking as if they had been hurled out of some giant's hand to land unexpectedly in the middle of meadow or range, and stay there forever, polished down by wind and rain. At the base of these rocks nestled wildflowers, and underneath were the lairs of small animals. Sitting quietly, watching, one would see the inquisitive small faces peering out, perhaps rock chucks, like grinning old men, perhaps badger, sometimes even a mother coyote with her cunning sharp-nosed pups.

It had been a hectic morning. Pearl had not appeared to make the breakfast. When Nell went looking for her she found her still in bed, groaning with the misery of a hangover. There had been a party the day before, following Penny's baptism and everyone on the ranch had partaken of champagne. But Pearl had also had a visitor, and the visitor had brought a bottle, and Pearl had made an occasion of it. Nell made the breakfast next morning.

Then the station wagon had left with Rob and Howard and Carey. Ken had disappeared somewhere on horseback in a very bad temper. Kim and Chaps had gone with him. The house was in a mess. Nell had dusted and tidied and made beds all morning, then given Penny her dinner and lain down beside her for a rest. When they awoke there was still no sound from Pearl's part of the house.

Nell took her sewing bag and sought out her favorite spot and settled herself here to spend the remainder of the afternoon. She was glad to be out of the house. She hoped Pearl would have slept it off soon.

Pilgrim was with her. He lay down on the edge of the shadow of the tree and put his head on his paws. He watched Nell. The bull was roaring, but far away. Nell was glad he was not close. Penny ran about, endlessly occupied by the things her bright eyes spied upon the ground.

Nell felt quiet and at peace. For one thing, she was alone on the ranch, or practically alone. And another thing, Penny's baptism had come off at last.

Penny had behaved well, that is, she had not yelled until just at the end, and had not demanded to be passed from Nell's arms to Rob's and back again more than three or four times. And she had looked simply ravishing as she had been carried into the church, on Rob's arm, in her tiny white frock with puffs at the shoulders instead of sleeves and the pale pink bonnet set back of three silky brown curls.

Two of Nell's women friends and Howard and Ken

had been the godparents.

"What is the name of this child?"

"Penelope Margaret."

"Dost thou in the name of this child, renounce the devil and all his works . . . wilt thou keep God's holy will and commandments and walk in the same all the days of thy life?"

"I will, by God's help."

Howard had taken it in his stride, but not Ken. He took his responsibilities seriously. Renouncing the devil and all his works for that little bundle of TNT—a big order! Ken had had a very funny look of despairing disapproval on his face when Penny had begun to be naughty.

Nell looked up. Penny was running along the barbed-wire fence. In the sky overhead some chicken hawks were tilting and circling. One of them gave a series of raucous cries. The bull had stopped roaring. There was no wind, the day was extraordinarily quiet. Pilgrim lay in the shadow, his eyes on Nell.

Nell took another piece of thread and threaded her needle. She took up the fine nainsook, found her place in the scalloped edge and began again the slow weaving of her needle.

She thought of the Reverend Richard McConnel, the pastor of St. Stephen's Church. He was an eloquent and ardent and spiritual man. Even the soles of his shoes prayed loudly to the Lord when, every Sunday before ascending the pulpit for his sermon, he knelt at the altar and bowed his black-thatched head on his arms.

This prayer before the sermon always touched Nell. It had touched her as a child when she had seen clergymen do it. It seemed so impetuous and passionate a thing, as if, about to preach, about to tell others what they ought to do and be, a wave of humility suddenly overcame the mere man and, like a boy, he flung himself on the altar, kneeling there oblivious of his congregation, his feet protruding from the cassock, tilted right or left, and prayed an utterly private prayer, begging pardon for his sins and inadequacies, pleading that the truth might be in him, that his words would be acceptable to his God and helpful to his parishioners.

The great doctor of theology, St. Thomas Aquinas, it was said, always prayed before preaching. Prayed, weeping. In imagination Nell could see him, kneeling and praying and weeping and the soles of his sandals praying too, but no more eloquently than the soles of the shoes of the Reverend Richard McConnel.

Nell swiftly prayed a little private prayer for Penny. "God keep her!" she prayed. "God keep and bless my baby."

And then she began to think about the party. How nicely it had gone off. It had been a buffet luncheon. Pearl had outdone herself with her creamed chicken, made with real cream and mushrooms and Parmesan cheese and scraped onion, her delicate tomato and cucumber sandwiches, the hot fresh potato chips and young peas, the first of the season, so tiny and tender and sweet that they were boiled for only two or three minutes. Strawberry ice cream and sunshine cake had ended the repast and there had been plenty of champagne—all their friends from Cheyenne and Laramie and from the ranches around had come. Penny had sat in a high chair until she began to get sleepy and fretful—and Rob had picked her up and she had put her face in his neck and sobbed "Dad-dee's ba-ba—" and he had carried her away and put her to bed.

How sweet he was with the baby—

She looked up to see what Penny was doing and could not find her.

Nell stood up swiftly, her sewing dropping to the ground. She looked at the creek running so close to her, but it was shallow—if Penny had fallen in she would have made an outcry.

Then she saw her. The baby was seated in the midst of a clump of the flame-colored Indian paintbrush, pulling at the stalks, gathering them in her hand. These flowers were at the base of a towering clump of rocks in the pasture beyond the barbed-wire fence— how had the child got there? Through the fence? She went everywhere.

Nell went and leaned on one of the fence posts. "What's baby doing?" she called.

Penny said, "One, two, fee, fi, ten, ate, two, fee—"

Suddenly the baby stopped counting. She pointed and said, "Doggie, doggie—" She gurgled with laughter. There was a little chipmunk darting across the rock above her. It came to a stop and sat up, nibbling its fingers.

"Not a doggie, darling," said Nell, "that's a chipmunk."

Then the corner of her eye caught a movement— something big and dark coming silently down the meadow.

Cricket. His eyes were on the white dress of the baby and the patch of scarlet flowers.

Nell dropped to the ground and rolled under the wire. Her skirt caught in the barbs. She attempted to force herself through, so embedding the barbs more firmly in the strong linen cloth. With a muffled scream she exerted all her strength and jerked and tore at it.

She saw Cricket reach the baby, lower his head and stretch his nose out, sniffing at her. Penny drew back a little at the sight and smell of the great dark head so close to her, and then said, questioningly, "Doggie?" She reached out a tiny hand.

Cricket's right hoof went back and under, gouging up the ground in a cloud of dust. A deep rumble came from within him, and at this terrifying sound, Penny burst into wild crying and tried to scramble to her feet. The bull turned his head and advanced it slightly, presenting the horn.

Nell flung herself upon him, bringing her clenched fist down across his nose. She snatched up the baby and leaped for the rocks. She felt the blow of Cricket's charge against her thigh and stumbled. She clawed at the rock with her right hand, clutching Penny to her with her left. She clambered up the first, the lowest of the rocks, and threw herself upon the higher one.

To get a grip on the stone with one hand, to pull up her skirts so that her bare knees could fasten upon it too—it was a frenzied effort that left her fingers and knees bleeding.

Pilgrim was barking and trying to deflect the attention of the bull. But a bull cannot easily change his target. With deep roars he swung his head low, this way and that, pushing Pilgrim aside as if he were a bothersome fly, but kept his eye on Nell. He forced himself through the smaller rocks at the foot of the great one, reaching his horn for Nell's body.

Nell screamed. She was slipping, she could not maintain her hold. Then her fingers caught in a crack and she clung there. Penny was striking out with legs and arms, trying to squirm out of her mother's clutch. Just above on the rock was a place where a piece seemed to have been sliced off, leaving a tilted shelf. Nell clawed herself up until she reached this shelf. It was not high enough to be safe, but she could climb no farther.

Suddenly Cricket, angered by Pilgrim's persistence, turned from the rock and galloped after the dog. Pilgrim fled, stopped, turned, the bull shot past him and ground to a stop. As Cricket swung himself around, Pilgrim catapulted himself at the bull's head and seized him by the nose.

In agony as the sharp teeth went into the tender flesh, the bull roared and swung his head in a great arc. Pilgrim was swung, too, but his teeth held, and when, at last, he went flying through the air, there was a small piece of bull flesh between his fangs, and blood streamed from Cricket's nose.

Pilgrim hit the earth with a thud and lay still. Cricket came after him.

Nell's head was bowed over the screaming child clasped to her breast. She was drenched with sweat. Her heart pounded so that it shook her whole body. She watched with despair. If Pilgrim was knocked out—

The bull was upon him.

With amazement she saw the dog crawl out from behind Cricket's forelegs and trot away to the fence before Cricket could be after him again. The bull had missed his aim and gone right over the dog.

Cricket came for the rock again. Frantic from the pain of his wounded nose, he raged around the base of it, forcing himself close, reaching up with his horns.

Nell's head wavered. There was a film before her eyes. She was afraid she was going to faint or to be so dizzy that she would fall off. "Dad-dee's—ba-ba" shrieked Penny with an accompaniment of wild howls, "Dad-dee's—ba-ba!"

Nell tried to quiet the baby. "Don't cry, darling— it's all right, baby—Mummy's here."

She looked wildly around. She could see the corner of the ranch house in the distance. Was no one there? No one to drive the bull away and get her down from here?

Within herself she was screaming for Rob, but Rob was far away—besides he had refused to get rid of the bull . . . and now this . . . it was all his fault—rage at her husband mingled with her terror.

She began to cry. How long was this going on? How long could she cling up here? If only Pilgrim would drive the bull far enough away she would slide down and dash for the fence.

Then her crying turned to laughing. The whole thing struck her as ridiculous. She could just see herself stuck up there on the top of the rock, treed by the furious bull with his bleeding nose. She laughed until it was hysteria—she was choking. She put one hand to her throat and there flashed before her eyes all those terrible scenes of impending tragedy. Here it was at last . . . she would faint, she would be unable to hold Penny—she felt her mind going—she summoned all her will.

She took off the bandanna she wore on her head, wound it into a rope. She tied this tightly around Penny's body and put the ends through her own belt, knotting it fast—then consciousness left her. Penny wriggled and squirmed, stretching out her arms, yelling pitifully, "Dad-dee's ba-ba—" but she was held fast and could not get loose from the inert figure that lay on the tilted shelf of rock.

With an impact like the crash of a wave, Nell leaped back to terrified consciousness.

Ah! As if he had heard her wish, Pilgrim was at the bull again and Cricket was galloping after him, head down, heels and tail high in the air. His bellows were like thunder. Pilgrim was agile. Again and again he saved himself, then bored in to nip at haunch or shoulder as the hot charging mass swept past him.

He was watching for another chance at the nose.

Ah! He had it! His teeth closed! Once again the frenzied beast swung his head and the dog with it. Pilgrim went sailing. But this time, when he hit the ground, Cricket was there. He made a sideways scooping motion with his head. It came up with a small twisted form on the horns. Down again. The bull kneeled. Pilgrim disappeared from view—the bull was making motions of grinding his head into the ground.

Nell heard the death cry of the dog, turned her face to the rock, clawing it to keep it from whirling out from under her. The whole universe whirled. She knew that she was fainting again—Oh, Pilgrim! *Pilgrim!*

Pearl groaned. She sat on the edge of her bed and held her head in her hands. She had been sitting that way some time, listening to Cricket and muttering profane epithets directed at him and his incessant noise.

She staggered to her feet, walked into the kitchen, wrung out a cloth in cold water and held it to her face and head. Again, and again.

She went to the stove, stirred up the fire, pulled the coffeepot forward, then walked the floor until the coffee was hot. She poured herself a cup of the black thick fluid and sipped it, standing near the window.

She heard a horse galloping up the road. Leaning to the corner of the window, she saw it swing off the road across the field. It was Ken on Flicka and they were going hell-for-leather. Where on earth was he going? He was heading straight for the barbed-wire fence! He would never try to jump it! No—he pulled Flicka up on her haunches and leaped off, then seized the post of the fence and vaulted over and vanished from view.

Pearl couldn't make this out. She was curious. She went out onto the terrace. From here she got a glimpse of something going on down there in the meadow but it was too far away, her eyes were dim and clouded. She hurried into Captain McLaughlin's desk and took his binoculars from the pigeonhole in which they were kept. She went out onto the front terrace, screwed the binoculars until they suddenly brought the whole scene vividly to her eyes. Nell on top of the rock! And Ken down below in the meadow fighting the bull with only his quirt. Cricket was in a frenzy. Ken had taken the offensive, he lashed and lashed him across the nose, forcing him back—the bull broke out from the blows and charged—Ken stepped aside and lashed again as the bull rushed past him.

At this point, Pearl dropped the binoculars on the terrace and ran screaming up through the Gorge. The men were in the corral, just returning with the light wagon from a day spent on the fences.

"The bull!" she screamed. "Gus! Tim! Get the pitchforks! The bull's killing Ken!"

# 27

"Ya, Boss," said Gus, "like I'm tellin' you, Ken, he held de bull off de rock wid his quirt while his mudder come down wid de baby. He go fur him gude. He give yells. He bang him in de face—eyes—nose—und Crickett he sqveel lak a pig, and he back off, an' he turn an' run, den he cum back at Ken, an' Ken, he yump yust in time, den he run after him an' he yell like crazy, an' he beat him an' lash him, an' Cricket turn 'round ag'in, an' back avay—he back an' back—an' Ken he give it to um in de face all de time—den we come wid de forks—"

Rob, Howard and Carey were hearing the story at ten o'clock that night. They had just reached home and were standing in a group on the front terrace in the darkness.

"He killed the bull, you say—" Rob's voice was slow.

Chills ran up and down Carey's back.

"Ya, Boss. De Missus, she faint, she cum to. She faint agin. Ken got her to de house while we drive de bull to de corral. He kep' roarin' and pawin'. He mak' a turrible racket. His nose an' his eyes hurt him. He smell blood an' he taste it. He's turrible mad. De Missus she cum down from de house holdin' de big express rifle. Ken he walk along wid her. She reach de corral fence an' put de gun troo de bars. Ken took de gun avay from her an' she begin to cry."

A harsh sound came from Rob's throat.

"Ken, he say, 'You stand avay, men.' He say it yoost lak dat, Boss. Ve get out de vay. Ken shoot de bull. De bull go down—mak' a big crash. De missus, she go down too. Ken he pick her oop agin, he say to me, 'Gus, you hitch chains to his horns, take de truck, cart him avay, dump him down de ole mine shaft.'"

"And you've done it?"

"Ya. Ve drug heem avay. He's oop dere—down de mine shaft."

There was silence for a few minutes. Carey thought of the truck dragging the great inert form over the half-mile of road, then across the prairie to the trees and the old mine shaft—of the great body hurtling down, as limp, as helpless as a little dead gopher and the crash at the bottom piling him up in a shapeless mass.

"Go—osh!" exclaimed Howard under his breath.

"And Mrs. McLaughlin wanted to go in to town?" Rob's voice was labored.

"Ya. Ken, he say he go for de doctor. She say, 'No, tak me to heem.' Boss, she hold her troat. Her eyes stick out. She bust out cryin'. Den she laugh. Den she pass out. Ve put her in de car. Ken, he drive her avay."

"The baby?" Rob's voice was sharp.

"Ken, he tuk her too. Vas nobody here but Pearl."

"Thank you, Gus." Rob turned to the others. "Go to bed, children. I'll go to town."

He walked around the house, got into the station wagon which he had just parked on the hill and drove off into the darkness.

Carey felt she could not go right to bed. Nor could Howard. They foraged in the kitchen for food and sat at the table with the red-checked tablecloth, and ate scrambled eggs and drank chocolate, discussing the events of the day—all that Buck Daly had told them of finding the horses in the canyon bottom three miles west of Westgate. And now this awful thing about Nell and the bull.

Carey felt awed. When, at last they went to bed, she lay awake, thinking it all over, thinking of Ken. Again and again she rehearsed the scene as Gus had described it. It was like Ken to do that . . . he was brave—hot tears filled her eyes—he was the bravest, most wonderful boy she had ever known or could imagine . . . she wished she had not been so mean to him, teasing him all the time. She turned her face to the pillow and burst out crying. She fell asleep at last, only to wake with a jump after some hours.

It was the sound of cars that had waked her. She ran to the window and parted the curtains. She saw the two cars coming. Headlights blazed, then wheeled past the house. A moment later voices approached her window. Rob and Ken came past, talking in low tones. They walked close together. Rob carried the sleeping baby in his left arm. His right arm was laid across Ken's shoulders.

Then they disappeared from her view. There was the sound of the front door opening, more low voices, then their steps going upstairs.

Ken was home. Carey lay thinking that they were under the same roof again, she and Ken. And Ken was certainly a hero.

It seemed to her that, far away, she heard the pitiful sound of a puppy crying. On the day of Penny's baptism all the puppies except one, little Willy, had been given to their new owners. The first night, Nell had put him with Daisy so that he would not be alone. But he had tried to nurse. Daisy snarled and snapped at him. Nell said he might as well sleep alone and get used to it. So a box had been fixed up for him against the wall of the tool shed under the wide eaves. The sides were too high for him to crawl out of.

Yes, that was Willy. The pitiful whimpers now and then burst out into desperate yaps, then became long trembling howls.

Carey yearned to comfort him. If she could only have him with her, in her arms, in her own bed, it would comfort her too.

She slipped out of bed, drew her moccasins on, and

without putting on a dressing-gown, stole out into the warm night. Walking down the terrace, she saw that two kittens were walking ahead of her. They, too, had heard Willy's pitiful crying and now and then they stopped and listened, then went on toward the puppy's box. Carey walked slowly, to see what they would do.

Willy heard them coming. His crying stopped while he listened, then began again on a different note, a note of eagerness, of frantic pleading.

The kittens reached his box, crawled up and over the sides and down into it. Willy welcomed them ecstatically. Carey stood over the box, watching. What happy greetings! The kittens purred, they licked Willy's face. Willy turned and twisted and wriggled. At last they all lay down again, snuggled close, Willy's chin resting on the kittens. So they would sleep.

Carey turned away from the box and went back toward the house. She was crying again; she didn't know why. The tenderness of the little kittens seeking out the puppy to comfort him—

Suddenly she saw a dark form before her.

When she realized that it was Ken, it was a shock. Of all people, she would have wanted to be with Ken; to say something to him about what he had done, to touch his hand and feel his eyes looking at her.

She stood there, her hair hanging on her shoulders, tears streaming from her eyes, her hands outstretched to him, forgetting that she was dressed only in her white silk pajamas.

"Oh, Ken! I do think you're so wonderful!"

Bewildered, thrilled, weary, excited, Ken moved hesitantly toward her. How close did he dare to go? He put his arms around her, he hugged her tight, he bent his head down upon hers. He felt the slim little-girl body against him, her arms went around him, and her hands held on to his waist. She cried and sobbed.

"Did you—did you—hear the puppy?" she sobbed.

"Yes. I—heard—the puppy—"

"And—you—c-c-came out to him?"

"Yes—" Ken hugged her tighter. He began to kiss the top of her head.

"Oh, Ken! So—did I—the poor, little p-puppy—"

Ken was beginning to feel weepy himself. His voice trembled. "Yes. Poor little fellow."

"I th-th-ink he's so path—thetic—" sobbed Carey.

Ken kissed her and kissed her. Carey's arms crept up around his neck.

"It's just a d-d-amned sh-shame—" muttered Ken.

"Oh, Ken! Ken—"

"Gosh, Carey—"

"We-ell—I guess I've g-g-got to go—" Carey's chest heaved and her breath came with catches. She drew herself out of his arms, and wiped her eyes with her hands. "Good-night, Ken—"

"Good-night, Carey."

He stood there while she pattered away from him. He looked up at the sky, all around, as if he were dazed. Then, suddenly, with fists clenched, he thrust both arms upward as high as he could reach—a gesture of triumph. Then he sped silently indoors.

# 28

Nell was kept under opiates for several days. The fainting, the incessant weeping stopped. She was to remain in the hospital until she had entirely recovered from the shock of her terrible experience and until the doctor had had time to make a thorough examination of her. A competent infant's nurse was sent out to the ranch to take care of Penny.

Howard and Ken walked up and down the platform of the Tie Siding station. Evidently each of the boys had something on his mind. They were not talking. Howard felt as if the solid ground had fallen out from under his feet. To go away from home and not have his mother there to say goodby to him! The doctor wanted no visitors at the hospital, so Howard had had no last words, no kiss, no little lecture on the love of God to take away with him. And his father was at a stockman's meeting, so there was only Ken to see him off. It made him feel like a stranger, drifting off into the world with no one caring.

At such a time one naturally thought more about religion.

Doubts! At times they shook Howard horribly. He had asked his father, when he was saying goodby to him, "Dad, you know all the religion Mother tells us about—do you believe it, too?" And his Dad had answered, "Yes. Certainly. I don't *know* as much as she does, don't study it as she does, but what she tells you is true and someday you'll be awfully glad you know it. The time comes in most men's lives when they've nothing but God left!" Rob had laughed. "That phrase always amuses me. It ought to be enough for any man."

*Nothing but God left*—Howard paced slowly along, his eyes on the boards of the station platform, *nothing but God left*—that would be awful. He was a long way from that.

Ken cleared his throat with embarrassment. Both

boys had been swept beyond their recent estrangement over Carey and yet it had not been thrashed out. It stood there between them.

Ken was whipping up courage, there wasn't much time, the train would be along any minute.

Finally he blurted it out. "Howard, you know that time you and I had the fight?"

"Yep."

"Well, I wish you'd tell me what had happened."

"You mean with Carey?"

"Yes. What had you done to make her so mad?" His heart quickened now that he had actually asked for it.

Howard turned his head in a haughty manner. He never permitted his younger brother to question any of his actions. But this was a different Ken, and back of the quiet intensity of his face and his questioning eyes was authority! Ken asked if he had a right to know. Besides, Howard was weakened by the sadness he was feeling about his mother.

He looked away rather sheepishly. "Oh, it wasn't anything like what you thought! I never kissed Carey, or even tried to."

Ken hid his jubilance. *He* had kissed her—he was ahead then—way ahead. "But she was so mad at you," he said. "I heard her."

"Oh, it was just a lot of kid nonsense," said Howard. "I pushed her off the rock up above Deercreek when we were fishing. She fell in that shallow pool—all mud. She looked so funny when she got out. I laughed at her. That was what made her the maddest, because when we came home I kept laughing at her. I tried to get some of the mud off her. And there were little leeches all over her legs and arms. I picked them off her and that made me laugh some more and I put one behind her ear, and then when she found *that*—"

"But you let me think—you said—you fought me—" stammered Ken, overcome with relief and happiness. No wonder Carey had told him nothing about this humiliating experience!

"Well, I was sore that you would call me to account for anything I did. Why shouldn't I kiss her if I wanted to, if she would let me? What business was it of yours?"

There was the train in the distance. Both boys fastened their eyes on it. Howard grabbed one of his suitcases, Ken the other. Howard looked around, almost wildly. He suddenly felt as if he were plunging into an abyss—he turned to his younger brother and Ken turned as eagerly, as warmly to him. Their right hands clasped—impulsively they leaned to each other and hugged.

"It's all right, Ken. Carey doesn't care a rap for me."

"Gosh, Howard—"

"That's right—"

"I'm awfully sorry, Howard—"

"Hey! I don't care a rap either—"

The train roared in. There was to be only an instant's stop for this one passenger. Even before it quite stopped the porter let down the steps, swung off and seized the bags. Howard got aboard, turning to wave to Ken. Both boys were lightened of their distress, their faces were flushed with love and happiness. Ken saluted smartly.

"Hi, Cadet!" he yelled. "Good luck!" There was a broad grin on his face.

The conductor waved his arm, the train picked up speed and Howard vanished from view as the steps and door clanged shut.

Ken stood proudly at attention until the train was just a speck in the distance, and then, when he walked to the car, he remembered the West Point walk, as his father had now and then showed it to them, and tried to walk the West Point walk.

Nell was watching the time. She knew at what hour that train was taking her boy away from her, and without a goodby. Without the little lecture which he had asked for. To fail him like this!

She asked her nurse for writing paper and pencil. She was supposed to keep very quiet and she had to insist that if she were not allowed to write the letter it would make her more nervous than if she did it and got it off her mind.

She sat up against her pillows, drew up her knees, and placed the writing pad against them.

She was feeling completely at peace. Whatever the awful fate was that had been threatening her, it was over now. It had struck her and done its worst and she was safe from it.

Moreover, it was a relief to know that there had been a reason for all her emotional storms and for the feeling of choking and the dreams and premonitions— just an enlarged thyroid gland that was growing inward and pressing on the windpipe. One of the goiters that grow in high altitudes where there is little iodine in the soil and water. If she had only had a check-up long ago. But no, this was better. To have gone right *through* the thing, the horror, the death . . . and come out on the other side—her thoughts jammed a moment . . . *Oh, Pilgrim!* . . . then went on—and then to have this long blissful rest in the hospital, knowing that she was under treatment that would cure her, that she would go back to the ranch feeling quite different, and begin again.

Ken . . . Carey . . . how would things go with

them? She smiled, holding her pencil, her eyes staring at nothing. It didn't matter. They would get on without her. Things would work out. Howard—he was the one to think about now, the boy who was going away from home for good, and who had asked her to teach him more about God.

But she hesitated to begin. Should she write him this that she had in mind? Was it really suitable for him? She had to think back and remember how young she had been when she, too, had wondered about God, everything about Him, and had wanted to know and understand. Young people, children have to know about God. That is when it is most important of all. They have to start out in life right. They have to start out, companioned by God—not alone. Besides, who knows, one of her boys might decide to be a clergyman!

At this thought, Nell put down her pencil and looked out the window.

Her father's grandfather had been the pastor of a little country parish. He had eked out his salary by farming and claimed that he got the inspiration for his fine sermons walking behind his plow. He believed that spirituality grew naturally out of the soil. The prophets of the Old Testament, the great preachers and poets, they were shepherds and farmers. They were close to the earth, and from the earth came their vision.

Her boys then, they, too, should have poetry and vision and spirituality, having lived as they had done, protected from artificiality, close to the earth, to the storms, to the skies, and to the simplicity and the passion and the obedience of the animals. Faith should be natural to them. They should, spontaneously, lean toward God.

If one of them chose to be a clergyman would it be Howard or Ken? Howard seemed to have the cool speculative mind—was it that which made him interested in these talks on religion, or was it the deep sense of personal need? He was so secretive—it would be hard to know. At any rate then, *sow the seed*.

She put her pencil to the paper and began to write.

July 2nd
In hospital

Hello darling!

You've got away from me! But not away from my thoughts nor my pen. And I haven't forgotten that we didn't have a proper goodby and that we have not had our talk about the love of God.

I feel that I had made an engagement with you, to tell you of my thoughts on this subject, and I don't like to break engagements. This letter will be the little lecture you asked for. I will write you many more letters, but first to get this one off my mind—

This is an ambitious subject for me to tackle. St. Francis de Sales wrote a *Treatise on the Love of God* and it is about six hundred pages long, if I remember rightly, and very fine print! I won't ask you to read that. I'll just send you my own ideas on the subject, quite simple, almost infantile, and hope that they will make sense to you, and that they will open a door for you.

The term "the love of God" is used so much. It is spoken of as if it should be taken for granted. Children are told, "If you loved God you wouldn't do that." The child never seems to have the sense to answer, "But I don't love Him. I don't know Him. I don't want Him or ever think about Him." Which would often be the truth. Also, it seems to be taken for granted in most sermons, that of course every Christian, every religious person has a true love of God in his heart. But this is not so. I think it is one of the rarest things in the world, one of the greatest gifts, really the pearl of great price. So I always say in my mind most urgently to the preachers, "Well, now, give us a sermon about the Love of God. How can you get it? Where is it to be found?" But I don't think I have ever heard a sermon about just that one thing (which is not to say that they have not been preached).

So the upshot is that I have done a great deal of thinking about it myself, trying to find out how that beautiful flame can be lit within the human heart. I have traced love, any kind of love, back to its beginnings, or tried to, and it seems to me I have found out a good deal about it.

To begin with—just one more word about the way LOVE bestows happiness. When you come to think of it, there is nothing that bestows happiness *except* love. Love is implicit in all praise, in admiration. You know how, in yourself, when you see some glorious thing, a sunset, or a beautiful face, or some of those exquisite scenes of nature that you now and then come upon, a great tide of praise, love and happiness rises in your heart until it seems that it will burst, and tears push up behind your eyes! Or perhaps it is the grandeur of a symphony. Or perhaps it is great courage or a noble, unselfish deed—and again that bursting love fills the heart. This can be traced down to the smallest thing. Imagine a young girl, about to go to her coming-out party. She sees her dress lying on the bed, clasps her hands (a classic attitude of praise and love!) and stands there in a trance of happiness. Or, a gathering of friends. Analyze your warm, happy feeling. You may call it good cheer, geniality, hospitality. These are other names for love.

And so I say that it is love that gives us all our happiness, and if only we could find some way to kindle it to a great flame in ourselves, which would never wane or die, and for some One who could never disappoint or abandon us, we could ask nothing more. We would be just bursting with happiness all the time.

This great happiness is what the Saints have, and is why they are Saints. This happiness is what the mystics have.

So now, back to our search—how to get it?

Well then, look at love. Wherever you see it (and you see it nearly everywhere) trace it to its beginnings. What started it?

Let's take a very simple example. Penny, when she sees me the first thing in the morning. Or the puppies. They almost burst with love. Where do they get it? Where does Penny get it?

Well, Penny needs me. Penny is helpless without me. From the mother a baby gets security, food, warmth, tenderness, companionship and a thousand gifts that change and increase as the infant gets larger and needs more.

So first there is *need*.

Now what next? Second, I should say, the recognition of the source of good. It isn't long before the infant knows that all these things come from its mother. And what next? Gratitude. And here we have love, the full cup running over.

There one sees the evolution of love. First NEED, then RECOGNITION OF THE SOURCE OF GOOD (I wish I could find one word for that—perhaps you can) and then GRATITUDE.

I think there is no love in the world that does not begin with those things.

The love of friends? Of course. The need, the recognition of that particular person as the friend, and then the gratitude.

The love of men and women? First, their great and permanent need, then the recognition of each other as possessors of all the gifts that could fill that need, then, if the gifts are bestowed—the great gratitude.

The love of God? First we find out how much we need Him. I think that a person who does not find that out, who is incapable of finding that out, who is always smug and self-sufficient, can never win this great happiness.

Then, needing Him, we grope around perhaps for years to find the source of good. And at last we do. Probably someone tells us, tells us in a way that we can accept and understand. The torch is lit from one hand to the other, and has been all down through the ages. We know where our good is and we turn away from the things of the world (or at least we know that they are not of final power and importance) to God, and our "hearts burn within us" and we know that He is with us, always has been, always will be, and we are filled with gratitude and we are so happy we could die.

This second step in the process I suppose is a miracle. It is a gift. It comes to some and not to others. I suppose it comes to those who *need* the most, who *seek* the most persistently. It takes thinking about. It might seem that there are many good things which do not come from God—the girl's pretty dress, the good dinner, material belongings which are bought, or achievements which are earned, but this is looking at it in a small way. The nobility of human character, heroism, courage, unselfishness, steadfastness, *conscience* above all—that inexplicable determination in man to lift himself up from his lower nature and live on the highest level he is capable of (and to this force can be traced all man's progress of whatever sort)—it is obvious that these come from God. And we are grateful for them. Try to imagine what life on this planet would be like if man had no conscience. Try to imagine it without beauty. Try to imagine the physical universe without order, plan, design.

If you think of things like that, Howard, perhaps, suddenly, your heart will "burn within you" and you will know that the flame of the love of God has been lit because you have recognized Him as the source of good.

Once you have the love of God it spills over onto everything, and your heart and your life and your world are full of love and therefore full of happiness.

Now, my dear boy, write me the moment you have any spare time. I will write you again soon, something of less exalted nature.

I am feeling better already. Much love to the Cadet.

Mother.

And while Nell finished her letter, handed it to the nurse to mail and then lay back on her pillow, exhausted, Howard was sitting in the Pullman car, flooded with intense happiness, wondering in a dazed way how and why that sudden rush of brotherly love, that quick and ardent embrace and the glimpse of Ken's salute and laughter, had swept all the misery from his heart.

# 29

Four black mares were in Thunderhead's band. Buck
had not been able to get close enough to them to
identify Jewel by the white mark on her forehead, but
he had seen Thunderhead more than once and also a
number of colts. They were feeding in the flats of the
headwaters of the Spindle River. This was a ravine
running north and south, three or four miles west of
Westgate. It was, roughly, half a mile wide, between
broken mountain ridges that converged at the northern end, nearly meeting, then opening up again. Here
would be the place to build the corral. It was a
natural. The mountains which formed the sides of the
ravine were ready-made wings. Within these, the
fence wings could be built. Line riders could guard
the ridges and the southern mouth of the ravine so
that the horses could not wander away while the corral was being built.

This information was contained in a letter from
Buck which was waiting for Rob McLaughlin when
the Goose Bar station wagon drove up to the hotel in
Westgate late on a hot July afternoon.

Ken McLaughlin and Carey Marsh jumped out and
began to unload the suitcases while Rob walked in to
register.

Behind the station wagon there drew up the Goose
Bar truck with Tim driving and Ross Buckley in the
cab beside him. In the truck were half a dozen of the
Goose Bar horses. Tim yelled to Ken that he'd drive on

and find a stable where he could unload them.

Ross was feeling his oats. Coming into a new town with half a dozen of Captain McLaughlin's famous hot-bloods in the truck behind him, on a mission of such importance as the finding and capturing of the outlaw stallion as well as the English filly, was something to live up to. He hung out the side of the cab, swinging his big hat and emitting a succession of war whoops. The horses, wild with curiosity to see and to smell all these strange new things, thundered from one side of the truck to the other, and Big Mohawk, who was only half broken because the Captain liked him that way, reared and crashed down again.

By the time the boys had located a stable, they had gathered up half the town.

As a matter of fact, Westgate was ready and prepared for these visitors. The day before there had arrived a large Cadillac limousine driven by an English groom and pulling a deluxe horse trailer. Out of the car had stepped an imposing lady who looked like the townspeople's idea of an English queen-mother, and a tall, thin old gentleman with a limp and an acousticon who was dressed in tan Cheyenne pants and ten gallon hat. He was soon recognized, Beaver Greenway, owner of the famous stable of race horses in Idaho.

The town was not much more than five or six blocks long. One of the state highways went through it, a narrow strip of asphalt, leaving a broad expanse of dirt road on each side of it. It existed because of lumber camps in the near-by mountains, and ranches on the North Platte and Little Laramie rivers. There was a hotel, a large square building on a corner, trimmed with wooden scrollwork as elaborate as the embroidery on an old-fashioned petticoat. Wide verandahs ran across front and side and it called itself the Grand View Hotel.

The view was, indeed, grand. It looked westward over a long low timbered ridge to a mountainous country beyond. The peaks rose, one behind the other spreading like a fan north and south until, reaching above the timber line, they became bare crags, and beyond these in the far distance, tips of the Mummy Range, snow covered, dazzling white in the mornings, pink at sunset time and purple in the long evenings.

Fortunate for Carey that there was this eye-filling beauty to the westward, for she spent many hours rocking on the verandah beside her grandmother in the next few days.

But, now, she was in the lobby of the hotel, clasped in the arms of her uncle. He gave her a resounding kiss and put her off and looked at her.

"Bless my soul, Carey! How I've missed you! The Blue Moon wasn't the same without you!"

"Oh, Uncle Beaver, I'm so glad to see you!" She flung her arms around him again. "I feel as if I'd been away a month!"

"Have you been having a good time? Let me look at you!" He studied her again, his face becoming more serious as he listened to her telling of the wonderful time she had been having. "Carey, you've changed."

"Have I, Uncle Beaver?"

"My word!" He looked at her, turned her around, seized her shoulders. "Why, child alive! You're a different girl. Carey, I feel as if I'd never seen you really happy before!"

"Why, Uncle Beaver, what do you mean? Of course I've been happy!"

But he shook his head. "I've got to think about this.

Something's happened, but I don't know just what. Maybe you've suddenly grown up."

"Where is Grandma, Uncle Beaver?"

"She went up to her room to take a nap. She ought to be awake now and ready to come down. Supper'll be ready soon." He turned to Rob who stood reading Buck's letter. "Did you get your key, McLaughlin? I took a room for you and Ken."

Rob looked up. "Here's a letter from Buck. Says the horses are right over there west of that ridge. He's camping out near by."

"Gee!" said Ken. "I can hardly wait! I'd like to ride out right away and get a squint at Thunderhead!"

"You hold your horses, young man," said Rob.

Carey laughed. "That's what he wants to do! So do I! Uncle Beaver, did you take a room for me, too?"

The clerk had come out from behind the desk with a key. "There is an extra bed in your grandmother's room, Miss. We've had that made up for you."

"Yes, Carey," said her uncle, "Your Grandma chose a double room for you and herself."

Carey spoke with calm decision and again her uncle looked at her with amazement.

"But I'll be getting up early to go out riding. I wouldn't want to wake Grandma. I'd rather have a room to myself the way I do at home."

"Suit yourself."

The clerk went behind the desk for another key.

Carey asked where her Grandma's room was, flew up the stairs, rapped softly on the door and without waiting to be answered, opened it and stepped in.

Mrs. Palmer, fully dressed for supper, was adjusting the shades, raising them a little to let in the air which was still warm, but not so hot as it had been at midday.

Hearing the door open, she turned, astonished that anyone should enter her room. Carey rushed forward, exclaiming, "Oh, Grandma!" and threw her arms around her.

In that instant's meeting Mrs. Palmer sensed that something was all wrong. With what assurance Carey had greeted her! How strongly those young arms held her! Where was the hesitation, the timidity that ought to have been there? Her face went pale. Her light grey eyes became stony beneath the fine black arches.

She extricated herself from Carey's arms abruptly and backed away from the girl, smoothing her gown as if it had been roughly disarranged by a dog. She spoke with biting sarcasm, she made graceful bows, she sneered, she put on a scene.

"Oh, how do you do? Who is this, may I ask? A young lady! Quite a grand young lady!"

The impact of this upon Carey was shattering. She felt in her grandmother that rage which seemed to well up so easily. It was shocking to discover that this was still there as it always had been. She had forgotten it in the happy weeks she had been away.

She stood back, her hands dropping to her sides. She was ashamed for her grandmother.

Mrs. Palmer raised her lorgnette and inspected the girl coldly. "But what a costume! You look like a stable boy!"

Carey had made the trip in bluejeans and pink-striped shirt.

"Where is your luggage?"

"Ken is bringing it up, Grandma."

"You will sleep there," said Mrs. Palmer, pointing across the huge room to a second large double bed in the other corner.

Carey's heart sank. "Grandma," she said hesitantly,

"you know I expect to get up early and ride out to where the horses are. I think I'd better have my own room—" She stopped short. Mrs. Palmer sat down very suddenly in a chair by the window and clutched her heart. She leaned her head back. Her face was contorted.

"Oh, Grandma!" It was the frightened child speaking again. "Is it your heart? Where are your smelling salts?"

Mrs. Palmer's head rolled helplessly from one side to the other but she motioned with her hand toward the bureau and Carey, running across the room, found among the toilet things a bottle of smelling salts. She held it to her grandmother's nose, supporting her head with the other hand. It began to seem very natural. The visit at the Goose Bar Ranch was like a remembered dream.

"There, that's better." Mrs. Palmer pushed her away, drew a deep breath, and sat up straight. "You were saying you wanted to have a room to yourself? Very well, then. Perhaps your uncle can find a woman from the village to sleep in here with me. The doctor says I must not be alone at night in a strange place."

"Oh, Grandma! Of course I'll sleep in here with you. I had—sort of forgotten. I didn't realize you had been having heart spells."

There were steps in the hall. With surprising agility Mrs. Palmer jumped up and went to the door, opened it and looked out. It was the hotel clerk and Ken, each carrying one of Carey's big suitcases. The clerk was unlocking the door of the room across the hall.

Ken dropped the suitcase he was carrying and turned to greet Mrs. Palmer. He was untidy and sweaty but at sight of his long sensitive face and the sweetness of his expression Carey had a sudden surge of the heart. It was the feeling a prisoner might have at sight of one come to set him free.

"Why, hello, Mrs. Palmer," he said.

She ignored his outstretched hand. "How do you do, Kenneth. Will you please put Carey's luggage in here."

"I thought she was going to have a room to herself? She said—"

"She will sleep in here, Kenneth." She swept back into the room. Ken glanced at the clerk. They picked up the cases and followed her in. "Put that big one there; the other over here." She pointed to two chairs.

Carey met Ken's eyes. Howard's eyes were opaque, you couldn't look into them, but Ken's were like deep wells of dark blue. Now, in those depths, she saw a sort of shock. He was horrified. Carey wanted to give him a look which would be a cry for help! But this was all wrong! Help for what?

The suitcases were put down where the old lady had indicated. She tipped the clerk and he left the room while Ken still stood there, hesitating, feeling that Carey was in a jam and he ought to find a way to help her.

"I'm going to the stables to see to the horses. Would you like to come with me, Carey?"

"Carey will not be going out again this evening, Kenneth," said Mrs. Palmer, so smoothly, with such expert finality that Ken, who had intended to put up a fight for Carey, found himself standing outside the closed door, marveling at how he had got there. What was it in that old woman that moved other people around as if they were chessmen!

# 30

After supper they all sat out on the front verandah.

A dignified gentleman who spoke with a southern accent came up and introduced himself as Ashley Gildersleeve, owner of the weekly paper of the town of Steamboat Springs. He explained that a valuable mare belonging to him named Lady Godiva had disappeared the year previous, that there was evidence that Thunderhead had been in the neighborhood and the general opinion was that the white stallion had stolen her. Hearing that a search for him was on, he had come down to be present at the round-up.

Rob shook hands with him, introduced him to the others, pulled up a chair for him beside Mrs. Palmer, and Ashley Gildersleeve sat down and proved himself a good conversationalist.

The old lady became very expansive. She chatted vivaciously, beginning every remark with some reference to herself, as "I can assure you, Mr. Gildersleeve, this is quite an experience for me." Or, "When I was a girl in Philadelphia—"

Mr. Gildersleeve had a habit of gallantry in conversation with ladies. When ladies called attention to themselves the proper response was a compliment! At the first compliment Mrs. Palmer relaxed and became expansive.

Meanwhile Ken and Carey were wandering down the street.

It was an ugly street, crowded for its few blocks

with gas stations, garages, drug stores, pool room, bowling alley, small dry goods and hardware shops. On the side streets were the small frame houses belonging to the townsfolk.

Ken and Carey turned into one of these and walked under the spreading branches of Chinese elms.

"Gosh, Carey, it isn't the way it was at home—that you and I could go off for a ride with each other whenever we wanted to," said Ken almost in desperation.

"I know, Ken. Everything has changed." Carey drew a deep sigh. "But that wasn't really *my* life, with you and your family. That was *your* life. My life is quite different. A person has to go back to their own life."

Ken almost choked on the words he wanted to say —that her life and his life ought to be together. They came to a little bridge and paused, leaning over the railing, looking down at the shallow creek.

"Do you—do you think I'm very—er—possessive, Carey?"

"About what, Ken? Thunderhead? But he's yours— why shouldn't you be?"

"I—I didn't mean Thunderhead." Ken's breath suddenly left him and with it his courage. "Now, your grandmother, Carey—*she's* possessive about you, too —but in the wrong way!"

"About me *too!*"

"Oh—I—" He could not go on. Bravely he looked into her face, then burst out, "Carey, do you—l-l-like me?"

"Why, of course! You know I do!"

"Oh, yes, I know that, but, well I mean, for instance, as well as you like Howard?"

"Oh, much better. Howard is superficial."

"Well, what am I?"

"You are mature."

Ken savored this. *Mature.* The word brought him over the edge of boyhood. It was wonderful—*mature.* Then he grew doubtful. She had said it so seriously, she was always so motherly to him that he would hardly have been surprised if she had suddenly taken her handkerchief and wiped his nose. He didn't know if this was a good sign or not.

The honk of an automobile horn startled them. He pulled Carey to him as it rushed by. It was a moment that might have turned into something and again Ken's breath left him, but there was Carey slipping her arm confidingly in his and saying, "I think we ought to go back—Grandma will be looking for me." And as they sauntered homeward she began to talk hesitatingly about her grandmother, saying she wished she didn't have to sleep in the same room with her, if only she had a room to herself she could get up early and go out riding with Ken—go out to the ravine where the horses were.

"Tomorrow morning," said Ken, "we're going to decide definitely just where the corral will be built. They've got enough men and the permit to cut the timber. We're going to have breakfast at five-thirty and ride out, your uncle and Dad and I. We'll meet Buck and the men out there. Why don't you come along?"

"Grandma would never let me. You know that, Ken."

"Carey, you know, I think it's awful the way your grandmother bosses you."

"Sometimes I—kind of—do, too, Ken. And when I was visiting at your ranch I made up my mind I wouldn't stand it any more. But when you're away from her, you forget what she's really like and how there's something in her that just makes everyone give in to her. But you find it out again the moment you're with her."

Ken had found this out once or twice himself. Even his father gave in when Mrs. Palmer blazed her eyes. But he stuck out his chest and insisted, "I don't see how you stand it! I'd just tell her to go chase herself!"

Carey gave a little gasp. People didn't talk about her Grandma that way. But presently she turned shining eyes to his and said in a low voice, "Maybe I will!" And then, more boldly, "I will, Ken, I will!"

Just as they reached the hotel a tall man in a business suit walked up the front steps and took off his ten gallon hat.

"I'm looking for Captain McLaughlin."

Ken and Carey sat down on the top step.

Rob stood up. "That's my name." They shook hands.

"I'm the Deputy Sheriff," he showed his badge. "My name's Elmer Barrows."

Rob introduced him all around and said, "Take a seat, Sheriff. What's on your mind?"

The Sheriff cut himself a plug of tobacco and put it in his mouth. "Well, it's about these horses you're going to take out of the state. I hear that's what you're here for."

"That's right," said Rob. "The black filly belongs to Mr. Greenway here."

"Is she branded, Mr. Greenway? I happen to be the Brand Inspector as well as Deputy."

"No, there's no brand on her."

"You understand I have to be satisfied as to the ownership of these horses before they can be moved. How many head are there?"

"There's between fifteen and twenty head not

counting the colts," said Rob. "Sure, we can prove ownership. Mr. Greenway has papers for his filly, and the groom can identify her. He brought her from England."

"And where do the others come from?"

"All over Wyoming and Colorado," said Rob, grinning. "Wherever the stallion had a mind to steal them. When we've got them corralled and have taken the two we're after I'll leave the rest for you."

"That'd be the best way," said the Sheriff.

"And save me a lot of work," said Rob. "You can examine the brands and notify the owners."

"I'll know Lady Godiva," said Mr. Gildersleeve.

"And this man will know his, if I'm not mistaken," Rob pointed to a ramshackle little Ford sedan which had just stopped before the hotel in a cloud of dust.

Out of it stepped a heavily bearded man with his two tall sons.

Rob went down the steps to greet him. "Jeff Stevens! Come after your two mares, I'll bet!"

"That's right," said Stevens, and Rob shook hands with the three.

"How'd you smell this out?" he asked.

"Oh, they was talkin' about it down to Glendevy, said you had the stallion cornered up here and was goin' to round him up and catch the mares. So, thinks I, I'll just trot up there with Tad and Hick and get my mares while the gettin's good."

He burst into a snicker.

"Suits me down to the ground," said Rob. "That means I can have my work team back again."

"They sure helped me out, Mr. McLaughlin, but they ain't a patch on Molly and Lizzie."

"Come up onto the porch and meet our friends here." He made the introductions. "This is Mrs.

Palmer—"

"Pleased to meetcher, I'm sure, Mum," said Stevens with his greasy hat in his hand.

"And Mr. Greenway—"

"Howdy, howdy—"

"And Miss Marsh. She is the owner of the filly we're looking for. You know my son, Ken. And this is the Sheriff—"

"I ain't no sight for sore eyes to Jeff," drawled the Sheriff.

"Do sit down," gushed Mrs. Palmer, "and tell us, did you lose some mares too? Dear me! This stallion of Kenneth's seems to be a regular Bluebeard!"

"Don't know as he's got a blue beard, Mum, but he's a son-of-a-gun fur stealin' mares. If the Captain here hadn't lent me a work team don't know how I'd have got my crops in this summer."

"How about that, Sheriff?" said Rob. "Is there any law says a man is legally responsible if his stallion goes around rustlin' mares?"

"Not as I ever heard tell of," said the Sheriff.

Jeff was immediately in a huff. "Ain't no man goin' to think I'd take it lyin' down—to have a rich man's stallion steal the mares I needs to make my daily bread!"

"Well, you got a team from the Captain, ain't you? You got no kick coming."

"The trouble I'm in," said Rob, "is that it isn't my stallion, but it *is* my responsibility. The horse belongs to Ken."

"Puts you in a helluva fix, Cap'n," drawled Barrows.

Ken, seated on the top step of the verandah, gave an embarrassed laugh.

Down the street, enveloped in a cloud of dust, came two riders. They were Ross and Tim who had not been able to resist the temptation to show some of the McLaughlin spindle-legs to the town. They pranced along sideways, Ross twirling the end of his rope and greeting all and sundry with jovial yells.

As they got abreast of the hotel, Rob called them to come and meet the Sheriff. The boys dismounted, tied the horses to the hitching pole and, standing below the verandah, leaned on the top rail of the porch and were introduced all around.

"This is Jeff Stevens," said Rob.

"The fellow that Thunderhead stole the mares off of?"

"I'm the guy," boasted Stevens, beginning to enjoy his fame. "I've come here to git mine from that fence-jumpin', mare-stealin', murderin' son-of-a-bi— I beg your pardon, lady, I was going to say, that murderin' hellion!"

"Gol-durn," said the little broncobuster slowly. "Seems like everybody in the state has seen that stallion but me. I'd give my eye teeth to ride him. Bet I could take him into a rodeo and win everything in sight. They say he's a buckin' fool!"

"Buckin' fool!" exclaimed Ken indignantly. "Bucking isn't all he can do. He can run. He's the fastest horse anywhere around."

"I can vouch for his speed," said Greenway. "Ken put him in my race over at Saginaw Falls two years ago, and that horse would have won if he hadn't taken it into his head to buck. He broke out into the middle, and did he put on a show!"

Half a dozen voices spoke up, with tales of some bucking horse they had owned or ridden.

Tim asked Jeff Stevens if he had been an eyewitness to Thunderhead's kidnapping of his mares.

Jeff Stevens raised his voice as he told the story. His

two boys, Hick and Tad, perched on the rail of the verandah, were smoking cigarettes that they rolled themselves with careless nonchalance.

"It was when the two mares were being taken from the plow, right there near the corral. They knew wot was comin' before any of the rest of us had caught on. They began to nicker and ra'r around. Lizzie she went up straight and Tad here, he wuz loopin' up the harness on her, and he lost his balance and sat down kinder sudden—"

Tad gave a sheepish grin and his brother dug him in the ribs.

"The harness cum down half off her, and before you cud say Jack Robinson, there was that son-of-a-gun, that white devil plunging right into us, neighin', screamin', lungin' at Liz, she giv a jump and run like hell with Tad still holding the reins and riding along on the seat of his pants—"

Hick burst out with, "Haw, haw, haw—he sure did."

"Well, he let go, and did he cuss! By that time all you cud see was the two of 'em, one white, one brown, tearing along, away off on the prairie. She stopped once, to kick herself free of the harness. The stallion, he tuk the collar in his teeth and tore it off'n her. Yes, sir, I seen that with my own eyes. A smart one and no mistake. An' I'm a son-of-a-gun ef he didn't come back a week later and steal the other mare. I tell you there's nuthin' a man kin do, lessen he was sittin' there waiting for him with a gun."

There was uproarious laughter, profane exclamations, more questions were asked, and the stallion's fame and stature grew.

Half the town, it seemed, was gathering around the front verandah of the Grand View Hotel. The Sheriff introduced them.

"This is Charley Gage, President of Stock-Growers and Lumberman's Bank of Westgate."

"Sit down, Mr. Gage."

"You boys down thar, come up here and meet Mr. Greenway who owns the racing stable in Idaho, and Mr. McLaughlin—these boys are our fire brigade—"

The guests of the hotel, transients, traveling salesmen, a few of the towns people drew their chairs around and joined in.

"It's this here stallion of Ken McLaughlin's is creating all the commotion," said the Sheriff. "He's come to the end of his tether now, and half of these folks you see here is men that have had mares stolen by him."

"Is he yours, sure enough?" asked one of the fire brigade of Ken.

"Yep," said Ken, uncertain as to whether he was a hero or a villain.

"Can you *ride* him?" demanded Jeff Stevens, slapping his two hands down on his knees and leaning toward Ken.

"Sure I can! I raised him from a baby!"

"Gee whittaker!" marveled Tad Stevens, shaking his head. "Put a saddle and bridle on that devil! Not me!"

Jeff Stevens still had his deep, bright little eyes fixed on Ken. "Say! Joe Daly was a-tellin' me—he's the fellow that tends your rams for you, ain't he?"

"Yep."

"Well, he had it that Jeremy told him that Gus had a yarn about your ridin' that stallion bareback way off in the mountings somewhere, when he was a-roundin' up his mares."

"That's right," said Carey loudly. "He did it. He told me so!"

"Carey!" exclaimed her grandmother. "Moderate

your voice, my child."

"Is it a fact, Ken?" insisted Jeff.

Ken was modest. "Thunderhead's easy to ride. I've ridden him bareback ever since his back was strong enough to hold me."

Tim and Ross were corroborating the story of Ken's exploit. There were murmurs of amazement and everyone turned to look at the boy again.

Greenway leaned to Rob. "Did he really do that?"

"Yes," said Rob. "The damndest stunt I ever heard of. He didn't know he was doing anything out of the ordinary. Stuck on for a mile or more, then slid off, came home covered with cuts and bruises."

"Good God!" said Greenway and turned to look at Ken with new respect in his eyes.

"He's a rider," said Rob. "With him on his back I've seen Thunderhead do a half mile in forty-seven seconds. He sails over fences, rocks, roads—cattle guards —nothing stops him."

Greenway was thoughtful, dallying with the idea that if Ken had been such a fine trainer for Thunderhead, he might be the one to get Jewel into form.

The Sheriff turned to Rob. "What are you going to do with this fairy-book hoss when you catch him?"

"Let's catch him first," said Rob.

"Gol-durn it," yelled Ross, "give him to me! I'll make him famous!"

"He's famous already," said Ken sourly. He felt himself in a spot. Just what should be done with Thunderhead had not yet been talked out between himself and his father. He avoided raising the question, he didn't want his father to commit himself. Catch the horse, get him off the range and put an end to his raiding—that was as far as they had gone. But Ken knew his father would not be content with that. Thun-

derhead would be just as much of a menace on the
Goose Bar Ranch as he was on the plains. Rob would
want him got rid of, gelded, sold, given away, shot!
*He* wouldn't care!

It made Ken feel tragic and bitter and desperate. If
only things would work around so that Thunderhead
could race again.

"Hi, Ken," said Ross, "how about it?"

"What you goin' to do with him, Ken?" persisted the
Sheriff. "You know you can't ever take a chance of his
getting on the range again."

"No," joined in Jeff Stevens loudly, "you got to keep
him off'n the range! If ye don't, us ranchers'll do it for
ye!"

"Dear me! What a violent sort of life!" said Mrs.
Palmer.

"I'm going to race him," said Ken, burning his boats
behind him. He didn't look at his father. This was as
good a way as any to ask permission to do the thing
he was longing to do.

"Sure enough, Ken?" asked Tim. "You figurin' to put
him in Mr. Greenway's Free-For-All again?"

Ken was gathering courage. "This time, I'll ride him
myself," he declared, "and he'll win."

"I believe he might at that," said Greenway, "if he
were ridden by someone who can manage him. He's
got the speed."

"I can manage him," said Ken bitterly.

"But he ought to be in a steeplechase," said Carey,
"because he's such a good jumper."

"Yes," Ken grew bolder. "That's what I was figur-
ing."

"Maybe the American Grand National at Belmont
in November? He and Jewel can both be entered."
Carey clasped her hands and rocked where she sat.

"Oh, wouldn't that be fun! I wonder which one would win!"

The Sheriff turned to Rob. "How about that, Mr. McLaughlin?"

Rob was busy filling his pipe. He answered quietly. "Ken goes to school. He's going to keep on going. How could a kid go around to race tracks with a stallion?"

"Lots of money in it," said one of the men.

"Sometimes. But what kind of a life? What father would want to make a race tout out of his son? *You* know, Greenway—what would you say to that?"

"Make him stick to his muttons, McLaughlin. If he gets mixed up with race horses and racing he'll descend to my level."

There was a guffaw of laughter which Ken took to himself. "But wouldn't *you* want to race your horse if he was a winner, Dad?" he asked passionately.

Rob grinned. "I'm just human enough, Ken, that I would. If a man raises horses, it's just about impossible to avoid having hopes for them. He wants them to turn out the finest there are. And that usually leads to the race course."

"But why shouldn't it?" inquired one of the fire brigade, mystified that there were any arguments whatever against so glorious a career as horse racing.

"Ask Mr. Greenway here," said Rob.

Greenway answered, "It's a tragic thing that the horse, the finest of all animals, has been so exploited. Though I am a racing man myself I must admit that by and large they are a tough crowd."

"It's the money," said Mr. Gage, the bank president. "Men make such a killing now and then that all the gamblers and slickers in the world hang around."

"That's it," said Rob. "And, too, there's a certain

self-glorification—"

Greenway laughed. "That's right. The owner gets to thinking he's the horse—does all the runnin'—wins all the prizes."

There was more laughter at this. Then Ross and Tim said good night and mounted their horses and rode away.

Mr. Gildersleeve and the banker were next to leave; the crowd melted.

Ken went to bed in an agony about Thunderhead. What would be done to him? Don't think about it . . . just think about having him again . . . standing against that arching neck, feeling those great muscles ripple . . . and to know him his own again . . . to get on that fierce back and be carried through the air . . . like flying or sailing. . . .

A strange feeling ran through his body. It felt like the electric heat that charged the stallion and that, when one rode him, fused them into one.

# 31

Going upstairs to her room, Carey kept rehearsing it. "Go chase yourself! Go chase yourself!" Her courage was still high. Of course it would not be those rude words, it would just be some act of independence that would show her grandmother, once and for all, that she was a little girl no longer.

What if her grandmother were really sick? But for the first time Carey was doubtful of this.

Late that night she rose up on her elbow in bed and looked across the big old-fashioned room to where her grandmother was sleeping in the other double bed. Her breath came slowly and regularly, now and then with a deep snore.

It was hearty, healthy breathing. As a matter of fact she never had attacks of any sort at night and yet she had said she must have Carey in the same room with her in case she had a heart attack. Thinking long and seriously about this, Carey decided that her grandmother's spells, convincing and pitiable as they were, occurred mostly when things did not go her way. Well, then, the time had come to rebel. She must turn on her inner alarm clock for five next morning, and if there was any interference, be ready to put her grandmother in her place.

It was too hot to sleep. Not a breath of air came in through the wide-open window. Carey put the sheet down from her and kicked it to the foot of the bed with a motion that said, "go chase yourself." Then she sat up, drew her nightgown off over her head and defiantly threw it aside. She put the pillow away and lay flat, a long slender shape of nakedness, her hair thrown upward so that it would not heat her neck.

Now she felt much more courageous. A car whizzed past on the highway outside the window. A train whistle, far away, echoed in the mountains. These sounds from outside gave her a sense of the world, of life beyond herself that she could seize and be one with, if only she could grow up and have courage.

She woke promptly at five. Her grandmother was still asleep. Downstairs there were sounds of people stirring in the kitchen—the stove being rattled. There were voices—that one sounded like Ken's!

Moving noiselessly she fastened her bra and drew on her small, white silk shorts. Her bluejeans were in the closet. Taking an enormous silent step across the room, she turned to look over her shoulder at her grandmother. She met the fierce grey eyes, wide open, blazing.

"What on earth are you doing?"

"I was—je-jess g-g-getting up—"

"Well, just get back!"

Carey leaped back into bed and pulled up the sheet, then lay there scolding herself and calling herself a coward.

Later, when it was time to get up, her grandmother played a different part. Carey was "Dearie" and "my pet," "my own little girl." Mrs. Palmer told Carey how she had missed her during the last month, how lonely she had been, how hard it had been to have no help when she was ill, only the servants.

Carey went downstairs to breakfast with her, then out onto the porch. And wrote letters for her grandmother. And held her wool. And took a walk. And rocked and rocked, her eyes on the faraway peaks of the Mummy Range.

That night Rob had a talk with Nell over the long distance telephone. They exchanged their news. Rob missed her awfully and told her so. He told her of the horses, so conveniently trapped near the headwaters of the Spindle River.

"They're in the bag."

"Are they really?"

"Yep. In a bottom between two ridges. At the north end we'll build a corral."

"Can you get men enough?"

"Get men enough! The trouble is in keeping them away. We've got some of the owners of the stolen mares. They've come from all over the state. And don't forget the local interest, the Deputy Sheriff, the Bank President, the Newspaper owner, the fire brigade and every male, sound in wind and limb, over fourteen. Why, the horse is famous!"

"Jewel?"

"Jewel nothing! Thunderhead!" Rob spoke proudly.

"How many mares are there?"

"We can't count exactly, they're in and out of the brush and I don't let anyone get close to them. Don't want to scare them. But there are more than I thought. He's picked up some more. Perhaps twenty."

"Twenty mares! That's a full band!"

"Yep. He's a rustler!"

"Have you seen Jewel?"

"There are a number of black mares. We can't tell one from the other from a distance."

"How about colts?"

"Lousy with 'em. He sure has done a good job with that band—fed them well—a colt running beside every mare. There are two Palominos."

"Any white colts?"

"Not one."

"Funny, isn't it?"

"No, it's natural. He's a throwback. The Albino didn't reproduce himself, he reproduced the dams."

"Have you talked to Ken about Thunderhead?"

"What about him?"

"About what's to be done with him."

"No."

"Well, what is?"

"Ken's got an idea."

"Oh, Rob!"

"Yeah! He wants to race him again!"

"*Rob!*"

"You might know."

"What do you tell him?"

"I don't even talk to him."

"You wouldn't consider it, would you?"

"Certainly not! Keep him out of school again?"

"He's been doing pretty well in school."

"Nell, don't you back him up in this!"

"No, Rob, I think you're absolutely right."

Rob fumed. "Racing! It's like a drug. It gets into the blood. Once you're bitten by the racing bug there's no hope for you."

"Well, what *are* you going to do with Thunderhead?"

"You know as well as I."

"What?"

"Well, I can't bring him home."

"Of course not."

"And he has to be kept off the range."

"Certainly."

"So there's only one thing left."

Nell was silent. The silence dragged on. "Hello!" said Rob. "Are you there, Nell?"

"Yes, darling, I'm here. I was just thinking. She gave a little groan. "Of course Ken will be broken hearted but I think you're right. Go on and geld him."

"Yep."

There was another long silence. Then Rob said, "There's a good veterinarian in town. I'll have him do it as soon as we get Thunderhead into the corral. I'll not take the chance of his getting away again. This way, we can have him at the ranch, he will be a magnificent saddle horse for Ken."

"Yes." Nell heaved a sigh. "It should really have been done long ago. Are you going to tell Ken?"

"Tell him nuthin'," said Rob gruffly. "When he sees it done, he'll know it."

There was another long silence from Nell, then a sigh. "Yes," she said.

Mr. Ashley Gildersleeve rented himself a horse and, in his business suit and with a large cigar in his mouth, attached himself to the riders who were guarding the ravine. Lady Godiva was not going to get away from him again if he could help it.

# 32

The sky was brazen. The trees on the mountains stood breathless, not a leaf moving.

In the dust holes out in the Spindle River bottom the mares lay down and rolled, kicking their heels. There was a delicious tickling as the hot sand sifted through the hair to the skin. The great bodies writhed on their backs, like big foolish fish with helpless bellies exposed. Not every mare could complete the roll-over. It took a big squirm and heave. They twisted until every inch had been scratched by the hot sand, then thrust out their forefeet and, bracing against them, lurched up. Then came the violent shuddering which shook them free of dust and sand and caked sweat. After the roll and shake every mare was as refreshed and invigorated as a lady after a Swedish massage.

On the borders of the ravine and between the winding washes and rivulets was an abundance of half-cured grass, burnt umber in color. This was its most nourishing stage. While the perpetually hungry mares grazed, the colts slept flat on their sides, or they pretended to graze a little, too, copying their mothers, trying to reach the grass which they could only do by stretching their little short necks and spreading wide their forelegs.

In the evenings when the light was low and tinged with a rosy gold, they romped like children. The delicate little bodies took on sportive attitudes, heads pulled up and back, little hairy chins tucked in. They bucked and kicked, they reared and pretended to fight one another, tiny forefeet flailing the air. Then they would drop to the ground and gallop wildly about making a small sound of thunder.

In the pine forests above the northern end of the ravine, a thousand poles were felled. Here on this government reserve were whole mountains of trees so straight they deviated from the perpendicular only about two inches in fifty feet. There were few branches, they stood too thick. Great numbers of them died, due to the overcrowding, and these the government was glad to have cut and taken out.

The work of cutting the timber and bulding the forty-by-forty-foot corral went on quickly and quietly. No hammers or nails were used. Posthole diggers made the holes for the uprights, the long poles were fastened against them by baling wire.

And then the wings, wings a hundred feet long, seven feet high.

"I should think," said Greenway as he and Rob rode slowly along the mountain side above the corral," that six-foot wings and fences would have been high enough."

"Six-foot fences would be high enough for the mares," said Rob, "there won't be any trouble with them at all. They've all been handled, they'd trot right into the corral and look for oats. Unless he has picked up some wild mares as well. Buck was saying he thought there were some wild mares in the bunch—but Thunderhead is the only one there will be trouble with, and if he really wanted to get over a six-foot fence, he'd manage it somehow."

Greenway whistled. "Six feet! Great Scott! Why, no corral or pasture will hold him!"

"That's the devil of it."

"What are you going to do with him when he's caught?"

Rob laughed. "Theme song! What to do with Thunderhead! You wouldn't like to buy him, would you?"

"If I did, the first thing I'd do would be geld him. How does it happen he hasn't been gelded before this? He's certainly not a horse for the stud."

"That young son of mine. Now and again a colt dies of the gelding, you know, one or two of ours have —Ken was determined no chances should be taken with this love-of-his-life. He'd manage it one way or the other—luck, too. One year, when I had the vet come out Thunderhead couldn't be found. I let it go till the next year and then Ken talked me out of it."

"Six feet!" Greenway was still marveling. "And no training except what Ken has given him. No wonder the boy has ideas about putting him in jump races. Why wouldn't that be a way out for you, McLaughlin? He might win, someone would buy him and your troubles would be over."

"It isn't practicable," said Rob. He was about to add, "Besides, it's not necessary—I'm going to have him gelded before he ever gets out of this corral we're building," but decided to keep this to himself. "Look over there," he pointed to a purple cloud just pushing over the mountains to the north. "We're going to have weather. This heat is due to break."

Greenway was wiping his neck with his handkerchief. "It would suit me if it was snow," he said. "This heat gets me."

"Maybe it will snow. No telling. Any time after the Fourth of July, comes winter."

"Rob, I want to ask you something."

"Shoot."

"I'd like to take Ken back with me to the Blue Moon for a visit of a few weeks—or as long as you can spare him."

Rob said doubtfully, "That's certainly very kind of you—"

"Not kind at all—purely selfish. Carey and he are great pals—have you noticed them together?"

Rob turned to face him and both men burst into a laugh. "I sure have!"

"Well, that child of mine doesn't have enough companionship with young people of her own age. She's had the time of her life with you and your wife and your boys this summer and it's been good for her and I want it to go on."

Rob asked, "How will your sister feel about this?"

There flashed through Greenway's mind the conversation between himself and his sister which had taken place that morning at the breakfast table. Carey had left the room and he had taken the opportunity to announce that, if Rob would consent, he was going to take Ken back to the Blue Moon Ranch with them.

Mrs. Palmer had expressed herself with her usual vigor. "What on earth has got into you! Surely you can see that the boy has fallen in love with Carey?"

"That's just the reason."

"You wouldn't encourage such a thing!"

"You've got the wrong slant on it. They're just kids. Carey's happy. Every girl is happy when she has a nice boy around. Carey has lived too much alone. It didn't matter so much when she was just a child, but she's growing up and I want her to have more freedom and to be more with boys and girls of her own age and we can begin with Ken McLaughlin."

That had just about floored her, and then, in case she should start something, he had added chuckling, "and don't pull a fainting spell or an attack of asthma, Caroline. You can't put that over on me. This time I've made up my mind and it stands."

Rob was looking at him, waiting for him to answer. Greenway cleared his throat with a little embarrassment. "In a matter like this, it's my say-so. But I don't mind telling you, Rob, that I'm quite worried about the way my sister has got Carey under her thumb. She's a very imperious woman. She won't have anything to do with anyone she can't rule. Except me. The way I've managed, I live my own life, keep out of her way, kid her a little bit, let her do as she wants. But when it comes to Carey—it's a—" He hesitated.

"Well," said Rob slowly, "I've noticed a good deal of that. Is she really ill?"

"I wish I knew. She has a doctor come to see her at home, a tame cat. In my opinion she makes her own diagnoses, tells *him* what's the matter with *her*, what she ought to eat, do, how people ought to treat her, then pulls that on Carey and me and anyone she wants to rule. He falls for it. She turns on her charm—she's got charm, you know."

"Yes, and knows how to use it," said Rob. "But surely, when it comes to Carey, you can do what you think best?"

"It's not so easy. I haven't interfered much so far because Carey is so young and, by and large, has been happy and well. But I admit I have often had a sinking sensation when I thought about what would happen when the time comes for the girl to marry."

"You'd better look out or Carey will never marry.

Many a time, a character like your sister's has made an old maid of a girl."

"I know it. She did her best to prevent her daughter's marriage, and she'll do her best to prevent Carey's."

"That accounts for the way she looks at Ken. As if she would like to poison him."

Greenway laughed. "Yes, he's the enemy right now. But it's more than that. Carey is growing up. Her life is opening out. And she feels Carey escaping her!"

"She won't let her," said Rob.

Greenway looked distraught. "The worst of it is, the thing that ties my hands, is that the child is so tenderhearted. And she loves her dearly! Always has!"

Rob was silent. He could understand. To be ruled does not to a child seem cruel. And the habits of love and obedience have tendrils that clutch and cling long into the years.

He said, "You look out, or she'll ruin your little girl's life."

"No," said Greenway, "I shan't give in to her. The thing that will do it is to send Carey away to college. Meanwhile, let me have Ken. There's another reason I want him, Rob."

"Yes?"

"He did a wonderful job training his stallion."

"Yes, I can say that for him."

"Well, Jewel is going to need a lot of training and I'd like your boy to do it."

"Jewel will be in good condition. This life on the range puts them into top form."

"She may have a foal."

"Even so, she won't be soft. I'll wager she'll be in racing form by October or November."

"All the same, she'll need training and Ken's the one

to do it."

Rob still did not answer. As between having the gelding done with Ken looking on, or away at Blue Moon Ranch, he preferred the latter. Then, when Ken returned he would be presented with a *fait accompli.*

"Well, all right, Greenway. I consent and I think it'll be a fine thing for Ken."

"That's settled then. I am delighted and I know Carey will be."

Rob pointed down at the camp. "Look, smoke! Time for lunch."

They rode down and dismounted, and joined the men.

Ross Buckley had got a fire going and a big pot of coffee was cooking on it. The men opened the lunch boxes and took out thick ham sandwiches.

Greenway sat on a fallen log and listened to the talk and looked around. He sniffed the warm air, pungent with pine needles and hot earth. He felt the simplicity and beauty of his surroundings. Carey should have been here—his eyes wandered, looking for Ken.

Ken stood at a little distance where the horses were tied. He was about to put the bag of oats on Flicka's nose when suddenly the mare raised her head, pricked her ears sharply, looked down the ravine and gave a ringing neigh.

Rob jumped up and most of the men did likewise. Greenway half expected to see the white stallion burst out of the brush and come plunging toward them.

"Look out what you're doing!" yelled Rob.

Ken was already turning Flicka around, trying to interest her in her oats. The other horses had looked up but were now quietly munching. There was no answering neigh from the ravine.

Ken came to the fire, took his mug of coffee and sat

down on a rock. Greenway studied his face, noting
something wistful in the eyes, something stubborn in
the mouth—all of it very sensitive, quick, and *handsome*. Gad! no wonder Carey—

"Ken," he said, "your Dad and I've been cooking up
a plan that concerns you."

Ken looked up, "You have, sir?"

"Yes. I'm looking for someone to train Jewel for me.
How'd you like to come to the Blue Moon with me
and put some good work on that filly?"

"You mean right now?" Ken's face flushed clear to
the top of his brow. He was thinking, *Carey! Carey*—

"Yes. As soon as we've caught her."

"Why, gosh! Mr. Greenway, that'd be keen—" His
eyes swung over to his father. "Did Dad say I could?"

"Certainly. I think it would be a nice visit for you."

Ken's eyes lingered on his father's face and his own
expression changed. He felt worried. There was
something so smooth about the way his father had
said that. Suddenly he gave a sharp exclamation,
"Oh!" and then was silent. While the men talked he
sat thinking. Thunderhead—he couldn't leave Thunderhead. As if his thoughts had been audible, one of
the men asked.

"What's going to be done with Thunderhead?"

Rob was silent. Every man present was willing to
contribute suggestions. No one had as yet had a good
look at either Thunderhead or the filly. The sides of
the ravine were timbered nearly to the top. To reach
the corral site the men rode out on an old lumber trail
along the outer side of the ridge. And Rob had given
orders that no one was to go close to the horses.

Ken answered in the negative. "I don't want him
gelded," he said.

"A lad of one idea," said Rob sarcastically.

Ken looked stubborn.

"Why Ken, geldin' won't hurt him none," said Tim.

"It *might* kill him," said Ken.

"Could happen, but ain't likely."

"Besides," said Ken, "he would never be the same again."

"Ken means," said Rob in the same mocking manner, "that he would never be the great Thunderhead, any more!"

The men gulped down their coffee from their big tin mugs.

"But gol'durn it, Ken, what use is he?" demanded Hank Percy, tall leathery woodsman from one of the lumber camps.

"What I tell him," said Rob, "is that, whether or no he wants Thunderhead gelded, it's going to be done, either by a good veterinarian with clean instruments or by a rusty old pocket knife in the hands of some enraged rancher."

"Better let me have him, Captain," said the persistent Ross as he tended the fire, "don't take any o' that ginger outen him."

Ken's face was pale and set. Here it was. The same jam he had been in after Thunderhead lost the race at Saginaw Falls, only now he couldn't say that there was a valley in which he could lock the stallion up and keep him out of trouble.

Greenway saw the look of despair on Ken's face. All about a horse! The boy must love him! He said, "You told us what you *didn't* want, but what *do* you want? What do you figure is the right life for that horse?"

Ken's eyes dropped to the ground and he said in a low voice, "What I liked for him was the life he lived up there in the Valley of the Eagles, and—" he jerked his elbow southward toward the ravine, "down there with his mares and colts. Only I'd like him close enough so I could ride him now and then."

The men laughed.

"And race him, too," suggested Tim, "that's what you said the other night."

They joshed Ken about the fairy story he was weaving.

"If he ain't to be gelded, you'll have to take him home and keep him," said Percy.

Rob answered, "I've got one stallion on the ranch already. And if I brought another stallion there, you can figure for yourself what would happen."

Ross said, "Only thing with a horse like that is, race him, or put him in rodeos. That way you can git the good of all his orneriness."

To race him! This was the conclusion Ken had come to a hundred times himself. The only way out. He stole a look at his father. But Rob was busy filling his pipe.

Lunch finished, the fire doused and Mr. Greenway said he was going back to town. Ken asked permission from his father to go with him.

As they rode along the lumber trail Ken said, "Mr. Greenway, I'm awful sorry, but I don't think I can go up there with you to the Blue Moon."

"Why not, Ken?"

"Well, because of Thunderhead. You see, we haven't really decided what to do with him, and I'd be afraid to leave him with anybody else."

"Afraid!"

"Yes."

Greenway pulled up his horse, Ken turned to face him and they looked into each other's eyes. "I'll be damned," thought Greenway, "he believes his father is going to geld the horse the minute his back is turned."

Without saying anything, they started forward again. Greenway was still in deep thought. By the time they had come to the place where the trail crossed the ridge, he had decided the boy was right. That was just what Rob McLaughlin was going to do.

"Don't know as I blame him," muttered Greenway. "But I don't blame the kid either. He'd better stick tight."

"What did you say, sir?"

"Just thinking out loud." He pulled up his horse again and slung the field glasses off his shoulder. He aimed them at the bottom, and through them could see the horses moving in the underbrush.

"Want a look?" he handed the glasses to Ken.

Suddenly there was an exclamation from Ken. "Oh, gosh! There he is!" He dropped the glasses and strained his naked eyes and saw the whiteness of the stallion crossing a patch of green. Mr. Greenway took the glasses, put them to his eyes, and had a glimpse.

"Well, there he is," he said, as they moved on again. "And little he knows that he has come to the end of his career of crime." He looked, smiling, at Ken. "Gives you a big thrill, I guess, at the idea of having him again?"

Ken's face was all lit up. "And how!" he kept turning in his saddle to look back.

"Ken, I'd like to help you out."

Ken looked at the old gentleman questioningly.

"Suppose we take Thunderhead with us to the Blue Moon?"

Ken's face went blank. He thought hard.

"You see, I want *you* to come and if I can't get you without the stallion—"

"Gosh, Mr. Greenway!"

"Well, will you come?"

"Will I come! You bet I will! Mr. Greenway, I'm ever so much obliged. You don't know what a fix this gets me out of."

"Does it? Seems to me it merely postpones the fix a few weeks longer."

But Ken's thoughts were racing ahead. With Thunderhead at the Blue Moon where they had a practice track and professional trainers—of course, Thunderhead would make a sensation—they'd all be out of their heads with amazement at what he could do—and Mr. Greenway being a racing man—and rich —of course, it would all lead to Thunderhead's going into another race— Ah-h-h! The starting bugle! The jockey's silks! the horses galloping around the track, and this time himself in the saddle!

Mr. Greenway was saying calmly, "We'll locate a double trailer and put Thunderhead and Jewel in it together. They ought to be good friends after this year spent together."

So Carey, after having felt toward Ken as she would feel toward a young lover from whose side she was to be torn in a few days, now had to feel toward him as she would feel toward a young fellow who was to be her companion for weeks. Quite different! She became extremely reserved.

And Mrs. Palmer, not knowing how to register her displeasure, adopted the attitude of piteousness and tremulous bravery which she knew from long practice was the hardest of all on her granddaughter.

And Rob, when he talked again to Nell over the telephone, said, "Isn't it the damndest thing how events work around so that Ken gets what he wants? What do you bet he doesn't get to race Thunderhead again?"

# 33

Now that Mr. Greenway had taken a stand, Carey went out every day with Ken on horseback. They had lunch at the corral with the men. Carey, in bluejeans, made herself useful, or tried to, anxious to be part of the activity. And riding home along the ridge with Ken they would stop and hold the binoculars to their eyes, excited if they caught a glimpse of the stallion or some of the mares and colts. And when Carey saw any one of the black mares through the glasses, she would cry, "There she is!" One of them must be Jewel.

Occasionally they joined Buck Daly where he had made his camp on the inner side of the ridge near the mouth of the canyon. He had found a place on the mountainside from which he could see the whole valley and every movement of the horses. Sometimes he rode up to the camp to see how the work was progressing. Sometimes, on foot, he wandered over the country with his silent Indian step. Buck never had much to say.

In spite of all this freedom Carey was not happy. Mrs. Palmer was ailing. The piteousness had turned into pain and dizziness and breathlessness.

One morning—it was the day on which the corral and wings were to be finished—Carey came down to the hotel dining-room in a dress instead of riding clothes. She explained to her uncle that she would not be able to go out to the camp with them, because her grandmother was staying in bed and she had to bring her meals up. Carey was downcast for tomorrow was the round-up.

Without a word, Mr. Greenway rose from the breakfast table and went upstairs.

He found his sister sitting up against pillows, a thin silk bed jacket over her shoulders and a copy of the *Westgate Weekly Sentinel* in her hands.

He drew up a chair beside the bed and took hold of her wrist at which she put her paper aside and looked at him in astonishment. He said gravely, "What is the matter with you, Caroline?"

"I am feeling very badly," she answered with hauteur.

"You need some castor oil, about five ounces."

"Don't be vulgar, Beaver."

"Well, what is it then?"

"My heart has been jumping and fluttering and I have dizzy spells. This intense heat is very bad for me."

"I believe there is a good doctor in Westgate, I'll try to look him up and send him in to see you. Perhaps we had better postpone our departure tomorrow?"

"We are leaving tomorrow?"

"The work is practically finished. We will drive the horses into the corral early tomorrow morning. Then there is nothing to keep us. We can leave immediately."

"I shall be very glad to leave this place." She sank back weakly against her pillows. "You don't know what it is like to be ill and alone in a strange place. Carey has been constantly away from me."

"For the last few days she has, because I insisted on it. But I do not want you to be left without attention if you are ill. That is why I spoke of getting the doctor. Or a nurse."

"I do not need a nurse. There is nothing that Carey cannot do."

"Carey cannot do *anything* today and tomorrow. She is going out to the camp with us today and when we round up the horses tomorrow. After all, Caroline, have a heart! Give her a chance to have some fun!"

Color came into the invalid's face, and rage into her eyes. She sat up with surprising vigor.

"Am *I* to have no consideration? Where do *I* stand in this household, I'd like to know!"

His lips set. "I am tired of seeing that child carrying trays and hot compresses and hot-water bottles. From now on, Caroline, you must have a nurse."

"I will *not* have a nurse! I will not be made into an invalid!"

At this, her brother burst out laughing. "I am delighted to hear it. If you don't need a nurse, you don't need Carey. I'll tell her to come up and get her riding clothes on."

Mrs. Palmer's rage boiled over. "You get out of my room and mind your own business!"

At that moment Carey entered carrying the breakfast tray. She closed the door and stood transfixed at sight of her uncle just rising from his chair by the bedside and her grandmother leaping out of bed in pursuit of him.

"Calm yourself, Caroline," Mr. Greenway backed away. "I think I had better stay and finish this discussion, now that it has started. Carey had better hear."

"Oh, Uncle Beaver, what is it? Grandma, what is the matter?"

"Get out, Beaver, get out of my room!"

Mr. Greenway made no move to obey.

Tremblingly Carey put the tray down on the table and said, clasping her hands, "Oh, Uncle Beaver, she'll have a terrible heart spell! You'd better go. I'll take care of her!"

At this, Mrs. Palmer sank weakly on the edge of the bed and dramatically clutched her throat.

But Mr. Greenway was prepared. "No. I shall not go until this is settled."

Mrs. Palmer sprang to her feet again, her bare toe caught in a loose strand of the rag rug which was beside her bed and she lost her balance. Her brother leaped to catch her but he too slipped and they crashed to the floor together.

Her screams were deafening. Mr. Greenway scrambled hastily to his feet and, exclaiming, "She's in hysterics!" seized the water pitcher and emptied it on her face.

Mrs. Palmer's hysterics turned to choking and sputtering. Carey brought a towel, knelt beside her grandmother and tenderly wiped her face. She looked reproachfully at her uncle who helped her raise the old lady and put her in bed again. She was now sobbing.

"Oh, Uncle Beaver!" reproached Carey, leaning down to put her arms around her grandmother.

"I feel like a brute," muttered Greenway. "Caroline, I didn't mean to knock you down, I hope you don't think that."

Wearily she turned her head and sobbed, "Oh, go away! Go away!"

He stood there stubbornly. "I want Carey to have her freedom. Let that be understood."

"Carey can do anything she wants to do." The old lady said this as if there had never been any question of the opposite. A loving smile broke through her tears as she looked into the face of the girl, which hung above her, tender as a Madonna. She laid her hand on her cheek. "Why, little childie! Do you think your grandmother does not want you to be happy? To have all the fun you want to have? Go, my pet, go with your uncle. Put on your riding clothes and ride off into the hills with that boy!" She ended with a tragic wave of the hand.

"Come, Carey," said her uncle. But his niece looked at him indignantly.

"Do you think I would leave her like this? Her gown is soaked. It has to be changed."

"I will wait outside while you do that."

"But she is fearfully wrought up. I will read to her and quiet her."

"If she is going to need constant attention, I shall get a nurse."

"I will not have a nurse!" It was a furious scream.

"Well, then, you'll have to stay alone."

"I'll stay today, Uncle Beaver—just today."

"What about tomorrow?"

Carey hesitated. Mrs. Palmer evidently decided that she had better consolidate the small gain she had made. "I shall be better tomorrow, I am sure. If Carey will stay with me today—"

"Let me, Uncle Beaver!"

"All right. But this is the last time."

As the door closed behind him, Carey brought a dry nightgown for her grandmother and helped her change. The old lady, with a sigh of relief, leaned back against the pillows, held out her arms and turned her gaze upon Carey.

Carey dropped on her knees beside the bed. The old arms closed about her. "My pet! My childikins! Don't cry so, it's all right! He didn't mean it. Your uncle is a good man."

"But oh, Grandma!"

"Now, there—there—" She smoothed Carey's hair. "What is this all about? Is my dearie unhappy? Is there something she should be telling her Grandma?"

Carey did not answer. She was crying.

"You aren't keeping anything from me, are you, pet?"

Carey withdrew a little and felt for her handkerchief. The old lady, with her charming, irresistible smile drew Carey's hands into hers and with her own handkerchief wiped away the tears. Carey was thinking furiously. Her grandmother had always wanted the most complete confidence. To keep anything from her was a crime. There must be no secrets. But Ken— she couldn't tell about Ken—there wasn't anything to tell—except those few kisses.

"Well, my precious?"

Carey could not lie, she was not expert enough to evade.

Her grandmother laughed softly as if she understood all and considered it no sin, nothing of great importance, only natural. "Tell me, Carey—"

"Well, I don't know," Carey hesitated.

"This boy—Kenneth McLaughlin—he seems a very nice boy and I like his parents. Has there been something between you? Is that what you want to tell me, dear?"

Carey clasped her hands and the hot color flooded her face. "Oh, nothing much, Grandma, only I do like him."

"Has he—said anything? Tried to—?"

Carey turned her face still farther away. Her ear was scarlet. "Well, he—" her sentence did not end.

"Kissed you?" said her Grandma playfully.

Carey nodded without speaking.

"When?"

"One night."

"Where were you?"

"It was outside the house. I heard the puppy crying. I went out to him. Ken came, too." Suddenly Carey was in a panic. In a moment it was going to come out that she had been in bed; had gone out in her pajamas—

But her grandmother's mind was on another angle of the scene. "Did you *let* him kiss you?"

Carey nodded silently. Her grandmother said nothing. After a long minute of suspense, Carey turned to look into her face and saw there a look of scathing condemnation. The grey eyes blazed from between narrow slits. The mouth was twisted in scorn. The face cried to her, *"So! I got it out of you! Now I know! I had suspected as much!"* And Carey, to the very foundation of her being, felt the shock of this betrayal! She jumped to her feet.

"Grandma! I'll never tell you anything again as long as I live!"

Mrs. Palmer reared up in her bed. "You won't tell me! *You* won't! It's I that will do the telling! And I tell you now that that boy is not going back to the ranch with us!"

Carey began to shake all over. She stood, battling her tears, not knowing what to do or say. The huge injustice of it! How could she! And she made her resolves, passionately, never to trust her grandmother again, to turn elsewhere for love, to put behind her, forever and ever, her childish dependence upon her.

She looked into her grandmother's face with eyes that were hard in spite of the trembling of her lips. Mrs. Palmer seemed suddenly to grow weak, sank back, turned her head sideways and allowed her face to quiver piteously.

"I feel very weak—I've had nothing to eat yet—"

Long habit made the girl penitent. "Oh, Grandma! Your breakfast! It's all cold. You just wait. I'll go down and bring you everything hot."

Carey brought another breakfast tray. Mrs. Palmer glanced at it with a pretence of indifference, but the pot of coffee, the pile of toast, the bowl of jam and the tempting odors made it impossible to conceal her greediness. She allowed herself to be helped to a sitting position, and a small table bearing the tray was pushed close to the edge of the bed.

She began to eat. Carey seated herself in the rocking chair and looked out the window, her face pale and woebegone. The atmosphere of the room was horrible. To be at outs with the one who had always been closest—it dragged at her heart. She did not know how she could bear it—did not know where to turn. And there was a great hollow sinking within her, because Ken was not going back with them. Today, tomorrow—these were the last days she would have to see him.

She realized that tears were running down her cheeks. She found her handkerchief and wiped them away.

The breakfast was finished. She drew away the table. Her grandmother looked up at her brightly. "I feel better! You know, dearie, I think the attack has passed over! I shall be all right alone. Now you put on your riding clothes and go out and have a good time."

Carey rode furiously along the ridge road. Her face burned. She was unhappy, she was worn out, she was full of bitter disappointment and full of fear and doubt for the future. It was good to give Redwing his head and to feel her body swinging to his motion, her hair blown back, her cheeks blazing hot. Ken—if only she could tell Ken all about it. If she did, *he* would not betray her, he would be on *her* side, he would fight for her. At any rate it was all lined up for tomorrow. She would see the round-up, would see Jewel! And suddenly all her care was tossed aside. With a surge of happiness she gave a loud yell and flung her head back and swung her arm. Redwing leaped and turned her head, wondering what had happened. Carey burst out laughing and galloped down the last incline to the camp with a face so happy, so starryeyed, that Ken as he came to meet her, smiled too, wondering what had happened. . . .

Next morning, Mr. Greenway was halfway through his breakfast and still neither Carey nor his sister had come down. It was nearly eight-thirty; Rob and Ken McLaughlin had breakfasted and left for the stables. Two or three other tables were occupied and the waitress was bustling in and out the swinging door which led to the big kitchen at the back of the building.

Mr. Greenway was mopping up the last of the maple syrup on his plate with the last piece of flapjack when he glanced up, his eye caught by a swift movement out in the hall, and saw Carey, carrying a blanket and a flatiron, coming out of the kitchen and going toward the stairs. She was dressed in her riding clothes.

He had seen his niece carrying blanket and flatirons before, and felt a quick anger which would almost have done credit to his sister. He rose abruptly and pursued the girl.

"What's the meaning of this, Carey?"

"Lumbago! I can't go out with you."

"Is it real or fake?" he roared.

"I—I—don't know!"

He dropped her arm and she hurried one way, up the stairs, and he the other way toward the kitchen door. He opened it. Three women were there: one waitress in her neat, striped cotton dress; the other waitress, the older one, a dark, weary woman, was cooking the breakfasts; and Mrs. Evans who was the proprietress of the hotel, and also the cook, was seated at the kitchen table having a cup of coffee. Mrs. Evans' bare arm, as she raised her coffeecup, was like a great ham.

"Anybody here know anything about nursing?" he called out, holding the door open.

Mrs. Evans put down her coffeecup, wiped her mouth, and pushed her chair back. Her bright pink face, framed in a fluff of blonde hair, was so fat that it sagged forward as she leaned over, propping herself against the table.

"I do. Anybody sick?" she boomed.

"Know anything about lumbago?"

She was already taking off her apron and moving across the room to hang it up. She must have weighed two hundred pounds, he thought, tall as well as broad and with the voice of a man.

"Did you ever use an iron on the back of a person with lumbago?"

She took off her apron. "My grandfather. Had it all the time. Red flannel's the best. Horse liniment's good —wait a minute, I'll get the bottle." She waddled to the corner where there was a wall cabinet and took out a bottle. They went upstairs together.

Without knocking they entered Mrs. Palmer's room. Mr. Greenway pointed to the bed where Mrs. Palmer was lying flat, her eyes half-closed in suffering. She emitted a faint groan with every breath.

Carey, standing beside her, had the flatiron in one

hand.

As her uncle entered the room she said, "She won't turn over!"

Mrs. Evans moved to the bedside and took the iron from Carey's hand.

Mrs. Palmer's eyes flew wide open.

Mr. Greenway took Carey's arm. "Come on. There's nothing more for you to do." He strode toward the door, dragging Carey along with him.

"But, Uncle Beaver! I must tell her how!"

He did not pause. Carey looked backward. "She's got to turn over."

"I'll turn her over."

Mrs. Evans spit upon her finger and touched it to the iron to test the heat.

"Come on, Carey." Mr. Greenway opened the door.

"What is the meaning of this outrage—Aouh—h—h." Mrs. Palmer's indignation turned into a howl of pain.

"And you have to press down hard!" cried Carey.

"Don't worry. I'll press down hard. You run along with your uncle. I'll take care of her."

Greenway closed the door behind them.

# 34

Thunderhead had known, all week long, of the men who were working at the northern end of the ravine. Now and then, as he grazed, he lifted his head, hearing and feeling the vibration of the feet of galloping horses. But they did not come down into the river bottom. He and his mares were never molested. There was something agreeable in the proximity of men and in the knowledge that work was going on within a few miles of his band. This was like being on the ranch again—the Goose Bar Ranch. Like being a colt, with men coming and going, the sound of voices and laughter and shouts. The smells were all right too. There was no fear, there was no tension or excitement.

In this river bottom was everything he and his mares required. There were thickets of brush into which they could thrust themselves when the flies were bad, scraping them off, scratching themselves deliciously. There were some old salt licks. There were rivulets of fresh water, there were the sand wallows. And in the evenings, when the heat of the day abated and sunset colors spread over the sky, there came something electric from the air which all the horses felt, and they ceased their incessant feeding; while the colts romped, the mares gathered in small groups, gossiping, and Thunderhead himself, standing near Lady Godiva, who was his lead mare, would become very erect, his head high, his ears cocked sharply as he watched over his herd, his body like a taut instrument played upon by waves of enjoyable sensation.

Because of the eastern ridge, the morning sun did not strike the river bottom until nearly six o'clock. When it did, the horses stood broadside to it, their heads hanging low, their bodies completely relaxed as they took their daily bath of ultra-violet.

On this particular morning, as Thunderhead stood, drinking in the level sunrays, he drank in something else too. It began like a feeling of uneasiness. In a human being, it would have been a premonition. In him, it was an increasing alertness. He began to investigate. Within the immediate proximity of his band, which was scattered over a quarter-mile area, there was nothing to cause uneasiness. He trotted a few hundred yards northward, stopped and searched the air. He got the scent of the horses, of the men who had been working on the corral, familiar odors which he had been smelling for a week. Today the air carried the taint of tension and excitement.

He went back to his mares and commenced grazing again, then jerked his head up as he saw the first of the riders advancing from the south. They were strung across the valley. They came slowly.

One mare after the other jerked her head up. The colts sensed the alarm and ran to their mothers, then faced about to stare at the oncoming men. A few of them began to trot away. Presently the whole band was moving northward.

Soon the horses realized they were being driven. This, to the half a dozen or so wild mares which were in the band, was a new and terrifying thing and their fear ran through the entire herd. A group of mares bolted up the western slope, but were met by two riders emerging from the trees. The mares jammed to a stop, wheeled and galloped back to the rest of the band which by now were coming to meet them. Colliding, they reared. Dust rose in clouds. They milled about, then started back down the valley in the direction from which they had come. But the riders bore down upon them.

"Hi, you there! Git a-goin'!"

The mares propped again, flinging up their heads, wheeled, and the whole herd burst into a run, fleeing straight northward toward the corral.

Thunderhead galloped along with them. They tore through the little thickets, leaped boulders, splashed through the shallows of the streams which wound across their paths. Occasionally half a dozen or so were bunched close, running like race horses. At other times they were widely scattered, each finding its own way.

A horse has almost miraculous vision, but fear affects the senses as well as the mind, and it almost blinded them. When, in the distance, the wide arms of the corral wings became visible, the horses did not at first actually see them. In a cloud of dust they rushed into them, their widened nostrils flaring crimson, their eyes ringed with white under streaming manes.

And now more riders burst out of the trees and with shouts and yells bore down upon them.

Thunderhead was in the lead. He did not intend that his band should be caught in that trap. He wheeled and tried to stop them. But the men pressed closer, swinging their ropes. Thunderhead was everywhere at once, snaking between the mares and the open gates, nipping, chopping, forcing them back, but a few rushed past him into the corral. The men came on. Finally all the mares were jammed through, carrying Thunderhead with them. Men quickly dismounted and closed the gates.

Now the frenzy increased. The wild mares milled, rearing to paw against the walls.

Thunderhead soon had them bunched and under control as if, somehow, he could deliver them from this trap. Then he made the complete circle of the corral, seeking an exit. The mares scattered again.

The men climbed the fence or crowded at the gates.

Ken sat on the top rail with Carey beside him. They were wildly excited and yet oppressed by the violence of the scene and the terror of the helpless animals.

Carey murmured constantly, watching the tiny, nimble foals as they wheeled and reared and danced and turned and sped off beside their dams.

"Oh, look at them! Look at them! Aren't they *darling!* The poor little things!"

But Ken was watching Thunderbird, his heart aching for him, understanding every movement the stallion made, every look of the wild eye as he reared up, flung himself around and reversed his direction.

Ross came up the fence beside him, rolling himself a cigarette, and just behind them, on the ground, were Greenway and Collins and some of the other men.

"Where's Jewel?" cried Carey, craning her head to see. "Do you see her, Uncle Beaver? Oh, there she is! Oh, I think I see her, there in the middle with a little black colt!"

The scene which followed was witnessed by all the men, and talked about for many months to come.

Thunderhead made one last tour of the corral, stopping now and then to rear against the walls, to reach up with his nose, seeking some weak place, some crack through which he could escape. There was none. Then it was as if he gave up. He quieted down; they were all quieting down. He still trotted around and around the enclosure, his ears cocked, the crimson lining showing inside his palpitating nostrils, but his pace was slower.

A rope sang out. It was Tad Stevens'. "Thar she is!" he yelled.

Another rope followed and, even while Rob roared, "Cut that out!" and then, frantically, "God-damn it!" the damage was done.

Thunderhead went into the frenzy which a singing rope creates in some horses. He hurled himself at the western fence, leaping as high as he could.

It was a magnificent jump. His great body lifted easily, and then, in the air, seemed forced upward by a second leap of will and determination. Thunderhead could clear a jump of six feet. He couldn't clear this. But his feet were over. He clawed the rest of the way. He balanced on the top of it. He rolled over and turned a complete somersault, righting himself as he landed with a flashing of white legs and flailing of hoofs. He was on his feet! He was unhurt! He was away!

There was complete silence from the spectators, even from the mares, as the stallion streaked up the farther slope and vanished in the trees.

The silence was cut by a shrill whinny from Lady Godiva. She trotted up and down the fence, calling to him again and again.

Suddenly the stallion appeared in a clearing of the woods and turned to look at the corral. A furious, squealing neigh rang from him. Bedlam broke out in the corral. Every mare neighed. Even the colts shrilled their excitement. A wild war whoop from Ross added to the noise, and then came a wave of laughter and profanity from the men.

"The son-of-a-gun!"

"Can you beat that?"

"Hi-ya! Go it, Boy!"

As if he had heard these words Thunderhead was off again. He disappeared into the woods.

"Waal—we got the mares anyway!" This was from Jeff Stevens. Tad had one of his mares roped. He slipped down into the corral, drawing her to him. By her side trotted a long-legged colt, dark brown, promising to be a perfect Morgan in type. Hick Stevens roped the other Morgan mare.

Buck Daly slipped amongst the mares without alarming them, slid a rope around the neck of one and drew her into a corner. It was Jenny. By her side was a perfect little filly.

"Dead spit for her mammy!"

"Oh, where is she? Where is she? I don't see her!"
This was Carey. She straightened her lithe body and
reached one leg down, and then felt the firm grasp of
her uncle's hand on the back of her belt.

"Don't you go into that corral, young lady!"

"But Uncle Beaver, I—"

"Nothing doing."

She went back over the fence to him. "But, Uncle, I
don't see her. I want to hunt for her. Come with me."

"I can't manage that fence." He held her tight. "Collins will go."

Collins went up the fence, puffing. Tim followed.
They got down into the corral and started moving
around the edge of the bunched mares, looking for
Jewel.

Ken sat fussing with the halter he held in his hands.
There was nausea in his stomach and his teeth
chattered slightly. He twisted the leather aimlessly.
Behind him, down there on a rock in the forest, was
Thunderhead's saddle and bridle. He had meant to
ride the stallion back down the ravine to the town.
More than once the triumph, the ecstasy of this ride
had been rehearsed in his mind. Ride him! They
didn't think he could ride him! They were all afraid of
him! And Carey would have seen him do it!

His father was going to be in a terrible rage over
this. Sure as shooting, Thunderhead would start right
in gathering another band of mares. His father—
where was he anyway? Ken didn't want to see him,
not even the back of his head, but suddenly he
couldn't help looking around and, as his eyes clashed
with his father's, it was as if he felt a blow. He looked
quickly back at the halter and bit his teeth together to

stop their shivering.

One after the other, men climbed over the fence into the corral. Dust and the hot smell of sweating horseflesh rose to Ken's nostrils. The mares were quieting down.

The Sheriff was examining the mares. "There's some slicks here," he shouted, and several of the railbirds, men or boys from the town who had come out just to watch the fun, yelled in answer,

"I'll take 'em!"

"Gi' me a chance at 'em!"

"I need a bronc!"

The Sheriff got out his brand book. They broke up the bunched mares. If, for a moment, a foal was separated from its dam, there were the wildest whinnyings, mother and child trying desperately to unite again, wheeling on hind legs, making sudden rushes.

"Got to break 'em first!"

"Break 'em this afternoon! Hold a rodeo here!"

"I'm on!"

Occasionally some man would be in the way when the mares plunged in his direction. He would dive for the fence and pull himself up amid yells of raucous laughter.

Carey's head came up over the top rail beside Ken. Her face was flushed with heat and excitement. Her linen hat was on the back of he head and damp tendrils of dark hair clung to her forehead. Her wide red mouth was open.

Ken glanced down at her.

"Oh, Ken! Ken! Have you seen her?"

Ken shook his head. The nausea was getting worse. He jumped down from the fence, made his way around the corral, and with Thunderhead's halter and rope still on his arm, picked up the stallion's trail and followed it up to the woods. The trail was plain. If he had been on horseback he could have followed it at a canter.

His heart was thudding hard. He sat down on a rock and tried to hold onto himself. Then he lay back flat on the rock and closed his eyes.

Without opening them he knew that the sun had gone behind a cloud. There was a sudden respite from the glare. A faint breath of cooler air moved over his face and he gave a deep sigh and felt his heart steadying. The nausea passed. Strength came back to his arms and legs. He wondered how it was that a disappointment—a really bad disappointment—could make you feel sick so quickly.

He could still hear the racket of the corral, the voices of the men, barking of dogs, the pounding hoofs of the mares, squealings of the colts, but he paid no attention to them.

Thunderhead—Thunderhead was gone again—should he go back and get Flicka and start right off trailing him? If he came up with him would the stallion let himself be caught?

He sat up straight, took his hat off, opened his shirt wider. He was getting himself in hand again. Whatever he had to do, he would do. He felt stronger.

His eyes automatically made the slow sweep which a plainsman's eyes make a score of times a day, taking in everything in the sky or on the earth, far or near.

Below him it looked like a Country Fair grounds; the horses, colts, men in the corral; saddled horses tied outside to the nearest trees; the earth beaten flat; clouds of dust rising and eddying; half a dozen dogs poking their inquisitive noses into everything.

There were a few clouds in the sky and a menacing

bank of them over the mountains in the north, but they hardly seemed to move. The sun had just tipped under the edge of one and now was out again, a brazen furnace in a brazen sky.

In the exact zenith were four motionless black birds. Large birds. Occasionally they tilted a little, slipped, circled up, steadied again. Ken was puzzled. They were not hawks. They did not have the lean lines, the bent wing-tips of hawks. They were heavier birds. He looked away to rest his eyes from staring, then quickly back at them, passing by them, not staring at them. In that instant's flash he saw them clearly. Yes—they were vultures. Vultures come where there are dead things to eat. His eyes examined the corral but there were no dead things there. Vultures are prophets. They come in advance of death. They hung there in the sky above the corral, waiting.

Ken felt all right now. He could go down and join in with the rest of them and forget about Thunderhead and see Jewel. How happy Carey would be! He could just forget all about his own disappointment.

He ran down the slope. A number of the mares had been brought out of the corral by their owners. His eyes scanned them quickly. There were the Stevens' mares and the two Palominos and Mr. Gildersleeve with Lady Godiva and three other black mares, but no mare that looked like the picture of Crown Jewel.

His father was talking to Mr. Greenway and Collins and Tim near the gates of the corral. Carey stood near them. As Ken reached them she turned to look at him. He saw her face. It was a white, tear-drenched face, the eyes glazed with weariness.

"Jewel isn't there," she said.

Ken stopped short. "Not there?" He couldn't believe

it. Thunderhead would never let a mare go once he had caught her. His eyes turned to the group of men.

"No, she hain't there," said Collins.

Ken looked at his father.

"The whole damned show for nothing," said Rob in a tight, controlled way.

Mr. Greenway's face was longer, sadder, than Ken had ever seen it. "I am convinced," he said, "that she was internally injured in that fall from the freight car, and even though she was able to run away with Thunderhead, she died later. At the time it seemed to me a miracle that there should have been no injury after so dangerous a fall."

Rob answered slowly. "You may be right. It looks like it. The stallion would never have let her out of his band—unless she were injured or sick."

"That's right, Cap'n," said Tim.

There was a silence, broken by a long sobbing breath drawn by Carey. Greenway turned to her.

"Come, Carey, you and I'll go back to the hotel. It's been too much for you."

"The boys are goin' to put on a rodeo," said Tim.

"A rodeo?"

"They're going to try to break those slicks in there," said Rob with a gesture of his head toward the mares that were still in the corral. "The Sheriff is taking the branded mares, the tame ones, into a stable in town. He'll keep them there until the owners come and get them. He's got to send some wires. But the wild mares are for whoever can break them and ride them."

"Goin' to be some show," chuckled Tim. "Ross, he says he's goin' to git him three of those broncs."

"They're not young mares," said Rob. "They won't give in. There's likely to be some cracked heads."

"And busted collarbones and ribs!" yelled someone.

"Say! Better git a wagon out here to carry off the wounded!"

"Git a hearse!" came an answering shout and joyous laughter accompanied the embroidering of this theme.

Greenway turned to Carey. "Want to stay, Carey?"

Carey shook her head. She was almost swaying where she stood.

"It's—so—terribly—hot, Uncle Beaver."

He put his arm across her shoulders. "You've had enough, my dear. So have I." He turned to Rob. "McLaughlin, I think I'll pull out this afternoon—as soon as we can pack our things. Nothing to wait for."

"No—that's right—nothing," said Rob.

"You're not coming in now?"

"I think I'll stay and watch the boys break their necks."

Greenway took off his hat and held out his hand. The gesture was like a blow to Ken. *They were saying goodby!*

The two men shook hands. Carey began to cry again and put her hands over her face. She didn't seem to know what she was doing.

"Untie the horses, Collins!" snapped Greenway and the groom ran to obey as his master took Carey's arm.

"Come on, baby," ssid Greenway tenderly. They walked toward the horses.


# 35

The Sheriff claimed that he could hit a moving target at three hundred yards with his Marlin thirty and every man in Westgate backed up his boast.

Rob picked up the gun and balanced it. The moonlight glinted on the blue barrel. He fitted the stock to his shoulder. The gun fell into position.

"It was a present to me," said Barrows. "It happens that I did a favor to the President of the Marlin Company without knowing it—tell ye about that some day. Anyway, he looked me up, said he'd like to give me a gun, the best gun they make. The plant's in New Haven. They sent me a circular with all the pictures of the different guns they make. I picked this 'un."

"It feels as if it would shoot itself," said Rob.

"It does. Sees, aims, drops on the target. Does everything but pull the trigger. I have to do that." He laughed.

"Give it here," said Ross. He balanced the gun. "Sure feels sweet," said he and passed it on. "Want to feel it, Ken?"

Ken tried the gun, handed it back to the Sheriff.

The four men lounged in comfortable positions on an outcrop of rock east of the corral. It was halfway up the ridge and gave them a clear view of all that lay below, the northern mouth of the ravine, the corral, the ground around it which sloped up to the mountains, the mares who stood quietly now, worn out with the beating they had taken that afternoon. Ross had subdued two of the three which he had picked and intended to take to his own ranch tomorrow. Others had been roped, broken, and ridden. But they had exacted a price. One of the boys had his thigh ripped open by a flying hoof, another his ribs crushed when his mount rolled on him, and there were still five unbroken mares in the corral, mares that never would be broken. They were at peace now, freed of the persecution of men, their little foals drowsing at their side or lying flat on the baked earth, sleeping. Their shadows cut black against the silver earth.

The Sheriff said, "Ought to get a wonderful shot from here."

"Be sure you give us time," said Ross.

Rob lit his pipe and pulled at it. "There'll be plenty of time, I think. The stallion isn't going to get panicky."

"What do you think, Ken?" asked Ross.

"No, he won't be panicky," said Ken. That afternoon, when he had told his father that he wanted to follow Thunderhead's trail and see if he couldn't catch him, Rob had answered, "I don't think it'll be necessary. Thunderhead won't leave his mares. He's probably hanging around close by right now, watching and listening to all that's going on. It's my guess he'll come back to the corral as soon as it's quiet, tonight probably. If you have such confidence that you can make him walk into that halter, you'll have your chance."

"Tonight?"

"Yes, we'll stay here and be ready for him when he comes."

"And if he doesn't?"

"Doesn't what?"

"Let me halter him?"

"I've promised Ross he can have one swing at him with a rope. Just one. I won't take a chance on two."

"And if he doesn't get him?"

"The Sheriff's got a gun that never misses. You understand, Ken, that I can't let Thunderhead get away again."

Ken sat in his corner on the rock, holding the halter in his hands. He turned and twisted it. If it could be a magic halter . . . if it could draw Thunderhead's head in, the way a magnet draws a needle. . . .

The hours dragged on. It was a still night. The black timbered mountains made jagged lines against the clear indigo of the sky and the moon was small and riding high, a coin of burning silver. To one side of it hung the wide, spreading cloud, so thick it seemed a carved shape with tinsel edges.

Ken and his father had dined at the hotel. The Greenways had not yet left because Mrs. Palmer was really sick and could not be moved. Ken had seen Carey and had told her that he couldn't go with them to the Blue Moon because he was going to stay and hunt Thunderhead—that was before he knew it was going to be all over, one way or the other, tonight. There was just one chance. This halter. If it didn't work, it would be all over with Thunderhead, and Carey would drive away to the Blue Moon with an empty trailer behind the Cadillac.

He put his hand into his pocket and took the whistle into his fist. He held it close. He counted a lot on that whistle. Thunderhead had learned to come at that whistle when he was a little colt. He had learned to love it. It meant oats, and friends, and shelter, it meant all the things that a colt loves.

He wondered. *If* he caught Thunderhead, would Mr. Greenway want him and Thunderhead to go to the Blue Moon with them even though there was no Jewel?

Probably not. The whole idea had begun with Mr. Greenway's wanting Ken to come along to train Jewel. And if Ken wouldn't come without Thunderhead, then the stallion would have to be brought, too. And now there was no Jewel—

An excited whinny split the air. The four men stood up quietly. All the mares were on the alert, every body tense, every head turned northwest, every pair of ears sharply cocked.

"This is it," said Ken in a low voice, "we'd better go." He and Ross walked very quietly down through the trees toward the corral.

Rob stood beside the Sheriff. Through the stillness of the night came the sound of a horse's hoofs and of brush cracking. It came from the fold of a mountain northwest of the corral.

One of the mares, a large black mare of fine conformation, an unbranded mare, one of the ones who had not been subdued, was in a state of great excitement. It was she who had whinnied. Now, turning away from the fence, unable to keep still, she trotted up and down the length of it, then again put her head through the bars, sniffing frantically, ecstatically, and her wild, eager love calls rang out again and again.

The other mares were infected with her excitement. They all began to prance about, whinnying, pausing to sniff and look through the fence.

The white stallion emerged from the trees and came cantering down toward the corral. He gave a fierce, triumphant cry, and every mare answered him. He shone silver white in the moonlight. The Sheriff cocked his gun, holding it loosely under his right arm.

"Wait," said Rob.

"Oh, sure," said Barrows.

They could see the inky black figures of Ken and Ross moving toward the corral. Now they were lost in its barred shadows.

The stallion galloped to the fence of the corral. The black mare was there to meet him. Their heads came together; their muzzles touched and clung; they breathed each other's breath, squealing softly.

Rob stood watching in a somber misery. To have to

do such a thing! His hand slowly closed into a fist in his pocket.

"God! What's the matter with Ken?" he muttered. "Why doesn't he call him with the whistle? No—no—he's right—he wouldn't answer the whistle now—let them get this nuzzling over with first."

Now the stallion trotted along the fence, seeking some place to enter. Ken's whistle rang out. Again and again the soft trilling notes pulsed on the air and every horse was shocked into attentiveness.

Ken stepped out where the stallion could see him. One hand held the whistle to his lips, the other was outstretched, the halter hung over his shoulder. Between whistles he called, "Thunderhead! Oh, Thunderhead! Come along, Thunderhead!"

He expected Thunderhead to hesitate, to advance toward him, to come close, perhaps to refuse the halter, but still to come close enough to smell him, but the horse did nothing of the kind.

He gave the wildest plunge Ken had ever seen. He wheeled, he tore away.

Ross's rope sang out and fell short. The stallion was a white streak, running away. Cursing, Ross pulled in his rope.

There was the crack of the gun. The white shape leaped in the air, the hoofs pawed at nothing, the horse crashed to the ground. Ken walked slowly toward it.

"I guess that did it," said the Sheriff.

"Good shot, Barrows," said Rob. He asked the Sheriff for a match. He took his time in re-kindling his pipe which had gone out.

"Go back!" said Ken viciously to Ross, who was at his heels. The little broncobuster stopped still. Ken did not know that as he reached the white mass lying on the ground he groaned.

Blindly he went down on his knees. He drew the head into his arms. Looking over the shoulder Ken could see the great wound and the dark stream welling from it. There was a spasmodic quiver, one deep sigh that answered his own, and all was over.

Ken sat there, staring. Staring at the muzzle which was not black as Thunderhead's was, but pink. Could a horse change the color of his muzzle? It was a long time before his mind really began to work. He examined the eyes, they were pink rimmed, white lashed. The ears—they were pink inside. Thunderhead had black muzzle, black eyelashes, the inside of his ears was dark. This was a true albino with no dark marking upon him anywhere.

Ken got to his feet and examined the horse all over. It was a stallion, about two years old.

Then he remembered. "Oh!" he said aloud.

Ross sauntered up to him. "What's up?" he asked.

The other men were coming. Ken walked to meet them. "It isn't Thunderhead," he said, "it's Ishmael."

"Ishmael!"

"Do you remember, when I rode Thunderhead in the Valley of the Eagles, there was one black mare with a little white colt? I told you all about it. She tried to run away from Thunderhead when he was rounding them up. I called them Hagar and Ishmael."

They examined the dead horse. The black mare, Hagar, neighed frantically.

"That's his mother," said Ken in a low voice.

"Gol-durn!" exclaimed Ross.

"Damndest thing I ever heard of! Shot the wrong hoss, did I? I didn't know there was two like this in the country."

Rob was silent. Ken said, "He must have brought

the black mare and her white colt with him when he left the valley last summer." The blood was pounding in his ears. Thunderhead was safe. . . . Thunderhead was free. . . . "He's a two-year-old," he added aloud. "You can see. He's not as heavy built as Thunderhead."

Rob straightened up.

"Might as well go on home, I guess," said the Sheriff.

Rob was sickened. "I'm going to let that mare out," he said, "we've killed her colt for no reason. Let her see the last of him."

He waved the men away. "I'll do it alone," he said, "just stand away over there."

Rob went into the corral, and talked quietly to the mares. At last they stopped their trembling and their rushing to and fro and stood watching him. With arms outstretched, he maneuvered Hagar and her little black foal away from the others. She saw the open gate and freedom. With one terrified eye on him, she gauged the distance, made a rush past him. He closed the gates and followed her.

She pounded past the corral, the foal trotting springily at her side. A high wild whinny broke from her as she saw the white shape on the ground. She hung over it, sniffing, then tossing the smell away with violent snorts. She did not whinny again. She knew all that had happened. Death was now mingled with the beloved smell of her son. It was finished. The foal nuzzled her bag. She stood for it to nurse. She lifted her head and looked away at the hills. She pricked her ears. At last she moved abruptly, plucking the teat from his mouth. Breaking into a canter she headed for the fold in the hills from which Ishmael had come. She turned a corner and was out of sight. The sound of her hoofs diminished in volume, faded to a faint thudding, ceased.

Riding away from the corral Ken turned to look back. His eyes lifted to the heavens. No vultures there now. Just the dazzling clear sky, the burnished moon —but they would be there the next day, earlier than that—at dawn. In imagination he saw them plummeting from the sky.

They had known all along, he thought, that it was to be Ishmael, not Thunderhead. And he had a sudden strange feeling that things were all in one piece, not strung out in time. Life was like a patterned cloth being drawn over a knife-edge. The knife-edge was the NOW and what was happening now—but the patterns were there on the cloth, all the same, before and after it had run over the knife-edge.

Cantering down the valley, waves of feeling went over him, one at a time, like undulations of the sea. He was lifted, then dropped into the deep. It seemed, he thought, like God passing over him in waves. He had had this feeling occasionally before, always in a crisis. Perhaps that was the reason for their being crises. It was an experience people ought to know, different from anything else—to feel God going over you in waves. It left you completely helpless, pulled out from yourself, saved from your little self. If he had known the words, he would have said "Thy seas have gone over me." Through it all, soundlessly, his lips were murmuring a prayer of thanksgiving.

# 36

Carey did not come down to breakfast nor to lunch next day. She slept the hours away in a room of her own which her uncle had taken for her. When he knocked on her door she roused long enough to tell him that she wanted no breakfast. She pushed the sheet down—it was frightfully hot already—and ripped off her pajama jacket, threw the pillows off the bed, then turned on her face, dragged her hair off her neck and, spread-eagled, her four limbs pointing to the four corners of the big double bed, slept again.

There is no more powerful sleep-producing drug for the young than a bitter disappointment.

Mr. Greenway and Rob went out to search for an osteopath, a chiropractor, or some sort of bone doctor with or without license to practice. It seemed that when Mrs. Palmer had leaped from her bed the other morning with intent to kill she had thrown something out—"perhaps the devil," said Mr. Greenway hopefully. "Sacroilliac," said Mrs. Evans—and this had brought on the lumbago.

Ross and the fire brigade were having another try at the wild mares in the corral.

Ken saddled Flicka and went for a ride. He rode out on the familiar road along the eastern ridge of the little valley west of town, then crossed it to the western side. No reason, any more, for avoiding that river bottom. The life had gone out of it. No more quietly browsing mares, no little dancing foals thrusting their pinhead hoofs into the soft loam.

The western ridge was unfamiliar to him. It was higher than the eastern and it was heavily timbered. He explored it until he was dripping with perspiration. Looking for water, he traced back one of the rivulets which fed the Spindle River and came upon one of those little pools, quite deep, perfectly transparent, fringed with grass and ferns and rocks which are often found half-hidden at the base of wooded mountains.

He dismounted, stripped and bathed.

The pool was fed by springs and very cold. Standing in it, the water, at its deepest, reached just to his neck. Looking down through the translucent brown color, he saw his white body, oddly foreshortened. Motionless, he watched the ripples die and the water grow quiet. A school of trout darted past him, stopped, turned with little flips of their muscular bodies, seemed to look at him, then darted on again. Three blue dragon-flies played over the pool, now and then pausing, their gossamer wings like tiny oars lifted over fairy craft, supporting them on the glassy surface. The air was drenched with the perfume of sun-warmed pine needles, of wild strawberries and of the fresh spring water.

It was deliciously cooling. Underfoot was firm sand. He trod water, went over backwards and floated. This was doing something to him, washing him of the fever and grief of yesterday. He had gone through the actions of last night without allowing himself to think or question. He had obeyed his father. He knew it was right. He had tried to do it all in a trance. But now he allowed his feeling about it to well up and overflow; his terrible acquiescence, the tension of those minutes when he held the halter in his hands, the agony of that walk toward the corpse. For that one endless minute he had believed Thunderhead dead. Now he was washing it all out of himself.

Parts of the pool were in sunshine. He paddled until his face caught the warm light and floated, smiling to himself, more and more washed and clean, more and more filled with strength and confidence and happiness. *Carey. Thunderhead.* His little "freemale" . . . his big stallion . . . what riches. He was not very close to either of them just now, perhaps parted for a long time, but they were there, alive, part of his life, part of his very self. His mind went off on a sudden, long journey with Carey. All that must happen, the time that must pass, before Carey was his wife and they could begin choosing names for those children. . . .

He got out of the pool and lay basking in the sun until he was dry, then dressed himself. It seemed to him he would like a smoke. It was hard to have to wait until he was eighteen—nine more months; it was time he smoked. Where had he put his boots? He had set them on a near-by rock. He reached for them. One fell off the rock and he had to stand up to get it. Leaning over, he paused. Near the boot was a mark on the ground, a circle. It was shaped like a horse's hoof . . . it was a horse's hoof . . . *big as a bucket* . . . Pete's hoofprint. No horse but Pete had a hoof like that. . . .

Ken's heart leaped. Jewel? . . . He stood up straight, his mind going in big happy swoops. If Pete had been traveling along with Thunderhead's band, not right in it but on an outside ring as Ishmael had, why not Jewel, too? Excitedly he bent his head, searching for more hoofprints. He found plenty of them. Pete's and the prints of a smaller, an average size horse. He did not know Jewel's hoofs. He could not tell. They were about the size of Flicka's—like Flicka's. Were they Flicka's? She had been to the pool

to drink, she had wandered over the banks. But no—
they were not exactly the same as Flicka's. They were
smaller, more rounded.

"Plain as day!" he suddenly yelled, hastily pulled on
his boots, mounted Flicka and put her on the trail.
The marks were conspicuous in the soft loam of the
mountainside. Now he was sure. Two horses had
traveled this way, one was Pete, the other a tall horse
with long legs and small hoofs. Where these two had
pushed through the brush, weaving in and out among
the largest trees, they had made a sort of path which
Ken and Flicka easily followed.

It was nearly noon when he came out upon a
clearing, high on a shoulder of the ridge. Beyond it
the path dropped off into space. Ken reined Flicka in,
leaned over, his eyes sweeping the ground.

The gravelly floor of this little clearing was stamped
all over with hoofprints, the big ones, the smaller
ones. Had more horses been here than the two? Or, for
some reason, had those two remained here a long
time, milling around? If they had, why? What had
held them here?

He thought he heard a faint shout. He would have
disbelieved his senses had not Flicka turned her head
and pricked up her ears. Ken pushed her forward
across the little clearing to the outer edge where the
scrub was shoulder high. Flicka put her head over it
and Ken leaned above her.

Way below him, and it seemed far away, was a
scene set for him as if on a stage. This clearing where
he was, way up on the mountainside, was like a seat in
the top gallery of the opera. The scene was the corral
where, yesterday, the mares had been caught and later broken. Today it was the same setting and a simi-
lar scene. Even as he watched he saw the corral gates

flung open and a team of broncs, harnessed to a light wagon, come out at a gallop. Probably that crazy Ross trying to break a pair of broncs with a wagon and a W. Little black specks ran around, closing corral gates, getting out of the way of the plunging team.

It was fascinating to stand here and watch. When the wind came in his direction he could hear their shouts and laughter and Ross's high yells as he urged the team forward. Progressing in great leaps like a pair of kangaroos they were headed for what seemed inevitable destruction by collision with a pinnacle of rock. Pulled around at the last moment by the dead weight of Ross on the reins they went leaping in another direction and here a group of immense trees blocked their way. This time there was no stopping them. Ross drew their heads clear around to one side and still they went plunging on. Suddenly both horses crashed to the earth. Ross had pulled the W and thrown them. They fought to their feet again, stood on their hind legs, then sprang forward in a gallop down the valley, the light wagon bouncing behind them.

Ken began to laugh. Watching Flicka's intense interest in this scene, her alertly held head, the sharply pricked ears, the way she would suddenly move, prance a little, give an excited grunt or whinny as if saying "I do declare!" he could know just how Pete had stood here with Jewel yesterday, seeing all that had happened, turning to look at each other in amazement like two human beings who would nudge each other and say "Can you beat that?"

He dropped the reins on Flicka's neck. In her excitement she pranced around the clearing, inspecting every part of it, then came back to her ringside position and again watched what was going on in the

valley below. Just so had Pete and Jewel pranced
around, covering this clearing with their footprints.
Where did they lead? Brush surrounded the place.
Had they gone back down the path up which they
had come? Ken dismounted and made a careful
search. He found the trail leading out from the
clearing around the shoulder of the mountain. For a
little way the tracks were upon shelving soil, then
they leaped a gulch, went up a wooded incline on the
opposite side and turned another shoulder.

Ken stood still, catching his breath. Hills, peaks,
mountains—an endless wilderness of them, reaching
farther and farther, higher and higher until they
soared up to the Continental Divide with its many
ranges, its vast snow fields.

Ken felt as if he had been dropped into the middle
of them. Loneliness, like a cold wind, blew upon him.

# 37

It was late that night before Ken and his father went
up to the room they shared, Ken more silent than usual because the thoughts and emotions that surged
within him were conflicting; one silenced the other.
He had led his father and Mr. Greenway and Collins
out to inspect the tracks on the mountainside, and the
little town buzzed with the results of that inspection.
The English filly was not dead; she had run off with
Pete. Ken was undoubtedly a hero, but—he had not
seen Carey again.

Rob did not start to undress but sat down in one of
the rocking chairs and lit his pipe. Ken sat down in

the other. Windows were wide open, the flimsy white curtains hung straight in the lifeless air. The room was left in darkness because of mosquitoes.

Rob began to talk. There was a note of jubilation in his voice. "Damned glad you found those tracks! Changes the whole picture. I was beginning to feel pretty small—bringing the gang out here to get Mr. Greenway's filly, costing him a lot of money, and going back with nothing and less than nothing!"

This made Ken very proud. Happy, too, as he always felt when his father gave him praise. At the same time his heart behaved strangely, because his father was talking as if the filly had already been recovered; and the truth was, before this could happen, Ken had to follow the trail through that lonely mountain wilderness he had seen this morning. For how long? Days? Weeks? It wouldn't be anything like spending a night or two camping out on Saddle Back, or down in the Valley of the Eagles. It would be doing an important work—difficult too—all on his own in Colorado, while the rest of them went back to Wyoming and Idaho.

All this had rushed through his mind that afternoon when he heard his father say to Beaver Greenway so confidently, "Sure! No trick to it at all! Ken'll trail 'em and bring her back!"

But there was excitement mingled with his dread. Never had he done such a thing before. And though any boy's throat would fill up and his heart drop at thought of such an undertaking, yet no boy would shrink from it, but would press into it, and love even the loneliness and the dread and the throat choking and the heart dropping.

"Now," said his father, "you can load up here with everything you need in the way of provisions. I won't leave until I've seen you off. Take plenty. You might catch her in a week, or it might be six. Let's see—what's the date today? The twelfth, I think."

"That's right. Howard left eleven days ago."

"Seems longer," said Rob.

"If I find her soon," said Ken, "maybe I could—er—take her to the Blue Moon and train her for Mr. Greenway."

"Don't count your chickens before they're hatched," advised his father. "It may be a tough summer holiday for you."

Ken's heart dropped again—but his father knew, too—that made it a little better. Did Carey know? Did she have any idea? Where was she now? He wondered if she were still up, talking to her uncle or her grandmother—no, it was late. Probably in bed. Maybe those same white silk pajamas which once he had seen —maybe that mane of glossy hair flung upward, maybe that smooth child's face, those full pink lips crumpled against the pillow—

"Dad," he said abruptly, and there was a slight hoarseness in his voice, "When are the Greenways leaving?"

"In the morning."

Ken was glad it was dark. He crossed one leg over the other, clutching his ankle.

"Is Mrs. Palmer well again then?"

"Yes, the old hellion!" Rob gave a little chuckle. "We found a bonesetter. He did some sort of jiu-jitsu on her, something popped, and her ladyship is herself again."

Ken's chair rocked nervously.

"I tell Greenway," continued Rob, "that he ought to give her an overdose of something the next time she has a heart attack."

"They aren't real heart attacks, are they, Dad?"

"She's a hypochondriac. No telling what's real and what's made up for the purpose of getting attention and sympathy. My opinion is, if she didn't gain anything by her sick spells, she would turn out to be a well woman."

A shutter banged loudly somewhere and the flimsy curtains of the north windows blew inward on a cool draft. Ken turned his head. If a storm came, the tracks might be obliterated.

"Ken."

"Yes, sir?"

"Thinking about those plugs again. If we're right in our guess that Thunderhead will join up with Pete and Jewel, and if you come up with them, you'll have a lot better chance to catch your stallion than if he was off with a band of mares."

"Yes, sir." Ken had thought of that himself.

"That halter you've got with you—Thunderhead's halter—you haven't had a chance yet to get it on him—"

Ken did not answer this. He thought of the other night when he was holding that halter in his hands, walking toward the white stallion in the moonlight, whistling, calling "Thunderhead."

"Ken—even though it leaves me in a fix, yet I'm glad it wasn't Thunderhead that was killed. Don't misunderstand me—if I had to do it again, I'd do the same thing, and if it was Thunderhead he would be killed if he couldn't be caught, yet, all the same, I'm glad it wasn't. Bad enough to have that other one lying dead out there. Ishmael."

Rob took his pipe out of his mouth and leaned forward. Accustomed now to the dark, he could see Ken's face, and noticed how drawn and nervous the boy looked. How intense he was—always breaking his heart for something—but *quick*. Alive, intelligent, emotional—

Rob placed his hand on Ken's knee and gave it a little squeeze. "It's all turned out pretty well, son, and now the rest is up to you. I know you can do it. I'm counting on you."

Ken's eyelids swept up, he broke into a vivid, charming, self-conscious smile. And Rob felt a pang, for the look in the dark blue eyes was like Nell's.

Again the curtains blew straight into the room. A rising wind swished around the building and there was a sudden crack of thunder.

"Here it is," said Rob, going to the window. Ken followed him.

Half the sky was clear and luminous, the bright moon in the zenith. The other half was a heavy bank of dark clouds that were moving rapidly, shoved up from the northern horizon.

"Goodby to Pete's tracks," said Ken dolefully.

The clouds were churning, one layer against another layer, great chunks torn loose by the wind and sent flying. Lightning split it again and again and thunder rolled and tumbled in the mountains. Northward, the storm was beating on the earth—rain—snow—they could not yet tell what it was. But even as they watched, the bank of clouds was shoved up and across the zenith, over the moon, and the world was inky black, crackling about their ears.

"Hail," said Rob into Ken's ear, as the familiar sharp patter hit the streets and the roof of the hotel. "You're in luck."

"Thank goodness," said Ken, knowing that hail would not erase the horses' tracks but freeze them into a hard mold.

The din increased. Rob went around the room closing the other windows.

"Better come to bed," he said, "this'll be over in a few minutes."

"I will," said Ken, but he did not move. The storm had swept away all his dread and given him, instead, exultance. The luck was with him. Thunderhead had not been shot, Jewel had not died. Neither of them was lost beyond recapture. Nor was the prospect of his visit to the Greenways entirely hopeless. If his luck held and he caught up with the horses soon, there were still weeks of summer to spend with Carey and with the horses on the practice track of the Blue Moon.

That night the gates of the corral stood open, for there was no living thing inside it to be confined. There was one dead thing—a mare. She had broken her neck in the fight with the rope and the snubbing post. Outside the corral there lay another dead thing, corpse of the young white stallion. Coyotes and vultures had been at both of them.

In the animal world, too, there is a news-carrying grapevine.

In the thick darkness of the night, before the storm had scattered the clouds, Thunderhead came down from the woods to stand and sniff and snort his rage upon the ground. A grey form slunk away, belly to earth. The stallion struck as swiftly as a cat. The cleaverlike hoofs drove through the backbone of the coyote and one agonized yelp died on the air. Rearing, coming down with stiff legs, he cut the coyote to pieces, then raised his muzzle and screamed a furious challenge to the world. He stood a moment as if listening for an answer, then turned to the clean hills and thundered away.

Other visitors came when the storm was over and the clouds broken into tatters that flecked the moonlit sky. Huge, plodding feet, each one with a skirt of heavy hair that swung as they were lifted, went to the corral gate, then braced with sudden nervousness against the earth. The smell of blood, of death, was overwhelming.

From some distance away came a wild, nervous whinny. Jewel trotted to his side. He rumbled deeply, she whimpered back at him. Snorts of horror rippled from the nostrils of both horses. Jewel went up on her hind legs, wheeled, plunged away.

Pete turned more slowly and trotted off. Jewel made a wide circle, cantering over earth which hail and moonlight had turned to silver filigree, in a figure of indescribable grace and beauty, her feet hardly seeming to touch the ground. She came back to Pete as he was passing the dead stallion. Two coyotes were feasting there now. Pete paused to look at them. They darted away, but not far. They kept their eyes on the great horse, and when he passed on they returned to the carrion.

Pete lifted his head and shook this corruption and grief far from him. He broke into a thundering gallop. Jewel ran up to him and together they cantered into the hills, the filly clinging to his side as a colt clings to its mother.

# 38

If you have a difficult decision to make, never force it, Rob had told his boys. Weigh each alternative singly, without prejudice. If they seem to balance evenly, no advantage one way or the other, do not be deceived. There *is* an advantage one way or the other. If you wait long enough, it will become apparent to you and suddenly the decision will be made without difficulty and it will be right.

Ken remembered this when he made his first camp, some miles north of the corral, and decided it was nonsense for so many decisions have to be made in the shake of a lamb's tail. Or, they spring to life, ready-made, the moment the issue arises, and don't have to be made at all.

Here was an issue, very important, because it might have far-reaching consequences.

He was on the trail of Pete and Jewel. Crossing it, near where he was now sitting by his campfire, was another trail. He knew those hoofprints. They were unusually large, the prints of a horse who had never worn a shoe. There were cracks in the edges, several big pieces of the hoof chipped off. These were hoofs that took care of themselves, had never been pared or shaped, good broad hoofs to carry a great weight without stumbling. They were Thunderhead's hoofs, and they went north. And Pete's and Jewel's, after having come from the corral in a northerly direction for fifteen miles or so, had then swung around, following a tiny creek. They were now heading due east.

Ken was dead tired. He had forced the pace that first day. He had been at the stable soon after dawn with his father where they had seen to the packing of a rangy buckskin named Sparks who had been hired for a pack horse. Upon him was put the sawbuck and pack with six weeks' supplies.

"I hope you won't need all this stuff," said Rob.

"You ought not to. But it would be just too bad if you got close to those two plugs and had to turn back because you had run out of supplies."

Sparks carried fifty pounds of oats, a slab of bacon, half a dozen boxes of Albers' pancake flour, a dozen cans of milk, powdered eggs, canned beans, molasses, honey, jam, coffee, sugar, salt and pepper. Ken himself carried gun, fishing rod, binoculars, compass, flashlight, slicker, blankets and one bath towel.

"Watch his back," Rob had cautioned. "Don't ever pack him unevenly."

Ken had curried the backs of both horses when he removed saddle and pack. Then they had rolled. Then he had hobbled them and put them to graze.

For his supper he had trout fried in bacon fat, trout that he had caught in ten minutes of fishing in the little three-foot-wide brook. Then he washed his things.

All the time he was thinking about the difficult decision he had to make.

Thunderhead's trail was the older. He had not crossed *their* trail, *they* had crossed his. If it had been the other way around, Thunderhead might have overtaken them. Did horses actually follow trails, smelling it out on the ground the way a dog does? He decided that they don't, they just sniff the air, smell horses from a great distance, know whether they are mares or stallions. He wondered if Thunderhead, from where he was now, somewhere to the north, could smell Pete and Jewel, off there to the east, and decided he probably could not.

Some distance away, a small brown cottontail crept out from a thicket and began to nibble the grass. Ken reached for his gun. The cottontail put up its long flannel ears, waved them, whisked around, presenting its little white powder-puff, and disappeared, Ken took a comfortable position, lifted his gun to his shoulder, cocked it, laid his cheek upon it, sighted it for the thicket and waited.

In a moment the cottontail emerged again, there was one sharp crack, and a few minutes later Ken was cleaning it at the edge of the brook. This would be his dinner for tomorrow. He would have no difficulty in having fresh meat every day—wild doves, rabbits, trout, sage hens.

He put away his gun and climbed a big rock and sat down on the top of it to watch the sunset. All afternoon the waning moon, tilted languorously on its back, had hung amongst the white clouds like a little roundish white cloud itself. But now it didn't look like a cloud any more. It was bright and faintly luminous, and behind it the sky glowed like a blue jewel.

The wind was cool. The hailstorm had broken the heat. Ken's eyes went to the line of bluish white behind the highest of the timbered mountains. Snow—fairly thick snow. There must have been a fresh fall up there when it hailed down here. Now and then the smell of it was on the wind. Now and then a current of air poured down, like a cold tide, delicious and oddly challenging.

The first stars came out. A pack of coyotes opened up a mile or two away, a few scattered yaps, then a rising chorus, then slow diminuendo and silence again.

He wondered why they should yammer. No need to hunt. They had two big horse carcasses to finish off. That would take them a good many nights.

As he thought of this his nose drew up fastidiously and a little shiver went through him.

Then, almost directly overhead, there poured out the clamor of one of those night birds who carry on an

entire noisy conversation with themselves when the
sun has set. Strident questions, squawks, and sudden
clattering exclamations.

Ken got to his feet, peering into the branches of the
tree from which the sounds came. He picked up some
loose shale from the rock and hurled it. There were
even wilder cries and a disturbance of the branches as
the bird flew away.

Ken stood there and took one last look around before going to bed. The dark and towering shapes of
the mountains were on all sides of him. To the south
was one far vista. It was like a window in the houses
of the mountains in which he was enclosed. The
slopes of the mountains came down and criss-crossed,
leaving the way open for him to see these three snow-
covered peaks, and they drew his eyes as, wherever
there is a way open into a beyond, a human being will
watch it, seduced by the haunting charm of the "far
away." It is the same with whatever is "long ago." Distances, then, in time or space, are romance.

Ken had come out from the corral in one of the
folds of the foothillls, for he had picked up Pete's trail,
not on the mountainside where he had first seen it, but
down near the corral. Pete and Jewel had followed
this little ravine, feeding on the pockets of grass which
lay, here and there, on the banks of the brook. If he
followed this trail he might come up with them in a
few days. Then, returning to this spot, it would take a
few more and by that time Thunderhead's trail would
be very old indeed. Rain might have obliterated it.

Ken flung his slicker on the spongy turf, a blanket
over it, another rolled up for his head, took off his
boots and lay down, covering himself with a third
blanket.

Then he remembered his prayers. He had made a

resolve. With so much at stake, he needed help. He would say his prayers regularly every morning and night. He would never skip them. He would not think of other things while he was saying them. After all, it was neither fair nor courteous to remember God only in crises—as when he had been trying to lash the bull away from his mother, as when his father had been going to shoot Thunderhead—such terrible crises that all you could do was breathe, "God help me!" or "God, don't let it happen!" No—perhaps if he prayed properly from the very start, he would be helped to find Jewel and Thunderhead and Pete, all three of them. And would bring them back safely. And would ride Thunderhead in a famous national steeplechase. *And would win.* He wouldn't need to ask advice as to which trail he would follow because, way down inside him, he already knew.

His father had given him some last advice. He had stood there in his belted, tan riding breeches and a blue cotton shirt which just matched his blue eyes. They had had their fierce staring look. His hands were tamping down the tobacco in his pipe.

"Don't go getting any wild ideas—"

"No, sir."

"Don't go off on any wild steeplechases on that white plug of yours."

"No, sir."

"Get your neck broke or something so I'll have to send out a search party *for you.*"

"No, sir."

"Remember, you're to bring back that English filly."

"Yes, sir."

"Remember, it's *your stallion* who stole her. In a way, *you're* responsible."

"Yes, sir."

"Damn it, *I'm* responsible! Because I didn't geld him when I had him!"

"Yes, sir."

"Yessir, nosir, yessir, nosir, and you're not even listening! You're starry eyed!"

"Yes, I am, Dad—I mean I'm listening, I'm not starry eyed."

"The hell you aren't! Well—"

All this ran through Ken's mind, but the immediate thing to be decided was, must he throw off his blanket and kneel up to say his prayers?

It was something he remembered all his life, the long time it took him to decide this point. Would it be a better prayer if he knelt up? He decided he could pray as sincerely lying down as kneeling up, and that if he limited his prayers to those occasions when he could kneel, there would not be much praying. There were times when he thought of his mother or father, talked to them in his mind, as he had just been doing with Rob, or asked their advice or help, in a way that made it seem as if they were with him wherever he went. Why could it not be the same with God? Except that it would be an even more constant companionship and guidance? He laid his arm across his eyes and went carefully through the Lord's Prayer.

To his surprise that was all he felt like saying. He began to think of Carey.

At school, the year before, his class had read Victor Hugo's *Toilers of the Sea.* The hero had been in love with a girl called Déruchette. He had never met her but once he saw her write something in the snow and, when he came up to it, he saw that it was his own name. After that he thought of her all the time. The author wrote these strange words, *"Déruchette was his abyss."*

Ken knew just what he meant by that. She was a deep place within him. She was there permanently. Whenever he was alone, he, as it were, fell into that abyss and there lived, silently and strongly, alone with her.

*"Carey is my abyss,"* he murmured.

He lay very quietly for a while. His mind went in big swoops over his friendship with Carey from the very first meeting to the last goodby, which was no goodby at all—just a pausing at the side of the automobile and her hand held out. "Goodby, Ken." "Goodby, Carey." And then the automobile driving away with the empty trailer rattling behind. Then he went back to the beginning and did it all over again. Each time it was a different story. Different scenes, different moments, different words, different looks in Carey's eyes stood out with significance. He remembered their talk on Castle Rock, the talk about all her children—*their* children—with discomfort. What he lingered over longest was the one time he had held her in his arms, the one time they had kissed. The trouble with that was, it was all about the puppy. They should have been talking about themselves. He should have told her, then, that he loved her. Another scene he remembered with still more chagrin, the time they had been out walking in Westgate and the automobile had rushed past—so close to them—forcing Carey against him. Right at that moment had been his chance. He ought to have had her in his arms.

Should he really? He searched himself more deeply. Did he really love her . . . *all* that love meant? . . . the eternalness of it . . . the each-one-for-the-other for good and all . . . the end of ever thinking seriously of any other girl or woman? . . . Or was it just puppy love? Did he want Carey for keeps?

A pain shot through him. And the pain was because it could even be questioned. It was a belittlement of his darling, of his sweet little love! Of course he wanted her! Anyone would want her. Oh, she was his own! She was the only girl he had even known or talked to who seemed important—who even seemed real. The others—the girls he had played post office with when he was a little boy at parties in Cheyenne and Laramie, the girls at the dances last year at school—they seemed sort of made up out of curls and eyes and giggles and pretty legs, but Carey was real.

The feeling inside him was as if he were groaning because he knew he would never marry anybody but Carey—groaning because there filled him a great wave of possessiveness. *My own—my own darling— my own wife.* He would propose to her, he would make her promise to marry him the very next time he had the chance.

He grew hot all over. He rolled over on his face and put his head in his arms. Carey . . . Carey . . . this was Carey . . . all his. . . .

In the morning he stood naked on the banks of the stream, rubbing himself with his bath towel after having bathed in the miniature waterfall. His teeth were chattering, air and water were cold and the sun was not yet up over the mountains. There was not a cloud to be seen. It was going to be a glorious day. He was in haste to be gone.

He fed himself and his horses, packed Sparks carefully and was off to the north on Thunderhead's trail.

# 39

Ken hurried. He must catch Thunderhead soon, so that he could go back and follow Pete and Jewel before their trail had grown too stale.

He was still in the Medicine Bow Forest Reserve, but the trail was leading downhill. Thunderhead was going back to the plains. He came to no ranches, saw no man, no other horses. Thunderhead was avoiding inhabited places. He followed grass from one little clearing, through the forest, or along a bare hillside, to another little clearing, always within distance of water.

Where the going was good enough, Ken went at a canter, with due regard to Sparks and the loaded sawbuck on his back. He had not realized how much slower traveling would be with a lead horse.

One day, two days, three days on the stale trail and it grew no fresher. The piles of dung were dry and odorless. All of Ken's confidence and happiness had gone. Far from thinking that in less than two weeks he might be at the Blue Moon with both Thunderhead and Jewel he began to worry about the six weeks—now five weeks that he had before leaving for school. It didn't seem long any more. It wasn't enough. He felt nervous and urgent. He sat by his campfire at night in a tense attitude, as if waiting, his ears keenly attuned to the sounds of the forest.

Little scurries and squeaks, footsteps, the crashing of branches, the hoot of an owl, or the eternal yapping of coyotes. He thought they sounded like cries of lost souls.

To be alone in the forest in the daytime and then come home to a warm supper, voices and smiles, the happy, close family life, that is one thing. To be alone all day and alone in the evening, too—sitting by a solitary campfire while the profound drama of the world changing from day to night takes place, while the light slowly fades until the earth is dark and shadowed and only the sky is light—that is very different.

Ken was much lonelier than he had been when he had gone hunting for Thunderhead the summer before. He wondered if it were because he had not known Carey then. Yes, he was lonely for Carey, and for home and people, and lonely with another loneliness, the loneliness of the wrong-doer. There was darkness and confusion in his soul. He had let go his silver thread of right behavior and it felt as if the world was against him. Right now he ought to be on the trail of Pete and Jewel—perhaps even catching up with them.

One day he lost the trail. He tied Sparks to a tree and, on Flicka, made wide circles, casting about. He found the trail again entering the forest. He could not understand this. It seemed aimless wandering on the part of Thunderhead. If he only knew where Thunderhead was going to, he could take the general direction and really make time. He turned Flicka around and climbed a mountain behind him, reaching so high a point that he could survey all the country for miles around. From here he could see why Thunderhead had entered the forest. It was a comparatively narrow belt, and beyond it the land dropped down in a series of grassy clearings. Way beyond the last of them, he could glimpse the shining of a river on the lowlands.

Just as he had thought, Thunderhead was going down to the Wyoming border and the plains.

After that he made better time, picking up the tracks of his quarry often enough to be confident. On the fifth day, he came out of the hills to the edge of the North Platte River. It brawled across his path, wide, shallow, rapid. Thunderhead's tracks led into it. He had crossed that river.

On the other side were flats, beyond that, hills again. There was plenty of grass on those flats. Ken's eyes swept it narrowly, right and left, expecting to see the startling splotch of white which would be Thunderhead grazing, but it was empty of life. He made sure of that. He mounted a rise of ground, took his binoculars and for half an hour examined minutely every foot of country which was spread out before him. Thunderhead was not there. Ken went down and crossed the stream on Flicka. He rode downstream a quarter-mile, then upstream. Here were Thunderhead's tracks coming out of the river and a pile of dung. It was not fresh. Flicka dropped her head and sniffed, then lifted it high and gave a ringing neigh.

Ken's heart skipped a beat. Was she neighing to Thunderhead? The wind reached them from the north and that was the direction the tracks led. Ken sat taut in the saddle, listening for a reply, but there was none. Flicka neighed again. Then came an answer, but it came from the trees across the stream. It was Sparks answering. Was it Sparks to whom Flicka had been neighing the first time?

He sat waiting but there was no more neighing. There was nothing in sight within miles of him. He would set out on this trail in the morning. He noticed with surprise that it was growing dark.

For some time clouds had been gathering in the

sky. Now, glancing up, he saw that a storm was coming. There was an enormous purplish thunderhead almost overhead, he knew that he was in for a wetting. He pulled the slicker off the front of his saddle and slipped his arms through it. There was a flash of lightning and a crack of thunder. Then it was as if bullets were hitting the surface of the river, each one causing a splash, at first single ones spaced some feet apart, then closer and closer together until the stream boiled white.

Flicka hung her head and drew herself together. In a moment his slicker was streaming. He put Flicka into the stream to ford it. The mare took a few steps then bent her head to drink. He loosened the reins. As he sat there it seemed to him that he heard the neigh of a horse far away to the north. Again his heart leaped and he turned to look. He could see nothing through the driving rain and the darkness. He wondered if he could possibly have heard aright. Flicka had not raised her head. If Thunderhead, from some distant peak, had seen him and given him greeting, Flicka would have answered. Unless, he thought, with her head down to the boiling stream and swallowing great gulps of water, she had been unable to hear anything. Now she raised her head and at the touch of his heel went forward across the stream.

The wind was rising. The downpour lessened, then the clouds were swept back into the zenith again, and again the torrents came down. Ken wondered how there could be so many tons of water in the sky. How did they get there? Then the storm moved southward, suddenly there was a streak of red light lying across the river, then it became dark again.

Ken made his camp under an overhanging cliff, back from the river a few hundred feet. Over him and on all sides of him was the forest, sighing in the rain.

He was wet through. He fed the horses and hobbled them. He changed his clothes, hanging his wet things around the fire on sticks. The saddle lay on the ground steaming in the heat from the fire. He cooked and ate his supper, cleaned up, put the things away, all in a state of confusion and misery which was almost panic.

Five days.

Five days to get here; if he started right back, five days to reach the trail of Pete and Jewel where he had left it—and what would these ten days and the winds and rains have done to those tracks? And if he went on and followed Thunderhead as he had planned to, what would this downpour have done to *his* trail? It might take him a day—two days—even to find it again.

He had wasted time enough hunting for Thunderhead. . . . Forget him . . . forget the race . . . forget all that he had so wanted for himself. . . . Do what he ought to do. Return to Pete's trail and go after him and Jewel and bring back, for Carey and for Mr. Greenway, the thing his father had made himself responsible for. His father's parting words sounded in his thoughts again. They were clear enough. Had he been crazy—going off on this wild goose chase when his duty so clearly led him elsewhere? There was even the horrible thought that, due to this long detour, he might not succeed in coming up with Pete and Jewel in time. This hit him a blow, and with it came a premonition that that was just the way it was going to be. He was going to fail, and serve him right if he did.

Damp and unhappy, he crawled into his blankets and slept the night through. The morning was dark and drizzling. Once again he climbed the little eminence near by and swept the flats across the river with his binoculars. Thunderhead *might* be near. Silly to turn and go back, when perhaps just a half-day's travel, just a few hours, separated them! He called at the top of his lungs, he whistled, he looked minutely, steadily, until his eyes were watering with strain. No sound but the urgent brawling of the river. No movement but the swaying of the trees, the low, windswept clouds.

It was a despairing goodby look which he cast upon those flats and hills. He put all thought of Thunderhead, of the visit to the Blue Moon, of the steeplechase, away, and ran down the hill, saddled Flicka, and headed back the way he had come.

He was able to follow his own trail without difficulty. He rode all day in the rain, having no mercy on himself or his horses. He must make up time. Again that night he had to strip and change clothes, setting out the wet ones to dry by his fire.

He felt exhausted beyond all reason. His thought drifted without direction. To lose Thunderhead, that he was resigned to. But what about Jewel? Carey? Everything? How had he happened to get in this jam? What about life itself? Would he achieve anything he wanted? What lay ahead? Suddenly he shuddered. It seemed as if all his needs and wants were known . . . they lay exposed to some malevolent eye . . . he was helpless . . . and all that he loved would be swept out of his reach by some power he could not control.

Attempting, with his inner vision, to see what lay ahead for him it seemed as if he could almost divine his future life as if it were a wide, mist-covered plain, dark. If there were waiting for him marriage, fatherhood, a life work, a home of his own, children, he could not see them. He could see no path leading to any of those stations and it did not seem possible that

they were really there. How could there come a
directive on the path of his life?

There was the soft steady rustle of the rain falling,
there was the hissing of the fire, there was the inde-
scribably sweet fresh smell of the earth and the grass-
es, and occasionally the sharp crash of a heavy pine
cone falling, scattering showers of water.

An hour passed. Still Ken sat motionless. How helpless he was . . . not only he, but his father . . . the
things you read in newspapers . . . what terrible things
happen to people because they are all helpless and
cannot save themselves . . . just little futile children,
unable to plan and do and achieve what they want to,
frustrated and defeated at every turn. He began to
feel surprised. He had not always known this. Lots of
times he himself had been defeated, but he had never
dreamed other people had it happen to them, too. He
had thought grown people had power and could propose and dispose, his father and the President and all
big powerful men. But they couldn't. . . . No. . . .
His father wanted Thunderhead to be found as much
as he himself wanted it. Besides, his father would die
someday; the President, too. . . . No. Everyone was
helpless and no one was complete or sure.

He reached this as a fact, as concrete as if it were
something he held in his hands. He accepted it.

Finding this and accepting it, there began in him
again the wild coursing; his mind, like a greyhound,
trying to find the very rim of life and beyond, trying
to find the power that was not in himself or other
men, the completeness that he now knew he would
never have in himself.

And suddenly his lips parted in surprise and he said
aloud, "Why! That's God!"

He stayed with this thought a long time in a kind of

wonder. So much he had heard about God, prayed to God, but not ever really found Him for himself—all of it just sort of a convention, a duty, a performance that as an obedient child, he had given himself to. Now he had found Him out of his own need, his own helplessness and the helplessness of all men, because, surely, power and completeness had to exist somewhere. How else would one even know about them or have the idea of them? Or discover that they were lacking? Or how could they be manifested in any field of human activity?

He wondered why all men did not find out that what they everlastingly searched and longed for was God. Then he realized that there were many men who never knew, at least, never admitted, that they were, in all fundamentals, helpless. Perhaps only a few did. Perhaps most men went right through life, either never looking forward to the end, or believing or bluffing themselves that they were really rr, could somehow pull it off, bull it through, somehow keep up the bluff and finally put it over. Well then, those were the ones that could never find God.

The wind again. The forest roared, a battery of pine cones pounded the earth, and Ken, his thoughts drawn outward, lifted his head and listened. *There* was power! An endless wild sweep of power! His eyes lit up, his lips parted, smiling. All alone there on the edge of the forest he was listening for God.

There came a sharp sound, a series of cracks, louder and louder, and suddenly the deep crash and great groaning of a tree going down. Prickles went up Ken's spine and he felt his scalp contracting. If you really listened for the voice of God, you began to hear it in strange places and strange ways.

He thought of his mother; he experienced again the

great deep chunk of living of those few minutes when he had seen her in danger from the bull, the terror for her mixed up with the dread that he might not have strength enough, determination and aggression enough to overcome the bull and beat him back. It had been a kind of madness in which he had not felt any timidity, only horror and hate and frenzied animal fear.

A deep sigh went through him, relief that she had come through that all right—that he himself had come through it and had been able to do as he ought to do. He would tell his mother about this thing to-night, if he could find words to tell her of it. He wondered what she would say. She always had something interesting to say about God, now *he* could tell *her* something interesting about God.

He looked about him almost fearfully, and in his mind he asked her, *"Mother, why did I feel, when the tree crashed down and when the great wind came and the whole forest roared and bowed down, that it was God?"*

As if in answer, he thought he smelled the perfume she used, lily of the valley. He inhaled it deeply. Then, thinking of her, he knew so exactly what she would say, that it was as if he heard her voice say it. *"These are the mighty works of His hands. In them and through them we find God."*

The wind was breaking up the storm. The rain stopped. Far off on the horizon the heavy cloud bank had lifted and there was a streak of yellow sky showing behind it, aftermath of the sunset. The wind was making a great noise in all the trees of the forest. It would be clear tomorrow.

Ken got to his feet and walked out over the soaked

ground to a place from which he could see the little clearing, bordering the forest, where he had put the horses to graze. With eyes accustomed to the dark he saw the shadowy undulations of the hills, one great pine standing out from the others, an inky silhouette.

He saw Flicka grazing, one foreleg slightly advanced, her head to the earth, jerking off the rich mouthfuls of nutritious mountain grass. Against the darkness she was a darker patch of darkness, drawn in a shape of intriguing beauty. His mother had once told him that, in Eastern symbolism, the horse represents understanding. So then, seeking a horse, he was seeking understanding.

Understanding of what? Of everything, really. Could one ever feel that one knew anything? There would always be something beyond, like the little crack in the mountains through which one could see that far vista of perpetual enticement.

The wind buffeted his face. The boughs of the trees were tossing. Here and there in the sky were clear spaces and, as the clouds chased each other across them, bright stars came and went.

Ken ran his fingers through his hair. He liked to feel the wind in it. He walked slowly forward to the solitary pine tree, stood close against the trunk looking upward, then, hardly knowing what he did, he bent his forehead against the bark and stood there motionless.

Different emotions went through him like great tides. There was fear. It was all too big, too marvelous, too much beyond him. And he was too small and futile. But there was love in him, too, a throbbing passion for everything wide and beautiful, which made him want, in spite of his fear, to continue searching forever to see if he could not get deeper and ever deeper into the heart of the world, into the very core of it and find the kernel—the last tiny kernel— and take it in his hand and hold it there and look at it, lying on the palm of his hand like a little nut.

In the morning the sky was clear and fair, there was not a cloud, there was a glitter of diamonds over the world and the forest was full of song. Ken could see the birds flashing through the branches and, here and there, one sitting on a sunny twig stretching its wings so that glints of scarlet and blue and gold shot from its feathers.

He said to himself, "After the storm comes the sunshine." His hand tightened on the reins and Flicka stopped. It seemed as if he had discovered a universal principle. He must always remember, when things were at the worst, fair weather would follow.

Ken was able to pick up the trail of Pete and Jewel again where he had left it. There was always the dung even though scattered. The two horses had followed a string of little clearings, upward, toward the higher reaches of the Medicine Bow Reserve.

Many days went by. Emotion, any sort of emotion, died in Ken. He continued his search with stoical determination, not concerning himself with anything beyond the day's travel and the care of himself and his horses.

At night he dreamed of Thunderhead. Over and over again, in that dream world, he would come up with the stallion, coax him with the whistle and oats until he got the halter on him, or would see him in excited play around Jewel. Often he would wake with the stallion's neigh ringing in his ears, so that he would lean on his elbow, his head turned, listening, unable to believe that it had not been a real neigh he had heard.

He grew quieter in mind and heart, able to make camp and lie down and sleep when the time and place were right for it, whether or not he had just lost a trail he had been following for days, or thought that the very next morning would bring him in sight of the two horses. Continual disappointment hardened him. In his loneliness there was a deep fusing of his innermost nature with the mountains and forests and skies.

# 40

Jewel was with foal by Thunderhead and her time was near.

August, and the summer heat pouring down the valleys. Grass, belly deep and still green, untrod, unseen by man, touched only by the winds that bent it into billows, marking it with undulating ripples of light.

How good it was to eat! Sweet, succulent, rich, tubular mountain hay, exactly what was necessary to provide milk for a foal.

It was not easy to find at this time of the year, when, on the plains, the grass had turned dry and brown. Only in the mountains were there these small valleys, occasional clearings, little pockets of lushness which the horses could find by smell, one patch leading to the other.

They grazed as they walked, one step at a time, the enormous mottled bay and the trim English filly, black satin beauty with a clean-cut diamond of pure white between her eyes and a long pear-shaped pendant hanging from it.

Pete's great size, inherited from Clydesdale, Suffolk Punch and Belgian ancestors, gave him a threatening appearance, but this was contradicted by the spirit of gentleness and humility which emanated from him, especially from the gaze of his large brown eyes. These beautiful eyes and the heavy black forelock above them gave him a look of a wondering, friendly child, peering out from under a dark bang.

Jewel had grown taller, her mane and tail were wild and sweeping and full, but her head was the delicate, beautifully drawn head of an English thoroughbred, and her body and long legs had the fine lines of a dancer.

Both horses were in top condition, their coats shining with a glossiness which would have been the envy of any groom.

Plucking great mouthfuls of the grass, they now and then paused to lift their heads and look at their kingdom, to chew what they had in their mouths, to prick ears and turn their eyes, seeing the sweet green valley cupped by timbered hills and ridges and shoulders, rising—always rising—to the mystery of those white ranges whose gleaming flanks, under sun or moon, flashed like diamonds and made the eyes blink, whose cool breath came like messages from some far world, perfumed, enticing, strange.

Jewel's nose would lift in tiny jerks, higher and higher, her eyes half closed, those delicate nostrils of softest black velvet quivering like sensitive antennae. And the images that were created in her horse-consciousness by these odors and sights and sounds could be compared to the images that would pour through the mind of an imaginative child if there were put into his hands a copy of the *Arabian Nights;* endless, avid, varied interest, endless beauty, endless seduction.

In the heat of the day the two horses would stand in the shade of the trees, almost motionless, resting, heads hanging low, half-asleep.

When the flies were bad they placed themselves alongside each other for switching. There was a definite technique. *Swish*—Pete's full black tail would be flung over Jewel's head, brushing off every fly, then as it was drawn softly across her face and eyes and for a second dropped, her tail would perform the same routine for him, *swish*. And so it went, *swish—swish*, *swish—swish*, a rhythmic performance that went on for hours without effort or thought and which, beside its practical use, was soothing as a drug.

Sometimes they found a spot to stand upon where there were no flies, some little ridge or promontory swept by a current of air. Here they would stand just resting in the happiness of being friends, close together, her muzzle on his back or neck, or with his head bent over her. Sometimes they touched each other with their nostrils, caressing each other, giving little soft lip-nips, sometimes even pressing the teeth into the skin, but tenderly, as a child might bite and nuzzle its mother's palm.

All summer their wanderings had been punctuated by violent storms. Since that one great hailstorm in which they had started out on their journey, hardly two days had passed without thunder and lightning crashing about their heads, without the heavens opening and pouring rain or hail upon them. Sometimes the clouds sank low and they were enveloped, barely visible to each other, seemingly the only inhabitants of the world, two dark ghosts looming through the mist.

There was many a sound that struck terror to Jewel's heart. The scream of a cougar at night. This sound, horrible enough to make a man burst into sweat, would make her tremble and press close to Pete with little whimpering whinnies. It was a sound that came fairly frequently, the sudden snarl rising swiftly to an ear-splitting screech, ebbing away in wails of agony. If, in her horse language, she asked him, "What is it? What is it?" he answered her with comfort, a deep grunt which said, "I am here."

But he took care, at night, to sleep in the open, not under the trees where, on some low branch, a cougar might be coiled, waiting to leap. This, Jewel saw one evening; a cougar dropping from a branch upon a deer that passed beneath; saw the deer's head twisted around, the neck broken in one split second; saw it go down beneath the tawny cat; saw the long ropelike yellow tail lashing sideways flat upon the ground; saw the great fangs close upon the deer head.

Pete led her swiftly away, crashing through the underbrush, hating the smell of the blood and the terror and the cat and the death.

They knew their enemies. Besides the cougars, there were the wolves. Jewel had heard them the winter before when she was in Thunderhead's band, and she knew that even the stallion was alerted by the faintest howl, miles away. Here in the mountains there were timber wolves, more formidable than the prairie wolves, standing tall as a calf, strong-shouldered, square of jaw, a rough grey in color with a long, trailing brush. They ran singly or in pairs or small groups. Their prey was deer, antelope, small game of every kind and the young of elk, horses, cows.

The deer and the horses were friends. Their natures, their feed, their habits were the same. They grazed together. Both were timid, had no desire to kill, depended on their speed for safety.

Here in these mountains Jewel saw her first grizzly
bear. It was neither friend nor enemy. She could not
feel any affinity for it. Her interest was curiosity and
dread, not pleasure, but the bear paid her no attention. It went its way.

Everyone was going somewhere, following little
trails, going to water holes to drink or to hunt,
returning to lairs or hideouts to sleep. Though each
animal located itself in one certain territory, within
that they were ceaselessly on the move. Only the
young, the little fawns tucked away in fern beds, the
bear cubs tumbling in play at the mouth of a cave, the
wolf pups hidden under a clump of rocks, stayed put.

. Pete and Jewel kept moving, too. The farther field,
the valley which is just over the mountain, the grass
on the other side of the river! Horses travel hundreds
of miles. The feed in one little clearing is soon exhausted. Their keen scent, bringing them the damp luscious-
ness of grass, sub-irrigated by mountain springs leads
them on from one pocket to the next. But there was
forest to cross between, there were barren hillsides,
there was far more danger from wolves and panthers
than on the plains below. Instinct makes the decisions
for animals, a fine line drawn between one hazard and
the other. They went on.

They crossed flat shallow rivers, noisy with swift
currents and whitewater. They crossed plunging
mountain torrents with water, like slabs of green
glass, pouring over waterfalls. Drinking at one of
these icy pools, before going on, Jewel would hardly
twitch an ear at sight of a muskrat arrowing through
the water under the bank, or the supple, strong-bodied
rainbow trout leaping in the falls, trying to surmount
them, hurling themselves high into the spray, falling
back into the churning pool, leaping again and again,

endlessly, tirelessly, leaping all day long. Over them, the sun pierced down through the trees and matched their colors in small rainbows spanning the falls or hanging in the spray.

But the horses stayed out of the forests as much as they could. A little valley such as this one which they had come to this morning would provide pasture for two or three weeks, then it would be time for circling back to lower altitudes, and, at last, to the plains. Within Pete's skull was a ranger, a philosopher, a geologist, a dietician—all called instinct.

There were springs in the hills that surrounded this valley and at dusk the two horses drank from a pool made by these springs, pushing their noses through tangles of wildflowers, bluebells on yard-long stems fine as hairs, mariposa lilies, forget-me-nots and asters of every shade of violet and lilac.

There came to drink with them a doe with twin fawns, two other does and bucks. Something frightened them. They jerked their heads up, stood listening, sniffing, then, in tremendous leaps, took themselves up the mountainside and vanished.

Pete and Jewel stood listening, too. That morning, coming into the valley along a hillside they had seen this band of deer feeding lower down on the slope, and across the bottoms, standing on the edge of the thicket on the opposite hillside, two panthers, watching the deer.

Now, here were the deer. No casualties. But where were the panthers? Pete's nose was often lifted, wavering, moving in infinitesimal circles, searching the wind. There was nothing, no acrid smell of cat— and the deer were gone up the mountain.

But next morning as the two horses grazed, there came swimming toward them over the sea of deep grass what might have been a flock of gulls. It was the heads of the deer, lifted above the grass as they moved through it. The little upheld noses of the fawns could just be seen. Now and then a buck sailed over a wide space with a tremendous jump.

Here they were again. Here too, somewhere, must be the panthers. And the sun was making a smaller and smaller arc in its day's journey, the nights were getting very cold, often an icy tide of air came rolling down from the glaciers, the season was late.

Between one mouthful of grass and the next Pete's head altered its direction, swinging around. He did not hurry. He went in a wide circle. By afternoon he was leaving the valley along the same hillside by which they had entered it yesterday.

Jewel followed him. She always followed Pete. Until a few nights later when she went off by herself. When he came after her she turned and plunged at him with sharp teeth that ripped a ribbon of skin from his withers, then whirled and kicked him in the belly. So, serving notice on him that the time had come when she must be alone, she trotted away and disappeared from his sight.

They had been grazing all day on a tundra where sheep had grazed before them. The place was saturated with the smell of them. Here, on the lower edge of the tundra, the forest came to meet it, and it was into the forest that Jewel had disappeared.

It was sunset time. Pete stood quietly waiting, his face turned in the direction she had taken. The dark was coming quickly and the sky was full of flaming colors and flying, tattered blue-grey clouds. There came a rush of wind and the trees on the edge of the clearing bent and soughed, sweeping the ground with their branches and then swinging up again. Not two hundred yards away three dark shapes trotted into the clearing and up the slope of the tundra. From far away came the long drawn quavering hunting howl of a wolf and within a few minutes it was answered three times, the last time by the wolves who had just passed Pete. He saw them now as they answered. They sat on their haunches with uplifted heads and the terrible sound poured from their stretched throats, more terrible because, falsely, it carried a tone of melancholy.

The wolves trotted off and disappeared. Though they were not dangerous to grown horses it was a good thing they had gone after the sheep, for a foal was coming.

Darkness came on. Uneasily, Pete turned his head and strained his ears, listening for Jewel, listening for a little bleat that would tell him he had a new responsibility. Now and then he lifted a great hoof and stamped it in nervousness, now and then he turned his head to the forest or the tundra, listening, sniffing the air.

There came a spatter of rain. The wind rushed down the mountain again, and again all the trees of the forest behind him bowed and soughed and swept their branches and moaned softly and again were still.

The rain came harder, fine and steady, the clouds sank lower. Pete took the rain comfortably, standing with his head low, his back slightly humped.

Hours passed. At last came the sound he was waiting for and his head lifted with a jerk. It could have been a cat meowing. And it was answered by soft deep gurgling whinnies in Jewel's voice, but a voice Pete had never heard before, a voice Jewel had never used before.

Pete trotted through the darkness to her and found

her against a wall of rock in the forest hanging her
head over a dark, wet little form which lay on the
ground, licking it ecstatically, talking to it with grunts
and murmurs. She swung her head up as Pete
approached, nickered at him in a greeting which had
a note of anxiety in it, then dropped her nose again
over her baby. Pete stood watching, a deep murmur of
sympathy rumbling out of him.

The foal raised its head. It was going to be black,
like its dam, with white markings on its face. There
came from it another little squeal. Jewel answered
and licked it more vigorously. It staggered to its feet
and stood wavering, then collapsed. The mare
continued her anxious licking with grunts of
encouragement and love. It struggled up again and
stretched out its little nose, already obeying the
command which would rule it all its life long, the
command to seek its food. The mare was in such a
state of delight—eyes, nose, lips so occupied with the
baby that she kept it from reaching her udder, and the
little thing trembled and wavered under her strong
licks and nuzzles, thrusting out its legs, bracing itself,
fighting for balance. At last she ceased her licking,
turned herself away so that her flank was close to it,
and waited. Pete waited. The wind died down. It was
very silent and very still and cool, with the fine rain
sifting through the leaves.

The foal put its little snout against its mother's side,
slobbering against her, and pushed here and there. It
was feeble, wavering, easily discouraged, making mistaken detours, correcting itself, getting nearer the udder, then going astray again, coming back, getting
close but missing the teat. At last it blundered against
the hot rubbery bag. The mare felt the foal's lips taking the teat, drawing it into its mouth, the foal felt the

hot swollen nipple. The mare became motionless, rapt, as her milk was drawn in sips and gulps into the baby's stomach. But the foal went mad with excitement, his first experience, his first triumph on earth. His pinhead hoofs pranced and stamped, his head butted and pulled, his wisp of a tail, crimped as if with curling pins, stood straight out and quivered and switched, wigwagging his ecstasy.

Pete stepped forward and sniffed the foal. Jewel turned her head anxiously and told him to watch what he did. But he nickered back that she ought to know better than to think he would hurt it, and again sniffed the little wagging tail, the bony, lop-sided haunch. This was his foal. Although Thunderhead was the sire, this was the foal of the mare Pete had taken for his own charge, to cherish, to love, to save from all danger. The baby was his little son, and his soft, big lips mouthed the tiny, bony rump. The curly switch quivered and whisked as if in response.

The foal nursed until he could drink no more. His stomach was as tight as a drum and the heat and life were all through him. He pulled his head away from the teat with a smack which made it flip and bounce, then he suddenly went down on his knees, then flat out on his side, his head sinking in blissful confidence upon the damp pine needles. The mare whirled to stand over him, drop her nose, sniff him, inhale his very essence.

There was something else that Pete was smelling. The smell of the blood of the birth. Others could smell this, too—and from a distance. They must leave this place. But the foal slept, Jewel would not wake him.

The two horses grazed while the night passed. The foal woke at dawn and nursed again, stronger now, rising more skillfully, finding the teat more quickly.

Again Jewel was overcome with the miracle of what
had happened, and turned to lick and sniff and caress
it, so jerking the teat out of its mouth. Then the little
one had to find it again, always quicker, always more
easily, getting expert with practice.

The rain stopped. Before dawn, came again the
sound that told all the world that wolves were out a-
hunting, and Pete started away from this tundra, Jewel following him, the foal staggering by her side, covering the ground with amazing swiftness, now and
then falling, but rising again, sorting out its long wob-
bly legs and controlling them with skill that seemed
uncanny. It was not a day old, yet it walked, trotted,
galloped at its mother's side.

They found rich pasture wherever they went. They
grazed, slept, wandered. The foal grew stronger.

Three wolves, drawn by the scent of blood, at last
found the place where Jewel had foaled.

It was not long before Pete knew they were on their
trail.

# 41

Pete kept moving faster than was good for the foal.
Often Jewel would not follow. If the foal lay sleeping
she would graze near by paying no attention to Pete's
whinnies which bade her wake the foal and come
along. Then Pete would act like a stallion, plunge at
her and nip her, wake the foal and make them both
come with him. But no matter how fast they traveled,
the wolves could travel faster and they never tired.

One night Pete saw them, a little pack of five, sitting some distance behind them on the hillside they had just crossed.

The foal was sleeping. A terrified neigh burst from Jewel as she, too, saw them. The foal, even in its sleep, heard the terror in its mother's voice and leaped up and fled with her. Pete still stood facing the wolves, as if daring them to come on. But they sat still, watching him. It was not him they wanted, it was the foal. He turned and pounded away after Jewel. Better not let her and the foal get out of his sight. Later on in the night, when they had stopped to rest, he was unable to graze for the anxiety that was in him. He stood sniffing the wind, listening. Now and again he smelled the wolves strongly, now and again there was no scent. He distrusted the wind. It veered this way and that. When next he heard the hunting howl it was not far away. He took the lead, trotting away briskly, Jewel following with the foal.

The foal was getting very weary. Their pace was slower.

It was night when the foal was five days old when suddenly the wolves were close around them, darker than the darkness, moving through the trees with only the fiery balls of their eyes showing.

Jewel and the foal were both lying flat, sound asleep. Only Pete was standing, dozing, but never entirely off guard.

Some sixth sense warned him, and almost before he heard the savage snarls with which the wolves, according to their habit, attacked, he had plunged to the defense of the sleeping foal and stood over it, giving a loud neigh which lashed Jewel with terror. She leaped up, whinnying wildly.

Pete's ferocious face, snorting fire, caused the wolves to draw back, their half-quenched snarls trembling against their bared fangs. The great forefoot, armed with a hoof that was like a cleaver, made a swift pawing circle, and one grinning wolf-face was pulp. The other wolf yelped as if it were he who had been hurt.

Another was at Pete's flank. As the foal, bleating with terror, ran to its mother, Pete felt the sharp teeth rake his haunch and lashed. Something burned in his throat even as his heels connected—another wolf—he shook himself free.

The foal thrust his muzzle under Jewel, seizing the teat as if, once he had hold of that, nothing could hurt him. But it was roughly jerked from his lips as his mother took to her heels, galloping away faster than she had ever galloped since he had been born.

Weaving his collapsible shanks with incredible dexterity he galloped beside her, attached to her by the invisible cord which never failed to hold him close.

Pete came pounding along behind them. He had killed one wolf and injured another. Behind there, the unhurt ones were having a meal of fresh meat. It would hold them for a time. But Pete himself was leaving a trail of blood. There was a deep gash in the side of his throat, from this a pulsing dark stream ran down his neck across his chest, down the left foreleg, over his hoof, staining the earth.

At dawn they stopped again, Pete and Jewel to rest and graze, the foal to nurse and lie down and sleep. But by evening the hunting howl was on the wind again.

Jewel was in a panic. Her lips brushed over her foal to wake him and he leaped up. They were away. Pete stayed behind, facing in the direction from which he had come, waiting and watching. For twenty-four hours his life blood had been draining from him. He was nearly done.

He moved around, touching the earth with his lips as if he would graze, but he had no desire for food, it was an automatic gesture. Presently, lifting his head he saw three wolves sitting, a hundred yards away, watching him. Their tongues hung out of their mouths. Now and then they put their heads back and gave a long quavering howl.

A mile away, this howl was heard by Ken and by Flicka, and by Sparks. Ken had been about to pitch camp for the night but the trail was very fresh. He knew that he was following Pete and Jewel and her foal and some wolves. There was still light enough— he would press forward.

His heart beat with excitement. Coming up with them at last! Wolves—they wouldn't harm a human being, but a foal—no doubt they were after Jewel's foal. He took his gun from the gunboot on his saddle, cocked it, put his heels into Flicka'a side and moved forward.

Pete was down. He had not gone down of intention, he had just sunk to the earth, a mountain of flesh, drained bloodless and weak, nearly gone. The wolves came closer and padded around him. He half got up— his forelegs braced. They came at him all three together. He lunged to his feet and fought savagely. Fangs ripped him, his great jaws opened, he seized a wolf by the neck, crunched, raised his head, flung it from him. A gun cracked. Another wolf leaped into the air and fell writhing.

Pete fell, too. If there was a living wolf left it vanished. He was alone. His head stretched forward on the ground.

He heard the thud of horses' hoofs, tried to stir, tried to rise, but a stinging weariness was through all his veins. Presently there were sounds, a human voice, "Pete, old fellow! Oh, Pete—" Footsteps, human hands —somebody was close to him on the ground, lifting his great head, cradling it, and the arms and hands were tender, the voice gentle and comforting—this was a friend. And there was that gun there, too—no more danger for Jewel and the foal—

His head relaxed in Ken's arms. Peace . . . his eyes closed in the final weariness. Ken held him an hour without moving. His arms and legs went to sleep. At last a great sigh shuddered through the big horse, then a convulsive quivering of all his limbs, and suddenly the head and neck were heavier. Ken withdrew himself and got slowly to his feet, straightening his stiff legs. He stood looking down at the dead animal with sadness, then mounted Flicka and rode on a mile, following the tracks of Jewel and the foal until he could see them no longer for the darkness.

He was following the base of the cliff. Here, at a place where it overhung a little, he could pitch camp for the night. In the morning he would take up the chase again.

But when morning came there was no need for him to take up the chase. It was about sunrise when, in his sleep, he heard the excited nickering of horses. This he had heard so often that even when he had opened his eyes he lay a few moments without realizing what had happened. Then he raised himself on one elbow and looked through the trees to the little clearing where he had hobbled Flicka and Sparks. There were three horses there now, Sparks and Flicka and Jewel. No—there were four. The tiny black foal pranced from one mare to the other, jealously called back by Jewel when it tried to nurse on Flicka, butted away by Flicka, sniffed and snorted at by Sparks. And all the time they talked to each other in a rapid fire of grunts and nickers.

Ken sat up, staring at Jewel. There she was, diamond and pendant and all! The long search ended! Confused thoughts of Carey rushed through his head. She ought to be here too! Carey and Jewel—they belonged together. He was so taken off balance by the sudden appearance of the filly that he felt dazed and could only stare at her, taking count of her perfect proportions, her small spirited head, all her keen, fine lines. She shone. Although her mane and tail were full and sweeping, every aspect of her proclaimed race and condition. She danced on her hind legs as she wheeled from one horse to the other.

"Gee—ee! What a beauty!"

The horses heard him. Flicka and Sparks whinnied and began to hop toward him, expectant of morning oats. Jewel, with the wariness born of forest dangers, leaped away, called to her foal to follow, and disappeared. Ken paid no attention to this. He took off the hobbles of Sparks and Flicka and filled their nose bags with oats. He filled a third nose bag. When he was feeding his horses Jewel appeared again, whinnying nervously. She pushed in between the two. She nipped at Sparks' nose bag. When Ken approached her she let him halter her and put her nose bag on. He fastened the halter rope to a tree and went about getting his own breakfast. When he started back on the trail he had come, Jewel was on a lead rope at his right side. She followed docilely.

It was late that afternoon when, again, he heard or thought he heard that brassy, faraway neigh. No—it was not imagined. This time the horses heard it, too. As he pulled Flicka up she turned her head and pricked her ears, and suddenly all three of them neighed. The challenging voice answered, there was bedlam for a moment or two, then silence.

With a beating heart, Ken dismounted. His chance had come at last. Was Thunderhead racing toward them through the forest at this moment? Now: to plan wisely, to keep his head, to make not one error. Halter and rope. Nose bag of oats. Lariat. The other horses tied to trees beyond any possibility of getting loose. Hobbled, too—that would be safest.

He worked furiously, quietly, his face scarlet. He led the three horses, excited and prancing as they were to a clearing so that, if he had to use the rope, he would have free play for it. He hobbled them, tied their halter ropes to trees—snubbed them up close. *There* was the danger—that if they got excited, if Thunderhead harried them, they would jerk backward, or rear, and break the catches of their halters or the rope itself.

While he was doing this he did not dare turn his head to listen for fear he would hear the crashing of the underbrush before he was ready.

At last it was done. He picked up his lariat and looked around for a hitch. That broken stump of a tree—solid as a rock. He fastened the end of the rope to it, laid the rest of it, neatly coiled, beside it. Then he took Thunderhead's halter and lead rope—strong new ones—from the pack and hung them over his left shoulder. He filled the nose bag—the biggest one of all. He had brought it along for just this contingency.

And now to wait. He had hardly sat down on the rock when the horses burst out with wild whinnies again, prancing, straining at their ropes. There came an answer from the forest.

Ken stood up.

Should he whistle?

There was not time. There was the sound of a heavy body moving through the forest and then Thunderhead stepped out into the clearing.

There were more whinnies. Grunts. Nickers. He paid Ken no attention but trotted to the mares. Ken had expected this. He walked slowly to them and began to talk to the stallion.

"Hey, boy! Hey, old fellow! Well! So you thought you'd come up and see us at last! Well—how's the boy?" He held out his hand, walked closer.

Thunderhead included him in his inspection. He sniffed at his outstretched hand, then reared and wheeled back to the mares. He smelled them thoroughly. He sniffed at the foal. He snorted at Sparks and gave an angry neigh at him. Sparks, frightened, drew away as far as he could. The mares whinnied coquettishly and excitedly. Thunderhead caressed them, going from one to the other, touching their soft muzzles. It went on for a long time.

"Oats! Thunderhead! Oats! Come and get your oats!"

Ken held the nose bag in his left hand. The lead rope was in his right.

Thunderhead walked to him, sniffing, a deep rumbling whinny acknowledging his master. As he came closer, Ken let the bag hang almost to the earth, and as Thunderhead stooped his head to smell it, stood close at his side, putting his right hand, which held the rope, against his neck. He rubbed the big muscles softly, up and down. Snorts rippled from Thunderhead. He smelled the oats in the bag but could not get to them. He lifted his big hoof and pawed at them. Ken let go the bag entirely, slid his right arm under the stallion's neck and up on the far side. At the same time his left hand reached up to the crest of the neck to meet his right hand and take the end of the rope. If he once got that arm around the stallion's neck—just so he had always put the lead rope on him. But the big head came up with a jerk and Thunderhead took a step away. All to do over again now—talk to him; coax him; tell him about the oats.

Thunderhead wheeled, trotted around the clearing to the mares and the grunting, the playing and whinnying and caressing began all over again. Then at last he came back to the oats. Ken opened the bag and let him eat some of them, but the moment Ken tried to put the rope around his neck, he moved away.

An hour passed. And another. Ken was exhausted by the strain. Thunderhead now and then would forget the mares, and begin to graze. Not even then would he allow Ken to complete that last step of drawing the lead rope over the top of his neck. Ken tried going up to him head-on, with the halter in his hands. He had always been able to halter Flicka that way. Thunderhead declined the honor. He walked away, dropped his head again, munched the grass.

Ken sat down on the rock, put his head in his hands and groaned. This might go on for days. He hadn't tried the lariat. Thunderhead didn't like it, no horse does, but after all, he had been well broken and trained. Ropes, halters had been everyday affairs in his life. If the rope was once around his neck—

Ken knew that he would not have two chances. Thunderhead was not moving, he was over there, grazing. Ken coiled his rope, stood up and gave it the first swing around his head.

Thunderhead gave a little start, looked up, watched. As the rope shot through the air it seemed that he waited until the last moment, then wheeled and disappeared into the forest.

Ken dragged in the rope, cursing as vigorously as his father ever had.

"He'll come back," he muttered, and got at the business of feeding his horses and making his camp.

He went to bed and found he could not sleep.

Thunderhead, he knew, would spend the night near the mares and probably be with them in the morning, asking for oats. He could catch him then. If not tomorrow, then the next day. Sooner or later the stallion would give in.

Thinking back to all the times he had imagined he heard that neigh, Ken decided that Thunderhead had been following them ever since the North Platte River. That detour had actually made contact with him, if only the contact of a scent carried on the wind and the sound of a distant neigh. When Sparks and Flicka had neighed to each other, undoubtedly Thunderhead had heard them and it had teased him to follow and at last come close.

That error he had made then—the trip north to find Thunderhead when he should have been following Pete's trail—it had turned out well. It had brought Thunderhead to him of his own accord. Ken thought long about this, remembering his sense of guilt, his feeling of being lost, and then the way he had found God in the forest—awfully queer, the way God can twist things around and bring them out right after everything has gone wrong.

He began to feel like a hero. He lay flat on his back and stretched both arms above his head. He yawned, and the big yawn turned into a grin there in the darkness. To bring Jewel home, riding her! Yes, he would ride her and lead Flicka—no, it would be better to ride Thunderhead. Ah! That would be a triumph!

He relaxed in his blankets, curled up and lay half-dreaming, picturing himself riding the famous outlaw home to the ranch with pack horse, two mares and the foal, following. Too bad Carey would not be there to see him arrive!

Anyway, it was a triumph. His father would have to admit that. All the same he knew he would get no praise from Rob. *Something* would be wrong.

Supposing he did not succeed in catching Thunderhead? Well—it wouldn't matter, for Thunderhead would follow the mares home, anyway. One way or the other he would come.

And so, as, in imagination, he brought his little train home, he began to see other things happening. The smile left his face. He went over it carefully in his mind. Finally he sat up. He clasped his arms about his knees and sat tense in the darkness.

Thunderhead running free behind him as he approached the ranch—yes, so far so good. But what when the smell of the Goose Bar mares on the Saddle Back reached him? Now, in his mental vision, Ken could see the white stallion cantering away, paying no attention to his frantic calls, his whistles—leaping a barbed-wire fence—galloping up the Saddle Back, disappearing over the crest of it.

Banner. What would Banner be doing? Of course, protecting his brood. Rounding them up, bunching them, going out to challenge any intruder.

Dawn, up there on the Saddle Back. The empty world of mountains and plains all around. The bunched, frightened, fascinated mares. The little colts, squealing, tense, feeling the danger. And the two stallions out in front, the white, the sorrel, facing each other, taut and bursting with the power and intention to kill.

Banner was an old stallion, worn out by a lifetime

of service. Thunderhead was young and strong. Thunderhead had killed the Albino.

Just as, when he had been looking at Jewel, Carey's face, Carey's voice, her whole person had seemed to be there with him, so now, thinking of Banner, he could see his father's face, the terrible, accusing look in his eyes. This was what had been griping his father all the time. This was why he had wanted to geld Thunderhead, to give him away, even to shoot him. *And he, Ken, was carefully bringing it about.*

He studied his predicament, every possibility. He did not know that a slight, steady quivering had taken him. At last he lay down again and tried to sleep. There was nothing he could do tonight. But tomorrow —yes, tomorrow—if he were good for anything, if he were any use at all, if his boasted power over Thunderhead had an iota of truth in it, he must catch the stallion, saddle him, bridle him, and bring him home between his knees.

# 42

It was about three in the afternoon of a grey day when Nell mounted Redwing and cantered through the meadows to the field where Rob and the men and the hay crew were putting up the last of the hay. Already, in the other meadows through which she rode, the big stacks were piled, shaped, tamped down, covered with weighted tarps.

Before she reached the crew she slowed to a walk, enjoying the sight of their activities, the light team of blacks, Patsy and Topsy, on the rake, trotting so swiftly, turning sharply on the two big wheels, the rake lifted and dropped as it bunched the windrows, the slow-moving wagon with three men on it going from pile to pile. Tim and Wink were on the ground, pitching up the hay. Rob drove the wagon.

Nell guided Redwing to Rob's side of the wagon and tightened her reins. Rob looked around and saw her.

"Hello."

"Hello, Rob."

"Came down to pay us a visit, eh? Want to pitch? We need another good man."

Nell smiled, crossed her right leg over the pommel and sat sideways. Redwing put his nose down and began to nibble the grass.

Rob's eyes, as usual, scrutinized her voraciously. "You don't look like the same girl, Nell," he said.

"I feel swell," she said. "It's wonderful what glands can do, either to you or for you." She put her hand in her pocket and Rob's hand reached out even before he saw what it was. She handed him a candy bar. "Here's some energy for you."

Rob's big white teeth bit into the chewy chocolate.

Let him eat that, said Nell to herself, and sweeten himself a bit before I break the news to him.

"How's Penny?" he asked with a full mouth.

"She's fine. Miss Sartoris has her out walking."

"Kind of gives you a holiday to keep the nurse, doesn't it?"

Nell nodded and two dimples showed in her cheeks. Nell had taken on ten pounds. The dark shadows were gone from under her eyes, there was a natural pink in cheeks and lips.

"We'll keep her a while yet," said Rob. "Have you got another of those things?"

Nell fished in the other pocket. "Aren't you about through work for today?"

"We've got to finish this. I think it'll rain tonight."

Gus, on top of the hay wagon, gave the yell which meant to move up to the next hay pile. Tommy and Big Joe moved forward even before Rob picked up the reins. The old wagon rocked and creaked. From it came the smell of the sweet hay, the pungency of the horsemint which had been cut from the creek banks, the sweat of the men. Nell moved along beside it without troubling to unhook her leg.

When Rob stopped by the next pile and the men began to pitch, Nell said, "Got a wire from Ken."

Rob's face changed expression quickly. He looked at her. She nodded her head smiling, "He's got 'em!"

"Both of them?"

"Yes."

Rob let out a yell which made the horses jump.

"Look out!" exclaimed Nell, grabbing Redwing's reins.

"Well, that ends my troubles," said Rob with a big grin.

"And vindicates your honor," said Nell smiling. "Now, you can wire Mr. Greenway that you've done what you said you'd do and he can come and get his million-dollar filly."

"Where is the kid?" asked Rob. "Where was the wire sent from?"

"From Beaufort," said Nell, "a night letter, sent last night."

"Beaufort," said Rob thoughtfully. "Why, that isn't fifty miles away! He'll be here any hour."

Nell nodded, and her eyes roved over the field. Something in her expression arrested Rob's attention.

"Anything else in the wire?" he asked.

"Well, yes," admitted Nell. "Something that has me worried."

"Shoot," said Rob with narrow eyes.

The wire said, *"Am riding Jewel, Leading Flicka and Sparks. Could not catch Thunderhead. He is following. Look out for Banner and the mares."*

For a long minute Rob stared at her, the smile leaving his face. And then, under his breath, he expressed his feelings by a burst of his best language. Nell appeared to be admiring the scenery. He then fell silent again, thinking, and presently said, "Isn't that the damndest?"

"It certainly is," said Nell, and she wanted to add, "What are you going to do?" But at such moments she was in the category of the boys, who knew that they would get their heads snapped off if they asked questions.

Rob's eyes roved over the horizon as if he expected to see the little cavalcade appear any moment. Then he looked at his watch. Then he studied the weather. Then he climbed down from the hay wagon.

"You get up there and drive, Nell, will you? And give me your horse."

"What are you going to do?"

"I'm going up to the Saddle Back and bring in Banner and the mares."

Nell slid off her horse and stepped up on the hub of the wheel. Rob gripped her riding pants by the seat and gave her a lift. Gus leaned over and took her hand.

Rob yelled the news to Gus.

"Yimminy Crickets!" said Gus.

"He might be here tonight or tomorrow early," said Rob. "And there's no telling—Thunderhead may be ahead of him. Once that horse gets close to home, he may come along on his own."

"Might be up there on the Saddle Back now," said Nell grinning down pleasantly at him as she took the reins in her hands.

Rob's blue eyes flashed at her as he called to Gus. "Get it all in, Gus, and get the tarps on before you come in tonight. It's going to rain."

"Ya, boss."

While Rob lengthened the stirrups on Nell's saddle, his eyes glanced over the field, checking what every man was doing.

"Where will you put them?" asked Nell.

"I'll put Banner in the stable."

Nell nodded. "He won't like it but that's the safest. If you just put him in the corral, Thunderhead would jump into it and murder him."

"And I'll put the mares and colts in the Six Foot pasture. *He* can jump *into* it and do whatever he has a mind to, but *they* can't jump out."

"Are they all bred?" asked Nell.

"Every one of 'em." There was vicious satisfaction in Rob's voice. "None of that wild-devil blood in my horses, thank you!" He swung up into the saddle, and Nell watched the way her quiet horse gathered himself and began to prance and champ the bit as he received the charges of Rob's powerful will.

Rob put his heels into the horse's side and Redwing jumped. He was off. Rob's head turned over his shoulder, "Be careful, Nell—"

"Goodby," she yelled to the figure that was flying down the field.

Rob's rage grew by the minute. That he should have to leave his work when they were pressed for time and every man was needed, that he should have to go out to the Saddle Back late in the day and round up the brood and take that grueling ride with them down the mountain when the day's work should have been ended and he should have been sitting in his chair, feet up, a highball in his hand. Might have known Ken would do something like this.

"But what else *could* he have done?" asked Nell at dinner that night when she had pacified Pearl for dinner being so late, when she had combed the hay out of her hair, tucked Penny into bed, and when Rob was washed and tidy but no less angry. "If he simply couldn't catch him, what could he do? Because the stallion would follow the mares, and Ken *had* to bring the mares, didn't he?"

"He had a gun, didn't he?" said Rob coldly.

"Rob, that's silly."

"Not at all. It was understood this summer, over there at Westgate, that since the stallion could not be caught, he'd have to be killed. Ken agreed to it."

"It wouldn't have been agreed to if I'd been there," said Nell so belligerently that Rob had to turn his face away to hide his amusement.

"Well, it'll have to be agreed to by everyone," said he, as they left the table. "He'll be caught and gelded, or he'll be shot. We're not going on year after year with this nuisance."

They composed the telegram to Beaver Greenway and sent it off.

"Be easy on him now—" was the last thing Nell said to Rob when they saw Ken leading his cavalcade up the road, across the Green and on up to the stables. Thunderhead was not with him. There was no sign of Thunderhead.

But there was too much seething in Rob's mind for him to hold it in long. That evening, when Jewel had been stabled safely in the cowbarn with her foal, out of reach of Banner, when Flicka and Sparks had been put out to pasture to forget their responsibilities, to rest, to roll and ease their tired muscles, when supper had been eaten and Ken's story told, Rob burst out.

"Why the devil did you have to wait till the last minute to wire me and let me know what I was up against?"

"Because," said Ken dully, "I kept thinking that I'd get him yet. I kept trying to all the time."

"What's the last time you saw him?"

"Back there—before we got to Beaufort. I heard some horses neighing far away. That's when he disappeared and I haven't seen him since."

"Stealing some more mares!" said Rob savagely, "I'll be hearing about that next!"

Ken made no answer. It was what he himself had been dreading.

They were in the living-room. The night was cool, a fire was burning on the hearth. Ken sat in an arm-chair, one long thin leg thrown over the arm, a position his father often took. Rob was unable to sit down. He stormed up and down the room, biting the stem of his pipe.

"Look at you now!" The words burst out of him. "This is the way it is, summer after summer. You're a wreck! You spend your vacation wearing yourself out, then go back to school to rest! I suppose that's the idea!"

Ken's drawn brown face, ringed under the eyes as Nell's had been, was turned over his shoulder to the fire. He made no response to his father—did not feel like making any.

Too tired, thought Nell, then, aloud, "Ken, you said you kept trying to catch him right up to the end. In the daytime, you mean?"

"Nighttime too," said Ken in the same dull voice without looking at her. "Whenever I'd hear him near, I'd go out with the halter and rope."

"How long ago was it that he first came up to you?"

"Oh, about ten days ago, I guess—I just don't remember exactly."

Rob bent a long, furious gaze on him and then glanced at Nell. She met his eyes. Ten days, they both thought. He hasn't slept for ten days. Rob started again his long plunging stride down the room and back.

"And what's it all for?" he roared. "A horse—a good-for-nothing brute who has been a pain in the neck ever since he was born—" he continued with Thunderhead's biography, rehearsing every disappointment, every outrage.

Ken heard him without listening. It made no difference what he said. He had done the best he could, and now it was over. Let him rave. His thoughts slipped to Carey. He had brought her filly back for her . . . thank heavens . . . yes . . . he had done what he said he would do . . . Carey . . . she would be coming now. . . .

Rob's roaring voice mingled with the crackling of the fire and the sound of the wind in the chimney. Kim and Chaps were lying on their cushions near the hearth. Pauly was on the davenport beside Nell. The puppy, Willy, was on her lap. Home . . . oh, what did it all matter . . . home . . . bed . . . sleep. . . .

His head sank lower on his shoulder and his eyes closed. Nell, watching him, smiled, for she saw that he was fast asleep. Rob continued his tirade, striding up and down the room. A good thing, she said to herself, smoothing the puppy's little domed head, let him get it all out of his system while Ken's asleep.

At last Rob stooped over Ken and looked at him. "I'll be damned!" he exclaimed. "He hasn't heard a word I've been saying."

Nell said nothing.

"Look at him, Nell."

"I'm looking," said Nell without moving.

Neither did Rob move. There was a long silence. Then Rob put his hand on Ken's shoulder and shook him gently. "Ken!" he said. There was no reply. Ken's head rolled on his shoulders.

"You'll have to shake him harder than that," said Nell, "if you want to wake him. Remember, he hasn't slept for ten days."

Rob put his pipe carefully in an ash tray, then leaned over Ken, gathered up the long spindly legs as he would gather up a colt, finally got the boy in his arms.

"He's almost as big as you," said Nell smiling.

"He doesn't weigh anything," said Rob gruffly, looking down at the tired face that hung over his shoulder. "I'll bet he's lost fifteen pounds on this trip."

"He did what he set out to do," said Nell shortly, and Rob carried the sleeping boy out of the room and up the stairs, walking softly, as if the sound of a step might wake him.

# 43

Halfway up the Saddle Back, an ancient pine thrust its gnarled trunk up through a split and caverned rock to spread wide branches over the hillside.

Here sat Ken the day after the Greenways' arrival at

the ranch. A pink and blue sunrise glowed in the east but Ken had eyes only for the gate far below him which led from the pasture out onto the County Road. She would come through that gate if she came at all.

For weeks he had been waiting for this moment. Since he had got home he had slept and eaten and wandered around and answered questions and groomed Jewel and ridden her. With his father and mother watching, he had put the mare over the three-foot stone wall, the brush jump made of wild goose-berry bushes, the five-foot rail and the broad jump over the creek. He had brought his mother his clothes for a last going over before he packed up for school. He had gathered together his books. He had got Gus to help him patch his suitcase. And when the big Cadil-lac arrived from the Blue Moon he had put Jewel through her paces all over again with Mr. Greenway and Carey watching.

But he had done everything as if he had been in a trance. Even when something happened that, a year ago, would have sent him out of his head with joy—when Mr. Greenway asked him to ride Jewel in her first race in November and his father consented—still he could feel no great elation about it. He was just waiting for the moment when he and Carey would be together and alone.

He sank back on the turf, laid one arm across his eyes and, in his mind, began the proposal. She would know, of course; she would meet him halfway; it would be easy—they would just go into each other's arms. It went on—he didn't know just how long it went on, but suddenly he sprang to his feet.

There she was, standing before him in her slim grey jodhpurs and white shirt. "Oh, what a climb!" She flung herself down where he had been lying.

"You—found my—note," said Ken, reseating himself, and he had difficulty in not stuttering.

"Of course! Under my door! I'm here, aren't I?" And Carey lay back on the hillside and looked up into the branches of the tree. "Why do you call it the Monkey Tree? I don't think it's a monkey tree."

"We call them that. There are only a few of them left on the ranch," said Ken. "Mother made up a rhyme—

Twisted old pine tree, I can plainly see
That you are just making a face at me.
You wink one eye and you bend one knee
And that's why I call you the Monkey Tree."

Carey laughed and Ken was furious at himself for reciting the rhyme. Everything was going wrong. To be talking about the pine tree was just as bad as to be talking about horses. Ever since the Greenways had arrived it had been horses, horses, horses. He had been obliged to describe every mile of his journey, all of his adventures. Then Carey had ridden Jewel and put her over the jumps. Then it went on all evening about the races Jewel would win. He hadn't even been able to *think* about his proposal. And now, when the time had come for it, it wasn't happening.

"How come your Grandma let you come without her along?" he asked casually.

Carey sat up quickly and turned solemn eyes to him. "Do you know something? I've found out that Grandma only gets sick when she can't get her own way!"

"What did we tell you!"

"She didn't want me to come here with Uncle

Beaver. And when I said I wanted to, she began to complain of her rheumatism and I had to get hot compresses for her."

"But you came anyway!"

Carey nodded but with a little chagrin at herself. "It was Uncle Beaver who stood up to her. I didn't dare."

"But why not, Carey? You oughtn't to be so afraid!"

She heaved a deep sigh. "But she gets so mad! That scares me. If only I could get mad! When one person's mad and the other isn't, the mad one always wins. Do you remember that time last summer when I wanted to go out riding with you early one morning?"

Ken lay there, silently, while Carey chatted about the episode. He felt quite desperate, because, no matter what turn the conversation took, it did not seem to get any closer to the proposal.

At last Carey, too, stretched out on the grass. "But," she said, almost forlornly, "I never *can* get the least bit mad."

Ken made no answer.

Carey added, "Besides, just suppose it *was* real after all? Even a little bit real?"

Still Ken said nothing.

Carey elaborated this theme, then at last stopped talking.

Around them the colors had changed. Brilliant green lay upon the hillside, the air was golden, the pink clouds were now puffs of snowy cotton. The hour was passing. The day—the last day was here! How could Carey be so oblivious?

Ken rose on one elbow and looked at the girl beside him. Reproaches welled up from his heart but got only far enough to choke him. The silence lengthened. In Carey's white blouse was a little pocket over the left breast and in the pocket a scrap of a blue handkerchief. Ken saw that the handkerchief was beating a quick tattoo, quicker than any heartbeat ought to be. His own heart suddenly galloped away in a mad flight. So she knew too—she was too—she—

Her face turned to him as he leaned closer, hardly knowing what he was doing, and he was aware, for a second, of the excitement in her eyes before he was too close to see them.

When Carey at last pulled away, she sat up and took the scrap of blue linen and pressed it to her eyes.

"I don't know why I'm crying!"

Ken sprang up and walked off a little distance. He stood there a few moments, then returned and flung himself down beside her and held out his arms. A deep sigh went through him—they clasped each other closely.

At last a sort of peace came to both of them. He held one of her hands, drawing it over his eyes and cheeks. One of her fingers traced the line of his eyebrow. Then across his cheekbone. That small finger was experimenting with this new intimacy. Now and then they turned their two heads until their lips just lightly touched.

At last, Carey sat straight up, turning her knees to one side. He watched every move she made as if he had never seen her before. She looked down at him and he smiled at her, a smile that made her heart quicken, that made it all so *exciting*—as if she did not half know him yet, not more than a fraction of him, and yet he was hers, hers to explore like a wonderful strange land into which she was just entering.

"Carey," he said and his voice was a little husky, "I've been waiting so long for this."

Her eyes wavered and her flushed face tucked

down over her white shirt.

"I knew it was coming, didn't you, Carey?"

She nodded, examining a bit of quartz she had picked out of the grass.

"We're engaged now, Carey."

Carey had no answer to this.

"Aren't we?"

There was just the least doubt on her face.

He sat up abruptly. "How can you look like that! You *know* we're engaged!"

"We—e—ll, *engaged*—yes, I guess so, but—"

"Well, that means married, doesn't it? Engaged to be married?"

"Ken, it just seems so far away. Too far even to think of. And then you know, there's Grandma—I can't believe she will ever allow it."

Ken exploded. "*That* is just what I was waiting to hear! You're not going to let *her* interfere between *us*, are you Carey?"

"*Us* is the one thing she really wants to interfere with. I guess she knows, Ken."

"Knows what?"

"Knows—this—"

"This" was another clasping of arms, another kiss. Then Ken took both her hands and held them tight. "Promise you won't let her ruin our life."

"I don't know what you mean."

"I mean—interfere with our marriage."

"But, Ken, we're too young yet anyway."

"I know it! Damn it!" he said. "I'll have to go to college next year, I suppose. Carey, if you would only go to college too, in the East, then we could see each other all the time, go to dances together, and be *really* engaged."

"I want awfully to go to college," said Carey wistfully, "but there it is. Grandma again. She doesn't want me to. She begins to get asthma at the very idea!"

"What does your uncle say?"

"He says it's entirely up to me. If I want to, he'll back me up." She drew a deep breath. "If I only dared!"

At this revealing remark, Ken's heart became tender. She was really afraid of the selfish old woman who had ruled her all her life. "You will now, Carey. Now you've got me. It'll make a difference." He kissed her again, and Carey, indeed, was beginning to feel that it would make a difference.

"Pretty soon there'll come a day," prophesied Ken with the wisdom of sixty, "that you'll just calmly say—"

"*Go chase yourself!*" exclaimed Carey, and they went into gales of laughter.

There was much for them to talk about. It crossed Ken's mind a dozen times that now he—practically— had a wife, he ought to have some idea of what he was going to do in life, how he would support her, where they would live. But as his thoughts on these subjects did not go beyond doing something very profitable with horses, he decided against mentioning it. They talked, instead, of the Thanksgiving holiday when Ken was to be the guest of Mr. Greenway in the East. He would have time to try Jewel out and study the course. If she was fit, if everything went well, he would ride her in the race. Mr. Greenway had said it would make up to Ken a little for all his trouble over Jewel and the disappointment about Thunderhead.

"You see," said Ken, "it's beginning already—our life together."

Carey was reflective. "I wish it was Thunderhead,"

she said.

"Don't you want me to ride your mare?"

"Oh, you know I do—"

It wasn't enough. Ken wanted more, and she beamed at him and said, "Ken, I would rather have you ride Jewel for me in a big race than anyone else in the world! No one could ride her so well! You're just *marvelous* on a horse!"

This was Ken's first taste of the sweet and intoxicating adulation given by a woman to the man she loves.

"It was only," continued Carey, "that I know how much you want to ride Thunderhead in a race. I hate to have you disappointed."

Ken wagged his head and was offish. "Oh, I'd just as soon ride Jewel! Honest."

"Besides," said Carey, "it seems as if Thunderhead belongs to me, too. I feel that way. It would be like seeing my own horse raced."

This touched Ken so deeply he could not answer. How wonderful for her to be possessive about *his* possessions! That proved they were really one.

She smiled at him shyly. "It would give me the greatest thrill in the world to see you win a race on Thunderhead."

"No chance of that now." He sighed deeply.

"Where do you think he is?"

"No telling. He may have got some mares and taken them away. Sooner or later something'll happen to him. Somebody'll geld him or shoot him."

There reached them the faint, musical sound of a bell ringing.

"The rising bell," said Ken, springing to his feet. He seized Carey's hand. "Don't let's think about Thunderhead, Carey. Let's think about Jewel." Once again they held each other close. The Monkey Tree winked its eye.

They walked slowly down the hill, their arms wrapped around each other.

There was a creek to cross, and at last Ken had his chance. He caught her up and held her across him, grinning at her, feeling that he really had her at last.

Carey laughed at him and put one arm around his neck. As he waded with her, she gave a few squeals of fear. Ken stopped mid-stream—put one foot on a high rock propping up his knee and sat her upon it. He laughed, teasing her. "Now, I've got you!"

Carey looked at him demurely, refusing to be frightened.

"I'm not going to let you go!"

"Don't," said Carey. "I like it. Ken—"

"What?"

"I've just been thinking. We might call the first one Penelope."

Ken looked disgusted. "Please don't start on those children!"

"Why not?" Carey suddenly threw her arms about his neck. "Oh, Ken! I feel as if you were my husband! You really are such a husband sort of boy!"

Ken tried to evade her arms, looking even more disgusted. "I don't want to be your husband."

"Why, you do! You know you do!"

"No—I want to be your lover. I want you to love me and forget all about those damned children."

"The oldest could have violet eyes like your mother."

Ken dropped his foot into the stream, lowering Carey so abruptly that she clutched him, screaming. Then he carried her to the bank and deposited her.

As she would have walked on, he held her back. She looked up at him questioningly.

"Carey, you *do* mean it all, don't you?"

"Of course, Ken," she answered softly, but there seemed to him doubt in her voice.

"Is it *the* love—the *real* love? It is with me, Carey. I'll never marry anybody but you. I couldn't. Could you?"

She shook her head slowly. "I don't think I could, Ken. But still—all that does seem very far away, doesn't it to you?"

"No, it doesn't! I'd marry you tomorrow! Elope with you! I wish we could. Lots of lovers have, you know."

"Oh, I couldn't!"

He took her by the shoulders and turned her face up to his. He looked long into her wide grey eyes—the candid eyes of a child.

"Tell me, Carey. Honestly—is it your grandmother? Are you afraid of her?"

Her eyes glanced away and the long dark lashes trembled a little. "I don't—know—" The happiness faded from her face, and the warm rosy color. "Oh, Ken!"

Silently railing at himself for having hurt her Ken said softly, "Oh, it doesn't matter, darling—darling—it's just that you aren't as old as I am," and again wrapped her in his arms. It was a frantic embrace that claimed her for his own against her grandmother or anyone else.

That was their last talk.

After lunch the Cadillac drew up before the ranch house and Collins jumped out. Greenway came from the cowbarn, leading Jewel. The foal ambled beside her.

Jewel looked nothing like the mare Ken had found in the mountains. Her mane and forelock were plucked and shortened and thinned. She wore a braided blanket coat, her eyes looked out from rimmed holes in a close-fitting cloth hood.

Collins took her from his master, clucking to her like an old hen. He could not get over his wonder. He had thought she would have to be treated like one who has suffered much and barely survived a grueling experience. Instead, when he had seen Ken take her over the jumps and run her on the track he assured his master that in his opinion Crown Jewel was ready for any race, any time.

"Gawdawmighty! The wind she's got! She don't even puff! That's because she don't have to *try*," said Collins. "She just sails. She looks two years holder than the filly Hi brought from Hengland."

Over and over again he had run his hand down her legs, exclaiming at the muscles, "Hard as iron." Or picked up her feet, one by one, examining the healthy hoof and frog. He marveled at the sheen of her coat, at her exuberance, the life that bubbled in her.

Her hair was too long. Nature had had no notice of the sudden change of plan and had been preparing for a winter in the high altitudes and zero temperatures of the Medicine Bow Reserve.

"We'll soon fix that," promised Collins, "wot with sweatin' and blanketin' and groomin'."

He led her carefully into the trailer which was hitched to the car.

It was an unusually constructed trailer. In it, against the right side, a small box stall had been built. This was so that on the long journey, the foal would have this little stall to himself, could not be knocked down or trod upon by an excited mother, could either stand and ruminate, or repose upon the thick bed of straw which covered the floor. When he got hungry the car must stop and the foal would be put in with his mother to nurse.

Now the small creature would not follow his mother into the trailer. She turned her head and nickered to it anxiously, but it paid no attention. It looked at the Green, at the people who stood around, at the fountain in the center, at the house, the barn, and it was as if it said, "This is all very interesting—let me have a little fun!" It began the ridiculous performance which is a foal's best attempt at bucking. The small curly switch stuck straight up, his nose went down, then his little body twisted and his hind legs shot into the air.

There was a roar of laughter which seemed to startle him. He righted himself, looked inquiringly around and whinnied.

Then he was almost destroyed by a tumbleweed that came bounding across the Green at him. He propped on four stiff legs and gave a loud squeal of fear. Jewel answered, nervously. The weed rolled past him and then stopped, hooked on a bramble. The foal stepped forward and stretched out his nose to sniff at it. The wind stiffened, the weed strained against its frail anchor, broke loose and sailed away with the foal galloping after.

There was another burst of laughter. Collins beamed as if he had given birth to the foal himself. But he wanted it safe in the little stall in the trailer which he and Gus had labored half the night to build.

"There's the name you've been looking for, Carey," called Nell.

For a moment Carey was puzzled, and then, "Tumbleweed! Of course! How perfect, Mrs. McLaughlin!"

"A gude name for him," said Gus smiling.

"He's been tumbling around the Rocky Mountains ever since he was born," said Rob.

"That'll stick to 'im," said Collins. "Eh, there's not

many thoroughbred foals that 'as 'ad such hadventures before they was a month hold and no worse for hit neither."

"Come, Tumbleweed!" called Carey, and she and Ken went to separate the foal from the weed.

"It seems to fascinate him," said Nell, watching, as they got behind the little fellow and steered him to the trailer. Jewel added her urgent nickerings and watched with great anxiety as they pushed him into the little stall beside her. She reached her head over the partition, smelled him, grunted softly at him.

The trailer was closed.

Presently Rob and Ken and Nell were standing at the end of the terrace seeing the last of the car and trailer as it swept around the shoulder of the hill. Ken turned away first. He went into the house, saying he had some more packing to do. A few minutes later, Nell saw him at the desk, his head bent over a letter he was writing.

# 44

Ken was sitting on the terrace, the next afternoon. He was alone on the ranch, his mother and father had gone to town. He was all packed up. In an hour or two, or whenever they came back, they would drive him into town to have dinner there and then catch the eastbound express.

Miss Sartoris, in her white uniform, came down the Gorge with Penny. Penny, now two years old, was dragging a tiny cart on wheels. In the cart was a doll about six inches long.

As they reached the terrace Ken called to her. "Come here, Penny—come here to see me."

"Go to your brother, Penny," prompted Miss Sartoris, seating herself in one of the terrace chairs and taking out her lacework.

Penny did not need to be urged. She loved her brothers.

"Come on, Penelope," said Ken, eyeing her thoughtfully.

Penny picked the doll out of the cart and trotted to Ken. She turned it upside down under his face. "See my baby?" she said.

"You, too," said Ken sadly. He inspected the dolly as Penny wished him to. He listened to her chatter. She showed him the blue feather, gleaming like a jewel, which Miss Sartoris had thrust through the eyelet of her little white dress.

She spoke so eagerly and hurriedly that there was a little stutter to almost everything she said, a breathless stutter, "I fo—fo—fo—fo—found it."

Ken did the same thing himself sometimes.

Miss Sartoris joined in the conversation and recounted the small adventures of their walk.

Ken sat half-listening, his eyes wandering.

Off on the Green a little grey kitten was playing all by itself. Leaping up at a flower nodding on a stem, catching it, rolling over and over with it. Bagheera came slowly out from the long grass on the hill, watching the kitten who was walking toward the spring house now, quite sedately. Bagheera following close, suddenly sank to the earth, placed a paw on the kitten's back and brought it to the ground.

"Oh, the cruel thing!" exclaimed Miss Sartoris.

"He isn't hurting it, he's just pinning it down," said Ken.

The kitten did not struggle but turned to look into Bagheera's terrible face.

"That cat!" laughed Ken, "the looks he gives! Black-hearted! And out of what a face! But it doesn't mean a thing."

"I wonder if the poor little kitten knows that?" said Miss Sartoris indignantly.

"It's probably scared to death," agreed Ken, but made no move to rescue it. "Did you ever notice his eyes? The pupils are like little black torpedoes in the middle of the yellow part."

Bagheera suddenly released the kitten, sat up and began to wash himself. The kitten fled through the crack of the door to the service court. Its tail remained visible, lashing from side to side in a small fury.

Ken pointed at it, laughing. "The size of it!"

Miss Sartoris turned to look. Under the heavy blue-painted door, only the small grey tail could be seen, lashing with no abatement of violence, as if, the more the kitten thought about it, the more outraged he was.

And now came another to join the play. Willy, waking up in a thicket of grass where he had been sleeping saw Bagheera washing himself on the Green —an irresistible invitation to a game. He galloped out and tackled him in rough play. The cat rose up, snarling, teeth bared, and one taloned claw lifted high to smite. But Willy leaped and seized the paw in his mouth. What a wonderful game! Bagheera fell over backward. Willy let go the paw and tackled the cat's throat, mauling him playfully and giving him such a dose of boxing with his soft padded paws that Bagheera suddenly extricated himself and with half a dozen great bounds, disappeared into the grass on the other side of the Green. Willy sat down and looked after him wistfully.

The sound of horses neighing came from the stables, then the sound of heavy hoofs coming down the Gorge.

Ken was sitting so that with the slightest turn of his head, the Gorge was in view. Now he saw the horse coming down it. The white horse. Thunderhead!

Ken did not move. Miss Sartoris went on chatting, Penny trotting from one to the other.

Thunderhead walked slowly to the fountain. Ken got up and went into the house, through the kitchen to the back porch where a halter and bucket of oats were always kept. He took the halter over his arm, the bucket of oats in his hand, and went out the back door, across the terrace and Green, down to the fountain.

As he approached Thunderhead and began to talk to him, he heard Miss Sartoris say, "Why, is that the horse everyone's been talking about?"

"I guess it is," said Ken easily. "Come on, Thunderhead, you've had enough to drink. How about some oats?"

Thunderhead swung his dripping mouth up, his head high. He turned to look at Ken, grunting. Ken set the oat pail on the stone rim of the fountain. Thunderhead put his nose down to it. Ken slipped the end of the rope up underneath the great neck with his right hand, took hold of it on the crest of the neck with his left, drew it over, tied it with the loop against a knot which had been put in the rope to keep the noose from slipping. Then, holding this with a catch around his arm, he put the halter underneath Thunderhead's chin, his arms on each side of his head. "Come on, boy! Stick your nose in this!"

Thunderhead thrust his nose through it and lowered his head into the bucket again as Ken fastened the buckle.

Ken's heart did not even miss a beat. He wondered at this. He led the horse around the Green, showed him off to Miss Sartoris. He said, "Want to see me ride him?"

There was the least bit of tension in him, for, after all, Thunderhead had not been ridden since Ken himself had ridden him when he shut him in the Valley of the Eagles. But the horse's training had been thorough, there was only a little crouching, shuddering, a plunge or two as he felt the boy upon his back. And now the old thrill went through Ken at the feel of the tremendous power coiled within that white hide. It made a lump come to his throat.

The horse was obedient to him. Ken's knees held him tightly. Neck-reining with the halter rope, Ken rode him slowly around the fountain, cantered in a wider circle over the Green.

Miss Sartoris was watching admiringly. "Say, Ken, that sure is a pretty horse!"

"Yes, he is pretty, isn't he?" said Ken bringing Thunderhead to a stop in front of the terrace. "Look, Miss Sartoris, what time is it? Have you got a watch?"

She consulted her wrist watch. "It's four o'clock."

"I want to go for a ride on him," said Ken. He slid off the horse. "First let's give Penny a ride. Want to ride the geegee, baby?"

"Huh?" said Penny cocking her head and looking at the horse. Without letting go of the rope Ken picked her up and held her under Thunderhead's nose. "Smell her, Thunderhead. That's my sister. That's my mother's baby. Get a whiff of her."

Penny was squealing, thrusting her fists against Thunderhead's big face which she did not like to have quite so close to her. Thunderhead's eyes bugged widely at her, he smelled her in loud snorts. She squirmed around, got a foot against his face and gave it a shove.

Pearl came out of the house to see what was doing. Ken lifted Penny up on to the stallion's broad back and the big black muzzle and face came around to watch her.

"Come along, Miss Sartoris, you hold her while I lead him."

Miss Sartoris clutched the baby by one foot and her sash and the little procession wound around the fountain. Penny laughed, pounding her little fists on the horse's withers.

Ken grinned at the nurse. "He's used to foals. He knows how they behave."

He lifted the baby off. "I'm going for a ride. Listen. If my mother and father come before I'm back, don't tell them Thunderhead came back. I want to tell them myself."

The nurse and Pearl promised. Ken vaulted on the horse again and rode off to saddle him.

Ken had his ride. . . .

It was only at the station, when he was saying good-by to his mother and father that he told them that Thunderhead had come home and that he had put him in the box stall in the cow barn, where Jewel had been.

He added. "So he's there now. You can do whatever you want with him. Are you going to shoot him, Dad?"

Rob answered this casually, "No, of course not, Ken. Now that he's been caught, there's no point in shooting him. I'll have Dr. Hicks up to geld him. He'll be a better horse than ever, all the trouble over, and you'll have him to ride for half of your life. A magnificent animal! I can't tell you how happy I am this happened."

Rob and Nell drove home along the Lincoln Highway in a state of excitement. The rebel, the outlaw home at last, and of his own free will! They visited him in his stall. He knew Nell's touch. His head curved to follow her, and she remembered the day after his birth, when, bewildered and frightened, he had run to her and hidden his eyes against her.

Next day Rob went for a ride on him.

With the thought in his mind of not putting too much strain on the stallion's self-control, Rob turned his back on the ranch house, the Gorge, the pasture where the mares were enclosed and took his way down the meadows, along Lone Tree Creek. Time and again he put Thunderhead at the stream to jump it—wider and wider jumps—jumps with a high wall of willows this side of the water—the other side, and every time the stallion sailed over hardly pausing to gather himself or to take off. What power! What reserve! Rob's blood began to run faster. He crossed the meadow to the place where the ground sloped up and away from the creek. One of the steep rock-slides separated it from the higher grazing land above. He put the stallion at the rock slide and let him have his head. He felt the muscles gather under him. There were slight roughnesses in the surface of the rock, here and there a vein of grass, an angle—nothing presented any difficulty to Thunderhead. The big hoofs seized every foothold unerringly. Where there was no foothold he seemed to advance by an irresistible inner force, there was a great leap at the end, and they were on the grass. Rob touched his heel to the curving arc of ribs and Thunderhead moved into a swift canter. Rob would try his speed now and prepared, with hands, heels, and the tilt of his body, to give the signal, but Thunderhead read his mind and anticipated him. The canter became a gallop, a run, then that incredibly swift floating pace which seemed more in the air than on the ground. The hoofs reached, slashed at the ground, man and horse sailed forward, the hoofs reached, slashed again—

The quickening of his blood became an excitement such as Rob had rarely felt. What horseman is there who has not at times dreamed of a ride more like the ride of the Valkyries than anything which takes place on this earth? And of a horse endowed as, occasionally, a man is endowed with almost supernatural abilities? Here it was—the supernatural ride, and the unearthly stallion between his knees, happy as he was happy, rejoicing as he was rejoicing, perfectly balanced by him, perfectly obedient.

Thoughts zigzagged through Rob's mind uncontrolled. They struck into his heart. Recollections of his long war against this animal . . . *give away* . . . *geld* . . . *shoot* . . . *kill.* . . .

A barbed-wire fence appeared straight in front of them. A moment's indecision shadowed Rob's mind and the stallion's pace mirrored it. Never, in all the years he had spent on the ranch had Rob put a horse at a barbed-wire fence or allowed anyone else to, but Thunderhead was different. His indecision passed. He needed to give no signal. Again the horse knew his mind, and effortlessly rose and cleared the fence with a good foot to spare.

Then a kind of wildness took possession of Rob. Why guide the horse here or there? He could go anywhere! Down again over a steep bank into the meadow, across the willows and the brook, up the other side clearing a fence with an uphill jump and onto the south grazing land which took them, in a big curve, up to Saddle Back. Saddle Back was empty now, no mares, no colts, no stud. Rob pulled Thunderhead to a stop on the crest and they stood together, surveying the vast expanse spreading below them. The stallion's crest lifted, his nostrils expanded, his eyes were wide, his head turned in swift jerks, this way and that as the wind brought him messages. He looked long at the Buckhorn Mountains to the south.

At last Rob gathered the reins and turned toward the ranch. This would be the final test. On the way home they would pass the Six Foot Pasture where the mares were confined.

Thunderhead did not pass them unaffected. His body gathered and trembled. Rob held him with hands, knees, and voice. There were wild neighs and answering whinnies from the mares. They collected at the fence, crying to him to come closer. But he had been well trained. Under the saddle, he gave obedience.

Rob unsaddled him and rubbed him down, fed him, led him to water. There was no sweat on him. The ride had not winded him.

That night he told Nell he was considering replacing Banner with Thunderhead as the Goose Bar stud.

Nell's hands crashed on the piano keys. "Thunderhead!"

"Yes, Thunderhead!"

"But you were going to have him gelded!"

"I am not going to have him gelded!"

"Rob!"

"Well, a man can change his mind, can't he?" He was sitting by the fire, staring into it, leaning forward, his arms set across his thighs. Now he sprang up, went to the mantel and nervously began to fill his pipe. As he did so he stepped on Chaps' tail and there was a wild yelp. Impatiently he shoved the dog away. Chaps went off and sat down near the piano, eyeing him reproachfully.

"But," said Nell slowly, feeling her way, "he has only half-papers. He's not entirely purebred. He has all that bad blood of the Albino in him."

Rob's voice was sharp and angry. "Bad blood! You can call it that from the point of view of wanting to play safe. If I was breeding race horses no doubt it might be considered bad blood. It *is* unruly and intractable. Yet see what Ken did with him! And look at his extraordinary natural endowment. He had it in him to win that race two years ago at Saginaw Falls and many another race. He has magnificent blood in him, too. Not only the spirit and power and speed he gets from the Albino but look at the rest of his blood, Appalachian, Banner, Flicka and a host of thoroughbred ancestors!"

Nell's hands dropped in her lap and then she leaned down to stroke Chaps' long ears, lifting one of them, absentmindedly rubbing it over his face then dropping it again. One of Chaps' eyebrows went up toward Nell, the other eye, with a comically wary expression in it, was fastened on Rob. The dog seemed to sense a strange tension in his master.

"What about Banner?" asked Nell.

"Banner will have the rest he deserves. The best the ranch has to offer. A pasture of his own, shelter in the winter, a box stall, oats and hay as long as he has teeth to eat them. He's given me a lifetime of service."

"And WhoDat," said Nell. "You had picked him to replace Banner."

Rob made an impatient gesture. "What of it? Anyone with half an eye can see that WhoDat is not cut out for a range stallion." He tamped the tobacco violently into the bowl of his pipe and went on in the same half-angry voice. "The purpose of all breeding is to produce the perfect—the superperfect individual. When you've done it—when you've got him, what sense is there in finding fault with the process that made him?" He struck a match, held it over the bowl of his pipe, puffed until smoke poured out of his mouth, then threw the match into the fire. "Besides," he added, "if Thunderhead had once won a great race, he would have a NAME, and his colts would sell because of that."

"Won a great race!" exclaimed Nell. "What *are* you talking about?"

"The Delaware Hunt Cup."

"But Ken is going to ride Jewel!"

Rob did not turn his head but the narrowed line of his blue eyes swung around to rest upon her face, his white teeth showed beside the stem of his pipe.

Nell sprang to her feet. "Rob! You wouldn't!"

"Wouldn't I!" he grinned. "I can't wait for the chance!"

Nell walked slowly across the room to stand near him. She could not find words to comment on this. Her mind struggled with the possibilities it opened up.

Rob took his pipe out of his mouth and said more quietly, "Nell, I'm aching to do it. And Thunderhead is aching to do it. And we'll win. Ken has never completely mastered that stallion. No boy could. He's a man's horse. He's my horse. And I tell you he knows it."

Nell looked down at the fire, then lifted her hands and examined a hangnail on one finger. She sat down abruptly and slowly raised her eyes to Rob's.

He was looking at her with a strange, questioning, almost humble expression. "Yes," he said, "I'm thinking of that, too. How would it affect Ken? After all, Thunderhead belongs to him—"

Nell looked back at the fire, placing herself first in Rob's shoes, then in Ken's.

Finally she said, "Ken's awfully happy that he's going to ride Jewel. That's tied up with Carey."

Rob nodded eagerly. He puffed at his pipe, he dreamed his dream, staring at the fire. At last he sighed. "It's up to the kid," he said. "I'll take Thunderhead to the race, just as I did before, with Ken not knowing. Then I'll give him his choice. I'll tell him I've brought the stallion for *him* to ride, but that if he prefers to ride Jewel, I'll ride him myself."

He sat down again, Nell got her knitting bag, and while a tiny sweater for Penny grew between the ivory needles, they discussed the plan.

"It was the mob and the noise in the grandstand that upset Thunderhead in the last race," said Rob thoughtfully. "I'll have time to give him a chance to get used to that before snow flies—take him to a couple of the local rodeos."

"And there's to be a big auction over at Pine Bluffs," said Nell. "There'll be mobs there. I'll go along!" she added excitedly.

"What about when I take him East?" asked Rob. "I suppose you won't want to leave Penny?"

Blue fire flashed at him from her eyes. "Not go!" she exclaimed. "Do you think I would miss that race with either you or Ken riding Thunderhead? We'll keep Miss Sartoris for Penny."

Rob's eyebrows shot up and he grinned. "Atta girl!"

Nell's hands dropped in her lap. "Thanksgiving," she murmured. "It might be very cold. A good thing

I've got my grey squirrel coat."

Excitement swept Rob again. He leaped to his feet. "I've got a chance!" he cried and gave a skip like a boy.

Nell smiled and Chaps came back from his corner eager to share the happiness which, mysteriously, had suddenly filled the room. He humbly begged pardon for having been stepped on and sat down before Rob, his stump of a tail brushing the floor ecstatically, his wistful brown eyes straining upward.

# 45

The day of the race was raw and cold. Fitful sunshine played over the course and the rolling Delaware country beyond. Although occasionally there was the smell of snow in the air the ground was dry and hard. It was weather to whip heat into the blood and make the horses dance as they stood in the paddock waiting to be saddled.

Nell pulled the collar of her soft grey squirrel coat up around her face. It was nervousness rather than cold that made her do it. Now that the race, *the* race, was about to be run, this feeling that was almost panic had taken possession of her. Rob, she whispered to herself, *Rob*—and her hand slipped inside the fur and clutched her throat, the old gesture, the old fear of choking.

"Oh, I wish they'd come! I *wish* they'd come!" Carey, standing in front of Nell in the box, swept the field with her glasses. Her little feet, from suspense and excitement, did a tattoo on the floor. Mrs. Palmer, ponderous in mink and broadcloth, sat beside her, one hand holding the knob of a stout cane—this because of her rheumatism—and the other occupied as Carey's were, holding field glasses to her eyes.

"Don't you, Mrs. McLaughlin?" called Carey over her shoulder. "I just simply can't *wait!*"

There was no answer from Nell. Carey cast a glance backward. "Are you nervous, Mrs. McLaughlin? Nervous about Ken?"

"No," said Nell, her voice steady but slightly hoarse.

"Sit down, Carey, and be quiet!" ordered her grandmother. "You behave as if you had never seen a race before!"

"I've never seen Ken McLaughlin ride Crown Jewel before!"

It was true that Nell felt no anxiety about Ken. This panic had seized her when Ken had made his decision to stick to the original plan and ride Jewel. Why had he done that? To win a victory for Carey's filly? Or because he saw that his Dad longed to ride Thunderhead? Nell suspected it was the latter. At any rate it had not been until that moment that Rob's riding of the stallion had become real to her. Now it was coming, now it was inevitable, and it was only a matter of minutes before she would see them ride out onto the track and take their places.

She had been insane ever to agree to it! Rob—middle-aged, tough and close-knit in bone and muscle—not like these little slim whips of jockeys, not like Ken who could take a dozen falls a day and not know it—*those terrible jumps!*

Her eyes swept the course taking in the brush, the rails and ditches, her mind trying to hide from her the fact that what she could see was not the half of it. She knew every jump. At the ranch, she and Rob together

had studied the course. Rob had duplicated every
jump and there was not one which had caused Thunderhead the slightest difficulty. Still—this was a race.
This was the Delaware Hunt Cup, the stiffest steeplechase in America. There would be falls—there never
was a steeplechase without falls—she had seen them
in movies, horrible falls, one man piling on another—

Nell sprang to her feet and leaned over Mrs. Palmer's
shoulder. "I'm going down, Mrs. Palmer. I want to see
Rob a moment. I'll be right back."

"Oh, I'm coming too, Mrs. McLaughlin! Wait for
me!"

Nell did not wait. She hurried out of the box and
started to push her way through the crowds down-
ward.

Mrs. Palmer dropped her cane, her hand shot out
and grabbed Carey by the wrist. "You'll stay where
you are!"

Carey tugged at her wrist. "Oh, Grandmother!
Please!"

Mrs. Palmer's face was bent on the girl. It was her
terrible face. The face in which the beautiful grey
eyes under their aristocratic black arches became
something so menacing they would not be met.

Carey's eyes stung with hot tears. She felt
frightened and indignant and ashamed. She ceased to
struggle. It would be indecent. She allowed her wrist
to remain in that iron grasp. With the other hand she
raised her binoculars to her eyes and directed them to
the spot where the horses would appear on their
parade to the post.

Nell's eyes did not see very clearly. The crowd and
the blaring of the loud-speakers confused her. She
made her way toward the paddock as fast as she
could. But there! She was too late! There came the

first one, a tall black horse on dancing feet. Nell's heart gave a leap. Crown Jewel! No! No white marks on the face and not Ken in the saddle but a cerise-shirted jockey with a young-old face and number 7 on his back. Another tall black horse exactly like the first one! Not Ken. Number 11 and colors green and gold—but surely those were the Greenway colors? Nell felt still more confused. Where was Thunderhead? Rob would be wearing a black shirt. She pressed her way forward. A tall man in a belted brown overcoat and soft hat was walking toward her. He blocked her line of vision. She tried to dodge to one side of him but he seized her arm.

"Nell!"

Bewildered by the voice, her eyes still strained to see the white horse, the black-shirted rider. *There they come!*

Rob squeezed her arm hard. She looked into his dark face, then flashed her glance to the jockey who was riding the big white horse through the opening. The shirt had the number 4, and it covered a very slim, boyish body. The horse—those great white haunches! the powerful legs!

"Rob!" she cried, clutching him. "Oh, Rob!"

A surge of the crowd almost upset her.

Rob's strong arms held her steady, he ploughed a way for her, drew her back against the grandstand, then, raising his knee, he braced a toe in an aperture of the boards and lifted her to his knee.

"Can you see?"

Her head was considerably above his own. She strained her eyes after the horses.

"Rob! What happened?"

"Watch!"

"But what happened?"

"I tumbled—that's all!"

"Tumbled?"

"Nell! It's about two months I've been in love with Thunderhead. Ken's been in love with him since he was born—get it?"

"He did it for you?—chose Jewel, I mean?"

"That's it. Now for God's sake watch them. I can't see. Where are they?"

"They're marching past the judges' stand," said Nell. "Who's that on Crown Jewel—number eleven, isn't she—with the green and gold?"

"Yep. That's Vickers, a crackerjack rider."

Nell felt so great a relief she could almost have fainted. She clutched Rob and stared into his face. She felt no fear for Ken. Whether he won or not did not matter. The stallion would carry him safely.

"What are they doing?" demanded Rob, and Nell looked again.

"Crown Jewel is skylarking around. Dancing."

Rob chuckled. "Wouldn't be surprised if she came in second."

"There's another horse looks just like her, number seven, with cerise colors."

"That's Gay Lady. She won this steeplechase last year."

One bay horse—he seemed an unruly beast—was being led past the judges' stand.

"They're collecting at the starting post."

There was a sudden crescendo in the roar of sound from the grandstand.

"What's that?" Rob asked.

"That bay horse that was led past the judges' stand —when he got near the other horses at the post he lashed out at several. He looks vicious to me."

"What's his number?"

"Ten. Blue and red stripes."

"That's Top Hole—a bad actor but a good 'chaser.' "

"They're putting him in the outside stall— Oh! They're off!"

The roar from the grandstand swelled as the horses swept forward and rapidly sorted themselves out into leaders, followers, tail-enders. Crown Jewel made a good start and held her place in a group of three just behind the leaders. Thunderhead ran alone behind the tail-enders.

Beaver Greenway joined them. Edging their way as the crowd surged and flowed, they gradually worked to the rail. How swiftly the first mile was covered! Four tough jumps and two horses down already, but-not Jewel, not Thunderhead. The stallion was running wide on the outside, gaining on the others a little, taking his jumps easily. And now the bright shirts and the straining horses were half hidden as they curved away through the rolling country beyond.

Greenway's field glasses were held to his eyes for a long steady inspection. As he lowered them he said quietly to Rob, "That white stallion of yours is going to win."

At the words Nell's heart leaped and across her memory there swept the panorama of Ken's long struggle with the stallion. To conceal her emotion she plucked Rob's sleeve. "You *will* be careless about tossing off sentences that are full of dynamite!"

"Me? Dynamite? What to you mean?"

"Long ago—how many years?—you said, *the only reason I've kept any horse of this line is because I thought maybe some day there would be one gentle one and I'd have a race horse.*"

"Yeah—" muttered Rob in answer. "If only he doesn't take it into his head to buck."

Carey had ceased to be aware of her grandmother's grasp on her wrist at the moment she had recognized Ken on Thunderhead and Vickers on Jewel.

The old lady made the discovery at the same moment. "Hah!" she exclaimed. "That Ken McLaughlin! He's riding his own horse after all, not yours!"

"I'm glad of it! I tried to get him to!"

"Why should you do such a thing?"

"You wouldn't understand," said Carey with barely concealed scorn.

There was silence for a few moments, both of them closely watching the track.

Mrs. Palmer sniffed. "Well! He's way behind. He hardly seems to be trying."

Again Carey felt as if she were going to cry. If only Nell had been there, or her uncle—someone who was sympathetic to her and to Ken.

"You just wait," she exclaimed bravely. "He can do whatever he wants to do— Ah—" The cry burst from her, as at the brush and water jump at the turn there was a bunching of the three leading horses. They disappeared from view, only one, Top Hole, emerged from the tangle. The crowd roared. Jewel and her close competitor, Gay Lady, were safely over. They had second and third place. Thunderhead, wide of the jam, sailed over easily.

And now Thunderhead began to close up the distance between himself and the leaders. He still ran wide, as if scorning the advantage of being closer to the rail. Down the backstretch he was abreast of Top Hole. The two horses took jump after jump with absolute precision. As Thunderhead forged ahead, running now with his strange floating gait, Top Hole seemed to lose heart. He dropped back. The crowd went wild. One length, two, three separated the white stallion from the six horses who were still in the running. They swept into the home stretch, the jockeys plying their whips, the crowd in a frenzy, all eyes fastened on the one jump remaining, the rail, the ditch, the wall and the water. Jewel galloped with might and main as if indignant that Thunderhead should run away from her.

For one second Carey closed her eyes. But only for a second. In the breathless, almost silent moment in which Thunderhead rode up to the last jump, Carey leaned forward and yelled, "Oh you, Ken! COME ON!"

It was over.

Carey drew a deep breath, hardly aware of the great roar of the crowd around her. Thunderhead first, Jewel second by a nose.

The grasp on her wrist tightened and she met her grandmother's blazing eyes. "What behavior! You ought to be ashamed!"

"Ken's won," stammered Carey. "He's won, Grandma! Let me go!" She gave a tug at her wrist. Around them the crowd was surging into the aisles of the grandstand. Announcements were being bawled through the loudspeakers.

"You stay here with me!" said Mrs. Palmer severely.

For one moment Carey stood, hardly aware of her grandmother, thrilling with the realization of the strange haphazard victory which, after so many heart-breaking years of struggle and failure, had come to Ken.

Then Carey turned on the old lady. "Grandma, there are some things I want to tell you!"

"Tell *me!*" Mrs. Palmer became inches taller. Her eyes bored into the girl's face.

"Yes—*tell you.*" Carey marveled that she was completely without fear. "I am engaged to Ken McLaugh-

lin. I am not going back with you to the Blue Moon.
I'm going to Miss Meredith's school in Washington to
get the rest of my college credits and next year I'm
going to Vassar. And I'll be visiting the McLaughlins
most of next summer at the Goose Bar."

"You dare to tell *me*, what you'll do and not do!"

For answer Carey smiled. She lifted her imprisoned
wrist, gave it a sharp twist, and she was free.

She said the word aloud as she stepped back, rubbing the skin where her grandmother's hand had held
her. "Free!" The next moment she was gone.

Mrs. Palmer could hardly believe that such a thing
could happen to her. She looked around to see whom
she could get to take her part, but the crowd was concerned only with the outcome of the race, the horses,
the announcements. She sat with lips drawn in, brows
pulled down over eyes which darted this way and
that.

Then a man in the next box saw the cane which had
rolled out of her reach. He entered her box, picked up
her cane, and courteously handed it to her.

She accepted it without a smile or a word of thanks
and continued to sit there as if waiting, the knob of
the cane in one hand, her other clasping her large
suede bag to her breast. At last her lips began to quiver and her eyes to fill.

She glanced furtively around, but there was no one
to see.

With an abrupt, angry gesture, she threw the cane
to the floor, rose to her feet and drew her mink coat
closer around her. Then, with an air of great hauteur,
and with steady gait, she left the box.

All the newspapers and racing sheets found material for something more than the usual announcement

of the winner of this famous event. The headline, RANGE STALLION WALKS AWAY WITH THE DELAWARE HUNT CUP topped an article of three columns, six inches long, which also contained a picture of Ken sitting on Thunderhead and wearing an amazed expression as he put out his hands to receive the trophy. The stallion had refused his share of the glory—the garland of flowers, and was photographed in the act of snorting his disgust. Something of Thunderhead's history was given, also that of Crown Jewel, who had amused onlookers by breaking away from her groom and running to Thunderhead to rub her nose affectionately against his shoulder.

The article was not flattering enough to satisfy Carey, but she liked the picture, and that night, as she pinned it to the edge of the mirror of her dressing-table and then stood looking at it, there was a warm, excited smile on her face. "You don't know it yet, Ken, but we're engaged—really engaged."

# 46

The June night was warm. Moonlight flooded the Saddle Back making strange shadows of the few, lonely monkey trees which broke the line of the hill, the sharp jut of rocks, the mares that grazed quietly on the rich, early summer grass, the white stallion who stood on the topmost peak, sloping, as if on a stair, his eyes taking in a vast sweep of country.

Below the Saddle Back, to the north, the buildings of the ranch nestled at either end of the Gorge, and from these came always sounds and smells that made his nerves tingle. He would listen, while an hour passed. He would lift his nostrils to catch the different scents, sorting them out, sorting out the voices, associating some experience with every sound, such as the rattle of a bucket, the slam of a door, feet walking up the Gorge.

The south, where twenty miles away the plains broke into folds, then higher hills, then the great crags and ranges of the Buckhorn Mountains—this drew him, too. Here was a deep fascination, a far call to which he must ever respond with an emotion that made his whole body quiver.

Closer at hand were his mares and colts. He and Rob had brought them up that day from their winter pasture in Castle Rock Meadow to summer pasture on Saddle Back. They were tired. The little foals, one or two months old, lay flat on their sides, some of the mares too.

A profound sigh went through the stallion. He slowly picked his way down the steep point of the hill and began to feed voraciously on the luscious mountain grass.

**FINIS**